# THE DOCTOR'S LOST-AND-FOUND HEART

BY
DIANNE DRAKE

*To Doctor Nance, the ID specialist who saved my life.*
*You made the diagnosis when nobody else could find the 'bug'.*
*Thank you.*

First published in Great Britain 2012
by Mills & Boon, an imprint of Harlequin (UK) Limited.
Harlequin (UK) Limited, Eton House, 18-24 Paradise Road,
Richmond, Surrey TW9 1SR

© Dianne Despain 2012

ISBN: 978 0 263 89793 7

Harlequin (UK) policy is to use papers that are natural, renewable
and recyclable products and made from wood grown in sustainable
forests. The logging and manufacturing process conform to the
legal environmental regulations of the country of origin.

Printed and bound in Spain
by Blackprint CPI, Barcelona

**Dear Reader**

I'm so grateful to be bringing you another book for the fabulous Mills and Boon® Medical Romances™. I love writing these stories. More than that, I love hearing from readers who ask me when I'm going to write a book featuring the Philippines or India or Barbados. It's humbling, knowing all the many places my books are being read.

THE DOCTOR'S LOST-AND-FOUND HEART takes us to Argentina, one of the most spectacular countries in the world. It also has the most amazingly friendly and resilient people, which is why I chose this setting for my story. It simply seemed like the place Jack and Amanda should be. Of course they're both a little resistant to that. Resistant to each other as well. But Amanda is transformed from a very unanimated woman when she's at home in Texas to someone who's positively hot-blooded the instant she steps foot on Argentine soil. So what's that about? You'll have to read the book to see.

Then there's Jack, a man from nowhere, going no place in particular. He wants to avoid Argentina at all costs, but when duty calls he will always put aside his personal needs and answer. In the case of Argentina, the cost of his call is the highest price he may ever have to pay.

THE DOCTOR'S LOST-AND-FOUND HEART follows Jack Kenner's story—a story begun in NO. 1 DAD IN TEXAS, which preceded this book. And there'll be another story to follow, also set in Argentina, featuring Amanda's brother Ben.

In the meantime, I'm finally joining the social media revolution. So please follow and like me at www.Facebook.com (DianneDrakeAuthor), and jump over to see what I'm tweeting @DianneDrake. Feel free to stop by my website (www.DianneDrake.com) as well, and e-mail me with suggestions for another amazing country in which to set one of my stories. I've just about exhausted my travel supply, so now it's time to start broadening my horizons.

As always, wishing you health and happiness.

*DD*

# CHAPTER ONE

WRAPPED around her pretty little finger. That was how he felt, traipsing around out here in God-forsaken nowhere, with nothing but a backpack full of testing supplies and a sneaking suspicion that there was going to be more to this mission than a couple of days. Way more than a couple of days...

Jack Kenner swatted a mosquito on his neck, flicked it away, then wiped the sweat off his face with the back of his hand. If he'd been smart about this, or had had time to plan, he'd have had his hair buzzed down to a bald cut, because collar-length wavy and summer jungle humidity weren't a good mix. And it was damn humid out here. Unseasonably so for mid-December. He'd have also had time to order adequate testing supplies—he never liked to go unprepared. But when Amanda had called him, told him what was at risk, and that it was urgent... First plane out. What could he say? He was a sucker for a beautiful face and a worthy cause. She certainly had the beautiful face, and a bunch of sick kids was a worthy cause.

Thinking about her brought a smile to *his* face. Amanda Robinson. More than beautiful, actually. Stunning. Exquisite. Wild, black hair when it wasn't all trussed up. Dark skin. Eyes the color of onyx. Exotic in every sense of the word. A real breathtaker who was totally unaware of the power she could hold over a man.

Outside a handful of professional encounters back in Texas, Jack hardly even knew the woman, yet here he was, somewhere in Argentina, because she'd asked. The hell of it was, he didn't do that kind of looking anymore. Kept it strictly off his radar. Except when Amanda walked by him that first time his radar had blipped. For him, though, one or two blips and that was as far as it went. His life was screwed up in every way that counted and he wasn't even sure he could define what a real life was anymore. So, why drag someone else into his confusion?

Easy answer. He didn't. Not even casually. Anything other than a passing glance and a wishful sigh got complicated, so he kept it uncomplicated, simple as that. The fewer lives he screwed up, the better.

On the other hand, being here was bordering on complicated since this was everything he was trying to put behind him. Medicine, unidentified outbreaks, epidemics... he wanted all of it out of his life. Problem was, controlling hospital-acquired infections, now called HAIs, was a growing specialty and the bigger problem in that was he was pretty good at what he did. It was hard to walk away from it when you were in demand. Harder still when he actually let himself think about the lives depending on his discoveries. But walking was what he'd been trying to do for the past two years. Walking, but always getting pulled back in.

So now, this Hospital de Caridad he was trying to find... He was promising himself it would be the last one. The last of the line for him, come hell or high water. Amanda Robinson had worked miracles with his nephew and this was paying back a debt of gratitude. Meaning, he'd find the HAI infecting the hospital she owned with her brother, then finally be done with it. Done with everything, without a clue what came after that.

Another mosquito dive-bombed Jack's ear, and he slapped at it, hitting it in midair. "You dirty little…"

"Dr. Jack Kenner?" a young voice piped up from the bushes just beyond the edge of the trail. "Are you Dr. Jack Kenner?"

"I'm Kenner," he said, quite surprised by an obviously adolescent voice. "Who are you, and does anybody know you're out here in the jungle alone?"

A scrawny scrap of a kid popped out of the bushes and walked right up to him. No shoes, no shirt, scraggly black hair, well-worn jeans, the biggest, widest smile Jack had ever seen on a face. "I'm Ezequiel," he said, extending his small hand to Jack. "I speak good English and I know all the roads and paths to the hospital. That's why they sent me to find you."

"That would imply I'm lost," Jack said, taking firm hold of Ezequiel's hand, amazed and a little amused by the adult and purely unexpected gesture. "Which I'm not."

Ezequiel's grin didn't fade in the face of Jack's solid grip, or his denial. If anything, it widened. "Okay, then I'll go back and tell them you're on the wrong trail, but you're not lost." He pulled his hand back when Jack let go and crammed it into his pocket.

"How old are you, kid?"

"Twelve," he said. Then quickly added, "Almost."

Jack chuckled. Smart kid. Smart in his head, smart in the world. "And why do you speak English so well?"

"Missionaries used to teach me in school. I was the best student. Now the doctors and nurses teach me."

"Not surprised you're the best." Jack pulled a stainless-steel bottle of water from his backpack and offered it first to Ezequiel, who refused. Then he twisted off the cap, took a swig, and replaced the cap. "So, if I were to admit that I might be lost, how far, would you say, I'm off the trail I need to be on?"

"Far off," Ezequiel responded.

"If I'm that far off, how did you find me? Or even know where to look for me?"

"Everybody makes that mistake first time."

Yes, very smart in the world. He liked Ezequiel instantly. Saw that same gleam of youthful enthusiasm he used to see in Robbie's eyes. "Then I suppose I'm lucky you knew I might get lost."

"I didn't, but Doc Ben did."

Ben Robinson, Amanda's brother. Admittedly, he knew nothing about the man. Amanda hadn't said and he hadn't asked. Kept things the way he liked them—uninvolved. "And Doc Ben would be the one who sent the Jeep for me... The Jeep with a driver who dropped me off halfway here and pointed me in the direction of *Aldea de Cascada* rather than taking me all the way there?"

"We had an emergency, Doc K. Only got one Jeep."

Doc K? A nickname smacked of familiarity, and he didn't want familiarity of any kind coming anywhere near him. Especially not with another kid. Jack's nephew, Michael, was the only one he was going to allow in his life from now on. He was Cade's son, and there was safety in that relationship. He could get as close as he wanted yet keep the distance he needed. "Call me Jack, or Dr. Kenner,"

"Okay, Doc K," Ezequiel said, giving him the thumbs-up sign.

Choosing not to correct the boy, Jack shook his head

in resignation. What the hell? He was only going to be here a day or two then he was going back to Texas, back to wondering what came next. "So, how about you lead, and I'll follow?" Follow an almost twelve-year-old boy to a village hospital with one Jeep, an unidentified infection spreading, and God only knew what else. Sounded like a mess to him, but that pretty much summed up his life these days, didn't it? A real mess.

"Okay, so maybe I shouldn't have interfered, but you're in over your head here, Ben. And not asking anybody for help. Not even me, which has got me a little angry, to be honest." Amanda Robinson dropped her canvas duffel bag next to the bed, then plopped down on the lumpy mattress. Her home away from home. She loved it here, loved Caridad, didn't mind the lack of amenities. In fact, back in Texas, she found herself always counting off the days until she could return. "So I asked him, even though you didn't want me to. He was hanging around, working a few hours here and there at the hospital, and I took the opportunity when I saw it because Jack's the best in the field, and we have a problem he can fix. What did you expect me to do?"

"Let me handle it since I'm the one who actually runs the hospital."

"But I had Jack Kenner at my fingertips. I'd be crazy to ignore that." The way she hadn't been able to ignore him all these months. A man who made her toes tingle. Except, when she looked, he didn't look back. Hence a whole lot of unrequited tingling going on.

"And I have a computer with a connection to a satellite. These are modern times, Amanda. We have communication, even in the jungle, and I've been in touch with a couple people who are experienced in these kinds of infections."

"Okay, so maybe I overstepped…a little. But your people *aren't* Jack Kenner."

"You overstepped a lot." He sighed, then sat down on the edge of the bed next to his sister and wrapped a supportive arm around her shoulder. "But I'm glad you're here, interfering."

"Because I care," she said, her voice giving way to tenderness. "Your vision, my passion. That's why I work my butt off to support this place. You…*we* do important work." There might have been only a year separating them in age, and no real blood relationship between them, but Benjamin Thomas Robinson was the person she most admired in this world. What he'd overcome to get here… "And I'm sorry if this is going to cause a problem between us, Ben, but…"

"But you were taking care of me, the way you always have."

"I can't help it. That's just what happens, and you should be used to it by now."

He chuckled. "I am. And most of me appreciates your… hovering, nurturing, mothering, whatever you want to call it."

"Then we're good with this?"

"We're always good," he said, wrapping his other arm around her to give her a hug. "And I'm glad you're back. Ever since Dad died…"

"I know," she whispered, feeling her eyes dampen. "It throws everything off balance, doesn't it?" Ben was a Robinson by birth, she was a Robinson by adoption. But there'd been no distinctions in the family. They were tight-knit, loving. And her dad's death a few months earlier had changed things…. Things Ben didn't know. Didn't need to know. He had enough struggles of his own, without taking on hers. Which he would do, if he knew.

"Look, it was a long trip down here. Any chance that fantastic hospital cook might have a bowl of *guisos* left over from lunch?" At the mere mention of *guisos* Amanda found herself suddenly craving the thick meat and vegetable stew. It was a simple concoction, quite traditional here, and something she could easily make for herself back home—onions, garlic, veal, tomatoes, carrots, sweet potatoes, squash, rice... But in Argentina it tasted better. Satisfied a certain craving that wasn't about food—something she couldn't explain.

"Maybe afterward a *palmerita* covered in *crema pastelera?*"

A flat, circular pastry covered in a vanilla cream. "Are you trying to get on my good side?" she asked, sniffling back her tears. He was about courage, and it was always good to be with him, to work with him. Be inspired by his strength. "Because if you are, it worked."

"Well, I sent Ezequiel out to find your Jack Kenner. I got word he was coming in by commuter plane, so I asked Hector to go to the landing strip to get him but, apparently, there was an emergency over in Ladera. Someone needs transport to the hospital, and Hector let your friend out somewhere down the road, pointed him in the right direction, or shall I say *some* direction, since it's been a couple of hours. So I decided someone should go out and help him find his way."

A smile crept to Amanda's lips. Jack Kenner, lost in the jungle. Good-looking man. Rugged. Large. Black wavy hair, dark brown eyes, stubble on his chin, perpetual frown on his face... The thought of Jack lost out there, somewhere, was funny. To a point. Because that moment of amusement would be followed by the reality that Jack wasn't any too friendly most of the time, at least, most of *her* time, and she didn't see him being as amused by his predicament as she was. At best, he was aloof and she didn't know why, didn't really care to find out. She needed his skill, not his personality. Although something about that gruff personality invariably brought a sigh to her lips.

Still, Jack Kenner, lost... "He's not very personable, Ben," she said, straightening up, as her smile got larger.

"Yet look at you smile. Am I missing something here? Something about you and this man you haven't told me yet?"

"Nothing to tell," she said defensively, as the heat rose in her face. "I barely know him."

"So the blush doesn't mean anything?" he teased.

"I don't blush, and if I did, you wouldn't be able to see it."

"Scarlet red against your complexion..." He leaned back to appraise her, then grinned. "Haven't seen anything like that on you before, so he must be one hell of a man to do that to you, Amanda."

"I don't know anything about how he is as a man, just as a doctor."

"All I'm saying is—"

"Nothing, Ben. All you're saying is nothing, because there *is* nothing. And don't go trying to marry me off to this man when he gets here. Okay? Because last time you tried that..."

"I was thirteen, you were twelve."

"And he stalked me for half a year. Kept telling me you promised he could have me. Then I found out you *traded* me for that bicycle you said you found."

"Seemed like a fair trade at the time. And he did *love* you."

"Until he got a better deal."

"Yeah, well, love is fickle, isn't it?"

"Except I'm not in love with Jack Kenner. Not even in *like* with him. He's simply a means to an end for us, and I just wanted you to know, in advance, that he can be a little...abrupt."

"I've done some research. Saw a mention or two about his personality in some articles I read. And you're right. He's a pretty somber guy, apparently, but good. So, the rest of it doesn't matter, does it?" He arched teasing eyebrows. "Even a less perceptive man than I could read something into your blush, though."

She chose not to dignify her brother's implications anymore. He'd think what he wanted for now, and observe, in due course, how wrong he was. "No, Jack Kenner's attitude doesn't matter, except for poor Ezequiel. Jack's going to chew him up and spit him out."

"See, there you are. Another denial. Denial by ignoring what I just implied."

"Would you stop it? There's nothing going on. I asked him here because he's the best, and I was only trying to explain to you that his personality isn't always pleasant."

"Yet, you're attracted to that rough type, aren't you?" He chuckled. "Anyway, I think Ezequiel will hold his own against your friend." Ben smiled. Nodded appreciatively. "He's a resourceful kid."

"And Jack does love kids..." she said, hoping her brother would back off the teasing. The truth was, she was attracted. What woman wouldn't be? But how did you tell your brother it was purely physical? The answer: you didn't. "Even though he'll never admit to having a soft spot for anyone." Jack didn't wear his heart on his sleeve as a rule, but in a few of their encounters she'd seen it there. Which was why she'd turned to him when she'd realized her brother needed help. Jack cared. He did a pretty good job of hiding it—most of the time. But sometimes it slipped out. With his nephew, the emotion was obvious. "So, about that food I was begging for…"

Smiling, "Ah, yes. My sister's priorities."

"Your sister's priorities," she said, trailing him out the door of the tiny hut she'd be calling home for the next couple of weeks. The only thing was, it wasn't really food she had on her mind. It was Jack Kenner. Back in Big Badger, Texas, he was a blunt force. But something about him being here in Argentina, in the jungle… That thought fascinated her almost as much as the jungle did. Almost.

Well, it was better than he'd expected. Nice little wooden structure. Probably ten or twelve beds in a central ward and a few private rooms. A small yet tidy surgery. Ample supplies. Well-kept grounds. Flowers planted here and there to give it a bright appearance. All of it perched on a little knoll overlooking the village called Aldea de Cascada.

Surprisingly, there were people milling around. Some appeared native to the area, some didn't. A few seemed to work here, others may have been visitors. All in all, he was more impressed by Hospital de Caridad than he'd expected to be. "Thanks for the tour, Ezequiel," he said, even more impressed by how the kid knew his way around the hospital. So, was it customary to tip the tour guide? He wondered about that since Ezequiel wasn't making a move to get away from him. In fact, if he hadn't known better, he might have thought the boy was latching on to him. "Is there something else we need to do?" he finally asked him.

Ezequiel shook his head. "Unless you want to see where you'll be staying."

"Sure. Show me."

"It's over there," Ezequiel said, pointing to a small hut adjacent to the hospital building.

It was nice enough. He'd stayed in far worse places, carrying out far worse duty, than what he was going to do here. "Okay," he said, still not sure what to do about Ezequiel. Then inspiration struck, and he slung his backpack off his shoulder and pulled out the stainless-steel water bottle. "You don't have one of these, do you?" he asked, holding it up.

Ezequiel shook his head.

"Then take it." He tried handing it over to Ezequiel, but the boy only looked perplexed.

"Back where I come from, when somebody gets lost, the person who finds them gets a reward."

"Reward?" Ezequiel questioned. "What's a reward?"

Jack thought for a moment, trying to come up with the right word to translate it. *"Recompense,"* he finally said. *"Regalo."*

"For me?" Ezequiel cried, sounding as excited as any child would who'd just received a gift.

Jack regretted he didn't have something better, something more suited for an almost twelve-year-old boy, and he wondered if he'd have an opportunity while he was here to find something else for Ezequiel. "Next time you have to go looking for someone…even if it's me…you can fill it with water and take it along in case you get thirsty." His second attempt to thrust the bottle at Ezequiel was met with success, and as soon as they boy latched on to it he opened it up and took a drink of the water still inside.

"Thank you, Doc K. I like it." Then the grin started, ear

to ear. And Jack's heart melted. Damn it, he wasn't going to do that again. Wasn't going to get involved. Wasn't going to let another kid get to him. Not after Robbie, or Rosa. *Shift, refocus, get his mind off children.* Clearing his throat, Jack inhaled a deep breath. "Care to help me get settled in?"

Ezequiel frowned, again unsure of what Jack had just said. So Jack tossed him the backpack and motioned for him to come along to the guest hut. Okay, so maybe he wasn't here to make friends, but Ezequiel was turning into the exception, with that smile of his, and that unassuming nature. Besides, what did a couple of days' interaction with the kid hurt? Interaction didn't have to equate to involvement, did it? Especially if he kept reminding himself that in another few days all this would be behind him. "Then you can help me find Dr. Robinson, if you have time."

"He's in clinic now." He pointed to another hut, a much larger version of the hut he was headed to. "Over there."

Hospital de Caridad, translated to mean Charity Hospital, was like a small village in itself. A well thought-out place, keeping the clinic out of the hospital. Even though he hadn't yet met Amanda's brother, Jack was already beginning to like the man. Or at least appreciate his vision. The care and concern surrounding this hospital had been obvious to Jack almost the instant he'd stepped into the compound, and he hadn't even seen the actual hospital operation yet.

"Then that'll be our next stop, after we go in here." He stepped up to the door of the guest hut, which was an opening covered by mosquito netting, then pushed back the gauzy material and motioned for Ezequiel to go in first. Then he followed, got halfway into the hut, and stopped. "What the...?" he said, obviously surprised by who he found there. "You never said you were coming to Argentina, too."

Amanda, who was stashing a few clothes in the small bureau next to her bed, spun around. "Maybe not, but here I am anyway."

"Precipitated by what? Your need to keep an eye on me?"

"Don't sound so defensive, Jack. I'm inspired by your work. Wanted to watch it in progress."

"So you just packed up and came here on a whim."

"Yes, I just packed up. But you don't get to call it a whim."

"Why not?"

"Because coming to Argentina on a *whim* makes me sound irresponsible."

"There's something wrong with being irresponsible? Lots of people do it every day, and do it well."

"You sound like you believe irresponsibility could be an admirable goal."

"Not admirable. But definitely a goal for some people. Me included, if I get my way. And don't pull out your analyst's couch and tell me to lie down because there's nothing there you'd be interested in."

"Don't underestimate yourself, Doctor. I think I'd find plenty to interest me if you were stretched out on my couch."

"Let me guess. You're psychoanalyzing me, aren't you? Because my goal is not to have a goal." It was said with a certain amount of amusement, because the idea of boots off and under her analyst's couch was suddenly the only thing on his mind. Boots off, belt off, stethoscope off...

"I don't psychoanalyze. I treat conditions."

"And I'm a condition to treat."

"You're entitled to your opinion," she countered, her smile never breaking.

"My opinion is I'm the challenge you may want to take on, which is why you're here. But I'm also the challenge you won't crack, which is why I came."

"Faulty logic," she quipped. "You're here because you did crack under the challenge. Caved right in when I asked."

"Or agreed because there was a need for my services, as simple as that." Caved right in was more like it, but he wasn't about to give her the advantage of letting her discover she was right about him. Amanda was resourceful. She'd find a way to use that kind of information again. Which, on second thought, might be interesting. Too bad he didn't even go as far as interesting. "Oh, and in case you're interested, I'm impressed by your hospital."

"Changing the subject, Jack?"

He laughed. "You bet I am. It's safer that way."

Her smile didn't waver, but the edges around it softened. "Then the conversation is changed. Wouldn't want you feeling uncomfortable."

"Sounds like you're not really changing the conversation, just twisting it around to suit your purposes. Only my opinion, of course."

"My only purposes are what concerns the hospital. But Caridad is nice, isn't it?" she asked, taunting him with her eyes. "I'm proud of what Ben's done here. Which is why, when I'm running off to Argentina a few times a year, it may seem like a whim to some, but I'm actually here doing something I believe in with all my heart."

Something about her looked different. He studied her for a second, realized her hair wasn't twisted into its usual tight, librarianesque knot at the nape of her neck. It was

loose, full of curl, wild. And her eyes had… The only way
he could describe what he saw was *los ojos del fuego*. Eyes
of fire. She was Amanda Robinson, but a different version from that he knew back in Texas. "So, I'm assuming
we're roommates?" he said, turning around and walking
over to join Ezequiel at his bedside.

"Yep, roommates. You over there, me over here, curtain down the middle." She bumped her bureau drawer
shut with her hip, then grabbed a handful of clothes she'd
left on the bed, and headed for a nook he figured had to
be the bathroom. "You don't mind sharing, do you?" she
called back over her shoulder, as she pushed back the door
to the nook and walked into the room behind it. "Because
the supply closet in the hospital isn't taken, if you'd rather
have that. But you'd have to sleep sitting up."

"I'm fine," he said, kicking off his leather cowboy boots
and letting them fly to the floor in the middle of the room.

"Good. Because the supply closet is a tight fit, especially if you're claustrophobic."

Except he wasn't claustrophobic. Right now, though,
he was feeling a little gynophobic. Afraid of women. One
woman in particular. Amanda Robinson was different, and
that bothered him. What bothered him even more was that
he was bothered about it in the first place.

In the tiny bathroom, the only place where'd she'd be able
to find privacy in their living arrangement, Amanda leaned
back against the door and drew in a deep breath to steady
her nerves. She was shaking. Actually shaking…hands,
knees, a few parts in between. So, what was that about?
She knew Jack, had been the one to ask him here. Now,
seeing him out of his Texas element… Even her breath was
shaking as she shut her eyes and conjured up his image.

Usual rough cut even rougher. Hair mussed, that sexy, *sexy* dark stubble on his face. Even the glisten of sweat on his face made him sexy. *Sexy...*

*No!* He couldn't be sexy. This wasn't about sexy.

Amanda's eyes flew open to stop the flow of pure sexual fascination with a man she was trying hard to repudiate as sexy. And failing miserably. Yet what had all that dialogue been about, especially the part where she had been getting him stretched out on her couch? Really? Was that what she'd said to him? Her analyst's couch, for heaven's sake!

Another round of shakes hit her because she didn't know what had come over her, and she didn't like it the least little bit that, rather than annoying her, his streak of opposition had tweaked something. Woken it up. Lit some kind of a fire.

It was like she was seeing Jack for the first time. Enjoying what she was seeing way more than she should. And now she was getting stressed out about sharing quarters with him, sleeping mere feet away from him. Forming an intimacy by proximity, something that had never bothered her all those years she'd slept in the hospital on call with colleagues and strangers alike. It was a bed, and everybody concerned was too tired to care who was in the bed across from theirs.

Except now she wasn't tired, and she did care, because...

Well, it was the jungle. It was *always* the jungle, and the jungle always made her feel like someone other than who she was. Why? No clue. But from the moment she arrived here—every single time she arrived here—the old Amanda started giving way to the new one. Sometimes it crept out of her by slow measures, sometimes it leaped, like a hungry panther.

Sure, there had to be a psychology to it, and as a psychologist she should have been able to figure it out. But maybe she liked the way she felt when she unpinned her hair and took off her pearls, which was why she avoided that little analysis. It just plain felt good to be Argentina Amanda.

So here she was, throwing off those figurative pearls by changing into something more comfortable than linen slacks and fitted blouse, anxious to get on with the panther inside her. Yet when she opened the door, she couldn't take that leap. That was the other Amanda fighting to take her back. The one who took control so completely now all she could do was stand in the doorway and stare at Jack, who'd apparently shooed Ezequiel away then stretched out flat on his bed. Either asleep already, or trying to bring on a self-induced trance.

She took a deep breath to calm herself, and to help her hang on to the last few shreds of that other Amanda... shreds she was a little afraid to let go of. "Look, Ben's in clinic for another hour, and I'm on my way to the kitchen to see what I can find to eat. Care to come with me?"

"Thanks...not hungry," Jack said.

"Thirsty? There's always a pitcher of fresh lemonade."

"Not thirsty."

This was the way it was going to be? "Are you always so non-responsive?" she asked.

"Pretty much."

"Why?"

"Why not?"

"Because you're a doctor, and doctors are supposed to be responsive." He rose up, arched the sexiest eyebrows she'd ever seen in her life, and simply stared so hard at her she began to feel self-conscious. "What?" she finally asked.

He didn't answer, though. Instead, he lay back down and shut his eyes. Then finally said, "You're being responsive enough for the both of us. No need for me to join in and interrupt what you're doing so well."

Now he was playing with her. Look out, Jack Kenner. Because as sexy as he was to look at, he was just that challenging to be around, and she did love a good challenge. A thought that added just a bit more jungle wind to Amanda's sails as she tossed the clothes she'd been wearing down on her bed, then headed to the door of the hut. "Well, here's one more responsive moment from me, Jack. Those boots...keep them under your bed. Not in the middle of the floor. In fact, keep everything about you on your side. I don't like messiness."

"And I don't like fussy roommates. Which makes this a stand-off, doesn't it?"

"Not really," she said, smiling as she spun around and marched straight back to the middle of the room, where she bent down, picked up those boots then strode straight to the window, opened it and hurled them outside. "Not when there's a simple solution."

Jack's only response was to rise up again, give her a good, hard stare, toe to head, then back down again. A stare so hard she could feel it graze her curves. Suddenly she was feeling self-conscious that her white shorts might be a little too short, or her white vest top a little too tight. Too much leg, too much chest.

"Okay, then," she finally said when Jack said nothing. "If you change your mind about that lemonade..."

By the time she was finally pouring that lemonade, she was back on course. Not as much as she wanted to be, though. Because that little episode in the guest hut, that up-and-down emotional swing—attracted, frustrated, attracted, frustrated—definitely wasn't her. These clothes weren't her. Nothing here was her. Not really. Yet it all felt so right. All except Jack, and she had no idea how what was going on inside her raised so many quivers, hackles, goose bumps and objections all at the same time.

The thing was, she knew she should avoid Jack. Maybe even wanted to. But could she? Truly, honestly, could she? And if she could, would she?

# CHAPTER TWO

"I KNOW you're familiar with the basic concept, but let me give you a little background on hospital-acquired infections," Jack said, settling into a wooden chair across the table from Amanda, trying hard to regard her professionally. Not easy considering the way she looked.

"Believe me, I've been reading. And I think my brother has probably spent some time on his hands and knees trying to sanitize the ward. The thought of being sick because of something we're doing..." She shook her head. "We've got to stop it, Jack. Whatever it takes, we've got to stop it."

"Might not be what you're doing so much as what's being done to you," Jack said. "Everybody blames themselves, especially in smaller, more contained hospitals like Caridad, but these *bugs,* as I'll call them for lack of a better definition, aren't predictable, and just when you think you're on to something..." He shrugged. "Everything changes. Like life, in a lot of ways."

He studied Amanda for a moment, saw absolutely no resemblance to Ben whatsoever. While Ben was fair, she was so... His guess would have been Argentinian, actually. Possibly from the Pampas region, Mapuche descent, which she wasn't, of course. But maybe that was just what he wanted to see in her because her eyes were the same color as Rosa's, and her skin the same tone. Odd, how coming back after all this time affected him, seeing Rosa everywhere he looked.

"Anyway," he continued, shaking himself back into the moment, "internationally, the incidence of a hospital-acquired infection makes up nearly nine percent of all hospitalizations, with pediatrics being even higher than that. Unfortunately, in Latin and South America, more of these infections turn into critical situations than in most other areas in the world. And we're talking things like methicillin-resistant *Staphylococcus aureus,* an Enterobacter species resistant to ceftriaxone, and even Pseudomonas aeruginosa resistant to fluoroquinolones. To name a few."

Amanda pushed a can of soda in Jack's direction, and leaned back in her chair. "So what do we do about Caridad to keep this thing from spreading? It won't take much to shut our doors, and the area can't afford to have us shut down for even a little while because the next nearest medical service is about half a day away." She paused, took a drink of her own soda, then set the can down on the table. "This is killing my brother. He blames himself."

"But it's not his fault."

"Logically, he knows that. He feels responsible, though. That's the way he is, taking on everybody's problems. I mean, the first time I ever met him, there he was all stalwart in his new brother duties, showing me around the house, the yard, the neighborhood. You'd have thought he was going to be my adoptive father and not my brother. Yet he has that sense of purpose…."

She was adopted? So, maybe he was right. "It's human nature to feel responsible when we're sidelined the way Ben is right now. He sees his world falling apart and there's not a damned thing he can do about it. But he's lucky to have a sister who cares."

"You have Cade."

"Cade and I are only now becoming acquainted. I think that kind of relationship is a long way off for us."

"I hope it happens, because you're right. I'm lucky. Ben and I are as opposite as two people could be in most regards, which is pretty obvious, but we formed a tight bond almost instantly." She laughed. "After he quit trying to find ways to get rid of me. He sold me a couple times, traded me, and then there was the time he simply took me down the street to the neighbor's house and told me to wait on the doorstep until they came home, then tell them it was their turn to be my parents."

"Did you?"

She nodded, and her eyes softened. "And Ben got in so much trouble. But he felt threatened, having this new sister just drop in from nowhere. Maybe if my parents had adopted me when I was a baby…" Pausing, the slight smile of reminiscence dropped from her face. "Jack, you're pretty straightforward. I don't think you'd soft-pedal something to spare someone's feelings."

"That's a pretty low opinion of me."

"But I heard you at the hospital back in Texas, the way you talked to people, your interactions."

"I've been accused of being blunt."

"Then be blunt with me. Tell me what you see when you look at me. You've traveled extensively, lived in so many places around the world—South America, Africa, the Mediterranean regions. More than anybody I've ever known. So, when you look at me, do you see anything you recognize? A nationality? The hint of something you've seen before somewhere? Because of your background, I've wanted to ask you almost from the first time we met. But how do you simply blurt out something like that? And I'll admit I'm a little afraid to know."

"It wasn't in your adoption records?"

She shook her head. "There weren't any adoption papers, no records. Nothing."

Jack swallowed hard. But didn't answer.

"I've tried to find out. But the best I've come up with is that the adoption agency told my parents they believe I'm from some sort of Mediterranean background. Except…"

"Except you don't believe that."

"Except when I look in the mirror and want to believe that I am, the image looking back at me doesn't have a clue. But you do, don't you? You're trained to observe, and you don't miss things. That's what makes you the best in the world at what you do."

"Hospital infections and what you're asking me to do are two entirely separate things, Amanda," he said, not sure what to do with this. "What I do with a hospital infection is make a logical guess based on what I see, then do the tests to prove I'm either right or wrong."

"How often are you wrong?"

He shook his head. "Never," he said, clenching his jaw so hard the ache was starting to set in.

"Then make a logical guess based on what you see."

"Why me?"

She smiled. "Remember the first time we met? You asked for a list of my credentials, even though I'd already worked with your nephew for several months, and his parents were pleased with his progress. But there you were all big and blustery and none too friendly, making your demands. Then what I found out later… You actually called and checked me out. Asked every last reference on my list about me. Which was fine. I wish more people would do that when it comes to hiring the people who take care of their children. And while that really wasn't your responsibility since you're Michael's uncle, not his father, I liked that you were so forthright. Pegged you for a man who would always be honest, maybe sometimes brutally so. And you have your suspicions about my heritage, don't you?"

"I'm not even sure why you'd come to that conclusion."

"Because of the way you look at me. Sometimes you stare, and it's so…penetrating."

"The way a guy stares at a gorgeous woman, you mean?"

She shook her head. "That's not it. Oh, I've seen *that* look, more here than back in Texas. But that's not what I'm talking about. You give it away in your eyes, Jack. Not for long, but there's this flash… I saw it when I asked you. Saw it before that, actually."

She was probably right. What had caught him off guard, and what he'd tried to cloak, was that he saw Rosa in Amanda. Same eyes, same beautiful wild hair, same delicate bone structure. It was a look he wouldn't confuse with any other look in the world because the person he'd loved most had had that look. He'd come unglued, tried not looking, but sometimes couldn't stop himself. He was like a moth attracted to the flame. So if Amanda had caught that flash in his eyes, she'd caught it correctly. "Maybe this is something you should discuss with your family."

"I have. Too many times. Which is why I'm talking to you now. Why I'm asking you. Please, be honest with me, Jack. Respect me enough to do this one thing. When you look at me, who are you seeing?"

"A beautiful Mapuche woman." They were words he

shouldn't have said, but words he felt bound to say because anything else bought into the lies that had cost Rosa her life. And for Rosa, he had no choice but to be honest.

"Mapuche?"

Nodding, he said, "Someone I loved once, a long time ago, was Mapuche. They're an indigenous people from the Pampas. I lived with them for a couple of years, working as a doctor in some of the villages."

"And you recognized that in me?"

"I did."

"Then thank you for your honesty."

"Amanda, I…"

She shook her head. "Just leave it where it is, Jack. I asked, you answered. It's what I wanted." More than that, it's what she needed, and she was numb with it, didn't know what to think, what to do. But Jack had given her something no one else ever had and for that she was grateful. "I think I always knew," she whispered.

"Knew what?" he asked gently.

"That what my parents told me was…off, somehow. Doesn't matter, though, does it?"

"Who we are always matters, Amanda."

"Or who we *aren't?* Anyway, I have a very important date in a few minutes, so back to the problem at Caridad. What's your plan?" She needed time to think about this, to readjust. To let the emotion catch up. But not here, not now. "And tell me what we can do to assist you."

"Are you sure? Because—"

She cut him off by nodding her head. "I'm sure." Not said convincingly enough, but Jack understood. The tone of his voice, the sense of concern emanating from him— yes, he understood.

"Fine." He paused, nodded. "But anytime you want to talk…"

"The hospital, Jack. Please, make this about the hospital now." No matter how distanced she was feeling from everything she knew.

"Well, then, no more cleaning, to start with. I need to find the source of contamination before I do anything else, then culture it to see what grows. Which means I'll look in all the usual places and get creative after that because in my experience the usual places don't really yield what I want."

"It's an odd specialty."

"But, as they say, someone has to do it."

"Why?"

"Public health was always what I wanted to do. You know, take care of the people no one else wanted to take care of."

"Because of Robbie?" she asked. Jack's brother Cade had told her once about Robbie, about how his parents hadn't wanted to raise a child with severe autism.

"You know about my brother?"

She nodded. "The child nobody wanted."

"After he died, I wanted to find a way to take care of people who were overlooked the way he was. He died because no one noticed him."

"He ran off, didn't he?"

Jack nodded. "No one saw that he had been missing for a while and he wasn't found until it was too late. When I became a doctor I wanted to make a difference for people who, like Robbie, weren't noticed until it was too late, which was why I chose public health. What I do now grew out of that as conditions in some of the places I chose to work in weren't good. So, you'd cure the patient and find the source of the illness in so many cases—fleas, ticks, four-legged critters, bacteria."

"But you quit or, at least, you've stepped away for a while, haven't you? That's what Cade told me. He said it's why you were hanging around Big Badger, why you were thinking about working with them at the hospital they were starting."

"You're right. I've stepped away. Not sure if I'll go back and work at the hospital, or not. Haven't decided…personal reasons. It's complicated."

Personal reasons he wouldn't divulge. She could see it in his eyes, like she could see the well-practiced resistance there, as well. Jack had given her what she'd wanted and now it was her turn to do the same. She'd broached a subject he didn't want to talk about, so she wouldn't pry. As a psychologist, it was her second nature to ask, especially when she saw so much distress. But for Jack she would go against that nature. It was the least she could do.

"Okay, well… You have free rein here, Jack. Whatever you need to do is fine, and if I can help you, let me know. We do have some funds…" She stood, then spun around to the beat-up old refrigerator behind her, opened it and grabbed a pitcher of juice—apple-pear mix from Patagonia. "But not a lot. So whatever you can do to be conservative would be appreciated. And right now I'm going to go have juice in the garden with Maritza Costa. Ventricular septal defect. Congenital." Meaning, a small hole in her heart. "She's feeling better today, and I think a nice walk in the fresh air will do her good."

"You're treating her how?"

At the mention of a child with a heart condition Jack's face turned to stone. Amanda saw it, saw the visible change come over him. Such a drastic turnabout, it made her curious. One curiosity among many, she was only beginning to discover. "With medicine only, for the time being," she explained. "And observing her. She got sick, probably a cold, and it lingered, so her parents brought her in and that's when Ben made the discovery. She's been a normal, healthy little girl, without any cardiac problems. So we're being cautiously optimistic we can keep her regulated with the most conservative treatments, because we can't convince her parents to let us send her to another facility for more sophisticated testing, maybe even surgery."

"What about a cardiac cath? They use them more and more these days to close small holes, and it's a safe procedure. Proving itself worthy of the task."

"Maybe it is," she continued, "if we had the means to perform a cardiac catheterization, which we don't. That equipment's on the list of things we hope to be purchasing in the next year or so."

"So in the meantime…"

"We keep a close eye on her and try to keep her as healthy as we can."

"Or go argue some sense into her parents."

"Believe me, Ben would have done that months ago if he'd thought it would work. But we have to maintain the balance here, because the people… While they want the medical help, they're always a little suspicious of outsiders."

"A little?" he snapped. "They'd let that child die because they're a little suspicious?"

"She's not critical, Jack. And we're doing the best we can."

"But what happens when your best isn't good enough anymore?"

It was a rhetorical question. She knew that, and decided to let it pass. "Look, it makes me angry, too. And my brother paces the floor he worries so much. But that's the way we have to do things here, because we want to get along. It's for the good of everyone, including Maritza. Things are changing here in the way we're accepted, and those changes have their own pace. I mean, you lived here, so you already know that. Probably better than I do."

"Look, I'm sorry. You have a nice facility here at Caridad, I'm not criticizing it. And I'm not criticizing either you or Ben. What you have works, and it's none of my business how you treat your patients, so forget what I said because I'm not the one trying to take care of medical services on so many levels with so few means."

Amanda stepped closer to Jack. "I appreciate the concern. No apologies necessary for that. And, Jack…thank you for earlier, for telling me who I might be." She bent and kissed his cheek, her voice catching as the words came out. "Sincerely, thank you."

As she was leaving, Ben was entering, and she gave him a bye-bye wave as she flitted out the door like a butterfly on a light breeze.

"She's…" Jack shrugged, not able to come up with the right word to describe her.

"A force," Ben supplied.

"A force," he repeated, just a little bowled over by Amanda's passion. She was so out there about it. In his life those kinds of emotions were kept hidden, and he wasn't used to being around someone like her, who showed all of it so naturally. It was a little off-putting to that self-admitted stodginess in him he tried to sustain. But it was also fascinating, much more than he would have expected. Still, should he have told her who she might be? It bothered him, made him uneasy being put in that position. Part of him was already realizing, though, that turning her down in anything she asked was going to be tough. Maybe damn near impossible. Because she *was* a force.

"Anyway," he went on, trying to shake Amanda from his mind, "about this hospital-acquired infection you've got going…"

"Seven diagnosed cases right now, all of them limited to the children's ward. General symptoms but not that serious—abdominal pain, nausea, vomiting, malaise."

"Fever? Cough?"

"Not yet. And the good news is we can do a limited amount of cultures here. But the bad news is, since we're not really set up for it, I'm not sure I'd totally trust the results, if we were getting results, which we aren't."

"Which means everything's turning up negative?"

"No positive test results for anything we've cultured. We're set up to treat patients, and our lab, well… Let's just say you're not going to be impressed with it. So let's just get this tour over with so you can figure out what to do with what we've got."

"You mean Ezequiel's tour wasn't a real tour?" Jack asked, smiling. "Great kid, by the way. Smart."

"We're fond of him."

"It's good you let him hang around. Gives him a purpose."

"And a home," Ben commented.

"He lives here?"

"For a little over a year now. His mom brought him with her when she came for treatment, but she died from cancer, and we couldn't find anybody who knew Ezequiel, let alone wanted him. No relatives, no family friends. So we set up a room for him…turned a large storage closet into a room, actually, and we all keep an eye on him. Make sure he's fed, clothed."

"Then he's one of the lucky ones," Jack said, thinking about Amanda, who'd also been one of the lucky ones. Thinking about Rosa, who hadn't been.

"Lucky maybe, but he's not getting a proper education, which is a problem. We're each taking turns teaching him, but there's no consistency to it. And he's not with a family, not getting that kind of nurturing, which is an even bigger problem, because all kids need that. Yet if we turn him in to the authorities we might as well give him up for good. He's too old to be adopted, probably wouldn't do well in an institutional situation, which is where he'd end up if he didn't run off. So we just…"

"Look the other way and hope for the best."

Ben cringed. "When you put it that way, it sounds bad, doesn't it?"

"No. Not really. I've worked in a lot of difficult situations and seen these lost children everywhere. Ezequiel's sharp. A real survivor. You're giving him more than he would have any other way, and he'll make it through."

"Let's hope so, but he deserves better. Anyway, welcome to our lab," Ben said, pushing open a door to reveal a closet-size space, set up with a table and two antiquated microscopes. "Like I said, don't expect much. I found these in storage in a public hospital in Buenos Aries. They'd upgraded, and told me to help myself. So I filled our communal Jeep with everything I thought we might be able to use, which makes us, officially, a hand-me-down hospital." Said with a big smile.

"I think the term today is repurposed." Jack stepped in, took a quick look, and decided it would work. Not well, but well enough for some basic cultures. "So, Amanda said I have free rein, which means I'd like to start by examining the ward where the kids have been infected."

"Well, since pediatrics is Amanda's specialty, she's going to assist you once she's done with Maritza. Oh, and while you're here, I've taken the liberty of adding you to our clinic schedule, if that's okay with you."

"You're good, slipping that in there when you think I'm focusing on something else," Jack said, laughing.

"We take our advantages where we can." He patted Jack on the back. "Anyway, I'm glad you're here, and until I hear otherwise, I'm going to consider you on call for general duty, starting tonight." Ben pointed to the door at the opposite end of the hall. "My sister's out there, when you're ready for her."

Jack didn't respond. Could anyone every really *be* ready for Amanda?

Slipping into a pair of plum-colored scrub pants, Amanda cinched the drawstring at the waist and headed for the pediatric ward. Actually, it wasn't a ward so much as one large room, sparse with equipment and other medical accoutrements. But there were beds, and sick children, and a growing problem that worried her.

Funny how Jack's mere presence brought with it peace of mind. She couldn't deny it, particularly since some of that peace was oozing into her. Peace in her medical life and, oddly, peace in her personal life. It was better knowing she might be Mapuche, she'd decided. Painful because that knowledge caused uncomfortable questions, but better. Although she owed him an apology because clearly he hadn't wanted to be involved in the disarray she called her personal life. Yet he'd allowed himself to be dragged in, which wasn't at all what she'd expected from him.

Something had changed him, though. She'd seen it happen. Seen the incredible struggle when it had flashed over him. But he had been so quick to grab it back, put it away. Leaving her wondering about the person he'd loved. Someone Mapuche. Perhaps a woman? The love of his life?

It occurred to her Jack may have returned to Argentina bearing some kind of pain, simply because she'd asked. "Who are you, Jack?" she asked, as her scrub top slid into place. "What kind of man are you?"

The kind who would fight to keep her from figuring him out. That was the answer that came to her on her way to meet him in Pediatrics. He wanted his distance, and she wanted... Well, she wasn't sure about that. Maybe all she wanted was to understand him. After all, their worlds did intersect in more than one place, so why wouldn't she want to understand someone who threaded in and out? Yes, that was it. A perfectly good reason for having Jack on her mind almost constantly. Which had turned into the case.

All thoughts led to Jack, but that was okay, because all she wanted was to understand. That was some mighty fine logical reasoning leading up to a half-believed conclusion. Who was she kidding, though? Because peel back all that logic and she just plain liked his gruff exterior, even his distance. That was what Argentina did for her, gave her different freedom than she was used to. Changed her perspective. It happened every time she was here, maybe because deep down she'd always felt the innateness of who she was. Or wanted to be.

"Anything going on other than what's being recorded in the charts?" Jack asked from his casual seat behind the old wooden desk that sufficed as the hub of the ward. One desk, one swivel chair, a rusty file cabinet, all of it tucked into the corner, out of the way. And Jack's size overwhelmed everything. An immense man in a small space made the man look even more immense.

Amanda noticed that, fought to keep her gaze steady. "Not really. Symptoms are mild, nothing you wouldn't expect. No one critical or even in danger."

"And you don't think that this might be some run-of-the-mill hospital infection, one that's not going to cause any real trouble." It was a statement, not a question. "Ben's downplaying it, so he's not the best one to go to for an objective answer. You, though, got me here, which means you're worried. So what's your assessment?"

"That's just it, Jack," she said, perching herself on the edge of the desk. "I don't know. Ben's been fighting this HAI for a few weeks now, it's isolated, but it's not going away. Not getting better or worse, either. With the way things mutate…and I'm not the expert on this, so bear with me. But you read how these various strains, bacterial and viral, mutate, and how so much of what we thought would stop the spread is rendered ineffective very quickly. My brother is smart, and he'll do whatever it takes to protect the hospital. Me too, because I'm also involved in this, and I believe you're what it takes or else I wouldn't have asked for your help."

"Well, for what it's worth, every hospital known to man runs some sort of HAI strain through it, Amanda. These kids have gastrointestinal flu-like symptoms. That's all. And according to what I've read, they've all been cured pretty easily."

"But per patient, our percentage is huge. One third of them are coming down with something we're giving them and that statistic, if nothing else, should be a warning. It's just that I don't know what the warning is about."

"Then it's a good thing you called me because warnings are my specialty." He glanced up. "So, it's time for me to meet the ward."

"Not the children?"

"Nope, not at first," he said, standing. "Sometimes not at all. I seem to have a better rapport with the contaminant than I do patients, so I try to keep to where I'm better received."

"Such a low opinion of yourself," she said.

"Or a high one, depending on your perspective. Anyway, with the symptoms that are manifesting themselves, the scope of what could be infecting the kids should be pretty limited, so I like to look at everything from a fresh perspective, which includes culturing areas that wouldn't normally be associated with what we're seeing. In other words, wear a sturdy pair of suspenders along with a belt, just in case."

"Overreacting?" she asked, smiling.

He didn't answer her at first. Instead, he merely stood and stared at her, eventually giving in to a half smile, then finally, "Reacting."

"Okay, then. If you're intent on reacting, did you bring the testing supplies with you, because we don't have —"

"I come prepared. Might even have another trick or two up my sleeve." He grabbed his white lab coat off the back of the chair, which she hated seeing because she liked his look now...cargo pants, and a crisp, white T-shirt. But everybody had something to cover up, didn't they? Jack covered something dark and despairing. Her parents covered something that scared her. She covered up so many things in herself, as well.

But what would happen once the covers started to peel back? That was a question she couldn't answer. And wasn't sure she wanted answered.

# CHAPTER THREE

"I DON'T suppose you've solved it already?" Amanda asked hopefully. "You know, one swipe of a trusty test swab and you have your answer." She plopped down on her bed, flat on her back, and looked across at Jack, who was busy reading, also trying hard to ignore her. "You know, Jack, the kids I work with back in Texas don't respond to me half the time for any number of reasons. They're slow processing the question, not sure what an appropriate response is. A lot of the time they're distracted, or they simply don't know that answering when someone asks them a question is the right thing to do. So when I don't get a response from them, I understand because my children, for the most part, are autistic, and I teach them how to respond. But you don't need to be taught."

He turned his head to look at her, not even bothering to push up the reading glasses that had slid halfway down his nose. "Your point being?"

"We're roommates. Roommates talk to each other."

"I don't have roommates, and if I did, we wouldn't have anything in common to discuss."

"Oh, I think you would, and a great place to start would be why you always set yourself apart from everybody else. People think you've got a terrible personality, that you're unfriendly or grumpy. I heard that about you all the time back in Texas, from my own receptionist, from hospital staff. But do you know what I think?"

"Could I stop you from telling me if I *didn't* want to know?"

"Just ask. I'll respect your wishes." True to form, he did what she expected. Ignored her for about thirty seconds. Then he finally pushed his glasses back up, specifically so he could look over the tops of them at her.

"Then don't tell." He cracked a half smile. "Or do. Whichever makes you happy."

She laughed. "So that's how you want to be?" He was like a breath of fresh air. No rules, no concern for what others thought of him. Basically, a man on his own terms, and she liked that.

"No, that's how I am. I learned a long time ago it's easier to let people just do what they want to do. It makes them happy, which makes my life a whole lot less complicated when it involves me. Besides, human nature... When someone asks you if you want to know what they think, they're going to find a way to tell you."

"Better watch out, Jack. You could be giving me insight into who you are, which means that if I do tell you what I think, I might be saying something you don't want to hear."

"Yeah, right. Like I haven't heard it all before?"

"Not from my perspective, you haven't."

"Human nature again. While you think your perspective of me may be unique, it isn't."

"But you won't know that until I tell you what I think."

"Which leaves the ball in your court. Tell me, or don't tell me. Either way..." He held up his journal. "Reading. Seven articles to catch up on. All of them on the HAIs *du jour.* You know. What's trendy, what's new, what's coming back into style."

She studied him for a moment, and saw something that surprised her. Devilment, maybe? Was he actually playing with her? "You don't ever just make the best of it, do you?"

"The best of what?"

"Your situation. The people you're with. You know, occupy your moment. This is Argentina, Jack. Argentina! It's Friday night, barely dark. We're in the holiday season now, and the people in the village are starting their celebrations. Making the best of your situation would be going down to the village, joining in or at least observing from one of the outside tables at a cantina. Talking to people, letting people talk to you. You know, having fun."

"You think reading medical journals isn't fun?"

"I think you're hiding behind a bunch of journals because you know you *will* have fun if you step out."

"Then you're challenging me."

"Not so much challenging you as…"

"Purposely distracting me."

"No. I'm telling you what I think."

"See, I was right. You wanted me to know, so you sneaked it in there when you thought I wasn't paying attention."

"Oh, you were paying attention. I doubt there's ever a time in your life when you don't."

He was definitely one tough nut to crack. Still, she wasn't giving up on him, and it had nothing to do with professional camaraderie. She just plain wanted to see Jack unwind. Wanted to see what he'd be like when his mind wasn't on such weighty things.

Okay, she was attracted on some weird level. She'd admit it. Back in Texas, the first time she'd met him, that attraction had crept up on her, but there had been nothing she could do about it as he'd been a family member of one of her patients. Yet here, in Argentina, they were doctor to doctor, and that attraction level was turning into something more than she'd expected.

"Oh, and fun is what you want it to be, Jack. If spending a dull evening reading journals is your type of fun, my brother's got boxes of them when you get done with these. But if you want to go meet the people here, mingle a little, see what makes them who they are, then fun is where I'm going, and you're invited along—to participate, or simply observe." Okay, maybe she was trying to distract him a little. Nothing serious, and not for long, though.

"Except I'm on call."

"So am I, but we're not going that far. And we've got adequate staff on to take care of anything routine that arises." She rolled over on her right side to face him, and propped her head up with her hand. "At a leisurely stroll we can be back here in ten minutes. Running, in less than two. Any more excuses?"

"Give me a minute to think, okay?"

"Said as the man is sitting up and putting his glasses on the table next to the bed. Which means you're coming to the village with me. Right?"

"Or getting ready to explore your brother's boxes of journals."

"Ah, yes. The way Argentinian Friday nights are meant to be spent."

"Are you goading me, by any chance?"

"Not goading. Just…" She paused, thought for a moment, wrinkled her nose when she couldn't come up with an answer.

"See, I was right, wasn't I? You *are* trying to distract me."

"Or show you something beneficial."

"Beneficial? How so?"

"A night off clears your head, lets you relax…"

"Oh, so we're weighing more medical knowledge against a night of bright lights and music? Now I understand." He gazed across at her for a minute—a solid gaze that gave away no aspect of himself whatsoever—then shut his journal. "I had this relationship once, back in medical school. Fine-looking woman. One of my professors, actually. At the end of her day she was done. She could go home, kick off her shoes, read a book, cook a meal, do whatever she wanted to do."

"Which was you, I'm guessing."

He arched a suggestive eyebrow at her. "The only problem with that was at the end of my day I had to work a part-time job to keep myself in medical school. When I wasn't delivering pizzas, I was studying. When I wasn't studying, I was sleeping. So I got maybe two hours with her, which gave her cause to think that we could have our *benefits* any old time she wanted them."

"You're comparing me to her?"

"Nope. Just saying two hours, that's all."

"What?" she sputtered, laughing. "The moral to your story is that I get two hours? I was expecting…"

"Something deep and profound, with a meaning that summed up the moral good? Sorry, I was just telling you that if you want me to go to the village with you, we'd better do it now because I still have reading to do."

In reaction, Amanda rose up, picked up her pillow and hurled it across the room at him, hitting him square in the face. "Want to know what I think?" she asked, standing up.

Jack groaned as he pushed himself off the bed. "Could I stop you from telling me if I didn't want to know?"

She produced a second pillow from behind her back, lobbed it at him, hit him in the face again. Then laughed. "Fun, Jack. That's what I think. In spite of yourself, you're going to have fun."

It was a few weeks until Christmas, and the village was already ablaze with lights strung everywhere. Some of them blinked, some didn't. There were lights hanging on bushes and trees, on house eaves, on fences and trash cans. Parked cars were decked with lights, as was furniture that had been dragged to the yard for sitting on outside on a hot summer night. Even a little terrier trotting up the main street behind a group of revelers sported blinking lights on his collar. All in all, the main street of the village took on an orange-red glow. "If I stop, are they going to string me with lights?" Jack asked Amanda.

"It's beautiful, isn't it?" she said, her voice filling with emotion. "Such a simple thing, yet it unites the village. Gives people the chance to come together, and be part of something bigger than the village itself."

Beautiful wasn't about the lights. What was truly beautiful was her reaction to everything around her, and watching her play in the middle of it all. "It's beautiful," he replied. Amanda had this effervescence about her, and it was catching. Even as he resisted being caught, he could feel himself bring dragged in. Disconcertingly, not kicking and screaming as he was being dragged.

"Then you do like it!" she exclaimed. "Because I knew I could find a sentimental spot in you somewhere."

"Sentimental is stretching it. Let's just say that I can appreciate what I'm seeing for its very nice attributes."

"But wouldn't that suggest a certain sentimentality for the holiday?"

More like a certain appreciation for what the holiday seemed to bring out in her. Which, of course, he wouldn't bother mentioning. "When I was a kid growing up, our Christmases were boring. Very regimented. One tree, all lights and ornaments the same color, packages wrapped to match the tree had to be lined up underneath according to their size. We weren't allowed to pick them up or shake them to guess what was inside. Weren't even allowed to be in the same room with the tree without adult supervision for fear we'd disturb something on it."

"Then it's time to make a new holiday memory for you. Something to balance out the bad one."

"That's assuming I want to balance it out."

"Don't you? I mean, don't we all want to balance out the bad memories, maybe even replace them totally with something better?" She tugged him to a stop, then pointed to a man stringing lights on his blueberry bush. "So, let's make a memory, Jack. Right now it may not seem like much to you, or even worth the effort, but maybe someday, when you look back, you'll feel differently."

She was trying so hard on such a lost cause. And he *was* a lost cause. But not so lost that he had the heart to tell her she was wasting her time. Honestly, he liked being with Amanda probably more than he'd liked being with anyone in a good long time. It would be short-lived, once she got to know him better and found him not quite the cause she'd thought him to be. But for now, who knew? Maybe there *would* be a good memory involved. "Why the blueberry bush?" he asked.

"Here, they celebrate the blueberries with decorations. It's a few weeks past the harvest, but in Aldea de Cascada people leave the berries on their personal bushes as long as they can so they can be ready for *El festival de los arándanos*. Festival of the blueberries."

"Which is?"

"What we're celebrating right now. A fairly new festival, but…" She pulled away from Jack, ran into the yard and picked up a strand of lights to help the man, named Alberto, with his decorating. "An important one," she called back. "Blueberry farming is new to the area, and it's turning into an important business. Here, in Aldea de Cascada, they pay homage to their good fortune by celebrating the blueberries." She gestured to another strand of lights on the ground, then nodded at a second berry bush. "And they like to party for any occasion, so it works out."

"So, if I string these lights on the berry bush, what's in it for me?" he asked, trying to hold on to a frown that simply wouldn't be held on to.

"The satisfaction of knowing you contributed to the pleasure of others."

"But staying back and reading my journals contributes to the quality of life of others."

She laughed. "And now you're being obstinate for the sake of being obstinate, aren't you?"

Rather than answering, Jack grabbed up a strand of lights, stepped up to the bush, plugged the end of the strand of lights into the lights on the other bush, then watched the colors light up. Reds, yellows, greens, blues…and all for a berry bush. "Not obstinate. Just stating the obvious," he said, as he started twining the lights about the bush.

"But aren't you missing something with that attitude?" Amanda countered. "You allow yourself to touch humanity, yet you don't allow it to touch back. Just look at the beauty we can create around us as humans. Beauty you may have part of, but won't let be part of you."

"It's a string of lights on a blueberry bush. Pretty by some definitions, useless by others."

"It's a festival, Jack. Very pretty and probably as useless as it is pretty. But you know what? Every time you look at a blueberry, for the rest of your life, you're going to have a memory of the festival celebrating it. And it's going to be a pleasant memory because, in spite of yourself, you're having a good time. Or else, why would you be stringing lights on a blueberry bush?"

He chuckled. "There's fault in that logic somewhere. Just not sure where."

"But I'm right. Admit it."

"You're right in that I'll have a memory." But of something much better than a blueberry.

"Good. Then let's go see what other kinds of memories we can make." For their efforts, Alberto presented them with a small basket of blueberries, and Amanda immediately popped one into her mouth. "Sweet," she said, plucking one out and offering it to Jack, who shook his head in refusal.

But Amanda wouldn't take no for an answer. She held it out again, and he refused again.

"You're going to eat this berry, Jack," she said, waving it at him. "One way or another, you're going to eat it."

"Oh, the mere scrap of a woman is going to force it down my throat?" he asked, quite amused by her determination.

"The mere scrap of a woman will pin you to the ground if she has to," Amanda countered, taking a step closer.

Her eyes simply sizzled with the challenge—a sizzle that started to catch fire in him. "All by yourself?"

"I've tackled them bigger than you."

An image that turned the fire into pure, pounding arousal. "What if I told you I'm deathly allergic to blueberries?" he asked, struggling to conjure up a focus on anything but Amanda. Images of trees and water and birds popped into his mind then kept on going, as hard as he tried clinging to them. Then he centered upon surgical instruments, and surgical procedures and post-surgical therapies, but none of that worked either, because as something popped into his mind's eye, Amanda came after it, taking a sexy hip-swing to it and knocking it away.

"What if I told you you're lying, that I can see it in your eyes?" She took another step closer. Stopped. Held out the blueberry. Then took another step. "Come on, Jack. Give in. One blueberry, and I'll leave you alone."

Except he wasn't sure he wanted to be left alone. "See, that's the thing. When you challenge me like you're doing, I can't give in. It's not in my nature."

"Or in mine."

"So we're at an impasse?" he asked, as she took two more steps, then stood so close to him that one inch farther and she would have been pressed into his erection.

"Not an impasse," she said, as she quickly raised her hand to his face to claim her victory. But instead he claimed her hand. Caught her by the wrist and held her hand mere inches from his lips, her fingers still clinging to the berry. "Victory."

"Mine, or yours?" he asked, his voice too thick to pretend anything other than the raw sexual energy between them.

"Depends," she purred.

And in that moment, he let his guard down just enough that she was able to slip the blueberry between his lips, and whether it was the blueberry that tasted so sweet to him or her finger lingering on the tip of his tongue just a moment longer than it should have as he devoured the berry, he wasn't sure. It didn't matter, though, because… victory. It was his. And, yes, it was sweet.

"See, Jack. That's what's in it for you. Something sweet."

Trying to regain his bearings, his senses and hopefully a little sensibility, he let go of Amanda's wrist and stepped backward. While his head wasn't spinning, everything else in his world was right then and it was time to stop it. Time to be Jack Kenner again and not the idiot who went all goofy over Amanda's persuasion.

"Sweet or not, your two hours are ticking away." She popped another blueberry in her mouth, didn't bother offering him one, then latched on to Jack's arm again. "Your two hours, Jack. These are *your* two hours. So let's go buy a strand of lights and find something of our own to decorate."

In his state of mind, with the throbbing in his groin not yet abating, all he wanted to do was go off somewhere and smoke a cigarette, and he didn't even smoke. "But I thought this was supposed to be my two hours. If that's the case, shouldn't I get to choose what we do?" A myriad of thoughts on that subject went through his mind, and not a one of them had anything to do with stringing lights.

"Under normal circumstances, yes. But this is my gift to you, which means I get to choose what it is."

She pointed to a vendor making his way up the road with a pushcart. Children were following the vendor, trying to get a peek at the goods he had for sale, while old ladies were scurrying to keep up with the procession, endeavoring to get a bargain. Not far ahead, a makeshift street band, made up of a saxophone, an accordion and a guitar player, rendered their version of popular Christmas carols while a grizzled old man peddled tamales and empanadas from the street corner.

"The vendor has lights. My treat. But since these two hours are yours to spend, you've got to decide what to decorate with them." She smiled as she chose three strands with mixed colors from the cart, and handed a five-peso bill to the merchant, waving him off when he tried to render change. "Does it seem like a good compromise?" she asked Jack, who was backing farther and farther away from the cart with each passing second.

"Do I have a choice?" he shouted, trying to sidestep a parade of revelers coming his way, all of them decked out with homemade kazoos and drums. Too late, though, for Jack, who got swept into the procession, was totally surrounded by at least a dozen music-makers who latched on to him like leeches, then pulled him into the bosom of the band as it marched its way on down the street.

Amanda stood there for a moment, watching Jack being literally swept away in a festive wave, a little surprised and very pleased he wasn't trying to forcibly remove himself from the merrymaking cluster. But he wasn't. He was simply, and quite literally, going with the flow. He wasn't exactly interacting with the people around him, or giving in to the dancing or the tin noisemaker being offered him. But he was going with them, nonetheless.

"You really find him fascinating, don't you?" Ben asked, stepping up behind her.

"I'm not sure why. But, yes, I do."

He handed his sister a cup of yerba *mate* tea, a traditional herbal concoction known as a national favorite.

"Well, maybe it's something about the lure of an unobtainable man. You know, wanting what you can't have."

"Spoken by the most unobtainable man I know," she said, lifting the drink to her lips. Stimulating, odd, definitely an acquired taste. One of the things she actually looked forward to when she visited.

"And you've put *yourself* out there to be obtained?"

She shifted her gaze to Ben, her lips still on the cup. "What's that supposed to mean?"

"I think you know exactly what it means. If you like the guy, go get the guy."

"How's that going to work when the guy doesn't want to be got? And that's assuming I even want to get him. Which I don't."

Ben actually laughed. "Good try, but I'm not buying it. I've seen the way you look at him."

"What if I do? I admire him, sure. I'm a medical doctor, he's a medical doctor, so I'm allowed to. What's wrong with that?"

"Again, I'm not buying it. You brought that look in your eyes with you to Argentina this time, which tells me this *thing* between you, or some variation on the theme, has been going on for a while."

"You're wrong, Ben. I mean it. You're totally wrong about what you're thinking."

"Maybe I am. Maybe I'm not."

She shrugged him off. "Then think whatever you want to, however wrong it is, while I go and rescue Jack. He's not enjoying the poncho and *boina* someone just put on him." *Boina,* meaning beret.

"And I think you're being too attentive for someone who's not interested in the guy with the poncho. So on that note I'm going back on duty."

"Yeah, run away instead of facing the fact that you're wrong."

"The lady doth protest too much, methinks."

"Methinks you should go away, Ben."

"I will, but it doesn't solve a thing."

"You two fighting?" Jack asked, handing her his *boina*. He'd already rid himself of the poncho somewhere in the crowd.

"Disagreeing. Not fighting," she said, putting the *boina* on her own head. "It's a long-standing tradition between us. He thinks he knows what's best for me and I tell him how wrong he is."

"Is he ever right?"

"Occasionally."

Jack smiled. "Then sometimes you *do* give in. That's good to know."

"Only about some things. But not the lights. Have you thought how you want use them?"

"You're still on that kick?"

"It was part of the plan, remember?"

"I don't make plans," he said. "They get too complicated, and usually take you in directions you don't want to go."

"But couldn't they take you in a direction you want to go or, better yet, need to go, even if you don't know it at the time?" She spied a couple of empty seats at a tiny tile-topped table in an adjacent cantina, grabbed hold of Jack's arm and dragged him across the street, then sat down. Except Jack didn't sit. He stopped just short of the little outdoor café and simply stood on the road and looked at her.

"Okay, you're right. So, I made a plan for my lights," he finally told her.

She knew exactly what it was going to be. Jack was going to pitch them into the nearest trash can, or shove them in the direction of the next person who strolled by him. Which totally mucked up her plans for the evening because no matter how much she wanted Jack to be part of this, it wasn't going to happen. He might go through the motions, but none of this was him, and that disappointed her. What had she expected, though? Take him to the festival and witness a miraculous transformation? Time to let Jack be Jack again. "Fine, take them," she said, trying to hide her disappointment.

"You coming with me?"

To face her failure in something where she was so positive she was right? Not a chance. "You go on. I've still got some party left in me." Party for one. And on a very blue note.

"I can come back later and walk you to the hospital," he offered.

She shook her head. "I'm fine."

He held up his cell phone and jiggled it at her—a reminder to call if she needed him. Then walked away. Yet as he walked he stopped when a little boy ran up to him, holding out his *boina* for pesos. He gave the child a handful of money and tousled his hair, which made her picture of Jack even more confusing. "I don't think I'm wrong about you, Jack Kenner," she whispered. Surprisingly, he was still carrying his lights in her last image of him before he faded into the darkness.

The hospital was unusually quiet. Most of the patients had checked themselves out to go to the festival, and it was almost eerie wandering down the hall, hearing nothing but the echo of his own footsteps on the cement floors.

So maybe being alone wasn't everything it was cracked up to be. He was used to it, though. It was what he knew, what he did. His comfort zone. But should he have stayed, tried putting on the pretense of fun for Amanda? She did try hard, and her intentions were so…so selfless. In fact, he couldn't remember ever knowing someone as selfless as she was. That, plus the village did put on a nice party.

Nice village, nice party, nice people… There'd been a time when he'd thought about raising Rosa in as much of her heritage as he could, and the festivals were part of that. Something he'd looked forward to for a little while. He'd pictured her in party dresses, with flowers in her hair. Dancing, playing…having fun. Pictured her older, too, with the little boys beginning to take notice, even though she was still clinging to her daddy's hand. Then pictured her even beyond that, when the boys grew up and he held on tighter.

Pointless memories that had never happened. A miserable reminder of his failings, and Rosa had never got to go to her parties or festivals.

Trying to blot out everything but the sound of his footsteps, Jack cleared his throat as he approached Ezequiel's room. "You in here?" he asked, pushing open the door. No answer, and no Ezequiel. He was probably in town, admiring the lights like everybody else. Which made this the perfect time…

Jack looked up and down the hall, saw no one anywhere, and crept into Ezequiel's room, shutting the door behind him. The boy didn't have much. Some books, precious few clothes, the water bottle, which sat prominently on a shelf. And a framed photo of a woman—young, vital, with Ezequiel's smile. Ezequiel's mother, Jack guessed, a lump forming in his throat. The boy had so little in the world, yet he didn't know that because he was happy. And optimistic. He was grateful for what he had rather than resentful for all those things he didn't have. There was a lesson to be learned there, Jack thought as he tossed the boxes of lights on the cot Ezequiel used as a bed and got to work.

Okay, so maybe he wasn't quite the grump he let on he was. The kid deserved something nice in his life, and while lights were only a temporary bandage on a much bigger hurt, sometimes a bandage helped. So Jack set about the chore, stringing lights over the two-drawer stand, the clothes rod hanging above the bed, the shelf, the door. If there was a place to string lights, he did, and when he left the closet-size area a little while later, purposely leaving the lights on so Ezequiel would see the effect the instant he opened his door, Jack was pleased. And melancholy. It wasn't much, not nearly as much as the kid deserved, but Ezequiel didn't measure his life in terms of what was much, or what he deserved. Jack vowed, though, that next time he went to the village he'd buy a couple of trinkets for Ezequiel, and wrap them for Christmas. He himself wouldn't still be here then, he hoped, but every kid needed a present or two.

Walking across the compound, where a mischievous light fairy had stopped and strung a few strands of lights, Jack thought back to Christmas mornings with Robbie, remembered his brother's excitement, not so much over what he got as the fact that he had presents to unwrap. It hadn't mattered to Robbie that they were all wrapped alike, or that there was a uniform consistency to them. It hadn't mattered that the decorations and lights on the tree were all one color, and every ornament was a precisely measured distance from the one next to it. No, none of that made a difference because his brother had looked at it with such innocence. And awe. In all those Christmases Jack had hated, Robbie had found so much joy and wonderment.

Jack missed that innocence, ached to have it back sometimes. But nothing in his life was innocent. He'd traveled too far, seen too many things, felt the pain of the ultimate failure. So there was no innocence left for him.

Except...Ezequiel. He still had that innocence, that honest expectation of life that everything worked out. For the boy's sake, he hoped Ezequiel could keep that for a long, long time. Hoped that he would find joy and wonderment in a simple string of lights.

So, now what? More journals? Read until he fell asleep? Stare up at the ceiling until the monotony dulled his senses enough to empty his head of the thoughts that usually kept him awake half the night? Go prowl the hospital, see if anything there clicked as a cause of the outbreak? Didn't matter. None of it did because that was the normal cycle of his life, the things he did out of habit. Had done before, would do again no matter where he was. Except tonight the music from the festival wafted over the hospital, and he could hear bursts of muffled laughter from the village. Some of it probably Amanda's.

*Amanda*... He had to stop doing this to himself. Stop torturing himself. Because what the hell good did it do, thinking about her when that was as far as it could ever go? He'd successfully gone maybe ten minutes without thinking about her, but there she was, right back in his head. He couldn't let her stay there, fought to get her out because why let her stay when the result would be something he couldn't hang on to?

But she was there again, like it or not, and as he trudged up the wooden steps to the guest hut, her name pounded rhythmically into his brain the way his feet pounded their rhythm on the wooden planks. *Amanda... Amanda...* "What the...?"

"Surprise!" she said, flipping the light switch that lit up the lights strung around his bed the instant he stepped through the door.

"This is payback, right? I left the festival before my two hours were up so you're paying me back by trying to electrocute me with Christmas lights?"

"Yep, Jack. That's exactly what I'm trying to do—electrocute you." Laughing, she circled around behind him then handed him an *alfajores de maizena*—starch cookie, along with a cup of thick juice. "Mango and orange," she said. "Since you wouldn't stay at the party, I brought the party to you."

"Lights on my bed is a party?" he asked, trying to hold back even though he was touched by her effort.

"It's also a thank-you for being honest with me earlier. Knowing where I might be from is very important to me, Jack. It doesn't answer all the millions of questions I've had for most of my life, but it's a start, and it's more than I had. So I'm grateful, and I'm also sorry if the way I pushed you into telling me caused you any conflict or concern, as that wasn't my intention. But I'm glad I did, because you told me something I needed more than you can know."

She walked over to him, stood on her tiptoes and kissed him on the cheek. "That's for being honest with me."

An honesty that already plagued him, as Amanda was building up hopes that could break her heart. It was not what he wanted and not what he'd intended to do. He might be wrong, but he was pretty certain that she was Mapuche, and how could he have lied to her about that? In truth, he couldn't. Still, her knowledge wasn't necessarily going to be kind and that, more than anything, was his regret. "I was afraid I might owe you an apology for butting in. It wasn't any of my business."

"Except you didn't butt in. I dragged you, and I would have kept after you until you told me. I saw it in you, Jack. Your eyes don't lie. When you looked at me…maybe not *at* me as much as past, me…you knew. Or maybe that was wishful thinking. Whatever the case, the truth is the truth. It scares me but I'll deal with it."

*Naive assertion,* he thought. The truth could be the most painful thing any person ever had to bear. That was what he knew on the deepest level, because the pain of his truths never left him. For Amanda, though, he was glad her naivety served as a shield. He only hoped it was strong enough to sustain her. "Well, I'm sorry, anyway. If not for any offenses I've already created, then I'm sure there'll be a few in my future. So, hold that apology on account, will you?"

"That sure of yourself?" she asked, breaking a pinch off the cookie he wasn't eating and popping it into her mouth. "Um," she murmured appreciatively, going back for a second pinch.

"Years and years of experience."

"And years and years…" she continued, looking up at him with wide eyes,

"Not that many," he grumbled, handing her his cookie.

"You sure?" she teased.

"Okay, well, maybe that many. I do have my reputation…"

"Hard earned and well deserved…or not." She broke the cookie into two pieces then handed half back to him. "So, earlier, when you said there was a woman, someone Mapuche…"

Just like that, all the niceness switched off for him.

One little reminder and he was thrown back into the past. He struggled against it, for Amanda. She didn't need that image, that ugliness touching her. No one did.

"Like I said, I lived in the region for a while. Went there to chase down a contaminant in an orphanage, and decided to stay because…because I liked the area. Got to know the people, became familiar with the Mapuche subtleties. Like your skin color, and the sculpture of your cheekbones. It's very characteristic, very…" He closed his eyes, pictured Rosa. Fought back the lump forming in his throat. "Very nice. When you travel as extensively as I do, chasing after the things I chase, you become good at observing everything around you."

"Did you fall in love there?" she asked. "When you were out in the Pampas villages, did you fall in love with someone?"

He shook his head. "There was this woman…. She caught my eye for a moment, but it didn't work out. Two different worlds. She didn't want to leave hers, I didn't want to leave mine. No, I didn't fall in love. Maybe got a little wiser…" What the hell was he doing, talking about this, talking about anything coming from that part of his life? And how was it that Amanda made it so easy for him to simply start rambling like he was, when that part of his life was off-limits to everyone?

She was getting too close, that was how it was. And he was letting her. Damn, he had to get a better grip. And fast. "Have you told Ben yet?" he asked, making an abrupt change in the subject.

"That I think I'm Mapuche? Not sure how I'm going to do that without implying our parents were…" She shrugged. "Tomorrow, though. And on that note, it's been a long day. For both of us. So I'm going to pull the dividing curtain and bid you happy dreams. And, Jack…really, thank you."

Even with a curtain dividing them, he wasn't sure he could sleep. Too many things had him wound up. Amanda, Rosa, Robbie. Even Ezequiel. "Think I'll go find a rocker out on the porch and read for a while," he said, grabbing his journal and heading for the door. Once there, he turned, only to find Amanda standing in the middle of the room, curtain half-pulled across, merely staring at him. After the longest half minute in the history of the world, she finally pulled the curtain the rest of the way shut, and only her silhouette shone through. "Enjoy the Christmas lights, Jack," she called.

# CHAPTER FOUR

"I THOUGHT you might like a cup of tea," Amanda whispered, trying not to break the silence in the dark of the room. Jack was seated at the desk at the edge of the children's ward, keeping himself to the shadows and simply staring at…well, she wasn't sure. Standing out in the hall, she'd watched him through the door window for a few moments. He'd barely moved. But for the rise and fall of his chest outlined in silhouette, he might have been a statue or a cardboard cutout of a guardian angel sitting there, looking over the children. "It's plain. None of the local spices."

"Thank you," he said, without stirring to take the cup from her.

So she set it down, took a step backward. Thought about leaving, but didn't. "What are you looking for?" she finally asked. He hadn't ever come back into the guest hut. She'd stayed awake a little while, listening for him then had finally drifted off. Later, when the that vexing little howler monkey who lived in the jungle canopy outside had decided to wake up and exercise his air-raid-loud call, probably in the hope of finding a girlfriend who, mercifully, didn't howl, she'd got up to shut the window and seen he still wasn't there.

"Don't know exactly."

"Then why are you here?"

"Sometimes I find the answers I need in the observations. Doing all the tests is fine, but too often the human element is left out of the diagnosis, and that's unfortunate because as doctors we need to stay involved. So while I don't actively treat the patients too often, I like to observe them." Finally, he budged. He looked up at her then drew in a deep breath. "What I observed tonight is that the girl, third bed on the right, has an elevated temperature…to the touch. It's not appreciable; I didn't take a reading with a thermometer. But by morning it will register enough for us to be concerned. That, and she's listless…something there's no test for, but it's a real symptom. Then another child, the boy, last bed on the far side, is more restless than he was earlier. Started about fifteen minutes ago with him kicking off his sheets, and I'm thinking he's getting ready to have a stomachache as he's curling up on his side." He took a sip of the tea. "So why are you here?"

"Monkey outside my window woke me up."

He chuckled. "You know those howlers are the loudest animal in the world, don't you?"

"Especially when he's looking for his lady love."

"Poor guy's probably frustrated as hell." He took another sip. "Can't blame him for trying, though I'd think all that bellowing would drive her away."

"Or make her fall madly in love if he's bellowing to his soul mate." Jack bellowed, she thought. Did he do it to drive people away from him? "So, we've got two more kids getting sick. What are we going to do?"

Jack shrugged. "Even though this bug is probably not communicable by proximity, we separate them from the rest of the kids in the ward. It's easier to watch for specific symptoms that way."

"Which isn't going to be easy as we don't have an abundance of extra rooms. But I'll see what I can find. What's your guess, by the way? I'm assuming you have some idea of what we're dealing with."

"Maybe. But it's something I always keep to myself until I know more. People panic, Amanda. They hear a word, get all kinds of ideas, do all kinds of crazy things. I learned a long time ago that while I'm at the guessing stage, it's better to keep it to myself."

"Makes sense," she said. "Except to the part-owner of the hospital. And she's pretty anxious to know *anything,* even a guess."

"So you're pulling rank on me, turning into my boss?"

Amanda laughed. "Has anybody ever truly been your boss, Jack?"

Smiling, he said, "Once, when I was a kid, I worked in this fast-food restaurant… Actually, I think I caused my boss to quit his job. As in turned in his paper hat in the middle of the shift and ran out the door."

"Because?"

"Kitchen was filthy. I called the Board of Health from his office phone, right in front of him. Probably called him out by name, although I don't remember that part. But it sounds like something I'd do, doesn't it?"

"Probably. But for the greater good, I think. At least, I hope it wasn't over some burnt burgers."

"Burnt would have been preferable. In my mind, I remember the hamburger meat having a greenish tint to it."

Amanda turned up her nose. "So, you've been chasing contaminants of some sort since you were a boy."

"That was my first time. Didn't really know much about contaminants except that green meat probably had something bad growing in it."

"So, what's growing here, Jack? Give me some idea, or at least some hope."

"Hope comes when I nail the diagnosis, because I've never faced anything yet that can't be cured. And this can be cured, Amanda, because the symptoms seem like they're water-borne. Haven't figured out how, but I do have a few culprits in mind, and that's all I'm going to say except that I don't want to move these kids until we know their room is as sterile as we can make it, even though I doubt the bug is growing outside a water source.

"But better safe than sorry. So, after we get them settled in, I'll want cultures of blood, urine, sputum, and other bodily fluids, as well as wound cultures if they have any open incisions, cuts, scrapes or lesions. I'd also like to get some general skin scrapings, just to see what's growing on the surface, because I'm tired of waiting and while I'm leaning in one direction based on a hunch, I need a definitive answer on if we're dealing with a bacterium, a fungal infection, a virus, or some other kind of microorganism… in the event I'm wrong."

"All this without getting any sleep?"

"I slept. Dozed in the chair on the porch for an hour or two."

Rather than sleeping on the other side of the curtain. She didn't know what to make of it. Felt a little hurt, maybe a little angry. But it shouldn't matter because he was doing exactly what he was supposed to be doing—solving the problem. So it was her hurt and anger to get rid of, or allow to bother her. Either way, it had nothing to do with Jack and everything to do with her.

Still, she'd liked that idea that he would be sleeping on the other side of the curtain. It made her feel…less vulnerable. So much for that, though. "By your own admission, you never get it wrong. At least, that's what you told me earlier today…actually, that would be yesterday now, wouldn't it?"

"About my *bugs,* as I call them?" He shook his head. "No, I don't get it wrong because in due course those are the easy things to deal with. They have a pattern, they make logical sense as they're wreaking their havoc. It's life in general I get wrong, pretty much on a daily basis because there's nothing logical about it. Nothing to make sense of out of the havoc it wreaks."

"Maybe if you think of life in terms of something that doesn't need to be fixed or cured so much as something that needs to be enjoyed, you'd be able to deal with it better."

"Easy for the optimist to say."

"I'm not an optimist, Jack. But I'm practical, and practicality in my life dictates I'm happier when I enjoy life, which in turn makes me a better person, which makes me a better doctor. It all works together."

"But practicality in my life is about the work, and the means to an end for whatever I'm trying to find. I don't need to enjoy it, and fixing or curing it isn't hinged on anything other than one goal, which is to stop the contaminant. No joy in it, nothing to make me a better person. Just a matter of something that needs to be dealt with."

"No pride in your accomplishment?"

"Sometimes. I mean, I do have some ego invested. But pride isn't the same thing as joy. Joy comes from another place…. A place I don't need to access."

"Then it's your loss."

"How can you lose something you've never had? Anyway, once I get the contaminant identified, I want to test it for its sensitivity to a range of drugs so that each child can be treated as quickly and as effectively as we're able to do with an appropriate medicine. Then in the meantime, while we're waiting for test results, I'd like to start preventative treatment with a broad-spectrum antibiotic such as penicillin. It's probably not necessary, but I don't want anything else creeping up on us."

"Poor Jack. All work, no play makes him a curmudgeon." But a very sexy one. And she wanted to be the one to break through the rocky exterior because underneath she knew she'd find something else entirely. Maybe something smoldering, or about to erupt. Maybe just a little joy waiting to happen, but not knowing how to do it.

"All work and no play saves lives." He shifted in his chair then stood. "So right now this curmudgeon is going to take himself to the pharmacy to see what antibiotics are available for prophylactic treatment."

Amanda laughed. "Now I get it. First you prescribe then you keep your fingers crossed."

He chuckled. "Something like that." Stepping away from the desk, he motioned for Amanda to follow him into the hall. "Don't want to wake the kids," he said, shutting the door behind him but turning his back to her so he could watch through the window to the ward. "I also want this ward disinfected once we get the kids separated. I know it's been cleaned, probably several times, but I don't want anything left behind."

"You're talking about a lot of resources, Jack. We'll do the best we can, but I can't make any promises. I mean, have you even looked at this place? We operate on nothing. We get expired drugs to give to our patients.... They're still good, still usable, but because they're past their date they can't be sold on the open market, which makes them affordable for us. Also, some of the pharmacies donate them to us, and we have to make use of prescriptions patients turn back in to us because they didn't take all the pills.

"We have used beds, used equipment, limited space. The cost of a single X-ray almost breaks our back, and if it weren't for the kindness of the village women who, as a courtesy, launder our sheets and blankets at their homes, I don't even know how we'd manage doing all that. Food is donated, most of our workers are volunteers. Villagers, who barely have enough to support their own families, leave coins and food on our doorstep to help keep us going.

"So we'll do everything we can to give you what you need. But be patient with us. It takes time. Sometimes it takes begging."

She appreciated his dedication, but appreciating it and knowing what to do about it were two entirely separate things and she was beginning to wonder if Jack was the kind of man who would pick up and leave if he didn't get everything he wanted, when he wanted it. The Jack Kenner she wanted him to be wouldn't, but the Jack Kenner she had standing in front of her right now, the one with expectations they couldn't even begin to fulfill—she didn't know how this was going to work.

"Begging," he grunted. "Fat lot of good that ever does. Especially when people hear only what they want to hear or see only what they want to see."

"Spoken like a man who knows."

"Spoken like a man who won't beg."

"Something from your childhood?" she asked, wondering about the bitterness he wasn't even trying to hide.

"Something from my entire life," he snapped.

See, that was just the way he was. Bordering on friendly one minute, shoving her away the next. It was frustrating. More than that, she was beginning to wonder why she even cared, why she even gave him a thought outside what she'd brought him here to do. It was clear Jack didn't want to be sociable, so why bother?

"Look, on that *sour* note, I'm going to go take my morning shower, then get started on the things you need. If you think of something else…" She shut her eyes, angrier at herself for reacting to his abrupt attitude change than at him for doing such a fast turnaround, nice to contentious in the blink of an eye. "Write it down and tack it to my office door." That said, Amanda spun away and walked down the hall, concentrating on each step she took, measuring her rhythm, keeping it even. Unlike her heart, which was beating erratically.

"I didn't mean to do that," he said, catching up to her and grabbing hold of her arm to slow her down.

"Hey, I'm not the one who's always at odds with the world." She stopped, looked up at him. "But you are, Jack. It's your business, and I'm not going to ask you what's going on because I refuse to turn this into an analyst-patient situation. Not with you. But let me warn you, *as a friend,* it's going to eat you up until there's nothing left. You can't go on living your life the way you do without hurting yourself. In your case, though, since you don't seem to care about yourself…"

"What do you want to hear? That my general loathing of all things happy and fun started in my childhood? Would it make you feel better knowing that I didn't grow up in the loving adopted family you did? That my father's wife, Cade's mother, by the way, adopted me for appearances, and we were forevermore a dysfunctional family of haters and malcontents. Except for Robbie, who was the only good thing…" He stopped, bit down hard on his lip.

"It wouldn't make me feel better knowing any of that, Jack, because I'm not the one who goes around with a perpetual scowl on my face and acid in my belly. But if telling me makes you feel better, then tell me."

"Always the shrink, aren't you?"

"No, Jack. Always the friend. I'm sorry you don't know the difference." More than that, she was sorry she couldn't make a difference for Jack because he had so much good locked away inside. She'd seen it as she'd watched him watch the children a little while ago. Too bad the Jack Kenner standing there frowning at her right now couldn't get to know *that* Jack Kenner. Odds were if he did, he probably wouldn't like him very much. She did, though. She liked *that* Jack Kenner more than she wanted to. Funny thing was, she liked this one, too. Go figure.

"It was like a miracle!" Ezequiel exclaimed. "I opened the door and they weren't there, then all of a sudden my room... It was full of lights."

"What kind of lights?" Amanda asked, knowing exactly where they'd come from. But it wasn't a miracle. It had been Jack, and it was exactly what he would do. Three strands of lights for one little boy and her heart swelled just a little. One minute she was ready to forget Jack existed, then the next minute she was practically weepy over something sweet he'd done for Ezequiel.

"All colors, like the lights in the village."

"And you're sure they weren't there when you left to go to festival?"

Ezequiel shook his head. "Just the one on the ceiling."

"Then I think it's a miracle!" she exclaimed, handing him a box of cotton swabs to carry from the storeroom to the ward. "And I'd like to come and see it later on, if you don't mind. You, um… You didn't mention this to Dr. Kenner, did you?"

"You mean Doc K?" He shook his head. "He had a hundred people in line to see him this morning. He didn't have time."

Jack was handling outpatient clinic this morning? He was certainly full of surprises. "Look, you take those swabs and give them to Nurse Consuela, and I think I'll go see if Jack…Doc K needs some help with those hundred patients."

One hundred turned out to be an exaggeration, but the dozen standing in line waiting for Jack's attention were glad to see her. So was Jack, who'd just finished examining a long-standing case of dry hacks from one of the village's most notorious smokers. "He thought I might have something your brother hasn't suggested," Jack said as Amanda entered the tiny office where Jack was washing his hands and getting ready to see his next patient.

"Did you?" she asked, fighting back a smile.

He nodded toward the trash can, where an almost full pack of *cigarillos* had been discarded, all wadded up.

"Do you know how much those cost him?" she asked, impressed he'd had the nerve to do what needed to be done, even though that wouldn't make him any friends here.

"Do you know how much of my time he wasted when he's not willing to make an effort to quit?"

"Señor Juarez sits on the village governing board. He's not really a good friend to the hospital. Doesn't like outsiders interfering with the people here. But it's a relationship my brother's been trying to cultivate, so I hope you didn't do something to…"

"Consider it cultivated." A slow, amused smile spread

across his face. "Better than cultivated, actually. More like rock solid."

"How, when you threw away his *cigarillos?* He loves those things, Jack. Would sooner give up his wife than his smokes. And he's got a lovely wife."

"I mentioned the wheezes in his chest. It caught his interest."

"He was wheezing?"

"A little. Nothing I'd consider serious. But I did say how wheezes could be an early warning of other lung disease—asthma, emphysema. Maybe I might have mentioned something about a lifetime of inhalers and oxygen. And that I couldn't make a proper diagnosis because I didn't have the right equipment."

"Am I going to regret the end of the story, where Señor Juarez vows to shut down the hospital if it's the last thing he ever does?"

"Oh, ye of little faith."

"Oh, me with lots of prior experience with the man."

"Well, in this case, *new* experience paid off because I think you'll prefer the ending where Señor Juarez promises to scrounge every hospital in Argentina if that's what it takes to find us some used pulmonary function testing equipment."

"Seriously? He's going to help us?"

He kept a deliberately stoic face. "And here you were, thinking the worst of me."

"Does he have some kind of chronic obstructive pulmonary disease?" she asked.

Jack shook his head. "Probably not. I prescribed some antibiotics for a mild case of bronchitis, though. With the promise that Señor Juarez will be the first one tested on our new equipment, once he finds it."

"You're bad," she said, smiling. Another one of those near-weepy moments.

"Been accused of worse."

"Do you ever just try to make things easy?"

"You mean, on purpose?" he asked, giving way to a half smile.

"Maybe not," she said. "Because sometimes bad is very, *very* good, isn't it?"

He felt the zing of her words, the heat and tension of them. Had to take in a deep breath to steady himself. Another time, another place, he and Amanda might have had a different ending to *their* story. Too bad he'd slipped ahead to the end of the book and knew what was there. Too damn bad.

"Anyway, I'm here to relieve you so you can get back to what you'd rather be doing. We turned the waiting room into your isolation room, moved the waiting room to the front porch, and I've got several people ready to start cleaning as soon as you give the word. So you'd better go take charge."

"What about the rest of my patients here? I can't just walk away and leave them."

"I'll make sure they're seen. Oh, and, Jack, those lights in Ezequiel's room…"

"What lights?" he asked, jotting down a quick note in a patient chart then snapping it shut.

"The Christmas lights."

"The kid strung up some Christmas lights? Good for him."

"You're not very good at acting innocent, you know."

"Innocent of what?"

"He thinks it was a miracle, Jack. One minute they weren't there, then the next they were."

"Lights are lights. Let the kid believe whatever he wants to believe. It doesn't really matter, does it?"

"Yes, it matters," she said, stepping up to him, standing on tiptoe and kissing him on the cheek. "It matters because it was a nice thing you did for him. In a more devious way, a nice thing you did for Señor Juarez, too. And the hospital, as we're going to get some equipment. Nice, all the way around."

Niceties made him nervous. They came with motives and obligations, and he'd given all that up years ago. "You're not going to kiss me again, are you?" he asked, laying his hand on doorknob, hesitating because he was actually hoping for what was turning into her customary thank-you.

"Maybe I won't…" She smiled and stepped up to him. "Maybe I will." This time, though, the kiss wasn't to his cheek. It was full on the lips. Not a brush to his lips, though, or lingering. More like a promise. And by the time he was out in the hall, his knees were shaking. Well, maybe not so much in the literal sense as the figurative, but he did stop, raise his fingers to his lips, and wonder.

"What the hell are you doing, Kenner?" he asked himself, quite aware there wasn't a rational answer in him when it came to Amanda. "What the hell are you doing?"

"You're setting up a new ward?" Ben called from halfway down the hall. He was emerging from a patient room, working at twice the speed of anybody else at the hospital, looking worn out even though the day had barely begun.

Did the man ever sleep? Jack wondered, because from the look of him he seemed like someone who would prowl the halls eternally. But everybody had their own way to avoid whatever it was they wanted to avoid. Life, people, love…that void where something you cared for was ripped away.

Jack had developed several means of turning away from what he didn't want to see, and he practiced them with the skill of a master. Not gladly, but necessarily. And he was sure Ben would share that same deep understanding. He saw it in the lines etched on Ben's face. "We need to get the kids isolated, not so much because of what they have but because I want to keep them restricted from what other people might give them. So I've got it in the works right now. Amanda turned over the waiting room to me."

Ben nodded his approval. "As you've noticed by now, I'm not much of a manager. So I appreciate you taking charge of this and moving forward."

"You manage in subtleties. Pretty smart and, as Amanda accused me of being, pretty devious."

"Yes, the pulmonary-function equipment. Good job, turning Señor Juarez around not only in our favor but sending him out to scrounge equipment. If you knew how many times I've tried to get that man to cut back on his smoking… Anyway, back to the bug."

"The bug… I made some calls. A few people owe me favors, and I've called some of them in. If you can find me the transport, I can get the testing supplies we need."

"Should I bother asking how?"

"Nothing illegal. And contrary to what your sister might think, nothing even devious. But when you travel as much as I have, you meet people, do some favors. People make promises. You know, *If you ever need anything…* I happen to be one of those who hangs on to those promises, because you never know when you'll need to call one in." Jack held up his cell phone. "I called. Now I have to work out the logistics of getting the supplies flown in."

"Amanda said you were different. She sure as hell was right about that."

"Have you talked to her since last night?"

Ben nodded. "Briefly."

"She told you what I said to her?"

"About her potentially being Mapuche? You know, I really don't have time to get into it now, but how could you do that? Without proof, *why* would you do that?"

Jack chuckled humorlessly. "She asked, I answered. But you already knew, or suspected, didn't you, Ben? You know the people. You know the differences between someone from a Mediterranean background and someone from the Pampas regions in Argentina."

"What I know... All I know is that our parents found life easier by taking the path of least resistance. Not searching for my sister's heritage made life easier for them."

"But you knew she wanted to know and yet you didn't tell her."

"Tell her what? Because I don't *know* anything. Neither do you. So why drag her through that when there's nothing to be gained?"

"There comes a point, Ben, when protection turns into suffocation. Then everybody involved gets hurt. But that's for you and your sister to sort out." He patted Ben on the shoulder. "I shouldn't have been the one to tell her, but I wasn't going to be the one to lie. She's strong, though. She'll work through it." He got why Ben was angry. What he didn't get, though, was why he'd kept the secret. Protecting parents was one thing, but weighing that against Amanda's right to know? Well, it was between Ben and his sister now. He hoped they could, or would, work it out. "Anyway, after I get the supplies we need lined up..."

"I'll call in a favor or two of my own. You do what you have to, and I'll make arrangements for a plane."

"Seriously?" Even though Amanda had unknowingly pitted him against Ben, he liked the guy. He was smart and resourceful. And being a devoted brother wasn't the worst thing in the world. Too bad he and Ben had absurdly different views on Amanda's well-being, or else they might have become friends.

"As serious as I am about protecting my sister."

So there it was, the implied threat. Except it was unnecessary. He wasn't the one who *would* hurt her, or *had* hurt her. "I'm not going to hurt Amanda, Ben. But I'm not going to protect her to her detriment, either."

Ben nodded, but didn't respond. Rather, he turned and walked away, not even glancing back when he rounded the corner.

Amanda stepped up behind Jack yet kept a proper distance. "He's always tried to take care of me, almost from the first day my parents brought me home. I was a toddler, and Ben just swooped in and hasn't ever really swooped out. That's what makes him such a good doctor. He truly cares."

"So why Argentina?"

"What do you mean?"

"Why is he operating this hospital in Argentina? He could have gone to Peru or Brazil, could have gone to any number of places in Africa, but he's here, and you have a heritage here."

"Coincidence?" she asked.

"Could be," Jack said, moving on past her. "Have you ever asked him why he came to Argentina?" There was so much protectiveness going on between brother and sister, yet Jack wondered what happened when you broke through that layer. There was definitely something else happening underneath, some kind of a riptide waiting to swell up and pull someone under. So, what was it? Ben hadn't admitted he knew Amanda was Mapuche, but what if he did? What if he *did* know, and…

*Damn.* Suddenly, it hit him. So obvious, so unthinkable. The beginnings of a truth that might be better off unanswered if he intended to keep his promise to Ben. He wouldn't hurt Amanda. *Wouldn't.* Not for any reason. Still, her Mapuche heritage… Ben suspected. He suspected the same thing Jack did. *Damn it to hell.* Why had she asked him—him of all people—who she was? And why couldn't he have simply left it alone? Stuck to his tried and true life course and kept his distance?

Because she was Amanda, that was why. Persuasive. Impossible to resist. Impossible for *him* to resist. Amanda.

A sudden, cold chill ran up Jack's spine. Not one that tingled but one that jabbed hard. *What have I done?* She was too inquisitive, she would want to know the answer to the question he'd posed: Why Argentina? She'd ask until she found out, and that was what he berated himself with over and over as his thoughts came together and his suspicions locked into place like pieces of a jigsaw puzzle. Pieces of Amanda.

*What have I done?*

He'd opened a door—that was what. Now he sincerely regretted that she wasn't Mediterranean. Wished he hadn't recognized the Mapuche in her.

On the other hand, maybe he was wrong about everything. Maybe Rosa's tragedy had jaded his life so badly he couldn't see anything through the haze except more heartache. *God, please, let it be faulty judgment.* It wasn't much of a hope to hang anything on. It was all he had, though. The hope he was wrong.

Somehow, however, he knew he wasn't. When that realization punched him, another cold chill shot up his spine, and this one settled in. What the hell had he done to Amanda?

"This is the last bed, Doc," Ezequiel called to him thirty minutes later. He'd been serving as translator throughout the whole cleaning process. "All clean. Ready for sheets."

Without real testing equipment, there wasn't much he could do. He still had a few swabs left, and some culture dishes not yet contaminated. It didn't come close to being enough, but it would work for now. On the bright side, the room was sanitized thanks to the generous efforts of village volunteers. Not sterilized, but as clean as it could be under the circumstances, and every one of the ladies who'd trooped in earlier with mops and pails had put their hearts and souls into the chore.

"Tell the ladies to go ahead and make up the beds," he instructed Ezequiel, as he climbed out from under one of the beds he'd been swabbing and stood up. "Oh, and after we get this transfer made, I'd like to see your lights."

"You would?" Ezequiel cried.

Jack forced a smile, even though he didn't feel much like smiling. His mind was still on Amanda, what he'd said, what he might have set in motion by telling her who she might be. "I want to see how they're strung, because I'm thinking about putting lights in here."

"All the rooms?" Ezequiel asked. "Could we put them in all the rooms? I can do that, Doc K. Please, let me be the one."

"You're not really allowed to go in the patient rooms, are you?"

Ezequiel's face dropped. "No, Doc Ben won't let me."

Jack fished a handful of money from his pocket and gave it to the boy. "Well, we're just going to have to figure where those lights will go, won't we? But first go down to the village and see how many you can buy."

"With all the money?" he asked, the excitement starting to return.

"All the money. Oh, and, Ezequiel…" He handed the boy a few more bills. "Stop and buy some empanadas from one of the vendors, and some of that *mate* tea. Enough for everybody who's volunteering this morning." He thought about the boy trying to lug all that back then had second thoughts. "Actually, you go get the lights, I'll get the food." Which was what he did. Trotted straight out the door, then halfway to the village Amanda caught up to him.

"I hear we're going to have a party this afternoon. That's so nice of you, Jack. I love parties, especially when they're impromptu."

He clenched his jaw when he saw her. In the past little while he'd reasoned himself out of believing that she would ask the Argentina question. He hoped she would, didn't know what he'd do if she didn't. Then come back to the one sure thing he knew above all else—Amanda was strong. If his mention of Ben's motives for being in Argentina opened up doors she found difficult, he'd help her shut them or move through them. He'd created the rift, and that was all he could do to make amends.

In all likelihood she was a child of Argentina, and wasn't it her right to know for sure? And it wasn't like she hadn't already been looking for herself. Still… "We're going to have food as in feed the volunteers for working so hard."

"Food and lights and tea. To some, that's a party, Jack."

"Let me guess. You're one of those people who believes everything can be a party?"

"It can, if you want it to be. It's all in your attitude."

"Then it's a good thing mine is perpetually bad, or else I might be partying every day."

Amanda laughed. "Your true colors are showing, Jack."

"You mean my evil, dark heart?" A heart that couldn't quite achieve any shade of dark when it came to Amanda.

"I mean whatever you're trying to hide isn't hidden very well. Lights, tea, empanadas…" Grinning, Amanda latched on to his arm. "Oh, and to go with the empanadas and tea, I'd think about buying something sweet. A pastry. Maybe some *facturas*. And just so you'll know, the best ones are stuffed with *crema pastelera, dulce de leche* or *membrillo,* then sprinkled with sugar or icing. Try the *panaderia* on the last corner on the left. Theirs are the best. So, now that I've fulfilled my mission in convincing you to buy *facturas,* see you back at the hospital." She unlatched her arm from his, and stepped away.

"You think I'm convinced?"

She wrinkled her nose. "I know you're convinced."

"But you're not going with me to make sure?" he asked, admittedly disappointed. The feel of her hanging on to him was actually quite pleasant. They'd been a nice few steps with her, and he'd hoped for a few more.

She shook her head. "I'm going to do a quick physical on each of the kids we're moving before we get them settled in. I know you checked them last night, but I want to see if anything's changed. By the time you get back, we should be well under way with the transfer."

"So you chased after me halfway to the village because…"

"Because I like *facturas*. And in case you're interested, *dulce de leche* is my favorite."

She smiled, spun around and headed straight back to the hospital. And Jack watched, couldn't help himself. Today, her shorts were more modest, her shirt a simple, oversized gauzy cotton, her hair tied up more the way he was used to seeing it. All of it so…sexy. Which was why he watched. Couldn't have helped himself if he'd wanted to. He didn't want to.

"All of them, Doc K," Ezequiel shouted, from the other side of the street.

The boy's voice broke though Jack's distraction, and he blinked hard to refocus. "What?"

"The lights. I bought all of them." His arms were stacked with boxes of lights, almost more than he could juggle. "We can light up the whole hospital."

Jack's mind wasn't on lighting up the whole hospital. It was on one bed only, already strung with lights, and the curtain that separated it from the bed across the room. Such an imposing piece of thin cloth, and while it wasn't yet noon he was already preparing himself to lose sleep over it tonight.

Had to be a bug bite, he thought as he headed for the *panaderia,* hoping for *dulce de leche.* Some uncharted bug must have bitten him and sucked out all his common sense. That was all it could be. Yep, definitely all it could be.

# CHAPTER FIVE

"Day after tomorrow?" Jack asked, steadying his thin thread of forbearance with a calming breath. The delay was nobody's fault. He understood that. Testing supplies were en route, but their free plane ride had been delayed a day while the plane was being serviced. Now all he could do was sit and twiddle his thumbs and at the same time try to keep up a facade of patience. Neither twiddling nor patience were his strong suits. But he didn't want Amanda to see his ruffled feathers because... Well, it mattered. He didn't know why, as he'd never really tried creating a good impression before. Accept him or not. Either way, it didn't matter because he got along with his life just fine, no muss, no fuss.

So this was quite an unexpected turn for him, trying to make a good impression. And he wasn't very adept at it. He felt that hot bother creeping along the edges of his collar, considered opening the window and just jumping out. "If that's the best they can do, it'll be fine. We'll make it work until then." Said with a clenched jaw.

Ben shrugged. "Wish I had better news for you."

"Me, too, since this morning we had our first adult patient come down with mild symptoms, and I'm betting there will be more to follow." Jack wedged himself between Ben and Ben's desk, trying to avoid the scent he knew had to be Amanda's shampoo. The quarters here were abysmally tight, and all three of them were nearly pressed together in this little conference. He didn't like anybody in his personal space, and he didn't like being in anybody else's personal space. Yet here he was, personal space overlapping all over the place, especially with Amanda, where the scent of her was reminding him of things he didn't get to have.

He needed room, air to breathe. Needed Amanda a safe distance away from him. But this spur-of-the-moment meeting had to be here, shoulder to shoulder, because Jack feared being overheard anywhere else. One misunderstood word turned into misconceptions, turned into panic. He'd seen it happen before. Seen all hell break loose. People getting scared. Out of control. Doing crazy things because they didn't understand.

That was what had happened with Rosa, why she'd died—misconceptions and panic. People who hadn't understood and conditions too chaotic to listen. So now better cramped than sorry.

Never mind he wanted to bury his face in Amanda's hair and nuzzle. "Like I told Amanda, I could take an educated guess what we're dealing with because I'm pretty sure it's some sort of water-borne problem. Depending on which one it is, the treatment would be vastly different, though."

"We're talking about what kind of life form?" Ben asked. "Protozoan, viral, bacterial, parasites?"

"Take your pick. The symptoms are all similar, with some distinctions, and right now I'm looking for those distinctions."

"And apart from the preventative antibiotics you're prescribing, is there anything else we can do?" Amanda asked.

"Treat symptoms like you've already been doing. Antinausea drugs, fight fever, restrict diet. Going after it with anything else could do more harm than good, so we treat what we can see…" It was getting too hot in there now, the early summer heat beating through the window without mercy, a bead of sweat trickling down Amanda's chest, on its merry way to some unseen destination between her breasts. Realizing that he'd been staring, totally fixated, and hoping no one had noticed, he glanced away. "Until we diagnose what we can't see."

"Could the contaminant be in the drinking water?" Ben asked. "I know that's the obvious question, and you've probably already considered it. But I have to ask."

"I don't think it's what anybody's drinking, because everybody would be sick, or at least a lot more people would be if they were drinking the contaminant. Something I'd like to do anyway, to be on the safe side, is filter the hospital's drinking-water supply, because that's where you always have to look first."

"What if we boil the water before we consume it?" Ben asked. "Will that get rid of the contaminant?"

"It can in most cases. But I still want it filtered as well, to be on the safe side."

"Leaving us in another dilemma, trying to figure out how to get a filter system." Ben sighed heavily. "These weren't the things they told us about in medical school."

"Med school teaches us to be doctors, real life teaches us to be doctors who know how to function in the world," Jack said, then shut his eyes and totally zoned out. Mentally stepped away from the office for a moment.

"I'll bet Jack's coming up with another idea," Amanda whispered, observing him, totally caught up by his process.

He didn't respond for another minute as both Amanda

and Ben stayed dead silent, observing him. Measuring their breaths. Then he opened his eyes, nodded, didn't smile, but his frown disappeared and Amanda and Ben finally breathed normally again.

"It's only a temporary fix, because at some point, when we isolate the bug we're dealing with, we're going to have to take care of it with more than a patch. But for now we could make a filter. Or filters. I've done this before and I'm betting we'll find everything we need in the village. Maybe put Ezequiel in charge of going down there and scavenging the parts. Then put his resourcefulness to use by letting him recruit volunteers to help in the assembly.

"Keep in mind this isn't a cure. Not even close. But we'll filter the water then boil it, and that goes for what we consume as well as what's used for sponge baths and washing our hands."

He finally managed to wedge himself between Amanda and Ben then opened the door, glad to make his imminent escape. "I'll make the supply list and give it to Ezequiel and hope we can get this project started later today."

"Then while he's out hunting for the supplies, would you like to make a house call with me?" Amanda asked, stepping in front of him, blocking his way out.

"House call?"

She nodded. "It's a dicey drive to one of the outlying villages. Nice people, fairly isolated. Don't really want to do it alone. Normally I take Ezequiel, but as he's going to be busy…"

He saw the corners of her mouth turn up, saw mischief start to twinkle in her eyes. "Something tells me you don't want me for my abilities as a doctor." He purposely avoided looking at the damp area spreading even more across the front of her T-shirt. Something about Amanda glistening with sweat was more provocative than he cared to deal with.

"And on my sister's less-than-clever attempt to manipulate, I take my exit," Ben said, sliding between them and on out into the hall.

"Okay, so maybe I do have an ulterior motive. The vehicle I'm going to use is a little touchy," she said, her grin widening. "Sometimes it needs help."

"As in?"

"A push start."

"Oh. You mean you push, I steer?"

"However you like it, Dr. Kenner," she said, sweeping out of the room. "I'll be ready to roll, *or push,* in thirty minutes. Wear your hiking boots, by the way. Half the journey's by foot."

A trek through the jungle with Amanda… He didn't know which would be more threatening—the pumas, skunks and wild boars they might encounter, or Amanda. Somehow, he thought Amanda. "This just keeps getting better and better. Next you'll be telling me we're going to have to ford a river."

She smiled. "Just a small river. You won't have to carry me, if that's what's worrying you. Currents aren't strong, water's not deep."

Actually, carrying her sounded like the high point. "Depends on whose currents you're talking about. And the water's always deep, Amanda. Sometimes you don't know it until you're in it." Or drowning.

One final sweep through the isolation ward to check on the kids, and he was on his way out the door. Truthfully, he didn't mind going to treat some villagers, but his preference would have been staying here, with the proper supplies, to do the job he was supposed to be doing. It was frustrating, being so…impotent. This HAI should have been diagnosed and treatment for it well under way.

What frustrated him even more than the fact that he hadn't even begun was what he knew he'd find when he did get started. It was going to be a simple bacterium. Easy to diagnose under normal circumstances, easy to treat. Except here it was turning into a convoluted mess because there was nothing he could do about it…*yet*. No control of what he should have been able to control…a situation that wasn't making him clamor to stay in medicine. At least, not right now.

Seeing Ezequiel running up the path toward him, though, made him wonder what he did clamor for. Was there anything any more?

"Now's a good time to come see my lights, Doc K," Ezequiel said, almost breathlessly. Jack rubbed his forehead, hoping it would quell his rising frustration. Then braced himself not to show it to Ezequiel. "Now's a *great* time to see your lights!" he said with more enthusiasm than he expected, then allowed Ezequiel to lead him down the corridor and around a couple of corners, until they reached the small room where the boy put on a grand ceremony of opening the door with a swoosh.

"Ta-dah," Ezequiel sang, stepping back so Jack could see every last one of them. "Isn't it beautiful?"

"It's beautiful." Jack was so touched by the sentiment, a hard lump formed in his throat, and he fought to swallow it back. A water bottle, a few lights…things no one ever thought about, yet they meant so much to Ezequiel. "What I want you to do now is to plan how we're going to string up the lights in the public areas."

"I don't know…" Ezequiel began shaking his head "…what they are."

"The waiting room, the place where the receptionist sits. The porch outside. I think Doc Ben's office would be good, too." He watched the boy's eyes grow wide from excitement. "Can you draw pictures, Ezequiel?"

"A little."

"Then here's what we need to do. I want you to draw a picture of each room, then draw in where you'd like to hang the lights." It was a little bit of a stall, but one, along with the water-filter assignment, that would keep Ezequiel busy until he returned from the house call. "We'll use those drawings to show us where to hang the lights."

"Tonight? Can I hang the lights tonight? And you'll help me, *please?*"

How could he refuse an invitation like that? Ezequiel was about as captivating a kid as he'd ever known. Shame the boy didn't have a real home. Damn shame he couldn't take him in, take him back to Texas since no one would even care, give him a real home and... No! This was what had cost him Rosa. That kind of thinking. The first thought that seemed so easy, so right. But doing the right thing, the easiest thing had turned so wrong. Wrong for her. Wrong for Ezequiel.

Besides, the boy was cared for. Being educated. Fed. Clothed. He was lucky. *Leave it alone,* Jack cautioned himself. Leave it the hell alone, or it would break his heart the way Rosa had. "Sure. After dinner. Don't know if we can get it all done, but we can give it a good start.

"But before you do that, I have something else for you to do. Something very important that will help keep people in the hospital from getting sicker. It's a big job, Ezequiel," he cautioned as he grabbed the boy's undivided attention. "And you're the only one I can count on to do it for me."

Jack spent the next few minutes explaining what they

were going to do with the filters, then he gave Ezequiel a list of commonplace supplies he needed from the town. Between that and the stringing of the lights, Ezequiel had some busy hours ahead of him. Hours, Jack hoped, that would be valuable to a boy who had so little in the world.

"He really idolizes you," Amanda said, once Ezequiel had scampered off to the village in search of filter materials. "Then after you gave him all that authority…you may have a friend for life, if you want it."

"I don't get involved," Jack said, turning on his gruff self.

"That's not what I'm seeing. Every time you look at Ezequiel, I see…something even bigger than involvement."

"Then you're not seeing right. Kids are okay as patients, but that's as far as I ever get involved with them. They're… needy. I don't need needy."

Amanda actually laughed. "That's supposed to convince who? You or me? Because I see need, Jack, every time Ezequiel comes around. And it's not his need I'm seeing."

"Then get glasses."

Jack started to march off, but Amanda ran to catch up with him. "Why is it so difficult admitting that you care for Ezequiel?"

"It's not. I like him. End of story." No way in hell he was one of those people who wore his heart on his sleeve. He'd loved a child once, she'd died. He couldn't go through it again. More than that, he wouldn't go through it again. And Amanda wasn't going to goad that story out of him because she'd get all sympathetic, try saying the right things, try being supportive, try making the situation better. But he wasn't the kind of person who required that. Being left alone was all he needed.

"If you say so, but—"

"But nothing. Let's go get that car push started and get out of here. Okay? Otherwise I'm sure I can find a few patients in the clinic who'd like me to see them."

"You're not really such a hard case, Jack," she said as they headed across the road, Jack trying his utmost to stay ahead of her and Amanda trying her utmost to keep up with him. "And I'm not fooled. But if you want me to pretend I believe you, I will." She added under her breath, "Even if I don't."

"You never let anyone get in the last word, do you?"

Pushing the door, she held it open for Jack then as he passed by her said, "Not if I can help it."

Glancing in the rear-view mirror, they were already off the hospital compound and Jack was still pushing the rusty bucket of bolts formerly known as a car. It was a tiny thing, two seats, no glass in the side windows, very loud once it got going, and right now it wasn't going. But watching him put his muscle into the effort was funny. Jack Kenner was all kinds of interesting, and the more she was around him, the more she admired.

Of all the times to meet someone like him, it had to be now. Sure, he wasn't responsive in the way most women wanted a man to be responsive. But she wasn't most women, and here, in Argentina, she *had* seen him watching her in off moments. The Amanda he was watching, though, wasn't really her. At least, not in the true sense, because in another two weeks, when she returned to Texas, she'd be back to her usual persona.

She was flattered, though, whichever Amanda she was. More than that, she liked the tingle she got when he was watching. No denying it was sexual.

But some of it was about knowing what her two different sides were about now. Jack had done that for her. Given her a part of herself no one in her life had even wanted to talk about, which better allowed her to understand why Argentina welcomed her, why she thrilled to that wildness it ignited in her, a wildness that didn't want to be tamped down. And why Texas tamped all that down in her, sent her back to the woman her parents had raised her to be… proper and reserved. She felt Argentina, she dwelled in Texas. Not quite polar opposites, she supposed, but definitely a night-and-day situation. Only which was night in her, and which was day?

Glancing back in the mirror again, she decided she liked being whichever one got to see Jack reasoning with an old car. Telling it to please start. No anger, no shouting, no grumpiness. Just gentle persuasion aimed at something that should have been relegated to the scrap heap a decade ago. "Maybe if you could push it just a little bit faster…" she yelled to him, then spun to watch his reaction in the rear-view mirror.

His reaction was fast, and totally unexpected. He sprinted from the back of the car to the driver's side, which had no door, and pointed to the ground.

"What?" she asked, amused.

"Get out."

"And do what?"

"We'll get another ride."

"This ride is perfectly fine. It always starts."

"And wastes time. So get out or I'll…"

"What? What will you do, Jack?" He wasn't scowling now, wasn't smiling, either. More like…simmering, ready to ignite. But ignite how? *How?* That was always the question with Jack. And she never knew the answer.

Didn't matter, though, because it stirred her up, thinking about all the possibilities. Jack good, Jack bad. All the same. All so sexy.

"I'm going to ford that stream," he said, then bent down and scooped her into his arms.

Next thing she knew, she was staring him straight in his gorgeous dark brown eyes. Giddy to be there, taken aback that she actually was because she and Jack were so close Amanda could practically feel the prickle of his rough stubble on her cheek. Causing definite heart palpitations, maybe some vertigo. "Make sure we don't drown," she finally managed, when she'd recovered her wits. Somehow she had the feeling she was already part way there.

As it turned out, Jack carried her to the end of the street, to the village's only taxi. A pleasant ride in his arms, all things considered. Then they got into the taxi, which would take them to the end of the next road, and from there they'd walk.

"Were you trying to impress me with your brute strength, Dr. Kenner?" she asked, fully expecting his usual sarcastic remark as she crawled into the backseat. Instead, he said nothing for what seemed like an eternity. His usual behavior and she was getting used to it—him staring at her. This time, though, he was staring so intently she felt a warm blush creeping to her cheeks.

Then, finally. "*Were* you impressed?"

She wanted to find an appropriate comeback. Wanted to say something sassy and provocative and pithy. But sitting there together on the seat, their shoulders touching, and their thighs, she didn't want to be touching because the more she thought about it the harder her heart pounded, and the harder her heart pounded the more she was afraid he would hear. Or she'd actually go woozy from the blood rushing from her brain to her heart. Or worst of all, in this moment of panic and panic attack and uncertainty, she'd open her mouth and say something totally, utterly stupid. So she simply nodded. Then looked out the window for the rest of the ride to the end of the road, wondering with every revolution of the tire what was coming over her.

The rest of the ride couldn't have come soon enough, because by the time the taxi let them out at virtually nowhere, she so wanted to get away from Jack that Amanda practically ran to the trail head.

"What's going on?" Jack asked, turning to watch the taxi drive away.

"Everything. The hospital's situation, trying to find out who I am. I'm not sure I know what I'm doing anymore."

"You're doing what you have to do," he said, picking up both their backpacks as they headed off toward the path leading to their house call. "Dealing with what you have to deal with."

"You don't think it's the right thing, do you? Trying to find out—"

"I don't think it's any of my business," he interrupted.

"You made it your business when you told me you thought I might be Mapuche."

"Your choice, Amanda. Not mine." He held out his hand to help her over a log on the path. "For what it's worth, would it do any good if I told you I think your search is going to be more frustrating than productive, that you're looking for the proverbial needle in the haystack? And that I know you're *going* to go through with it no matter what anyone says? Which I admire."

"Probably not," she said, enjoying the feel of his hand.

Rough, used to hard physical work. Not like most doctors with their velvety skin. "Or maybe a little."

He sighed heavily, still holding her hand as they continued down the trail. "Let me get through the crisis at the hospital, then I'll make a call or two and see what I can find. But I'm not promising anything. Understand that, I'm not going to promise you anything."

"You already did," she said, afraid to even wiggle her fingers lest he remember he had her hand and let go. "They lied to me, Jack. I don't know why they did, but I do know my parents lied to me." She'd never said that aloud before, but to reveal such a dark secret to Jack was easy. He made it easy. "By not lying to me, you're giving me the biggest promise I've ever had."

"Have you talked to Ben about any of this?" He actually gripped her hand a little harder, started to squeeze.

She shook her head, forced to pull her hand from his when his grip started to become painful. Wondering why he'd gone from tender to tense. Probably because he truly didn't want to be involved, she decided. None of this had been in the bargain when he'd agreed to come to Argentina, and she'd so handily dragged him into it. Something she was beginning to regret but didn't know what to do with.

"It would hurt him, and I won't do that. My brother's had his own share of problems over the years, and I won't add to them. The thing is, I just want to know. It won't make any difference in who I am, or what I do, but..."

"But you have the right to know who you are. I supposed we all do, don't we?"

"Then even though you don't agree with what I'm doing, you understand."

"I understand. And you're right, I don't agree, but if I were in the same place, I'd probably be doing the same things you are, the same things you did in the past. So, couldn't you simply ask your parents?"

She wanted him to take her hand again, stepped up next to him in case he wanted it, too. But the offer wasn't there. In fact, Jack took the lead, went a few steps ahead of her. Seemingly protective, but was he really just trying to keep his distance?

"I never told them I was looking for my records, but my dad found out. Then my mother was diagnosed with cancer, and he begged me to stop. Said it would kill her if she ever found out. So I stopped. Called off my lawyer. Mother survived the cancer, but now…she's frail."

"Your dad?"

"Died," she said. "Begging me, on his death bed, not to continue looking. The thing is, Jack, my parents weren't monsters who bullied me or ever treated me badly. I was cherished, they gave me everything. So while I want to do this, and I need to do this…"

"You're conflicted."

"Like you can't even begin to imagine. And maybe starting the search again is selfish of me, because it really *won't* make a difference in my life."

He stopped, and turned to face her. "Except there's this hole in your soul that needs to be filled. It's awful not feeling complete, and I'm sorry you have to go through it."

She looked up at him, a stray tear sliding down her cheek. Sniffed. Then nodded. "I wasn't sure anybody could sympathize. You know, great life, every advantage, what difference does anything else make?"

"It makes a difference." Stepping forward, he stopped and brushed away a tear with his thumb. "I don't know how I can help you, but if you give me a few days, until I can get the HAI isolated and figure out a way to prevent it, I'll make those calls. See if I can get back in touch with an old friend who runs an orphanage down there. He may be a good resource for you."

"Thank you," she said, her voice subdued. "That means more than you can know."

Impulsively, she stood on tiptoe to brush a kiss on his cheek, but as she pressed herself closer to Jack, it was far closer than any friendly thank-you kiss would ever call for, and their proximity, mixed with the blistering noontime heat… It was smothering him, betraying him in ways he'd never experienced before. The melting of will, the melting of soul… The physical throb of need arising so quickly and intensely there was nothing he could do to stop it.

Just this once he wanted to give in to it. Not tamp it down or deny it, but satisfy the curiosity, the hunger. It was all he would, or could, allow. But his heart…it was beating so heavily against her chest she would feel it. Would she know that she did crazy things to him he wanted to control? But couldn't? Would she hear the crazy thoughts in his head? The confusion? The argument?

It was either time to step up or step back. And nothing in him was going to let him step back.

One quick kiss to his cheek, her usual, but it was different. And the way he was staring at her…could he see it? See the feelings she'd fought in the taxi ride, that urgency to have more of him when he clearly didn't want the same thing? Or else why this hesitation? Why the stare? Maybe he felt it, too? That rising heat? That convulsive urge? Felt it, didn't know what to do with it, didn't want to get sucked in? Yet he wasn't backing away.

Amanda instantly felt self-conscious about this untempered emotion about to erupt in her, but not enough that she could, or would, look away from him once their eyes met. And fixed. The total awareness passing between them in that moment… For the first time in her life she understood the difference between what she needed and what she wanted.

And it didn't have the dizzying effect she might have expected. Rather, it inspired in her more appreciation for this man—his looks, the lingering trace of aftershave, the tender way he took another step forward, and rather than crushing her with urgency slid his hand around her waist, to the small of her back, and simply caressed her in this moment of uncertainty. With so much patience. And, oh, he had the patience of a saint.

"This is dangerous," she whispered, tilting her face to his until her lips were so close to his she could almost feel the quiver of his flesh on her.

"You're dangerous," he whispered back, his caress hardening as he pulled her against him.

Her lips curved into a sensual smile. "Want to see how much?"

"Here? In the open?" He arched wicked, wicked eyebrows over those dark eyes of his. Eyes that promised to burn right through her.

Amanda drew in a breath, felt it shudder all the way down to her lungs, then pulled him just that fraction of an inch closer, that tiny little measure that made all the difference between possibility and reality, then covered his mouth with hers in a hungry kiss.

Jack responded instantly, returning a kiss much more demanding than her own. And his mouth…so warm. The caress of his lips much softer, yet harder than she could have ever imagined, as he tasted with his tongue, and she opened her mouth with a low moan to welcome all he was offering.

There was nothing tentative in this first kiss. Nothing to explore, nothing to discover for the first time because the need was too great, too fast. The kiss was so new yet so familiar.

Then, as Amanda curled her fingers around Jack's neck, pulling him even closer, Jack pressed his erection into her pelvis, and suddenly the place, the time were gone to them as the ancient cadence doubled its tempo, infusing them with its beat.

Never before had she snaked her leg up a man's leg, yet as her left leg found its way along his, moving ever so slow upward over his thigh, there was no hesitancy in going where this was leading. No thoughts, only responses.

But when he slid his hand underneath her ascending leg, and caressed the back of it, she gasped with pleasure, allowing her pelvis to join in the primal sway with his. Slow, sensual movement. She was caught in the feel, a pure, raw savoring. Couldn't stop. Didn't want to stop. Swaying…pounding…

The feel of his hand slipping under her shirt, pushing aside her bra, finding her breast…

She moaned at the sensation, ready to start the fumble of zippers and buttons and all the things that stood in the way, but when the second moan escaped her, she felt him stiffen. Felt him pull his hand back, slip it away from her.

"What?' she whispered, opening her eyes to see…regret. Then feel her own regret start to slide down over her. "Jack, we…"

He nodded as he let her leg slip back down his. "I know," he said, his voice hoarse. "Duty calls."

"Duty calls," she repeated, tugging her clothes back into

place, trying to tug her heart back into place. But it was the stubborn one. The one refusing to budge. So it was up to her to step away, which was what she did. Stepped away from Jack, bent to pick up her backpack, then sighed the biggest sigh of regret in her life. "So…"

Grabbing his own backpack, he nodded. "So…"

And that was all they said for the next few moments as they both turned longing glances at the Pampas grass, and what that particular patch of grass might have turned into. A memory. *Almost* a memory.

# CHAPTER SIX

As the crow would fly, the hike to *Santo Maria del Rastro* was just at a mile. On that hike, with every last step of it he took, he alternately kicked himself for what had almost happened, and what hadn't happened. Of course he'd wanted that kiss. Wanted more. Had known he shouldn't, but hadn't been able to stop himself, no matter what he'd known. Sure, Amanda had been playing with flirtation almost from the moment he'd arrived, and he'd been enjoying it. All of it. That was all it should have been, though, and all it would have been if he'd had a clear thought in his head. Or an ounce of will.

But the woman was driving him insane in ways he hadn't known he could be driven, and there was only so much resistance in him.

He wasn't whole, though, and she deserved someone who wasn't broken, the way he was. Needed someone stronger to help her through what might be coming. Right now he might be the best available, but in the long-term…

Long-term? Hell, what was that? He didn't have a long-term, which was ultimately what had smacked him into the realization that he had to keep his distance now, even though they had amazing chemistry. She needed more than that chemistry to get her through. He knew that, she didn't. Not yet. But in time…

Damn, this wasn't working out the way it should.

"So, I'll be seeing the women and children in the church," Amanda said, breaking into his thoughts. She was pointing to the bare white wooden structure standing prominently in the middle of the road, the village focal point with everything else growing up around it— the houses, the handful of shops, the school. "Men are going to see you…"

She spun around, smiled mischievously, and nodded in the direction of an old gas station. Dilapidated, with thirty-year-old outdated pumps, and weeds half as high as the windows, not to mention an old hound dog napping lazily in the dirt outside the front door, it hadn't seen much attention for a while. But, then, neither had the proprietor napping alongside his dog, not in the dirt but in a rusty old yard chair that had passed its prime a decade previously.

To refocus his thoughts, pull him back into the moment, Jack blinked hard. "I thought we were making a house call, as in one stop."

"We are. One stop for you, one stop for me. That's the way it usually turns out. They hear a doctor is coming to the village, and aches and pains pop up. Oh, and expect payment for your services. People here want to pay for what they get, usually not in money, but we do take fruits, vegetables, handcrafts… We can use the food, and sell the rest and use the funds for the hospital. But we don't take animals, because we don't kill animals for food, and we can't afford pets, unless someone gives you laying hens or a goat, in which case I'll send Hector up with the Jeep tomorrow to get them. The hospital can always use fresh eggs and milk."

"You can get here by Jeep?" Jack asked.

"From the other end of town. It's a long, winding road in, takes forever, but it's accessible."

"Then why did we walk?" The Jeep would have made things so much less complicated.

"Because walking is faster and the overall distance is shorter. And I love the scenery coming in from that direction. It's good exercise, too, and I like to walk. Don't get the chance too often."

"If I'd taken the lead, would I have gotten to examine my patients in the church while you saw yours in the old garage? Or do I pretty much not get choices in any of this?"

Amanda forced a laugh, one that sounded like she was still under the effect of the Pampas grass. "Oh, I think you took the lead."

Of course he had. He'd wanted to. But she'd been a willing participant. Something he wasn't about to point out for fear of where it would go. "Let's just get on with what we came here to do, okay? I've got to get back to Caridad, and standing here talking isn't getting anything done." He really wasn't so grumpy as he and Amanda parted ways in the middle of the road. Frustrated, maybe. And disoriented, because even with all the cautions and warnings he'd been mulling over since that almost-moment, he still wanted to kiss her. Didn't matter where it would go, or not go, he still wanted to kiss her.

"Okay," he called, struggling to sideline his rising frustration and focus on the work, as he signaled for the few men standing around to follow him, instructing them to step around the hound dog. Which didn't matter, as the dog only barely opened an eye, saw no threat to his domain, and went right back to snoring. Pretty much the same thing his owner did, too. In an unsettling way, he wondered if that was his life in the future…life without medicine if that was what he decided. Or without Amanda.

Well into the third hour, and too busy to think about Amanda, Jack had patients everywhere. On stools, sitting on the floor. A couple of them were tinkering with auto parts and watching a rerun of an old American movie, translated into Spanish, in black and white. Two of them were engaged in a game of checkers, while another one was actually huddled over a workbench, repairing a small motor. Amazingly, the garage was clean. Not spotless, but good enough to serve its function as a makeshift exam room. He'd found an old chrome-plated table, pushed it to the back, and discovered it sturdy enough to suffice for the cursory exams he was performing.

So far he'd seen nothing startling, nothing even noteworthy. Some arthritis, a sinus infection, indigestion, a wart. Then Alfonse Macias appeared, and that's when Jack's uneventful day turned itself completely around.

"Where does it hurt?" Jack asked the gray-haired man, recognizing excruciating pain the instant he saw it. Alfonse was ghost-white, his eyes hollow and vacant. His hands trembled. Every few seconds he flinched in paroxysms of pain. *"Dónde duele?"* Jack tried again in his best, fractured Spanish, kicking himself for not learning more of the language when he'd lived here before.

*"Aquí mismo. En mi vientre."* Alfonso pointed to his lower belly and Jack got the meaning.

Rather than poking the exact spot Alfonso was indicating, Jack probed off to the right, the lower abdominal quadrant, to be specific, and he was pretty sure what the response to that would be. Alfonso groaned then doubled over, giving Jack his answer. *"El dolor. Cande tempo?"*

How long have you been in pain? Simple question, and he wished to God Ezequiel was here to do the translating, because Alfonso answered him but too fast, and Jack didn't catch a word of it. So he turned to the three or four men still waiting to be seen and asked, "Did anyone understand what he just said?"

An older man, one fully invested in watching the TV, didn't bother turning around when he answered, "He was sick to his stomach for two days, then the pain started, and he's had that for three days."

Yet he was still up and walking around. Apparently, Alfonse Macias was a man with strong stamina, because most people would have dropped dead from some kind of infection by now. Acute appendicitis would do that, except, apparently, not to Alfonso. At least, not yet.

"What are our options?" Jack asked Amanda, minutes later.

"Do you think he's perforated?" she asked, rushing behind him across the road, on the way back to the gas station.

"It's hard to tell. He's in a lot of pain, but the man's been sick for a little while, so there's no way of knowing if he's perforated, has some kind of periappendiceal abscess, or even diffuse peritonitis. He told me he wants pills so he can feel better when he goes to work later on today. I told him he couldn't work, he told me I couldn't stop him. I told him that I wouldn't have to stop him, that his appendicitis would. And let's just say an argument ensued."

"Who won?"

"He will, if we save his life. And that's assuming he's still at the gas station and hasn't gone on to work or some other place a man in his condition doesn't need to be going."

"Well, we can give him pills, but not until after we get him to the hospital and get his appendix out. He'll just have to know it's not negotiable."

Easier said than done. Jack knew that, so did Amanda. But she was an incurable optimist, and he liked watching that in her. Liked her sense of purpose. In this case, though, no matter how much optimism she had, or how large her sense of purpose, the longer the delay between diagnosis and surgery, the more likely there would be serious complications arising. Good stamina or not, Alfonso had a rough road ahead of him, and Jack even doubted the man would consent to go to the hospital, let alone stay there for the few days that would be required.

"So, while it may not be negotiable, tell me how we're going to get him to the hospital, because he's refusing to budge for me. Which makes me wonder, is there anything we can do here?"

Amanda stopped just short of the door, looked down at the old hound dog, which hadn't budged an inch in the past hour, then she looked at Jack. "We can't do an emergency appendectomy here, if that's what you're thinking. Wilderness-type procedures are fine if there aren't other options, but we have other options."

He shrugged. "I'm just saying…"

"I know what you're saying, and I know you're used to working miracles in places no one else could, but, Jack…" She stepped around him and went inside first, only to find Alfonse Macias sitting straight up in an old wooden chair, out to the world. Totally unconscious.

"When did this happen?" Jack asked the man who was sitting next to Alfonso, leaning his shoulder into him to keep him upright.

"Right after you left," the man said. "Shut his eyes, fell over on me."

"I guess this solves our first problem." Amanda was already on her knees next to Alfonso, taking his vital signs. "Jack," she said, discovering only a faint, thready pulse.

He didn't even have to look at her to recognize the tone in the way she spoke his name. They were in serious trouble. "How long will it take to get transport?"

"We don't have transport, except the Jeep, and at its fastest..." She sucked in a sharp breath as she wrapped the blood-pressure cuff around Alfonso's arm. "If we're lucky, from the time we call to get Hector started on his way here until we have Alfonso on the operating table, two and a half hours. Maybe three."

Jack groaned. "So, I'll make the call," he said, pulling out his cell phone then going outside, hoping for clear reception. Which, of course, he did not get. No signal, not a crackle, not a buzz. Nothing. Damn it to hell, that man was going to die and there was nothing they could do. They couldn't operate here, they had no equipment, not to mention the huge fear of the infection they'd find once they opened him up. No matter which way this went, Alfonso was a ticking time bomb. Yet how could they get him to the hospital?

He was the problem solver, wasn't he? The one called out to places all around the world to fix something. Relatively speaking, this was a simple problem. Getting his patient from point A to point B. Simple...

Sighing, Jack shut his eyes a moment and cleared his mind. Then he opened his eyes to an entirely new focus, turned round, looked at the various people wandering up and down the road. Assessed his options and came to the immediate conclusion there was only one thing to do. He needed a truck. Right now! "A truck!" He shouted at the top of his lungs. *"Necesito un camión. Por favor, alguien. Necesito un camión."*

Several people looked at him, one old man even started to approach, then changed his mind and turned off in another direction. Of course, why would anybody respond? They didn't know him. Had never seen him before. And here he was, some lunatic standing in the middle of the street shouting for a truck. But without a way to get Alfonse Macias out of here, he would die. Even with a way to evacuate him, his chances weren't good. A truck, a car…anything. *"Necesito un—"* He started to call out again, but was interrupted by a tap on his shoulder. The old man who'd almost approached him was standing there, holding out a set of keys.

"Behind my house," he said in broken English. Then pointed to a white, wood-frame house half a block away. "My truck."

*"Gracias. Gracias tanto,"* Jack said, grabbing the keys and running toward the truck as fast as he'd run in a good long time.

Last time he'd run this hard and fast he'd been looking for Rosa. They'd taken her, he'd been trying to find her, frantically running from house to house, building to building, searching… Blinking hard, he tried shutting out that image, shutting out that day. But it never completely shut out. Even as he engaged the twenty-year-old pickup truck and headed toward the garage, he was still back at that day, at that moment when they'd ripped her from his arms and surrounded him, pinned him to the wall so he couldn't go after them…go after Rosa.

For a moment he wondered about Amanda, almost pictured her being ripped from the arms of someone who loved her. But that image he blanked out as he ran inside the garage, flying by the hound dog so fast the beast actually got up and moved a foot away, then plopped down and returned to its nap. "It's not the best transportation, but we can make it work," he said, watching Amanda, who was still at Alfonso's side, but now prepping his arm to insert an IV.

"He's running a low fever," she said, while she swabbed the skin of his underneath forearm. "And he did respond to me, said he's not in too much pain." She smiled. "A lie, because he still wants that pill so he can go to work later on. So, where'd you get the truck?"

Jack shrugged. "I asked, someone answered."

"Amazing people," she said, taking the IV catheter and nodding toward the bag of normal saline. "Would you hook it up when I get the needle in? I figured you'd find a way to get him to the hospital, so I thought I might as well get the IV in him now, in case…"

She didn't say the rest of the words. Didn't have to. The implications were dire. They were about to haul a critically ill man over a bumpy road for the next hour in the back of an open pickup truck. Getting him to the hospital alive would be the miracle. What they'd have to do to keep him alive, he wasn't even going to guess. "Can somebody here drive us?" Jack asked the group of men that had now grown to well over a dozen.

One intrepid soul stepped forward. He didn't look to be much more than Ezequiel's age. But he held out his hand for the keys and Jack didn't refuse. Instead, he instructed several of the men to carry Alfonso to the truck, to keep him flat, to try and not bounce him around. Surprisingly, when they got there, the back of the truck, which had been stacked with crates, was empty, except for the fifteen or so blankets and pillows that had been spread out. And no one was around. Not one single, solitary person loitered to watch. It was as if they did their good deeds as a matter of course, then went on to the next thing. *The way every society should be,* he thought as he crawled into the bed of the truck next to Alfonso, then offered Amanda a hand to crawl up into the back with him. "I didn't get to see all my patients," he said as the truck rolled slowly down the road, with the boy driver in charge of their journey now. "I think I'd like to come back."

Amanda smiled. "It's addictive, isn't it?"

"What?"

"Practicing medicine this way. Practicing it at this basic level. It's different. Exciting."

"If you like practicing medicine," he said, placing his hand on Alfonso's wrist to take a pulse.

"If you like practicing medicine," Amanda repeated, "which you do, Jack."

He shook his head. "Past life, different man."

"Why?"

"I'm not the same man I was when I graduated from medical school."

"We all change. Hopes, dreams, goals. They always change when we get into the real world and assume our own responsibilities. I'm not the same woman I was when I graduated, and I pray to God I'm better, more compassionate, more observant, not only of a patient's physical condition but of his or her overall condition."

"I'm glad it works for you," he said sincerely.

"But it works for you, too. Just look at what you do."

"I diagnose HAIs, or isolate a virus or bacterium. And I don't even do that anymore, except when I get dragged into it."

"Dragged? I don't think you staying involved has anything to do with getting dragged. I mean, I don't know why the reticence, Jack, but your heart isn't in being reluctant. Because you do get involved. Just look at you right now, riding in the back of this truck, saving this man's life on a bumpy road. How much more involved does it get than this?"

"I'm not some inhumane bastard who'd let someone suffer. But I'm not…you. Not a do-gooder. Not someone who has to be involved on the very basic or personal level of patient care. Not anymore. Been there, done it all, discovered it wasn't for me." Because failure was the deepest, darkest pit of misery he'd ever known. And that failure was the hole in his own soul.

"Look, I know what you're doing. I recognize the lead-up to the pep talk. Rah, rah, stay in medicine. I appreciate your concern, but it isn't going to work because I don't know what I'm going to do after this. Maybe leave, maybe stay, maybe spend the rest of my life in indecision. That's who I am now. I'm impermanent. No commitments to anything other than the job I'm doing at the moment. And, sure, I can help you at Caridad, and I probably will from time to time when I can.

"But I'm not you or Ben or any of the other doctors who can do this in the way you all do because I just… I just can't get that committed. To anything. So if that makes me a bastard, then I am. But I'm not going to hang around and pretend I'm something I'm not just because you and I might…"

"Might what, Jack?" she asked.

"Might, at some point in time, get something going. It's out there, Amanda. You and me. We're both adults, we see what's going on between us. The flirtation, the looks. The kiss. It wouldn't take much to tip us over to the next level, and I'm a man who could be tipped. I'll admit it. You're driving me crazy in that regard. But anything we do, anything we have…" He shook his head. "Just don't go getting any ideas that this will lead to a happily ever after, where we both stay here together and help your brother with Caridad. Like I said, I don't do that."

"Well, aren't you just about the most pompous piece of…?"

Alfonso Macais took that moment to stir. In fact, he bolted straight up and tried to rip the IV from his arm. But Jack got hold of him, and helped him back down to a flat position. Then took his blood pressure, listened to his chest, took his pulse, while Amanda readjusted the IV then explained to Alfonso where he was going and what they were doing to help him. It took several minutes, but the man finally did settle down again, shut his eyes, and either went to sleep or simply tried blocking it all out, because he didn't stir again, except for the clenching and unclenching of his left hand.

"Pompous piece of what?" Jack asked, several minutes later. He was pretty sure what she would have said, and he deserved it. But this was the way it was, and it was easier to be clear about who he was rather than let something happen that would hurt her. She was flirting now, having fun with it, no true feelings involved, and that was how it had to stay. Because he cared for Amanda. Truly, deeply cared, and if there was anything in him that would let him get involved more than he already was, it would be his feelings for her.

But in his life he'd loved twice, and watched them die because he hadn't been enough to take care of them. He couldn't do that again. Wouldn't let himself get anywhere near it, especially not with Amanda because she deserved happiness when all he had to offer was grief and letdown.

"Do I really have to answer that?" she said, settling back in at their patient's side. "Because I'd think you already know the answer."

He smiled, but sadly, thinking about his own life without the things he wanted. But at least he knew his limitations. Maybe that was some kind of starting point, if he ever got around to starting again. "I suppose I do, and I deserve it."

"And it's okay with you that people think that?"

"Do I seem like the kind of man who cares what people think?"

"You seem like the kind of man who goes out of his way to fool himself."

"And everybody's entitled to his, *or her,* opinion."

"You were seeing patients in a garage, Jack. That's above and beyond the call. So, yes, I do have my opinion, and I'm entitled to it." She folded her arms across her chest and looked him straight in the eye. "Because I'm right."

Jack's response was to try his cell phone, only to discover he still couldn't get a signal. Well, so much for trying to deflect the moment. Amanda was one persistent woman. And pretty sure of herself. He liked it, actually. Was surprised to find how much he did, as all the women in his past had been…manageable. Submissive. Easy to let come and go without a bother. Amanda was none of those. No one could manage her, and she sure as hell wasn't submissive about anything. But she was worth the bother, and that was what worried him more than he wanted to admit. "So, will the hospital be set up for an appendectomy?" he asked. "I know it can handle simple surgery, but Alfonso isn't going to be a simple case once we get him opened up."

"Can you manage his infection?" Amanda asked.

"Me?"

"You're the infection specialist, and if ever there was a patient at risk for getting some sort of HAI…" She shrugged. "Getting his appendix out will be the simple part."

Rather than answering, Jack simply sighed. One way or another, she was going to keep dragging him in as long as he was here. Only thing was, as long as it was Amanda doing the dragging, he was a willing participant. Too willing, damn it. Way too willing!

"He's stable," Ben said, pulling down his surgical mask. "Pretty sick, but it could have been worse. His appendix was perforated, a fair amount of infection spreading, but I think we got it in time. Good job, getting him here when you did." He gave his sister a warm smile then turned his attention to Jack. "Your supplies will be here first thing tomorrow. You'll have to go down to the landing strip to pick them up. In the meantime, Ezequiel's recruited quite a few people to help you assemble those filters, so anytime you want to get that started…"

And here he'd thought he might take a couple hours off, kick back, enjoy the warm Argentinian evening. Maybe even contemplate the stars. But he'd been on the move from the moment they'd rolled into the hospital and Alfonso had been whisked away to surgery. He'd done rounds on his patients, discovered two more admitted to the ranks of HAIs. He'd done some white-glove cleaning, not because anything in his wards needed it but because he felt helpless, standing around, waiting, trying to fight back thoughts of Amanda always trying to creep in.

Then he'd gone to his hole-in-the wall lab, hoped to find

some kind of results in the few little samples he was trying to grow, only to discover nothing. Which led him to believe he was using contaminated medium dishes or faulty swabs. Whatever the case, in a fit of anger he'd swept everything into the trash, kicked the wall, then gone back to his wards and cleaned some more. "Filters," he mumbled.

"Jack's had a rough day," Amanda piped up. "It happens when someone forces some insights on you that you don't want to see, or understand, or admit exist."

"Sounds too complicated for me," Ben said, backing away from the two of them. "Think maybe I'll go grab a quick shower, see if I can find something to eat then check on a few patients before I turn in for the night."

"And I need to make a call to check on some of my patients back in Texas," Amanda said. "I've got good people looking after them, but I still like to keep up." She brushed by Jack. "Oh, and just so I can get my usual last word in, you *are* the kind of man who cares what people think, Jack. You care what they think, how they feel, and most of all you care about taking care of them. Maybe care too much, which leads to a whole different discussion which I don't want to get into right now. The one person you don't care about, though, is you."

"Says the psychologist," he snapped.

"Wrong again, Jack." She paused, laid her palm flat against his chest then looked up at him. "I'm your friend, like it or not." Then she stepped back. "Have fun with Ezequiel and his battalion of volunteers," she said, then slipped away, leaving Jack standing there feeling numb.

This time he didn't watch her walk away, the way he usually did. He was too tired to deal with it. As much as he braced himself against the desires that still gnawed at him, he simply couldn't brace himself well enough. Something to add to his list for a good berating later on. Jack Kenner, willpower of a starving dog standing before a plate of dogfood. But, oh, was Amanda tasty.

# CHAPTER SEVEN

"GIARDIA," he said. It had been diagnosed now, and the result wasn't unexpected, given the symptoms he'd seen. The medicine to treat it was en route, and his work here was, for the most part, close to being done. Most likely he'd be leaving here in the next day or two. Return to Texas, and… Well, he wasn't sure what came after that. He didn't have a life there. Not anymore. Didn't have a life anywhere else, either, and wasn't sure he wanted to get involved in anything that resembled one for a while because of one kiss, five days ago, and he'd been a mess ever since.

"The filters are in place, our patients are recovering, no new cases, and you know how to handle it until I get back to the States and see what I can do to secure a permanent filtration system—I know a couple of corporations that will always make a donation to a good cause. Then I'll oversee the installation when the time comes. But for now…" he shrugged "…there's no reason for me to stay on."

"I think there is," Amanda said stepping up behind him. "New case. Child, aged nine. Post-op two days for a compound fracture, right tibia. She fell out of a tree, had a fair amount of bone exposed in the wound. We're lucky that Dr. Clayton is volunteering this week because he's one of the best orthopedic surgeons I know, and his repair to the fracture was beautiful. So now the patient's on antibiotics due to the probability of infection stemming from how dirty the wound was when she came in.

"The water filters went on three days ago, Jack, but she was admitted a day after that, and she first started showing HAI symptoms last night. Which means we've still got something the filters aren't getting."

"Damn," he muttered, pounding his fist on the desk. They were standing in Ben's office again, a tight squeeze he'd come to like when he was squeezed in there with Amanda, and hate otherwise.

This morning, though, Jack took particular care not to stand anywhere close to her. In fact, he'd done a brilliant job of avoiding her for the past one hundred and twenty hours, give or take an occasional glance or word in passing, and it had truly been his intention to make his phone call to Richard Hathaway, as he'd promised her, then vanish. Not the best style, but the least complicated in the middle of a situation that had all the potential in the world of turning hugely complicated.

In the long run, better for Amanda, too. Besides, he hated messy goodbyes and this one, he feared, would be very messy. Or maybe he was simply taking the coward's way out, not facing up to the one thing that could actually stop him from leaving. "So, you're sure the symptoms match?" he asked.

"Not only match, they're bad. She's critical, Jack. Yesterday afternoon she was mildly sick. It looked like it might have been a post-anesthesia reaction. Then the overall downgrade of her condition started a couple hours ago, so I'm going to have to arrange transportation to a hospital with pediatric critical care because of her Giardia symptoms, as well as a wound infection that isn't clearing up." Amanda swallowed hard then lowered her voice. "I think one thing is exacerbating another, and we're not equipped to handle it. She's dying, Jack, and we can't save her here."

Without saying a word, Jack spun around and almost knocked Amanda over in his hurry to get to Pediatrics.

"I'm not sure how long it's going to take to get her out of here," Ben said. He was already riffling through his phone index, looking for the right contact. "I'll do the best I can."

"I know you will," Amanda said. Pure, merciless agony was written all over her face. "It's always so difficult when it's a child, isn't it? I mean, it's not easy when it's anybody, but a child…"

Turning away from Ben, Amanda focused on the window opposite him, her mind too preoccupied to fix her attention on anything outside. "Look, there's something I've wondered about lately, Ben. It's been bothering me, but there's never a good time to ask." She shrugged. "Don't think we're going to have one, so…so I'm just going to ask." Pausing, she drew in a deep breath to steady herself. Then turned to face him. "Why did you choose Argentina?"

"What?"

"Argentina. You could have set up a hospital anywhere in the world, but you chose Argentina, and I don't know why you did that. You never told me, and now that I'm discovering who I am, I'm curious. Did you suddenly wake up one morning and think that this is where you wanted to spend the rest of your life? Or was there another reason you chose this country? *This* country. That's what's been bothering me most. Was it a coincidence, or something else?" Now she'd know, once and for all, if her brother stood with her or against her. No turning back.

"I'd read about it," he said, clearly uncomfortable. "Seemed like as good a place as any for a hospital. There was a need. The government's receptive and even welcoming of medical care. So..." he shrugged "...I guess it fit."

"That's it? You read about Argentina, and something in what you read had so much appeal this is where you ended up? Then all these many years later, lo and behold, I'm transformed from Mediterranean into Argentinian because one person in my life saw fit to tell me the truth?" She shook her head vehemently.

"Until today, Ben, I'd have never believed you would lie to me. But that's what you're doing now, isn't it? Lying? And I don't know if you're doing it to protect our parents or to protect me."

She backed away from him, not sure whether to stay there and fight or simply walk away. This was her brother, and she loved him dearly. Nevertheless, he was wrong. Whatever his reason, he was wrong to hold back the truth from her. "I want the truth, and I'm going to get it, one way or another. With or without you, that's a promise. I'm going to find out, because it's my life and I deserve to know."

Drawing in a deep breath, she backed up against the wall across from his desk, needed it to hold her up. "I love you, and that's not going to change, but after I've learned the answers to the questions I've always had, I hope that doesn't change our relationship. It could, though. Because you know something I should know, and you're like Dad, who spent his last breath telling me to quit searching. Well, I'm not quitting, and I only pray you're not caught up or hurt in this, because this time I'm not backing down. So, let me ask you one more time. Why Argentina?"

"There was a need," he said, without conviction. In fact, he looked miserable.

Ben knew the answers she wanted and wouldn't tell her. What devastated her most, though, was that when Jack had predicted her broken heart, she hadn't expected it this soon. And not because of Ben. Yet his refusal to tell her the truth broke her heart. Probably the first of many other heartbreaks to come, and for a moment she wondered if she really wanted to go through with this. Maybe Jack was right about everything. Maybe she shouldn't.

But it *was* her right to know, no matter what Ben said or did. So she braced herself for her next words…words she'd never thought she'd have to say. "Then I'm sorry it has to be this way, Ben," Amanda said. "You, of all people, were the one I trusted. The one I've always believed in. But I can't. Not anymore."

"You don't have to do this, Amanda." He held his place apart from her, emotionally and physically, the weight of the world crushing him. "I can—"

"What, Ben? Tell me more lies and hope one of them takes? Hope that I'm gullible enough or desperate enough to believe you again?" She swiped at angry tears then turned toward the door. "I'll be with my patient. Let me know when you've arranged to get her transferred to another hospital."

Perhaps Ben was caught in the middle. Maybe his loyalties were being torn the way hers were. Bitterly torn, but of his own choosing, and there was nothing she could do except hope that someday she'd understand why he'd done what he'd done and be able to forgive him. Now, though, she felt so…alone.

That was the only thing on her mind as she trudged down the hall to the tiny isolation room where her patient was being examined by Jack, who was so totally oblivious to everything but his patient, he didn't even notice Amanda coming up behind him.

"How's she doing?" Amanda asked, watching the meticulous way he changed the dressing on Renata's incision. "Any better?"

He shook his head gravely. "Why didn't you come get me as soon as all this started?"

"What would you have done differently than I did?" she asked, still defensive from her argument with Ben. "And why do you think I'm not capable of taking care of my patient without your interference? You, Ben...you're both alike. You look at me and you think I'm...I'm... You know what? It doesn't matter what you think. What *either* of you think. I'm a good doctor, and I—"

"Amanda," Jack said, his voice barely above a whisper, "can we talk about this when I'm done here?"

"What's there to talk about?"

"Apparently, a lot more than I was aware of."

"Or nothing at all." Because she was talked out, tired of words. Jack and Ben could say or do what they wanted. So could she. *So could she.* "Look, let me help you with this," she said, snapping on gloves and taking her place at the other side of the bed. She looked down, cringed at what she saw. Then her bottled-up anger turned to concern for the child. "It's..." She mouthed the word *"worse."*

He nodded. "But Renata and I have been having a chat," he said, gesturing for Amanda to take the girl's blood pressure. "Even though she won't open those gorgeous brown eyes and look at me, we've come to an understanding. Haven't we, Renata?"

This was Jack at his best, Amanda thought. Where he shone. The man he was meant to be. "If he didn't promise you ice cream, Renata, I'd make him add that to your understanding." Of course, the child didn't understand a word of English. But she truly believed that many people in comas, the way this little girl was, could hear. A voice could be a lifeline. "Or a *palmerita.*"

"Both, if she opens her eyes right now and looks at me," he said, finishing the last of his bandaging.

"Blood pressure's still the same," she said, once she'd removed the cuff from Renata's arm. "Not getting better, not getting worse. Which is good. She's fighting." Lessons to be learned from a child, she supposed. Renata was waging her valiant fight while Amanda was wavering in hers.

"Look, I know she's your patient, and you've got her on metronidazole, but I'd like to suggest adding quinacrine to that."

"Both?" she asked.

"She's got at least one, if not two underlying conditions going on, and my goal right now is getting one of the problems knocked out of her as fast as we can."

"What do you mean, she may have two conditions?"

"Her leg wound is the first thing that worries me. The infection in it's going to turn out to be *Staphylococcus aureus,* a surgical site infection. Probably something she brought in with her when she broke her leg—something that got into the wound before we got to it. Normally, I'd want to diagnose an infection like that with a positive laboratory culture of a swab from the infected site, which we know isn't going to happen. My other choice, something I like to resort to when there are no viable bacteria to culture, is making the diagnosis on the basis of a blood test demonstrating an immune response to toxins following a compatible illness."

"Which we can't do, either." But, oh, how she loved hearing him talk about it. It was technical and exciting, and while to most people it was probably boring, hearing Jack in his element gave her goose bumps. "So, what's your third choice?"

He smiled. "I make a guess. Given the circumstances, the appearance of the wound, and how the surgical site infection developed, then factor in her age and a whole lot of unscientific variables, I'd say it's staph."

"Because Giardia won't erupt in a skin wound."

"Exactly."

"But you said a second diagnosis."

"I'm guessing she's also diabetic. It causes the body's defenses to go crazy, and even after a night of aggressive treatment she's not responding. *Staphylococcus aureus* and diabetes have a strange little song and dance they like to do together. They act in tandem to force the body's defense systems to hide their antigens to avoid an immune response. They also gang up to kill infection-fighting cells.

"Because people with diabetes are more prone to certain infections, the underlying condition can help the intruding bacteria survive within the host infection-fighting cells, which helps develop resistance to antibiotics. She's resisting the antibiotics you prescribed, so there's something else going on."

Sexy talk again. Okay, so maybe not traditionally sexy, but she was still having goose bumps, and wondering if her feelings for him were deepening because he was her only port in the storm or the only port she *wanted* in her storm. Being around Jack just made things seem manageable, and it was a feeling she liked. One she hadn't had much experience with. "So what you're saying is that one thing doesn't cause the other but assists it."

"Exactly. And because she's at a higher risk for Type 1 diabetes due to her heritage. Probably has a family history of it. Also, I took her blood sugar." He pulled a monitor from his lab-coat pocket. "Over two hundred."

"But she was normal last night when I took it," Amanda said, then let out an exasperated sigh. "And she doesn't sustain the fast." Meaning Renata was one of the rare individuals whose blood sugar elevated rather than dropped when she didn't eat. "Which I totally missed."

"Because you weren't looking for it. It would have manifested itself eventually. And in the meantime, you were treating the obvious—an infection, a fracture. But in my medicine I have to look for something other than the obvious."

"Or, if you're like me, you don't see it even when it's slapping you in the face every day of your life." She drew in a ragged breath, shut her eyes, rubbed her forehead. "I don't even know what's going on anymore. Can't focus…"

"You didn't make a mistake."

"Then why do I feel like everything's a mistake?"

"Probably because you're overwhelmed. People who take on life the way you do go through that from time to time."

"As opposed to people like you who take on people like me and tell them they're okay when they're really not?" She didn't want to be angry, didn't want to be hurt. But she was, at herself. "Look, I should have seen it. But I didn't and now look at her."

"Amanda, meet me in the hall. Okay?"

"Fine," she said, wanting to kick a hole through the wall in the hall to which she was being banished. The truth was, he was right to send her out. She wasn't being objective. Wasn't being the doctor Renata needed. So the hall suited her. So did the wall she leaned against to wait for Jack. And the floor she stared at. And the baseboard she kept kicking with the heel of her shoe. It all suited her and if she didn't get a better grip, it would be the only thing suiting her for some time to come.

"She's going to be fine, Amanda, once she's transferred, all the tests are done and her various conditions are diagnosed and treated." He handed the medical chart to the nurse who walked out of Renata's room with him, then went to lean against the wall next to Amanda. "In the meantime, I ordered—"

"You ordered insulin, and simple penicillin, which works best to treat the S. aureus. And the quinacrine. Jack, I..."

He held up his hand to stop her. "It's what I do. Not a big deal."

"Not a big deal? Tell that to Renata's parents. I have an idea they'll tell you what a really big deal it is. So how dare you *not* know this is where you belong? Because people are going to die without you, Jack. There's going to be another outbreak of something someone can't identify, or another child like Renata, who... How can you not see it? Tell me. How can you not see it?"

She slapped her hands on her legs in frustration, spun, and marched out. Out the door. Out into the courtyard. Didn't stop until she was halfway up the steps to her quarters. Even then the only reason she stopped at all was because Jack caught up to her, grabbed hold of her arm and forcibly held her in place.

"What's this about?" he asked.

She didn't spin to face him. Didn't want him to see her anger, her frustration. Her tears. So she stood her ground, stayed rigid, drew in a bracing breath. "I made a mistake."

"What?" he asked. "What, exactly, was your mistake?

Because you treated that little girl the way she was supposed to be treated."

"And missed the fact that she's diabetic."

"Because she wasn't displaying symptoms. And the tests haven't been done yet, Amanda. She could be having some kind of blood-sugar reaction due to the trauma. A one-time incident."

"You know that's not true, Jack. If I'd been thorough…"

He let go of her arm. "You were thorough, Amanda. I read your notes, saw what you were doing with her. You conducted the test you had available, and it's exactly what I would have done. Exactly what I did."

"No, it's not, Jack." She whirled to face him, not caring anymore what he saw on her face. "And quit trying to placate me with things that don't matter. Maybe I didn't mess up, but I—"

"What's this really about?" he interrupted.

She shook her head, afraid to speak for fear she'd burst into tears. "Argentina. That's what this is about. I asked him, Jack. I asked Ben why he chose to practice medicine here, and he wouldn't tell me. More than that, I believe he lied to me." Her voice broke into a whisper. "He knows something and he'd rather lie about it than tell me." Finally, the tears came, not in an outburst but in an intermittent trickle down her face.

Without a word Jack wrapped a supportive arm around Amanda's waist and led her up the remaining steps and into their cottage, where he shut the door behind them. "Talk to me," was all he said as he guided her to her side of the room. But she didn't go to her bed, or even to one of the few chairs that sat at odd angles in various corners of the room. Rather, she guided him to the window and looked out, trying to find a shred of composure.

"You know, I don't believe in coincidences, and I told him so. I also told him this could come between us, but it didn't make a difference. I know he cares, I know he loves me, but... How could he do this to me?" Stepping up behind her, Jack wrapped his arms around her, allowing her to relax into his chest, and she was glad for his support, his strength, even if it was hers only for a moment. "I don't understand."

"Did he say anything at all that would give you a clue about what he's hiding?"

"Just that he came to Argentina because there was a need here. But that's not it, Jack. I know my brother, and he's not good at lying. So Argentina *isn't* a coincidence, and Ben would rather split up our family than tell my why he came *here*. We've been so close, and now all I feel is..."

"Betrayed."

"Yes. I guess because I didn't expect he'd ever do something like this, especially after... Ben had this accident years ago, and we didn't know if..." Her voice broke. "He wanted to die. He wasn't fighting back. So I stayed with him, sat in that hospital room day and night and fought for him. Missed a whole semester of school because I refused to leave my brother's side.

"Then fought for him again and again over the next couple years when he needed someone there to help him through. And I promised him that no matter what happened, I would take care of him and make sure he got better. When nobody else could get him to eat, I could. When he refused his medications, I was the only one who could get him to take them. And it went on like this for months, Jack.

"It's when I knew I wanted to be a medical doctor. I saw my skills, not only at whatever kind of simple medicine a child could administer but I saw the psychological side to it as well, and how a person's psychological makeup is so important to their physical health. Which is why I became both a doctor and a psychologist.

"Anyway, later, when Ben and I were talking about how bad that time had been for him, he promised me he'd do the same if I ever needed it. I mean, it was one of those stupid promises you make in a moment of gratitude or overwhelming emotion, but I've always counted on it, counted on Ben to come through for me. Except he didn't because he's part of the lie. Part of what my parents kept from me."

"Maybe because he *is* trying to take care of you?" Jack asked.

"Take care of me?" She shook her head. "He's hurting me, and he knows it."

She turned to face him finally, and looked up at him. Tears were still glistening in her eyes. "I may lose everything… Maybe I already have. But I can't quit. You told me part of who I am, and now I have to find out the rest because…" she swiped at the tears sliding down her face, then sniffled "…because I was always different. The dark-skinned girl in a fair-skinned family. The one people whispered about. The one the kids made fun of. And, sure, it really doesn't seem like much of a big deal, but when you're growing up different, and people are always staring or pointing fingers, it hurts. People can be cruel."

"I know," he said, thinking back to Robbie. Sweet boy, and people had pointed fingers and stared. Robbie hadn't seen it so much, but *he* had, and sometimes his rage on behalf of his brother had ripped so hard at him he hadn't known what to do with it. Once he'd slammed his fist through the wall, broken a couple of fingers. "People can be cruel."

"The thing is, I want to vindicate my parents. Right now I have such mixed feelings about them, and I hate it. I loved my dad, love my mom and Ben, and I don't want that to change. But it is and I want to stop it. Want things the way they used to be. Want to think about my dad the way I used to when I was daddy's little girl and he called me his princess. I adored him, Jack, and I want to hang on to that. Which means I have to settle it." She drew in a deep breath, squared her shoulders. "Please, tell me. Am I doing the right thing?"

"If this search is what it takes to settle yourself, you're doing the right thing." He hated saying it because he knew the kind of hurt that would inevitably ensue. But he knew what it was like to not know yourself, to stand alone in a crowd. That was where he'd been standing for most of his life. "Let me tell you about the Mapuche, since that's where it all starts. Theirs isn't a prevalent culture in Argentina, as I'm sure you've already discovered. Mapuche, by the way, means native people, or people of the land."

"People of the land," she said, sniffling. "I like that."

Jack chuckled. "So do I. It fits you, because they're a very practical people. They embrace life, and have this way of just being part of their surroundings in vital yet subtle ways."

"It fits you, too. Maybe not in the way the Mapuche would define it, but you do belong to the land, Jack. To the people you serve, in vital and subtle ways."

"Used to," he corrected.

"Still do." She turned around in his arms, and tilted her face to his. "You still do, and I want to help you find that again."

"For me, there's nothing to find." He lowered his head, came within a breath of her lips, and stopped. "But for you, as soon as I figure out why we have a new case of giardiasis here, we'll go south."

"You'll take me?"

"Yes, I'll take you." Take her to his own personal hell so she wouldn't have to face hers alone.

The kiss that came after that was sweet. Tender. Familiar and comfortable. And before he got to the point of arousal or pure, raw desire, he slid out of it. Not because he didn't want more but because he'd just made a promise that scared him. Helping her was one thing. He'd created the monster she would surely discover, and it was his duty to protect her from it. But his feelings were changing. Softening. And that was where the scare factor came in and walloped him in a big way.

"Look, there's this area in the Pampas," he started, hoping his voice didn't sound as uncertain as he was feeling. "It's south and west of Buenos Aires. It's where that orphanage is I mentioned, and the records there go back at least for thirty years. So since your search is going to be like looking for the proverbial needle in a haystack, that's as good a haystack as any to start with."

"Jack," Amanda cried, as a new gush of tears started. "I…I don't know what to say except thank you! I've never had any support in this, and now you… You're doing so much."

"I won't stay, Amanda. Maybe a little while, but this isn't the start of any kind of change of heart for me. I'll help you get situated, make sure you have everything you need, but then I'll be leaving. You've got to understand that. I will not stay."

"I didn't think you would," she said, almost sadly. "But I'm so grateful, Jack. You can't even begin to know what this means to me."

Her gratitude, combined with his confusion and awakenings, then a kiss as passionate as anything anyone had ever laid on him, and in the blink of an eye nothing else mattered. Her arms were around his neck, and he wanted them there. In the second blink, her lips were pressed to his and tongues were already probing, as if this was customary foreplay between two longtime lovers. In the third blink of an eye, he was aroused beyond all reason. Arousal mixed with the hot, humid air of the Argentinian jungle surrounding him, and the drumming rhythm of her untamed heartbeat against his own chest...

Now or never, that was all he could think. He did want it now, wanted her now. And she wanted him. There was no mistaking her intention in the way she pressed her pelvis hard into his erection and gyrated. There was no mistaking her intention when she broke their kiss, leaned her head back and looked into his eyes. This was everything the Pampas grass along the side of the road had promised to be, and more.

Now or never. There was no way in hell he was turning his back now. No way in hell he was turning his back on Amanda. So, in the fourth blink of an eye, Jack scooped her into his arms and carried her across the room. Definitely now, he thought as he laid her on the bed. But what about later? It was a thought that had no place between them, a thought he put away the instant her gauzy blouse came off. After that, Amanda consumed him in every way a man could be consumed, and he was a man who wanted to be consumed.

No regrets. No thoughts. Nothing but the moment they both wanted. Or the night. And once he looked down at the beautiful woman undressed and opening her arms to him, he knew a night would never be enough. Another hell to endure.

# CHAPTER EIGHT

"No way!" Jack exploded, wadding the test results and hurling them at the wall. "We're having the water filtered and boiled, so there's no way in hell the Giardia is getting in." Which should have been the case by all logical standards, except there'd been two new cases diagnosed in the past twelve hours, making the day go from one of the best in his life to one of the worst. From afterglow to aftershock. He was reeling from it, seething, angry. "So, we've got another source, and I don't even know where to start looking for it."

"It's not your fault, Jack, but if we don't get this thing figured out soon, we're going to be forced to close down temporarily." Ben ran a frustrated hand through his hair. "I can't keep putting my patients at risk. Giardiasis in itself is treatable and not life-threatening, but if someone else with an underlying condition comes down with it…"

Jack's thoughts instantly went to Renata. As of an hour ago she was still critical, still fighting for her life. Her doctors were optimistic, but optimism didn't fix the problem because Ben was right. There might be another Renata out there, one who wouldn't get the vote of optimism from her doctors. That wasn't acceptable. Neither was his failure to locate the source. "How long have I got?"

"Twenty-four hours at the most, if we don't have another case of it diagnosed. If we do, then we're shutting the doors immediately and sending the patients we have to any hospitals that have beds for them, which is going to make for one hell of a difficult transport. But that's all I can do. I'm already dismissing patients I'd like to keep around a little while longer, and closing down new admissions, except for dire emergencies. I've also postponed a couple of noncritical surgeries." He shrugged. "I should have gotten you here earlier, like Amanda wanted, before it all went to hell."

"She wanted me here earlier?" He was surprised yet pleased.

"I thought she was overreacting. Apparently I was underreacting. Either way, none of this is on you."

"Except the onus," Jack snapped, thoroughly irritated and not trying to hide it. "Look, I'm going to have to start again, so buy me time, Ben. Whatever it takes, buy me time." He shut his eyes, trying to visualize, trying to mentally see something he'd missed. All the usual water sources, anything with running water. All the unusual sources, anything with standing or accumulating water. He'd looked. Cultured every last one of them. So what was it? What the hell was it he was missing? "Did Amanda ever tell you what happened in Big Badger, Texas?" he asked, opening his eyes.

"You mean that E. coli epidemic?" Ben's eyes indicated he wasn't interested but was trying to be polite.

"Lots of people got sick, and I kept checking all the usual places and coming up empty."

Ben cocked his head, his attention a little more stirred now. "What's that got to do with Caridad?"

"Crazy thing. I found it in the least likely place...an innocent little jar of jam people were buying right and left from one of the locals. She was known for her strawberry jam and half the people in town bought from her. The same half who came down with E. coli."

"Strawberry jam?" Ben frowned, shook his head. "I'll be damned. Who would have ever thought…?"

"Exactly. Who would have ever thought? But she was using contaminated strawberries and made freezer jam, not the old-fashioned kind you jarred up in a water bath."

"So what might have been killed by the heat of the boiling wasn't."

"And I was looking for E. coli in all the wrong places… which in that case were the usual places. What I didn't take into consideration was that the least likely place was the most likely because the medium for growth was different."

"Which has what to do with our situation?" Ben asked. "Giardia doesn't have a myriad sources, like E. coli does."

"Don't know, but I'll get back to you with the answer in twenty-four hours or less," he said, on his way out the door. Then he stopped but didn't turn back to face Ben. "And when I give you your answers, I'm going to ask you a question to which I'll expect an answer. Last time I wasn't involved enough to be part of it. This time I am."

"I don't want to hurt her, Jack. That's not what any of this is about. I just want to protect her."

Finally, Jack turned back around. "I wanted to protect someone once. Someone I loved every bit as much as you love Amanda. So I understand what you're trying to do. But what I also understand is that she believes you know something she has a right to know. I think you do, too. What I also think is that it's not your right to keep it from her. She believes you're betraying her, Ben, and I agree with that, as well. You are."

Ben shut his eyes for a moment and rubbed his temples. "I heard you're going to the Pampas with her."

It wasn't a place he ever cared to see again, but for Amanda...anything. "Yes. Because she can't do this alone."

"You're right. She can't. But she's not going to listen to me if I tell her."

"Do you expect me to stop her? Is that what you're saying?"

"What I'm saying is that if you love her, you'll do what's right."

"Yet you love her, and you won't." He drew in a jagged breath, trying to fight back his anger. It wasn't a good situation, not for anyone, and he truly didn't blame Ben. But he didn't agree with him, either.

"Look, this isn't between you and me, and I don't want to make it that way. Okay? But I want to help Amanda find what she needs. Or be there to support her if she doesn't. Either way, she's made her decision to go and I've made mine to help her. I only hope you can live with what you've decided to do, because losing Amanda from your life..." Jack didn't finish the sentence because he'd thought it through to the end, to the worst possible scenario. Not having Amanda there in any way shook him to the very core.

"Can I help you, Doc K?" Ezequiel asked, running up to Jack as he simply stood in the hospital kitchen, staring at the sink, visualizing the slow drip coming from the faucet and the plumbing beyond that was hidden by the wall. "I can look at things good, just like you do."

Jack chuckled. The innocence of a child transcended

cultures. Last night, with Amanda, the desire to be a father had hit Jack again.

It was the first time he'd felt it since Rosa's mother had delivered Rosa then died, leaving him with that precious little baby to care for. For a moment back then he'd had so many dreams, a lifetime of them for Rosa. One minute there had been no entanglements in his life, no plans for his own future other than doing more of what he was doing.

Then the next moment…those beautiful brown eyes, too young to even focus on him, yet with the way Rosa had looked up at him everything had changed in that instant. Everything he'd known about himself had suddenly been different because a child had been born, and she had become his.

But he'd thought ahead, to a child with Amanda. And he'd had to stop it. Stop the thought, stop the delusion and, more than anything, stop tempting himself with the notion he could have a future with her. The desire was there, but it took a hell of a lot more than desire to build a life, and he'd thrown out his building tools when Rosa had died because then, more than any other time in his disjointed life, he'd caught the clear vision of what he wasn't supposed to do.

Now he had last night to deal with. The best night of his life, but ultimately another delusion. "What I want you to do for me, Ezequiel, is take me on another tour of the hospital, of the surrounding buildings, of anything connected to the hospital. That way, we can look together." Suddenly, his thoughts shifted to the boy. What would happen to Ezequiel if the hospital closed? Would someone take him in or would he be shuffled into living on the street?

See, there he was, doing it again. Thinking about the things he couldn't have. Because he couldn't take Ezequiel home with him, and he couldn't stay here to take care of him. Why did he always do that? Why did he always go to these places he didn't belong? "Okay with you?"

"Okay with me," the boy said, giving Jack a thumbs-up sign.

"Good, then let me go..." Go and see how Amanda was doing? He'd left her at daybreak, when the promise of a new day had caused him to see what he was doing. She was vulnerable, depending too much on something that wouldn't come through for her. Because she expected, had the optimism to expect that life worked out. He didn't, because he already knew that life didn't work that way. Did she love him? Dear God, he hoped not. Did he love her? "Go grab some testing supplies, and I'll meet you in the storage shed outside the hospital."

Ezequiel scampered away to his task, leaving Jack *and* his quandary to stare out the window and figure out a way to focus harder. Or split himself in two.

"As they would say, a penny for your thoughts," Amanda said, stepping up behind Jack and slipping her arms around him.

He stiffened, not because of her closeness but because he loved the feel of her and she was already stirring him up again. "My thoughts? Giardia, and where it's sneaking in."

"Well, that sure was my penny's worth," she said, sounding surprised and stepping back.

"Look, I'm sorry. But Ben's on the verge of closing the hospital temporarily if I can't find it," he said, "and I'm on a deadline to figure it out."

"What?" she asked, her face draining of color. "Are you serious? He's going to close us?"

"He's already reducing services, and that's probably the best thing to do as I haven't found the real source. I mean, people are getting sick while I'm..." He didn't finish the rest of it. Failure was failure, no matter who or what he failed. It was all the same, and the reasons didn't matter.

"I knew it wasn't cured. I should have spent the night..." He didn't say the word. It was hurtful, and he didn't want to be hurtful to her. "Look, I'm sorry. But I'm preoccupied. Frustrated. I need some space so I can just..."

"You've got your space, Jack." She took another step back. "There, space." And another step. "More space."

"Amanda, we started something I can't finish. I'm sorry, but that's how it is."

"I suppose you're right," she said, fighting to keep her composure. "That's how it is, and it's not like you didn't tell me. You did. Every step of the way. But you know what, Jack? While you may have your regrets over getting involved with me, I don't regret anything with you. You're an amazing man who just doesn't get what's amazing in himself."

"No regrets, Amanda. Not about you." He took a step toward her, reached out his hand to take hold of hers and pull her closer. But she wrenched back, like she'd touched her finger to a flame.

"Don't, Jack. Just...don't. We had our night. It's all I ever expected from you. Although I'll admit that I didn't expect to wake up alone. Guess I should have seen that coming, too, right?"

"I don't have time for this," he said, so torn between duty and Amanda his head was spinning. "But later. We'll talk later. Okay?"

She took another step back. "Look, I've got to go and make a maternity call, and Ezequiel's out there now, waiting for you."

He glanced out, clenched his jaw. "Later," he said again, regretting that he had to go. "And, Amanda, please, don't ever think I have any regrets." Confusion, though, was an entirely different matter because falling in love shouldn't be so damned difficult.

Amanda watched Jack from the kitchen window. Watched him walk across the hospital compound and meet up with Ezequiel at the shed. Jack's stride was angry, his physical comportment even angrier. But with himself? Or with her? Either way, it didn't matter anymore. He was everything he'd promised he'd be—a man who wouldn't stay. Too bad she hadn't listened to him before she'd fallen in love.

"You've got it that bad for him?" Ben asked, from across the room.

She didn't turn to face her brother. "Why would you care?"

"That's not fair, Amanda. I've always cared. You know that."

"Then tell me what I need to know," she whispered, so close to tears she wasn't sure she could hold them back. Yet she wouldn't let Ben see. Wouldn't let Jack see. Everything hurt, and she didn't know how to stop the pain. But she was Amanda Robinson. Strong, adopted kid. Good doctor. Totally devoted to the humanitarian causes. Yes, that was who she was, and that was who Ben saw when she finally turned around to face him.

"Clearly, you won't do it because you love me as a sister. I can deal with that. But you owe me, Ben. I helped build this hospital with you, and I work myself to death to keep it funded. So, if you can't respect me as your sister, then respect me as your business partner. I have the right to know why we built this hospital in Argentina." She leveled a cold gaze on him. "Tell me, Ben. Or I'll get on a plane right now and go and ask Mother."

"You can't do that!" he warned.

"She's fragile, Ben. But her mind is clear. She knows the answer to my question."

"That's ugly of you, Amanda."

She shook her head. "Not ugly. Desperate. And tired of begging. Everybody I've ever loved has kept secrets about me. You don't know how that feels, and I can't even describe it. But it's like everything I've ever counted on has disappeared, and all I want to do is get it back."

"Then answer one simple question for me."

"What?"

"Do you love Jack Kenner?"

"What does that have to do with anything?"

"Because at the end of this, I want you to have someone, and I don't think it's going to be me."

"No," she choked, so close to tears again she didn't care now if Ben saw them fall. "I'll still have you, and Mother."

"Do you love him?"

She nodded. "Doesn't matter, though. Jack doesn't love me. I think he tried, or convinced himself he was trying. But I'm not sure he *can* love."

"Maybe he can love, but he can't accept it."

"And I'm not the one who can help him with that because I love him and he knows that, and it tortures him." She wrapped her arms around herself and sighed heavily. "Talk about all the worst possible elements for a relationship. Or, actually, there's nothing to talk about since there is no relationship."

Ben shook his head. "See it for what it is. Give yourself some space, some time, and I promise you, you'll see it for what it is. So now let me open another wound for you, because that's what I'm about to do. And I'm so sorry…"

"I can take it," she whispered, reaching out for Ben's hand.

He shook his head, refusing her gesture. Blinked back his own tears. Then steadied himself with a deep breath. "I don't know much about our parents' fascination for Argentina because, like you, I was told not to ask questions. Dad was a pretty exacting man when he wanted to be, and he loved Mother... I can't even begin to understand that kind of love. But it was so fierce, Amanda. Sometimes I'd see it just in the way they looked at each from other across the room. Or the way she'd simply lay her hand on his arm."

"When he talked too loud," Amanda said, smiling. "That was the signal."

"Then you saw it, too?"

She had but, unlike Ben, she believed she could understand a love like that. Or was just beginning to. "All the time."

"I only wish..."

"No regrets between us, Ben. We move forward from here. No matter what you're about to tell me, we move forward, together, from here. I promise."

"Don't give away your promises so quickly, Amanda. You may regret it."

Now she was scared. For herself. For Ben. For the memories she was afraid she was losing. And for Jack, who would be lost to her for reasons she couldn't change. "They lied, didn't they?" she asked, the words so jagged and sharp she could almost taste the blood on them. "Our parents lied to us, didn't they?"

Ben nodded. "I used to listen to them talk. Usually around us it was always about family things, school, work, you know, ordinary stuff. But after we went to bed at night they'd talk about earlier days in their marriage, when they…" He swallowed hard. "Amanda, our parents were volunteers for an organization that traveled around the world providing services, like teaching or physical labor, to impoverished areas. Dad taught agricultural techniques, Mom taught school. Young children, mostly."

"What? Why didn't they…? I don't understand." Growing up, the only thing she'd known about her parents' profession had been what she'd seen every day. They'd owned a ranch, raised sheep for the wool. Had been very successful at it.

"Neither did I. Not at first, anyway."

"Then how did you find out?"

"When they first brought you home, I was insecure. I thought they were going to trade me in. You know, replace me with you. Remember how I used to try and find ways to get rid of you?"

She nodded.

"Well, part of that involved spying. I used to listen to their conversations when they thought I was in bed. And I snooped through some of their personal belongings. It wasn't right and I knew that. But I did it anyway because I was just looking for something that would convince them to keep me." He grinned devilishly. "Or blackmail them into keeping me."

"And here I thought you were the perfect big brother."

He shrugged. "A kid's got to do what he's got to do. In my case, it worked out for a little while. I was gathering all kinds of information. One thing I discovered was that they lived in Argentina for two years. In fact, I'm pretty sure I was conceived in Argentina, because that's how the timeline worked out, according to some old pocket calendars I found. So that's probably the reason they returned to the States—to have me here. But who knows? Maybe I was actually born in Argentina, too. They lied about other things, so…"

He broke off his words. Swallowed hard. "See, that's what I didn't want you to know."

"That they lied?"

"If they lied, how do we know the truth about anything? Maybe I'm adopted, or… That's just it. How are we supposed to know *anything?*"

"And you've been carrying that around…"

"For years. When I was a kid, I didn't really understand it. But as I got older…" He shrugged.

"But Argentina. If they worked for a charitable organization here, it would have been a noble thing. Maybe they didn't lie so much as they didn't want to talk about it because that would make them seem like they were bragging or seeking some kind of praise or attention for it. Couldn't that have been it?"

Ben shook his head. "I kept asking them to tell me about when they lived in Argentina, and they ignored me every single time. So I went into the attic one night—"

"And found my birth records?" she interrupted, suddenly hopeful.

"No birth records. But I did find pictures, and clothes… fajas, ponchos, one particularly impressive rastras." An elaborate gaucho belt made with leather. "It was decorated with old coins, had a silver horse silhouette on it. I found a picture of Dad wearing it, along with full gaucho garb. He and Mother were at some kind of festival, dancing. And they looked so—so happy. Happy in a way I'd never seen them look. Anyway, that belt never made it back into the trunk. I kept it hidden, would sneak it to school with me and put it on. Dad showed up one day, unexpectedly, and caught me wearing it. So I told him what I'd found, that I'd seen all these pictures of them when they lived in Argentina.

"And he denied it, Amanda. Rather than ignoring me the way he usually did when I asked questions, he said they'd never lived here, never even been here. But I know what I saw—including their old passports, which clearly showed them coming to Argentina numerous times, even after I was born."

"I—I don't understand why they'd do that." Ben did, though. She could see it in him, some awful truth he was still holding back. Maybe this was the awful truth that cut him so deeply that what she was seeing was his own wound, the one that might never heal.

"That's what I've been asking myself for years. Never could figure it out so I gave up on it, because it's not easy going around telling yourself that your parents deliberately lied to you. Especially when we had such a good family. You know, close. So I gave up on thinking about it. But Argentina loomed over me like a big mystery and it turned into an obsession. Eventually, I started studying about it, trying to figure out what our parents were hiding. It made it better calling it a mystery rather than a lie, by the way."

"You never solved your mystery?"

"No. But the reason we built the hospital here is because I fell in love vicariously. Through my studies, Argentina became my passion. I knew the land, knew the people, became aware of the needs."

"And you never told me any of this? Why not, Ben? Maybe you didn't know I was from here, but why didn't you let me know what you'd found out?"

"Dad warned me, too, like he did you when you wanted

to search for your records. Told me not to upset Mother. Then with her cancer..."

"What could we do?" she asked.

"All I ever meant to do was protect you from finding out they'd lied."

"But who protected you?" She ran to her brother and threw her arms around his neck. "I'm so sorry."

"Then we're good?" he asked.

"The way we always have been." And she felt better. Still, she sensed there was more. More information, more lies? Or simply more confusion? She didn't know. In fact, what Ben had revealed actually raised more questions and gave her no answers. Yet she had her brother back, and maybe that was the most she could hope for. "I'm still going to look," she warned as they headed out of the kitchen together. "I won't involve Mother in it, but it's my life and I have to keep searching."

"I never thought you'd do otherwise."

"But not with Jack. I have to do this alone. Have to find the strength in myself to do it, rather than relying on him to get me through. I think I was hoping for easy answers, and that relying on Jack would help me find them. He's a man of his word, and I know he wants to help me, but I need...me."

"Even if he loves you?"

She shook her head. "No. Because I love him. I've seen his choice even though he tries hard to hide it. So it's time I respect that, because I can't spend my life with a man who tries hard to love me but can't ever get there. I want to wake up in the mornings with someone I love, who loves me just as much. Make a home with him, have children with him, grow old with him." She brushed a tear from her cheek.

"Not with someone who's simply making the effort. It

wouldn't be fair to me. Or to him. Jack may want to love me, but he can't. And maybe I should be able to figure out why but…but it hurts so bad. Which is why I have to go to the Pampas alone. I love him, can't have him, and I have to figure out how to reconcile myself to that." Swatting back another tear, she went on, "So, Ben, you owe me. And I expect you'll do this one thing for me."

"What?"

"Stall him. Don't let him know I've gone. Keep him occupied, send him off on a wild-goose chase if that's what you have to do. I need a head start. Twenty-four hours. That's all I'm asking."

"Then what?"

She shrugged.

"What if he comes after you?"

"Jack reads the subtleties, sees things no one can. He'll understand."

"In other words, you're walking away. Just turning your back on the man you love and walking away?"

"No. I'm letting him walk away. He'll never do it if we're together because above everything else Jack honors his obligations and, in the end, that's what I am to him. So this gives him his out." Because she could never walk away from him. Yet she could never bear to see him stay.

An hour later, her duffel already packed, and Hector on his way to drive her to the landing strip, Amanda watched Jack immersing himself in his process. He was standing outside the storage shed, simply staring at it. He was frustrated. She could tell from the rigid way he stood—shoulders squared, fists clenching at his sides. Angry with himself for missing something. Berating himself, thinking about turning away from medicine.

"Any progress?" she called to him, fighting to maintain

a steady voice. Certainly their paths would cross again. Maybe here in Argentina. Perhaps back in Texas. Before then there would be distance and separation and different perspectives. Next time she prayed she would be able to stand face-to-face with him without struggling with a lip that wanted to quiver, tears that wanted to fall. A heart that wanted to shatter.

So for now she was faking her bravery.

"I think my perspective is too narrow," he said, as she walked over to him. "I keep looking at this scenario in terms of regular water sources, but there's something else, something I'm missing."

She stepped up behind him, nearly leaning into him. Wanting to touch him so badly she ached, yet knowing she couldn't or it would hurt more than it already did. "Or maybe you're not missing it at all," she said. "Maybe it's right before your eyes and you're not seeing it because something's standing in the way."

"What are you talking about, Amanda?"

"You and me, Jack. Under these circumstances…it doesn't make any sense. Can't make any sense. Especially when you consider how we could have started this back in Texas, yet I don't think you ever looked at me as anything other than your nephew's doctor."

"I looked," he admitted, fighting visibly to keep himself reined in. "Every chance I got. And it wasn't my nephew's doctor I was seeing."

"Did you? Because I never saw it." And she would have loved seeing it.

"You in your prim and proper white lab coat, hair pulled back…" He paused, frowned. Mumbled, "Lab coat. *You in your lab coat!*"

She saw the figurative wheels start to turn. Knew she

was totally shut out now. Something was going on with Jack. His eyes were closed, his breathing almost non-existent. The way he always was when he was solving it in his head. In spite of her confused feelings, it was so exciting watching him in this process that she literally started tingling from head to toe. Barely risked taking a breath herself for fear she would interrupt an important moment the way she'd interrupted his life.

So she waited, watched the process churning in him, saw his face in deep frown, saw that frown begin to dissipate, heard his breathing get deeper, saw his shoulders relax. Felt on pins and needles until, finally, he opened his eyes and smiled. "I know," he said. "I know where the Giardia is coming from."

Two words. *I know.* Words that meant everything, and nothing. For she knew, too, only not the source of the Giardia. "Tell me what you know," she whispered, knowing his next words wouldn't be the words she wanted most to hear.

"The bedsheets."

"The bedsheets?" she asked, once again caught up by his process. "I don't understand."

"You said the local women launder them, right?"

"But Giardia has to stay viable in a wet environment."

"Unless it encapsulates into a cyst. In other words, dries out and goes dormant."

"Then what would make it come back to life?"

"Maybe someone continually exhaling into the sheets." He smiled. "Just a guess, and it's off the charts as a standard explanation, but if you put cyst-contaminated sheets on every bed, chances are some of the cysts will become activated by someone breathing on them, then invade that person."

"What made you think of the sheets?"

He grinned. "You, in that lab coat. Mentally, I took it off you and you were naked underneath. Then we were in bed, and afterward you were snuggling into me, sleeping. You sleep on your side, Amanda."

"I know that." It was an image she didn't want in her head now. Didn't want any images of them together in her head, because those images and that reality hurt too badly.

"Your breath on me when you slept…warm, moist."

"Then what you're telling me is that I have breath to awaken the sleeping Giardia," she retorted, trying to keep that proverbial stiff upper lip. "Which means you've got work to do now."

"Work to do. Blessed, sweet work!" He picked her up, twirled her round and kissed her hard on the lips. "But we'll talk later, like I said," he said, setting her back down. "Because maybe we don't make sense, but neither does Giardia in the bedsheets."

Giardia in the bedsheets. She turned round and walked away in relief as Jack sprinted back to his makeshift lab. Stopping for a moment, she pressed her fingers to her lips, the taste of him still there. Then she braced herself and continued on to the Jeep, where Hector was awaiting her. Jack wouldn't see her crawl into the seat, wouldn't see them drive away. All he'd see would be the results of his efforts the way it should be.

*Different paths,* she thought as they pulled away from Caridad, and she refused to look back. Different paths that couldn't converge. For a moment she'd thought they could. But she'd fooled herself.

# CHAPTER NINE

"WHEN did she leave?"

"Late yesterday. Oh, and in case you're interested, I was supposed to give her a twenty-four-hour head start before telling you."

"You should have told me right away. Before she had a chance to get on the plane. Or even leave the hospital."

"What would you have done if I had? Dropped everything, let the giardiasis go for another few days while you went after her?"

"I would have stopped her from going alone. Convinced her to wait another day or two."

"How, Jack? Tell me how, because this is Amanda we're talking about, and nothing's ever stopped her before."

"Okay, then. I'll go after her now."

"And do what? She went alone because she wanted to go alone, so what is it you think you're going to change by going after her?"

"It's not about what I'm going to change. It's about what I'm going to do when her world changes all around her. She can't do this alone."

"I know that," Ben said. "Which is why I broke my promise and told you."

Jack shut his eyes, rubbed his forehead. "Look, have you got one more favor you can call in? I need a plane ride."

"I can get you a plane ride, but make sure this is what you want, because Amanda's going to push you away with everything she's got."

"Then I'll push back."

"I hope so, because…"

Jack watched the color literally drain from Ben's face, and everything he'd suspected was suddenly confirmed. "Damn it to hell, Ben. You know, don't you? You know what she's going to find if she keeps looking."

"What do I know? That my parents didn't adopt her? That they walked into one of the villages and just took her? I don't know that. How could I, when all they ever did was…?"

"Lie?" Everybody was doing it, coming in taking abandoned children like they were shopping in a grocery store. Thousands of children disappeared. The assumption was they were going to good homes, people desperate for children were circumventing adoption because it was easier. Still… "They lied to you, they lied to Amanda. And you let her go down there by herself?"

"I didn't let her go, Jack. She went. And I couldn't leave the hospital."

"And neither could I," he said. "Damn it! That's why she left when she did. Because nobody could go after her."

"With Amanda, that's what you get. She makes her opportunities. Oh, and she figures you'll take the hint that she wants to be left alone, or more likely that I'll tell you she wants you to leave her alone. She's giving it to you as your way out. But I think you'll get on the plane that will be waiting for you on the landing strip as soon as you can get there. And that's why I didn't go after her. Because I would have, Jack. I swear to God, I wouldn't have let her do this by herself if I hadn't thought you'd be there to help her."

He wanted to be angry...at Ben, at Amanda, even at himself. But there was no point. Short of tying her up, he couldn't have stopped her. "Does she know what's happened to the children? Has she ever given you any indication that she's aware of any of that?"

"No. She doesn't know."

"You're sure?"

"You've never seen Amanda go after a worthy cause. If you think what you know in her now is stubborn and aggressive, you don't have a clue. If she believes, she believes with her whole heart. And if it's about children... Look, Jack. She adored our parents, and they doted on her, however they adopted or didn't adopt her. It's not going to be easy on her, accepting what they may have done, accepting that even after I'd promised her the truth, I gave her only half of it. And you...I'm not even going to tell you what's going on in her head about you. That's one for you to solve."

"So if I leave right now, you've got things under control here? Because if you don't, I can't go. You know that, don't you? As much as I want to go after Amanda, I won't if we're not squared away here."

Ben nodded. "We're good. Plenty of medical help. And now that we know Mrs. Ortiz was washing our sheets in a creek, trying to save money, we're going to let all the volunteers come here to do the laundry. In filtered water."

"For what it's worth, you protected your sister the way you should have, and you protected your parents as well by never saying anything. Not an easy thing to do because I know it's been tearing you up. But in your place I would have done the same thing. In the end, that's what it's about. We take care of the people we love." Something Ben had done far better than he had.

He blinked hard, trying not to think about Rosa. But she was always there, always reminding him. So now it was time to face up to it, face up to everything he'd done, everyone he'd failed, because this was about Amanda. Only Amanda.

Paso Alto, the homecoming he'd never wanted. Not thinking about it the whole way down here had been one way to avoid it, but now here it was, at the end of the dirt landing strip, waiting there for him the way it had been the first time he'd ever set foot in this village.

Except two years ago he'd come to cure a village illness. Malaria everywhere. People had been wary. He had been an outsider, not one of them. Not even close to being one of them, and he had never kidded himself about that. His life had been about traveling to these remote areas and dealing with issues, not people. But here he'd decided to stay and deal with the people.

The people…up ahead of him as he walked down the road to the center of the village, he saw them watching the plane taxi out and take off. Had they changed? He had. And the hell of it was he wouldn't recognize faces. Not most of them, anyway. Or maybe he didn't want to recognize faces because what if he did? What would he do if he came face-to-face with one of the people who'd stolen his precious Rosa?

"Not easy coming back, is it?" Richard Hathaway asked. He was the only friend Jack had here, the only one who'd tried to help him find Rosa. And the one who'd stood next to him at Rosa's grave the day Jack's world had ended. "Wasn't sure I'd ever see you again."

"Wasn't sure I'd ever do this," Jack said, thrusting out

his hand to shake Hathaway's then pulling the man into his embrace.

Richard Hathaway, a rotund septuagenarian with shocking white hair, ran the local orphanage and school. He'd come here thirty years before as a missionary, met the love of his life in another missionary and found his place. Lucky man.

"Well, it's a good thing. We all have our demons to face, don't we?

"Did Amanda find you?"

"She came to the orphanage last evening, asked to look through the records."

"And?"

"We took her in. Now she's still looking. Things are in a bit of a mess, and I never was very good at the paperwork." He grinned. "Which may work out since I know exactly where your young lady is right now. She's with my *young* lady, enjoying lunch at the village fountain."

"After I phoned earlier, did you tell her I was coming?"

Richard shook his head. "Over the years I've had hundreds of people coming here, looking through my records. People just like your Amanda, trying to discover who they are, how or if they were adopted. They walk away heartbroken, because what most of them hope to find isn't out there. Most of the lost children were never recorded. And while I raise orphans and school them and give them a place to eat and sleep and be safe, I don't know what it's like to be out there alone, not knowing who you are. I can only observe it. But what I know is that Amanda needs the kind of support I can't give her. The best I can do for her, or for anyone like her, is give them a bed while they search, let my Martha cook them a few meals, grant them access to whatever I have and hope they discover what they need. So go and do what you have to then afterward you'll know where to find her."

"Do you know how difficult it is just to walk through town?"

"The most difficult step was getting off that plane. The rest will be easier."

He hoped so, because after he and Richard parted company farther up the road, the same nervousness returned to haunt him that he'd been feeling all the way down here. So it was one step at a time, past the marketplace and the little outdoor café he'd stopped at nearly every day when he'd lived here that now he refused to remember. On down the road, past a family lumber mill and a bakery that pounded the best tortillas he'd ever eaten in his life, but refused to think about because just beyond that was the office. His office. His little house next door.

At first he thought about crossing the road, pretending it wasn't there. But out of the corner of his eye he saw the window to the front bedroom. Tiny. Pink. Rosa's. The curtains were yellow-striped now, and the chair on the front porch where he used to sit and hold her had been replaced by a swing. Same house, though, and he couldn't refuse to acknowledge that because to do so would be to blot out the few memories he wanted to hold on to. Painful as they were, they were all he had.

However, he didn't stop. No, he continued on because he had to put away his past to help Amanda through her future. Because she could continue to look and, one way or another, he was determined to be at her side. He owed it to Rosa, the little lost child of his heart. But he also owed it to Amanda, who'd found her way into his heart when he'd thought there was no room for anyone other than his daughter. In her way, she was a lost child, too.

Jamming his hands into the pockets of his cargo pants, Jack held his head up, looked down the road to the church and the hill behind it that concealed the graveyard. It wasn't good. Not yet. But it would be. It *had* to be.

Amanda glanced down the road, blinked twice, took another look. "That's…" she started to say.

Martha Hathaway looked up from the bowl of fruit she'd been picking from, smiled and nodded. "As handsome as ever. I'm glad to see him return. He was an outstanding doctor, so good with the people here. A very generous, caring man. Always figured he would come back someday. Just didn't know what would make him do it."

"Why wouldn't he return?"

"When it's time, that's for the two of you to talk about. But I'm so glad he's here because Richard and I are quite fond of your young man, Amanda."

She glanced at Jack again, standing on the road. Not moving. And her heart lurched. She'd always seen that distance and sorrow in his eyes in those off-guard moments. It was what he tried to keep hidden behind his gruff facade but she observed the emotions the way he observed his bugs. And what she observed…what she knew now was that it was connected to this place. "He's not my young man," she said, still watching him. "Just a colleague."

"A colleague who causes you to stare off into space and sigh." Martha capped her bowl of fruit, patted Amanda on the hand and stood. "If you catch up to him, bring him round tonight. Argentina dinnertime. Tell him I'm going to make a lovely stew with sausages. He's partial to that, you know." She laughed. "Or maybe you didn't."

With that, seventy-year-old Martha Hathaway dashed away with the agility of someone half her age, leaving

Amanda alone on the edge of the fountain, her attention still fixed on Jack. For the first few hours she'd been here she'd hoped he would follow her because she was so… uncertain. But then it got back to what she already knew, that Jack kept himself apart. Whatever his reason, he *was* that solitary man down the road. He kept himself to himself because that was what he chose to do and, no matter how strong her feelings for him were, loving Jack would turn into a lifetime of loneliness. Alone, in a love affair for two… She was only now beginning to understand the hopelessness.

Yet here he was, and while her intellect was telling her one thing, listing all the reasons she should avoid him, her heart hadn't caught up to her intellect because she still wanted to run to him. Yet she was afraid to go. But her betraying heart beat a little faster, refusing to let in the knowledge that she shouldn't do this, shouldn't go to him, shouldn't watch him.

Watch was what she did, though, while her intellect weighed the battle to keep her in place. Watched him walking by the café, the lumber mill, the bakery. Curious how he slowed down at the little house near the bakery, like he wanted to look at it yet didn't, or wouldn't. Or…couldn't.

Was he looking for her? Wouldn't he have gone to the orphanage first, if he was? It didn't make sense, especially seeing how hesitant he was, standing there alone. She could feel the struggle in him, even from so far away. See the physical manifestation of it crush him down in a way she didn't understand.

*He was an outstanding doctor, so good with the people here. A very generous, caring man.* That was what Martha had said, and those things were still true of him, but now they were buried too deeply for anyone to see. Yet there had been a time when they hadn't been. "Jack," she whispered, still watching. "What happened to you here?"

Suddenly she knew that what she was watching wasn't about him coming for her, looking for her as she'd thought he was doing. It was more. This had been where Jack's life had begun to stagger, where he'd pulled himself away from the world, away from medicine. His own personal hell to face, yet he'd come here for her.

Which meant he loved her. Jack Kenner loved her! He *could* love, and he'd proved it, walking through hellfire to find her. It was a realization that should have set her to tingling. Except there wasn't a thought in her head other than Jack. *He needed her.* She didn't know how, didn't know why, but none of that mattered. He needed her and now it was time for her to prove to Jack that she loved him.

The dreaded walk. He'd thought about this day for two years. Hoped and prayed he wouldn't have to trudge along this road again, see the same sights, be reminded every step of the way. Yet he'd always known that he would have come back someday. To say goodbye. To put a proper headstone on Rosa's grave. To forgive, even though that was the one thing he didn't want to do. Something he'd fought hard against every day for the past two years.

Now, though, he had a reason to move on and he wanted to. With all his heart he had to. But doing it meant forgiving. That was where he had to start otherwise he'd stay stuck in the same place—alone. Without Amanda.

Yet going back was the worst thing he'd ever had to do. So he kept his eyes down to keep from looking at the old white church looming ahead and the burial ground behind the little hill on the far side of it. Because he didn't want to look at the grave. Not again. He had to, though, because the last time he'd taken the road he'd been blinded by…by so many things. Grief, anger, loss. *Hatred.* All because of that tiny mound of dirt with the hastily made wooden cross that bore the name *Rosa.* Not even a last name, because no one in the village would give her what was rightfully hers. Just "Rosa," plain and simple.

On his last trip here he hadn't been able to say the things he'd wanted to say, which he'd regretted ever since. Because he wanted to tell Rosa how profoundly sorry he was for failing her. Tell her one last time how much he loved her. Beg God to let him trade places with his daughter. No, he hadn't said those things because too many people had watched, and yelled, and threatened to drag him out of town.

So, after two mired years, today was that day. He prayed he could find the strength to move on, for Amanda. It was what she needed from him, what he needed from himself. Not an easy thing, but it was time to put Rosa's memory in his heart where it belonged, time to move past the ugliness so he could hold on to the love. Put aside his heartbreak. Rosa deserved that. So did everyone he loved.

Then he would help Amanda through her heartbreak because when she learned the truth about who she was, her heart would surely break. And he would be the one to hold her.

"One minute at a time," he told himself, as he picked up his pace. That was all he could deal with. One minute, followed by another. He wasn't deluding himself into believing that those minutes would cure everything, but as he pushed open the creaking, rusty gate to the churchyard and headed round to the back, while his willingness waned, he could feel his conviction grow. "One minute at a time, one step at a time," he kept telling himself as he approached the tiny grave and came to a stop.

Odd, but no feelings rushed in the way he expected. No pain, no anguish. Just numbness. Was it because he'd fought so long to keep himself in a place where feeling nothing was easier? It had to be. He was still holding it all inside out of habit, afraid of what would happen when he let it go. Afraid to face the fact that his daughter was lying in that grave because he hadn't been able to save her.

His daughter…his flesh and blood. She should have been holding his hand now, tugging on it, looking up at him with beautiful brown eyes that clearly showed him she wanted to go and get ice cream, or play in the park, or find a puppy to adopt. That was the life he should have been living now. Not this empty existence where nothing mattered.

Because Rosa mattered. And Amanda… There was so much in his life that did still matter, and as he thought about it, thought about all the joy Rosa had given him in such a short time, and all the joy Amanda was giving him in spite of himself, that was when the emotion started to trickle back in. "Rosa," he said, dropping to his knees to run his fingers over her wooden marker. For the first time trying to remember, rather than trying to forget. Beautiful baby.

"I tried," he whispered, his voice breaking the words into shards. "But it wasn't enough…I wasn't enough." He could cure epidemics, diagnose the unknown, solve the impossible. Yet when it had come to Rosa… "I'm sorry," he said, swiping at the tears now sliding down his face. "So sorry."

"Sometimes it seems like we can never do enough," Amanda said, stepping up behind him. She stopped short, though, allowed him his distance. "We try, we give everything we have, and we fall short no matter what we do. And it hurts so badly we want to die. Then we blame ourselves for so many things…things we might deserve, things we don't deserve. And it consumes us, changes us, turns us into the kind of people we never thought we'd become. And the pain…"

She stepped forward and laid her hand on Jack's shoulder. "It doesn't go away. But it changes, and yet it won't let go."

"Sometimes living inside that pain is the easiest thing to do," he said.

"Until you find a reason to step outside it. Jack, when my father died, we'd been at odds for too long. I hurt him because all I could see was what I wanted to see, and he hurt me because he was trying to protect my mother. Neither of us deserved to have it end on such a dissonant note, yet it did. What you have to remember, though, is that love prevails. But not on its own. You have to let it prevail, otherwise it's just a word without meaning.

"Jack, I don't know what you're going through, don't know who Rosa was, but I love you and I want to help you face whatever you've got to face. You're not alone now."

"I don't remember a time in my life I wasn't alone. Except for those few weeks I had Rosa. And she made me realize how nice it is having someone to love, to take care of. I miss that. Miss her so badly there are days when I hope the sun doesn't come up so I can sleep through and discover that when I wake up tomorrow I'll realize it was all a nightmare." He turned to face her.

"Rosa was my daughter. I didn't want a child, never thought of myself in terms of being a father, yet there she was one day, in my life, in my heart…" He paused, reached out to touch the marker. "Her mother and I…it was…" He shrugged. "Brief. And we saw, early on, there was nothing… So we ended. No hard feelings. I didn't know she was pregnant then one day I was called to go help the midwife with a difficult birth. And there was Carla, fighting to survive."

"But she didn't?" Amanda asked, stepping forward then sitting on the ground with him.

He shook his head. "The real fight was to save her baby. Then in Carla's last breath she told me the baby was mine. But she didn't have to tell me. I knew it the instant I held Rosa in my hands. There was this feeling... I can't describe it, but it was like everything in my life changed in the blink of an eye. Everything got better.

"Except it didn't because Carla had spent months lying to everybody she knew, including her family, about who Rosa's father was. Apparently she'd told them he was one of the locals, a love affair gone bad. Don't know why but I suppose it made life easier for her that way. Maybe less prejudice to face. Can't fault her for that since all I've been doing since then is taking the easiest way for me."

"So you were the only one who knew Rosa was yours?"

"The only one."

"Not even the midwife?"

Jack shook his head. "The thing is, at the time I didn't think it would be a problem. I'd planned on taking Rosa home with me and we'd have a life together. Stupid, simplistic dream."

"What happened?"

"She was ill. Had a congenital heart defect that started showing in her pretty quickly. But there was no place around here with the means to perform the surgery she needed. It should have been an easy problem to solve— take my daughter back to the States for surgery. I'd made the arrangements with a buddy from med school, and I was on my way to the airport, but...they stopped me."

"Who?"

"The town. They literally stopped me on my way to the taxi and took her away from me."

Amanda gasped. "How could they? I mean, didn't they know who you were? Maybe not as Rosa's father but as the doctor?"

"A lot of the people knew me, most of them trusted me, I think. I'd come down to chase after malaria, decided to stay for a while because…" He shrugged. "They needed a doctor, I suppose. The thing is, even the people I treated turned on me." He shut his eyes. "They took her, and hid her. Shuffled her from house to house, family to family, village to village so I couldn't find her. But I looked. Everywhere. Kept looking, kept knocking on doors. Then after weeks of it I suppose Rosa's frail little body couldn't take it any longer because I received a hand-delivered note from the village priest telling me that her funeral service would take place that very afternoon." He swallowed hard. "I wasn't allowed in the graveyard until after she was buried."

Amanda gasped. "I'm so sorry, Jack. I can't even begin to imagine…"

"I know they were trying to protect her, but I kept telling them I was her father, and they didn't believe me because too many people had taken too many children, and to the people trying to protect Rosa I simply looked like one of the many. Because of that she died, Amanda. I loved that baby, and she died, and there wasn't a damn thing I could do about it." He swallowed hard. "And nobody can understand what it feels like, knowing you failed your child in the worst way any parent could ever fail their child."

Amanda scooted closer to Jack and put her arms around him. For her support, for his, there wasn't a distinction now as the grief settled down over both of them. But finally she broke that silence. "Why, Jack? Who was taking the children? I don't understand."

Jack braced himself for this. It was time. Time for things to end, time for things to begin. Doing it here with Rosa was right because, like Amanda, she was part of the cycle of sadness that had touched and broken too many lives. So he shifted, took Amanda's hand and held on for dear life because nothing would be the same again, not for either of them. "First, just let me say I don't want to hurt you with any of this."

"What do you mean?"

"I didn't want to come back here. Not ever. Didn't want to face what they'd done. Most of all didn't want to face myself because living in my own little isolated world was what I deserved. Or believed I deserved. Then I met this wild, crazy woman who kept trying to turn my world upside down, and it's damn hard to stand firm when she's feeding you blueberries and stringing your bed with Christmas lights."

"This doesn't have anything to do with Rosa, does it?"

He was surprised her face was the picture of calm considering what he knew *she knew* was coming, but it was. Beautiful, serene face. "It has everything to do Rosa, and Ezequiel, and you, I think."

"Then tell me, Jack. Tell me what I believe Ben knows and you suspect. And how it all connects to your daughter, and to Ezequiel. And to me."

If only there was a way to shade her from this like the leaves of the massive ombu tree overhead shaded them. But there wasn't. She was sitting there, looking so brave and determined, yet he saw the uncertainty in her eyes. And here he was, faced with the moment, dreading it and hoping, at the same time, there was merit in the old adage that the truth would set you free. Still, all he could see in this truth was pain.

But it was time to quit protecting Amanda. She needed more. Returning to Paso Alto had been his starting place. Now it was time to give Amanda the same thing—her own starting place.

So he drew in a deep breath and began. "All the years I've traveled, I've seen so many orphaned children. Everywhere. Internationally, it's believed there are about one-hundred and forty-three million. In South America alone close to eight million. It's sad, Amanda. I've seen them everywhere and wondered why all the people who want children can't just go to these places and find them. Cut through the red tape. Give the children a home. You can't even begin to imagine…" He sighed.

"Happily ever after for everyone. In so many ways it makes sense. But there are laws and procedures that have to be in place so these children aren't exploited, and I understand that because they have to be protected above everything else. Unfortunately, the laws are broken anyway. Children have been taken without going through the proper procedures. Sometimes they're literally abducted. Picked up off the streets and carried away.

"The people who live here have seen that happen over and over, lived with it, watched the children being…stolen. That's why they stopped me. They didn't know I was Rosa's father and to them, doctor or not, I was just another one of the outsiders who had merely wandered in to take a child."

Amanda looked at Jack and the color from her face drained away. But she didn't ask. So he continued before the full realization of what he was telling her sank in. "I think, or I hope that most of the time the people who took these children did so with the best intentions. But the sentiment became *See an abandoned child, save the child.* Still is in some areas. I know that sentiment, understand it probably better than I understand almost anything else because all I wanted to do was save Rosa, and she wasn't an abandoned child. Even Ezequiel—my gut reaction to him was to take him home with me when I go because nobody will notice. So I know how so many of these people felt when they came here, or any number of other places, and saw these abandoned children literally up for grabs.

"Yet taking a child without doing it the proper way is wrong, and in some cases children who weren't orphaned were even taken. See an abandoned child, save the child, but don't bother to see if the child is really abandoned or part of a family. In the rush to grab *free* children, mothers and fathers lost their sons and daughters, and there's nothing right about that, no matter what the intention."

He brushed her cheek. "Children in South America were especially desirable...beautiful skin, beautiful eyes. There were so many orphans here, and since so much of the land was still rural the assumption was that in many of the areas no one cared. Or noticed."

Her breathing turned ragged as she struggled with the next words. "Is that me, Jack? Was I one of the children who was taken?"

"I'm so sorry, Amanda, but I believe you could have been," he said, his voice barely above a whisper.

"And Ben? Does he know about these children? Does he think that I was...?"

Jack nodded. "That's something the two of you will have to work out, but he's devastated by this, devastated by the feelings he has for your parents and what they might have done."

"Yet he never told me."

"Because he was trying to protect you. And trying to protect your parents, as well."

"But they loved me, Jack. I know they loved me. So how could they...?" She shut her eyes, shook her head. "So how could they tell me the truth if they stole me? Yet how could they *not* tell me the truth if they didn't?"

"We don't know yet if it *is* the truth. There were many legitimate adoptions going on as well, especially in the early years. And now. So maybe the records really weren't kept, or your records got lost. Your parents were humanitarian workers here..."

"Who lied to me. Who would have had easy access to an orphan child. Which would make them part of the reason you weren't allowed to leave with Rosa. Because of what my parents did." She paused, and in a flash the pain on her face turned to pure, raw anger. "Jack, I...I don't know what to say. I can't even..." She paused again, shut her eyes, then pulled away from him. "You knew this, didn't you? You knew this all along."

"I suspected. Once I understood the confusion behind your adoption, I knew that could be the case. That your parents might have come here and taken you. Then when I found out how they'd lied..."

"Rosa was Mapuche. That day when you said you loved someone who was Mapuche... That's why you can't love me. How could you? My parents, what they did... And Rosa. I thought it was you, Jack. All this time, when you've pulled away or distanced yourself, I thought it was you. But it was..."

"Me," he said gently. "But not because I couldn't love

you, Amanda. I have. I do. But I've been filled with so much hate and anger there wasn't room for anything else. Michael got in first, though. Just knocked right through it all and found a little place. Then you, and Ezequiel. But you all deserve more than a little place in my heart, and I couldn't let go of all my emotions to give you what you needed. When you left, when you came here alone, I knew what you'd be facing sooner or later, knew you shouldn't have to face it alone. But to be what you needed I had to get past all this."

"It can't work now. Don't you understand? My parents were part of your suffering, and every time you look at me you may want to love me, think you do love me, but what I came from will always be a reminder of what happened to your daughter."

"I've known that from the day I arrived in Argentina and you twisted my arm into telling you that you're Mapuche. And it hasn't changed the way I feel about you. But that's something you're going to have to trust, and I think you will when you're past the initial shock.

"The thing is, Rosa died because people cared about her. I've known that all along, but didn't want to see it. I knew the people here didn't want to harm her. And if your parents did simply take you, it's because they cared, too. What I want to believe is that they saw a beautiful child who needed a home, and loved her the way every child deserves to be loved."

"And you can just accept that, and move on?"

"Not alone. My daughter died, Amanda, and I'm still grieving. Still struggling with how I feel. Maybe I'm only just beginning to grieve the way I need to. But I can't do that by myself because I'll go right back to being myself—

that grumpy recluse you met back in Texas. The one who finds it easier to stay numb."

"Always on the verge of quitting medicine," she added.

"Not medicine. I've never truly been on the verge of quitting medicine. More like on the verge of quitting me. I don't want to keep living with the pain, but being a doctor who failed to save his daughter is a pain that just keeps beating me down. Until you, I never had a reason to want to get back up again. To need to get back up."

"But you didn't fail her, Jack. The failure came from something you couldn't control. For Rosa, you were a perfect father who would have given his life to save his daughter. There's no failure in that. Only sadness for a little girl who didn't get to see how very loved she was."

"I want to stay here," he said. "In Argentina, at Caridad. Maybe come back here from time to time to put flowers on her grave and do some doctoring at the orphanage. But I don't want to stay here without you, Amanda. I don't want to be alone anymore."

"I keep thinking back to the first time I ever saw you… standing there in my office doorway, demanding my references."

He chuckled. "I remember that man. Pretty surly, wasn't he?"

"Surly, maybe. But I also saw the way you looked at your nephew later that day, at the hospital. You'd never even met him, yet that first look at him…"

"You saw that?"

"I saw everything." She blinked back tears. "And knew everything I needed to know about you. That's why it hurt so bad when I didn't think you could love me, because that was the man I fell in love with. Maybe not at first sight. But at second sight, when I saw you with Ezequiel. And third sight, with Renata, and fourth with Alfonso... Everything I saw was someone you didn't see, or couldn't see, but I never, ever couldn't see that man. And he's the man I want to see every day, for the rest of my life."

"I'm still going to be grumpy sometimes. Can you put up with that?"

"And I'm still going to get obsessed with trying to find out who I am. Can you put up with that?"

"I'll have to go when there's an outbreak of some sort."

"And I'll be going back to Texas a couple times a month to check on some of my patients."

"But I won't be eating blueberries again."

"No blueberries?"

"Allergic. They really do make me break out in hives."

She leaned her head on his shoulder. "Yet you ate one for me."

"Because you were cramming it down my throat."

"Because you were being grumpy."

"Because you were making me happy."

Sighing, Amanda reached over and brushed her fingers across Rosa's marker. Then smiled. "It's better together. Whatever it is, whatever we've got to face, wherever we have to go, it's better together."


"I guess I've never had a Christmas without a Christmas tree, but this works," Jack said, grinning as he studied the outline of a Christmas tree Ezequiel had formed with strings of Christmas lights on the wall. It was rather amazing, actually. Quite ingenious. Made Jack wonder what kind of talents he would discover in his soon-to-be son. One perfectly good kid in need of parents, two not-so-perfect parents in need of a kid. It was a great way to start a new life—as a family of three.

Ezequiel grinned from ear to ear. "And there are presents," he squealed, pointing to the wrapped packages sitting on the floor underneath the pseudo-tree. "Look at them! There are so many."

"All of them for you," Jack said, smiling. He'd avoided Christmas for years. Too much sentiment, too many memories. Yet today what he had was a life full of expectations. New things, good things. Journeys with Amanda as she went to look for her heritage. A son. The occasional call out to hunt down and take care of an epidemic. A home to build in Argentina, a hospital to help once he endowed some expansions, including a bigger office for Ben—although he was partial to the idea of taking over Ben's former office with its cramped space just because he had fond memories of being cramped in there with Amanda. Just the beginning of so many memories to come. "Except a couple for Amanda."

"Maybe one for Jack," she said, looking particularly pleased with herself.

They hadn't told Ezequiel their plan yet, but his adoption was in the works. It was going to be tricky because neither Jack nor Amanda were Argentinian citizens. But a strong recommendation from Richard Hathaway went a long way. So did a letter from the Paso Alto priest. The official assigned to Ezequiel's welfare was also optimistic. In fact, she'd promised her support. So it was all looking good.

"And me?" Ben asked, winking at Ezequiel. "Is there anything under that tree for me?"

"Your Christmas gift," Amanda told him, "is a holiday. You haven't been out of this hospital in ages, and considering all the stress you've just been through you need it. So Jack and I are going to take over for two weeks while you go someplace else and do whatever you want." She plucked an envelope from amongst the wrapped packages and held it up. "I know you've always wanted to see Tuscany, so this ticket will take you to Italy. Or you can exchange it for anywhere else you want to go."

Jack held up an envelope of his own. "And these two tickets will take us back home so I can take care of my personal effects and buy you a proper engagement ring, then maybe go and talk to your mother, if you're up to it."

Amanda glanced at her brother. "Maybe she'll tell me what I want to know, maybe she won't. I'm not going to press her for answers. But she has to know that, whatever she did, I love her and I forgive her. When I was in Paso Alto I saw too much guilt, too much pain, and it occurred to me our mother has lived with it herself all these years because of what I think she and Dad did. Just the way you've lived with the guilt, trying to protect me from it. So I have to let her know that, no matter what it was, I do love her.

"And I love you, too, Ben, for being the best big brother a girl could have." She reached out and took Ben's hand. "I'll be gentle with her. I promise."

"I know you will," Ben said.

"And two more presents, one from me and one not from me." Jack looked at Amanda. "Both for you."

"I love presents," she said, nudging Ezequiel to start unwrapping. So far, he was so caught up in simply looking at the presents, but at the prompt wrapping paper started to fly. And for the next half hour Amanda and Jack enjoyed everything about their first Christmas with their son.

"Now Christmas for us," Jack finally said to Amanda. "And your first gift comes from Father Garcia."

"The priest in Paso Alto?"

Jack nodded. "I never told you, but he was the one who literally took Rosa from my arms. His convictions were strong that he was doing the right thing, but since she died he's never been able to forgive himself. So I talked to him that day, after we left the grave. It's where I had to start to make things right again. Start to forgive. And he was so…sad, and so appreciative that I would stop to see him after what he'd done. Anyway, he's promised to help you by making contact with every priest he knows in the Pampas areas and ask them to search their records for any that might be yours."

She leaned over and gave him a proper kiss on the cheek. "Thank you for what you did for the father. You did a good thing, Jack. A very good thing, helping him get past it."

"Well, I hope this next present gets me a kiss on the lips."

"But I don't see anything else under the tree."

"Too big to wrap. Except the computer, which will be delivered in a couple of weeks."

"You bought me a computer?" she asked, smiling, but slightly puzzled. "Because we have a computer here."

"A hospital computer. But I'm having this one installed with software being designed especially for you and the foundation I'm endowing. Something we're going to run together with the help of Richard and Martha. Even Father Garcia."

"A foundation?"

He nodded. "That day in Paso Alto when Richard told me how many people like you show up at his orphanage, looking for records, I started thinking about how we could help their search."

Amanda's eyes widened, but she didn't say anything.

"We can do it from here, and from Paso Alto. Transfer

existing records to a searchable database. Search other databases for whatever we can find. It's not the perfect solution, but it's a start."

"I…I don't know what to say, Jack. I'm…"

"Speechless?" he asked, laughing. "Does that mean I'm finally going to get the last word?"

"And I'm going to learn the computer," Ezequiel said, grinning.

She looked at him, fighting back a laugh. "You knew about this, and you kept it a secret from me?"

"Doc K promised me a video game. I don't know what that is yet, but I think it's good. So I had to keep it a secret."

Amanda got up on her hands and knees and crawled over to Ezequiel, who was sitting in the middle of all his presents. Then hugged him. "It's very good," she said. "Everything is very good.

"Do I get any of that?" Jack asked.

She crooked her finger to beckon him over, and just as he leaned in for what he expected to be a kiss, she stopped him. "Thank you for doing that, Jack. It's important. It's something that can make a real difference. And it's worth more than a kiss," she said. "To help people find themselves…it's worth everything." Taking his hand, she placed it on her belly. "It's still early, just barely begun, but by next Christmas we'll be a family of four. My gift to you."

Speechless, he simply stared at her belly for a moment then stared into her eyes. "We did that?"

She nodded. "We did that."

Smiling, he pulled her into his arms, brushed a tender kiss to her lips then leaned down, pulled up her shirt and kissed her belly. After that he raised up and whispered, "Everything."

\* \* \* \* \*

# THE MAN WHO WOULDN'T MARRY

BY

## TINA BECKETT

MILLS & BOON®

First published in Great Britain 2012
by Mills & Boon, an imprint of Harlequin (UK) Limited.
Harlequin (UK) Limited, Eton House, 18-24 Paradise Road,
Richmond, Surrey TW9 1SR

© Tina Beckett 2012

ISBN: 978 0 263 89793 7

Harlequin (UK) policy is to use papers that are natural, renewable and recyclable products and made from wood grown in sustainable forests. The logging and manufacturing process conform to the legal environmental regulations of the country of origin.

Printed and bound in Spain
by Blackprint CPI, Barcelona

# CHAPTER ONE

WHY was he here?

Mark Branson's eyes slid for the hundredth time to the small child standing beside him at the altar, the boy's dark suit and red tie a miniature version of his own. They could almost be father and son.

But they weren't.

His gaze automatically swept to the left, coming to rest on the bridesmaid across the aisle. The woman he'd once planned to marry in this very church, before life had intervened, and she'd married someone else.

And having her child propped against him as they waited for the wedding to begin was pure torture.

'Do you have the rings?'

Mark blinked and switched his attention back to the priest, the man's gold-embroidered robes and matching cape seeming as ancient as the ornate carvings inside the small Russian Orthodox Church. Candles of all shapes and sizes adorned the altar, placed on glittering stands by the people in attendance. The flickering glow added a sense of awe and mystery to the room, and also provided the only source of illumination. The absence of electric lights in the church had always seemed strange to Mark but, then again, he could count on his fingers the number of services he'd attended here.

The last time had been for his father's memorial service. He could still remember his mother's tears. Her grief so misplaced. Mark had never visited the man's grave. Not once.

A throat cleared. 'The rings?' The concern in the priest's tone echoed off the high ceilings. The groom shot him a look, his best friend's brows lifting in question.

Mark cleared his own throat to make sure it came out normal. 'I have them.'

Okay, good. The steady throbbing behind his temples hadn't crept down to his voice box. Digging in his pocket, he located the pair of rings and handed them to the boy, who in turn trudged up the two steps to the top of the platform, giving one to the groom and the other to the bride.

The bride, a relative newcomer to the Aleutians, bent down to hug the child and watched as he skipped back down the steps. She then wrinkled her nose and smiled at her soon-to-be-husband, who gazed back at her with besotted eyes.

Mark barely restrained himself from rolling his own. His buddy had it bad.

Willing the child to go and stand beside his mother, who hadn't met Mark's gaze once since they'd taken their places on the steps at the front of the church, he gave an almost audible sigh of frustration. Because the boy wound up back at his side, leaning against him. The turmoil already raging within his gut turned into a firestorm of the worst kind.

Worse than his years in the military. Worse than what he'd returned home to six months ago.

'Do you, Blake Taylor, take Molly McKinna to be your lawfully wedded wife...'

The voice droned on as a curtain of red slowly rose behind Mark's eyelids. Could this get any worse? When his friend had asked him to be best man, he'd known it was a bad idea.

Churches and weddings?

Not for Mark. Not any more.

He'd become adept at drifting from relationship to relationship, never allowing things to become too serious. Never willing to risk the hurt that came with discovering someone you'd cared about had married someone else—had another man's child. It was his own fault, but he'd had no choice. Not at the time.

'Muster Mark?' The words brought his gaze back down to the boy beside him. 'Are we almost done? I'm thusty.'

The slight lisp sent a half-smile tugging at the corners of his mouth, before he cranked them back down. The child had to be almost six years old. A surge of hope had flashed through him the first time he'd seen the boy. Hope that he had been *his* son. But he had been aboard an aircraft carrier in the Arabian Sea at the time, flying missions to Afghanistan, so there was no chance.

He swallowed the bile that rose in his throat. He'd told her to move on with her life, and she'd done exactly that, Two years after his plane had left Dutch Harbor that final time.

Which brought him back to his original question. *Why was he here?*

A question that had nothing to do with witnessing his best friend's wedding and everything to do with moving back to his hometown. He swore once his dad died, he'd never come back, but his mom had seemed so...

Frail.

Terrified of being alone for the first time in her adult life. So he'd done what he'd tried to do as a young boy, protect her from the bad things in the world. He wasn't any better at it now than he'd been all those years ago.

He glanced down at the kid, who was about the same age Mark had been when he had realized something was terribly wrong with his family. That they were different from the families of his classmates and friends. Hence the fights he'd frequently got into. The need to prove he was tougher—better than them all. It had also kept anyone from focusing on the truth behind his bruises.

Almost against his will, his hand went to the boy's head, resting for a second on the dark silky hair—so like his mother's. 'A few more minutes,' he whispered, realizing he'd never answered the child's question.

The kid blinked up at him, eyes trusting. Innocent.

Hell, he hoped Sammi knew enough to protect that at all costs.

He glanced over at her again, this time finding her brown eyes staring at him, brows drawn together in worry. He had a feeling if she could snatch her child away from him without causing a scene, she'd do it in a heartbeat.

Mark removed his hand from the boy's head, and crossed his arms over his chest, staring back at her in defiance. She jerked her attention away and faced the bride and the groom, her teeth digging into her soft bottom lip.

Her customary braid was gone today, her long dark hair left free to spill over her bare shoulders and halfway down her back. Thick and glossy, he knew firsthand how decadent those silky strands felt as they flowed across his hands...his body.

He shifted in his spot to keep from remembering too

deeply, knowing this was not the time or place. Later, when he slugged back his first shot of whiskey and tried to push away the horrors of the last eight years, he could afford to nurse his regrets.

But he wouldn't go back and change how he'd done things. It had been the right thing to do under the circumstances. The only thing. His father had made sure of that when he'd cracked open the tiny velvet box and discovered Mark's secret.

*Well, well, boy. What have we here?* The slow, ugly smile that had made Mark's insides tighten with dread had appeared. *Don't worry. I'll make sure the girlie is given a proper Branson welcome.*

He'd left for Anchorage the next day, the engagement ring tucked into the pocket of his jeans, a duffle bag slung over his shoulder. He'd shown up at the first recruitment station he could find…and the rest was history.

Soft clapping around him made him realize the bride and groom were now in each other's arms, their lips locked together.

He couldn't bring himself to applaud, so he dropped his hands to his sides. When his gaze wandered back to Sammi, he noted that she was standing as still as a stone, her knuckles showing white as she clenched the stems of her bouquet.

How soon could he get out of there?

There was no reception planned, which was a big relief. He didn't have to mingle and make small talk about how great it was that the bride and groom had finally gotten hitched. Or how wonderful it was that they were moving permanently to Anchorage. Mark had never thought his buddy, of all people, would ever leave the island.

*Love conquers all.*

Wrong.

Sometimes love just turned you into a victim.

His friend's desertion, though, meant it was now Sammi…and him…doing the island's medevacs. Why he'd agreed to take the job, he had no idea. He should have said no, that he was strictly a tourist pilot, sticking to a fluffy job that required nothing more than a smile and a canned speech. Nothing like the life-and-death missions he'd flown in the military—or the terrible images that still invaded his thoughts and woke him in the night. But it was either that or stand in the way of his buddy's happiness.

And his friend knew how to lay on the guilt. He always had.

The pair at the front of the church broke apart amidst laughter. They pivoted towards the small assembly and started down the aisle to the pipe organ's piercing rendition of the 'Hallelujah Chorus', drawing more chuckles from friends and family. The groom put his arms around his bride and pulled her close, stopping for another kiss before they'd gone a half-dozen steps.

All Mark wanted to do was escape.

The rest of the wedding party—he, Sammi, and Sammi's son—turned to follow suit. He started to hold out his elbow for Sammi as he'd been instructed by his friend—under threat of death—but found her boy's fingers grabbing his hand instead.

Sammi shot him a glare that could have scalded milk and swept in front of him, perfectly rounded curves showcased by her snug emerald dress. The thing actually shimmered with each angry swish of her hips. It took several seconds and a tug at his hand before he realized he was still standing there, rooted in place, as Sammi drew further and further away.

He forced himself to move, having to dial back on the length of his strides to match the kid's. By the time they caught up with her, she was standing in the reception line by the front doors of the church, and he was once again trying to figure out why he was there.

Samantha Grey Trenton sucked down a deep breath and tried not to let her rising panic overwhelm her. Her son Toby's sudden fascination with Mark was nothing more than the fact that he was tall and dark like his father, her ex-husband. Despite the physical resemblance, though, Mark was not the kind of person she wanted her son hanging around. The kind that led you on for as long as it suited him and then left with barely a word.

'I think I have something of yours.' Low and deep, the murmured words slid over her, his breath ruffling her hair.

She swallowed, then turned to face him, realizing with relief he was talking about Toby and not some sentimental relic from the past. That thought caused a warning prickle behind her eyelids that she forced back with a single harsh blink.

Mark's hand came out, her son's small fingers still gripping it like a lamprey. No choice. Her only hope was to try to take possession of him without touching anything but Toby.

Except it ended up being impossible.

In order to take her son's hand, she was forced to wriggle her fingertips between their palms. Mark's warm skin sizzled against her icy flesh, and for a split second all three of their hands were sealed together: Hers, Toby's, and a stranger's.

The prickle reappeared. Oh, God, she was going to lose it. Right here in front of all these people.

The image of the funny, laid-back boy who'd asked her to be his date for their senior prom—whose desperate kisses had awoken something deep inside her—appeared in the back of her mind. But that person was gone for ever, destroyed when he had announced he was going into the military. That shocking decree had come just weeks after he'd professed his love for her, his face turning a charming shade of red as he'd said the words.

It had all been a lie, however. A way to get her into his bed, because there'd been no promise of a future when he'd left. Just a few tight-jawed words spoken at the front door of her house. Then he had gone. The remembered humiliation of that night still had the power to crush her heart in a giant fist.

The tall, rugged man who'd returned to Dutch Harbor eight years later was indeed a stranger. Flippant, arrogant and who now chased anyone in a skirt.

Anyone but her.

With a start, she realized Mark was now eyeing her, their hands still joined together. She gulped and with a quick move, prised Toby's hand free. She moved a few steps forward in line, needing to put some distance between her and Mark.

*Please let me get through this in one piece.*

That tiny prayer seemed doomed the second she sensed the heat from Mark's body close behind her. Too close.

*Ignore him. You've done it for the last six months. You can do it now.*

Not so easy this time as Toby had twisted around to look, a contented sigh lifting his thin chest. She listened for the warning wheeze, but it didn't happen. A dose of self-righteous anger whipped up at the deadly charisma her former beau gave off in waves. She would not let him hurt her son the way he'd hurt her.

She leaned down. 'Just a few more minutes.' She realized too late those were almost the exact words she'd heard Mark whisper to him earlier.

Thank heavens she hadn't waited around for Mark's return. Because he now barely gave her the time of day. And she wasn't much better. She avoided him whenever she could—not an easy feat on an island like Dutch Harbor—and the only times he'd appeared at the clinic over these last months had been to deliver a tourist who'd gotten a scrape or a bruise.

Her turn to offer her congratulations to the happy couple. *Finally!*

She pasted on a smile as she reached out her free hand to Blake, the groom. 'So you went and did it.' She tried to keep her voice light, but it betrayed her by shaking just the tiniest bit. She pushed on, anyway. 'I can't believe you're leaving the island and taking Molly with you.' Blake, Mark, and Sammi had joined forces during their childhood days, becoming a kind of mod squad—inseparable and lifelong friends. Those strands were now tattered and worn—she doubted they could ever be woven together again.

Blake laughed, evidently not noticing the strain she was under. 'I think if Molly had a choice, she'd never leave Dutch Harbor.'

Molly had worked as a doctor at the tiny clinic with Sammi for the last year until her funding had dried up, forcing her to move back to Anchorage. She and Blake had met while doing medevacs and, after a rocky start, realized they were meant for each other. Once she left, Sammi would be stuck doing medical evacuations with Mark, not something she was looking forward to.

Who was she kidding? She was dreading it.

Pausing to gather her thoughts, she tried to keep her mind on the happy couple and off her own problems. 'Treat her right, Blake. Or I'll come and find you.'

'I intend to.'

While Blake squatted to talk to Toby, Sammi moved over to embrace the bride. 'Be happy,' she whispered.

'You too.'

If only it were that easy.

She sensed Blake rise to his feet to greet Mark. At the sound of awkward male hugs—complete with palms delivering a few resounding smacks to the other's back—she had to fight back a smile.

She tried to tune out their words, but Mark's 'You caved, bro' caught her attention, the wry tone as flip as ever.

The bride's voice brought her back to the present. 'Okay, you two, I'm tired and starving.' She crinkled her nose. 'And I still have a three-hour flight to Anchorage to get through.'

That drew a laugh from Sammi. Her friend had married a pilot, yet she didn't like to fly. At all. Talk about opposites attracting. She gave Molly another quick hug. 'You'll be fine.'

Molly smiled. 'I know I will. I just like the extra hand-holding it gets me.'

Those words made Sammi's heart ache. Although she was over the moon that her two friends had found each other, she was sad she'd never found that same perfect happiness. Her ex-husband had done his best, but in the end they'd both known it wasn't meant to be. When Toby had been one, they'd separated. They'd finalized their divorce two weeks before Toby's second birthday. Her ex, now living in Anchorage, had remarried and was, to all appearances, blissfully happy with his second wife. Even Toby liked her.

A throat cleared behind her, making her jump. She realized she was holding up the line and that Mark couldn't get around her in the narrow gap between the door and the newly married couple without touching her. Again. The thought made her quake inside. She squeaked out a quick 'Sorry'.

Then she grabbed Toby's hand and did the only thing she could think of.

She fled.

# CHAPTER TWO

SAMMI pumped the inhaler twice and waited.

Toby, still half-asleep, lay on his back propped in a nest of pillows. The terrifying rattle in his chest slowly eased as the albuterol flooded his lungs, widening his breathing passages to allow more air flow.

As Community Health Aide for the island, she knew better than to panic, but when it was your own son... She closed her eyes. Who could maintain any kind of objectivity under those circumstances?

Not that she had much of that anyway. Molly had continually fussed at her for rushing from one house to another to check on patients she'd just seen the day before.

'You're going to wear yourself out this way' had been the rebuke *du jour*.

Her friend was right, but she hadn't been able to stop.

Now that Molly was gone and with only one other physician's assistant on staff at the clinic, she wouldn't have the luxury of taking off at any hour of day to check on her patients. And either she or the PA would now have to accompany any medevac flights headed to Anchorage. The good part was that she'd be able to meet up with Molly periodically. The bad part was that she was stuck flying with Mark—although Blake could still handle cases that weren't life or death and who could wait the three hours it took him to reach Dutch Harbor.

'Better?' she asked her son, his breathing now almost back to normal.

He nodded sleepily, trying to squinch his way back into his cocoon of warm covers.

'Not so fast, bud. Let's just wait another minute or two.'

His impatient sigh made her smile. Okay, if he could do that, instead of gasping for each breath, she could afford to let him go back to sleep. She tucked him in and stood over his bed, watching him for a second. Before putting the inhaler back on the book-packed nightstand beside his bed, she shook it to see how much of the medicine remained.

*Were they going through it faster than normal?*

She couldn't shake the feeling that Toby's attacks were coming more frequently than in the past.

Checking the child monitor before she clicked the lights off, she headed back to her own room, hoping she could squeeze her eyelids shut long enough to turn off her brain. She needed the sleep, or tomorrow promised to be a long, exhausting day.

'Mrs. Litchfield is in room one. One of her joints is swollen to almost twice its size.' The receptionist handed Sammi a file folder.

She tossed her braid over her shoulder, catching a movement outside the front plate-glass window as she did.

Mark. He was striding by on his way to the airport, hands stuffed into the front pockets of his leather bomber jacket, long, loose limbs moving in a way that drew the eye. Not quite a swagger, his stride gave off an air of easy confidence that said he didn't care what the world thought of him.

And unlike Sammi, who couldn't seem to look away, the man didn't spare a glance at the clinic, or at her. With a sigh, she forced herself to turn away and head to the exam room.

As soon as she arrived, all thoughts of Mark evaporated when Barbara Litchfield, a woman in her mid-fifties, climbed to her feet and greeted her.

'Sorry to come back so soon,' she said, the regret in her voice unmistakable.

'What are you talking about? I told you to get back in here at the first hint of trouble. Arthritis is nothing to play around with. I know you need those fingers whole and strong.'

A retired orchestral pianist, Barbara had moved to the Aleutians with her husband when he'd retired from a corporate job a couple of years ago. At a time when most retirees sought refuge in the south, hoping for warm, sunny days of golfing and fun, the Litchfields had bucked the trend, fitting right into the harsh landscape of Dutch Harbor. Barbara taught piano lessons—free of charge—to a few of the local kids. It meant a lot to both the former pianist and the kids she worked with. Those fingers were important, and not just for her physical health.

Sammi snapped on a pair of gloves. 'Let's take a look, shall we?'

Taking the other woman's hands in hers, she spotted the affected joint immediately. Swollen and angry red, her left ring finger didn't look happy, and for good reason. Molly frowned when she noted the woman's wedding band. 'Why is that still on?'

'I tried to get it off this morning when I realized how bad it was, but it wouldn't budge, and when I tried to force it…' Her voice trailed away.

'It's okay. The base of your finger isn't swollen at the moment, but if it begins to swell, we may need to cut the ring off.' She put a hand on the other woman's shoulder. 'We won't unless it's absolutely necessary, okay? In the meantime, I'm going to give you a shot of cortisone in the joint. Then I really want you to see a rheumatologist in Anchorage. I'll make a phone call and get you in as soon as possible.'

'I can't just keep taking Advil?'

Sammy shook her head. 'That used to be how we treated arthritis, thinking if we could get the inflammation under control, we could preserve the joint. But newer research suggests the real damage happens much earlier in the disease, even before it shows up on X-rays.'

Just like the damage to Sammi and Mark's relationship. Just as their feelings for each other started to gain a foothold, unseen currents swirled around them, eating away at the foundation. By the time she'd realized just how deeply she'd fallen for him, the mysterious corrosive agent had done its job. The silver cord joining them had snapped and Mark had bolted.

So why did seeing him walk down the street this morning still tug at something inside her? And why had seeing her son's hand enveloped in his at the wedding a week ago turned her heart inside out?

She shook off the questions. It didn't matter. She'd gotten married, had a child with someone else. Mark had dated plenty of other women since his return.

There was nothing between them any more.

'Let me make a quick phone call then I'll give you the injection.' Sammi scribbled a couple of notes down on the chart. 'I'll be right back.'

The phone call took less than five minutes. A bit of

arm twisting on her end, the promise of a jar of home-made salmonberry jam when the season rolled around, and Barbara had her appointment. Two weeks from today, record time for that kind of specialist. But she and Chris Masters went way back. One of the few islanders who'd gone to medical school and left the Aleutians, he was now a highly sought-after rheumatologist. Appointments with him could take months.

Satisfied, she made a note to herself that her debt to fellow doctors was now up to ten pints of jam and a pie. Not to mention her son, who'd made her promise on her life not to give all their jelly away again this year.

Speaking of Toby...

She jogged back to the reception area. 'What time is it?'

Lynn's raised brows told her even before she spoke. 'Two o'clock, and you've missed lunch again.'

'Right. I'll eat as soon as I'm done with Mrs. Litchfield. Promise.'

'You'd better. I've already locked the front door, just in case.'

Sammi laughed. 'Thanks.'

'I'm going to start heating your food in the microwave, so don't take long.' She paused. 'I'm heating mine too.'

In other words, if Sammi delayed, her receptionist would also go hungry. 'I'll be there by the time you pour the coffee.'

The injection was given and Sammi unlatched the front door to let Barbara out—a sheaf of papers and instructions clutched in her hands. She pushed the door closed again, twisting her head around when Lynn's threat reached her ears. 'Coffee's going into the mugs.'

'I'll be right—'

The front door started to blow open, probably a result

of the gusty conditions today. Sammi was leaning her entire weight onto it to force it shut when a harsh yelp, a colorful string of words and something squishy stopped her in her tracks.

Eyes wide, she turned to look. The doorway she'd sworn was empty a second ago was now filled with Mark, and that squishy thing…

Yikes, she'd just crunched his hand in the door!

'Coffee's getting cold.' Lynn's warning was drowned by the realization of what she'd just done.

She jerked the door wide. 'Oh, God, Mark. I'm sorry. I had no idea you were there. Or I'd have never…'

'Never what? Slammed the door on me?' He shook his injured hand, the graveled accusation bringing back the fact that she'd done exactly that once upon a time. When he'd announced his intention of moving away to join the armed forces, she'd slammed the door in his face with a 'Don't bother coming by before you leave'.

But that was all in the past, where it would stay.

'Come in so I can look at that hand.'

'It's fine.'

'Seriously. It could be broken.'

He gave a wry laugh. 'You really think I'd let you set it if it were? I'd probably end up with permanently crooked fingers.'

'I can think of at least one finger I'd like to fix permanently.' The one he showed to the world. Not a visible gesture, but one he exuded with his attitude.

In answer to her statement, he laughed. A genuine chuckle that moved from his stomach to his mouth…to his gorgeous green eyes. It took her breath away, and she had to force herself not to gasp.

'I'm not *that* bad, am I?' His brows went up.

*Worse.* The word came and went without her uttering a single sound.

Before she could give him an actual answer, Lynn peeked out from the other room, her mouth rounding in a perfect 'O' as she realized who was standing there. She'd grown up on the island, knew about Sammi and Mark's infamous past.

'You're going to have to start without me,' Sammi said. 'Mark's gotten an…injury that should probably be checked out.'

Mark grinned in the receptionist's direction and the woman's color immediately deepened to an ill-looking salmon, before she nodded and withdrew.

Damn him. How could he have that effect on every woman he encountered? And why had she been so stupid to fall for it herself all those years ago? Well, no danger of that now. She'd found a cure, and that was her son. She'd protect him from being hurt at all costs. And Mark could do exactly that with very little effort.

Jaw tight, she led the way to one of the exam rooms. 'Hop up on the table.'

He leaned against it instead. 'Don't I get a gown?'

'Don't push your luck.' Despite her irritation, the man still had the power to make her lips curve from the inside out. She pressed them together so he wouldn't see as she started toward the dispenser on the wall.

*Gloves? Really?*

*Yes.*

Wearing them would give her a measure of protection that had nothing to do with disease and everything to do with self-preservation. She glanced into his face. Would he know the reason?

Yep. It was there in the brow that lifted a quarter of a centimeter.

Forget it. She wouldn't let him know how terrified she was of touching him or how taking her son's hand from his had twisted her heart and left it raw and vulnerable.

She stopped in front of him and tilted her head to meet his gaze. 'Where does it hurt?'

'Seriously?'

'No more games, Mark. You could have broken something.'

His cocky smile disappeared and something dark and scary passed through his eyes. 'Did I, Sam? Break something?'

For the longest moment she couldn't breathe, couldn't tear her gaze from his. No one ever called her Sam.

No one, except Mark.

And she had the distinct impression the broken thing he was asking about had nothing to do with his hand and everything to do with her. No, that couldn't be right. He hadn't cared one iota about the damage he'd caused when he'd taken off without so much as a 'Why?'.

She shook her head, but had to avert her eyes as she did. 'Let me see your hand.'

He held it out, and she winced at the long diagonal stripe of discoloration already showing up just below his metacarpophalangeal joints. He must have had his hand wrapped around the frame of the door when she'd leaned against it. 'Wiggle your fingers.'

He obliged, and Sammi watched for a reaction as he curled his fingers into a loose fist and released them. Only there was no reaction. 'It doesn't hurt?'

'It was slammed in a door. What do you think?'

The amused sarcasm was back in place. She decided not to rise to the bait this time. 'Palm up.'

It was only when he turned his hand over that she realized she was avoiding touching him. But she was going to have to eventually. She'd have to X-ray his hand at the very least.

*Suck it up, Sammi.*

Sliding her fingertips beneath the back of his hand and desperately wishing she'd gone for the gloves after all, she tested the swelling on his palm with her thumb. 'I don't think anything is broken, but I do want to take an X-ray.'

She glanced up, surprised to find a muscle tic in his jaw. 'That bad?' she asked.

'You have no idea.'

'Hmm…' She looked closer at his hand, turning it gently. Maybe there was more damage than she'd thought. 'Follow me.'

Leading him into the tiny X-ray room, she fitted him with a lead apron, forbidding herself from thinking about exactly what she was protecting. She lined up his hand on the table and used the flexible arm on the X-ray tube to pull it down over the injured area, glad to be able to keep her mind on the job. 'I should be able to get this all on one frame, but if not, we'll take a couple more. Hold still for a second.'

She went into the control booth and took the first film, then rejoined him, swinging the tube away from his hand. 'All done. Let's see what we've got.' A thought occurred to her as she pressed buttons on the computer to call up the image. 'Why did you come to the clinic anyway? Are you sick?'

The correct X-ray flashed up, and Sammi zeroed in on the injured portion, not seeing any obvious breaks. Before she could heave a sigh of relief, though, several areas of calcification on his middle phalanges caught her attention. Fractures. Each apparently healed and running across his hand in a line. If not for the location of the bruise from where she'd slammed the door, Sammi would swear she was looking at his current injury. Except these were old. Already fused together.

As she stared, trying to work out how he could have broken a succession of bones like that, Mark's voice came through. 'I'm not sick. I came by to tell you I'm...'

His voice faded away as her eyes met his, horrified realization sweeping through her chest. 'Oh, my God, Mark. Did your father do this to you?'

# CHAPTER THREE

IT TOOK a second or two for Sammi's words to filter through his head and another few to register the horror in her eyes. How had she…?

His gaze went to the X-ray still displayed on the computer screen, and he knew what she'd seen. Hell, the days of his father's anger were long gone, replaced by things that were a whole lot worse. And the last thing he wanted now was her—or anyone's—pity. 'Is the damn thing broken or not?'

'Not this time, but—'

'That's all I needed to hear.' He did *not* want to relive the moment when reining in his temper—and being too stubborn to run—had resulted in a steel-toed boot crunching down on his hand, snapping four of the teenage bones with little effort. Sammi had asked about his father once in high school, and he'd blown her off—just like he had everyone. 'As I was saying, I came by because I'm flying some customers back to Anchorage this afternoon. I thought I'd see if the clinic needed me to pick up any supplies from Alaska Regional while I'm there. I didn't realize… I thought today was Hannah's day to work.'

He swore at himself the second the words had left his mouth. There was no reason to let her know he'd been avoiding her or that the need to stay as far away from her as possible had grown since enduring Blake's wedding. He'd caught a glimpse of what his life could've been like had things been different. If he'd given Sammi that ring.

But he hadn't.

So he'd keep doing what had worked for him over the past eight years: put one foot in front of the other. No reason to think it wouldn't keep on working. In fact, he was due for his weekly trip to the local watering hole. Since he was going to Anchorage anyway, he could kill two birds with one stone. And hopefully stave off the nightmares, which had come back with a vengeance after holding Toby's hand that evening in church.

'Hannah went to Akutan for the day. I offered to fill in for her.' Sammi's words were accompanied by a tilt of her chin, but he could swear a tiny glimmer of hurt appeared in her eyes before it winked back out.

He swore silently. This was exactly why he needed to stay away from her at all costs. She could knot his insides into a big ball of guilt without even trying. 'Right. So, can you think of anything you—the clinic, that is—needs?'

She stood to her feet. 'Nope. I—*and* the clinic—have everything we could possibly need.'

Well, that certainly put him in his place. Sammi had just let him know, in no uncertain terms, that the *last* thing she needed was him.

The state ferry chugged through the dark waters of the Gulf of Alaska, the rumble of its engines sending subtle vibrations along the length of the vessel. The noise was familiar, comforting. She'd made the trip from Unalaska to Anchorage hundreds of times over the years—the intricate tangle of the Alaska Marine Highway routes burned into her subconscious.

Elbows propped against the railing, Sammi glanced down at Toby. 'Are you cold?' Worried that the chilled air might irritate his bronchial tubes, her gloved hand went to the pocket of her down jacket for the hundredth time, making sure the precious inhaler was within close reach. It was one of the reasons she always reserved a cabin on-board for the two-day trip—despite the extra cost—rather than pitch a tent on the deck like other travelers often did. Especially as the summer air gave way to the frigid gusts of late fall.

'I like being out here.' Toby's words were muffled by the scarf Sammi had draped across his nose and mouth in an effort to keep the air as warm as possible.

The trip to see Toby's father was one she always dreaded. Not only because she hated to be away from her son but because the trip meant she wouldn't have access to her clinic or a hospital during the time it took to get from one place to the other. And flying was an expense she couldn't afford. Toby's father was footing the bill for the trip by water as it was.

*You could have asked Mark to take you.*

*Right. After he'd stalked from the clinic two weeks ago?*

She had been wrong to bring up his father, but the words had flown from her mouth before she'd been able to stop them. She doubted many people knew what he'd gone through as a kid, and he'd never openly admitted it to anyone. Even when they'd been together, Mark had avoided talking about his dad. But she'd seen little clues here and there, and she knew in her heart of hearts her hunch was right.

But to say the words out loud...

She cringed. If things between them had been bad before her outburst, they were a hundred times worse now.

The figurative arctic freeze they'd retreated into was more palpable than the real thing—on the open deck of the ferry. If anyone was going to break that frosty silence, it would be him. Not that there was much of a chance of cracking through all those layers without some kind of major thaw. And after more than eight years of icy accumulation, Sammi didn't see that happening.

Her thoughts went back to the X-ray and her initial horror at seeing those old breaks. Once the shock had faded, though, her brain had clicked into gear and worked through some other possibilities. He could have broken his hand in any number of ways. Like having it slammed in a door in a similar fashion to what had happened at the clinic. Only she would have expected one bone to have cracked in that case. Not four. The X-ray she'd taken had been merely a precaution.

Had he gotten them as a result of his military service? Because he hadn't come to the clinic with any injuries since he'd returned to Dutch Harbor—and she didn't remember seeing a cast on him during that time.

He'd never spoken of those years in the navy to anyone on the island, or word would have gotten back to her. Surely Blake knew something. They'd served in the military at the same time. But Blake seemed just as close-mouthed about that period in his life as Mark did. They'd both been pilots in Afghanistan, dangerous work, but Mark had never once bragged, even to impress any of the local girls, which shocked her. She couldn't think of a better way to pick up women than to present yourself as a bad-boy hero who thrived on danger.

In fact, he didn't mention his past at all, something she

found a little strange, now that she thought about it. She'd talked about the stuff that had happened in her life on a regular basis, from cute childhood moments to embarrassing tales of teen stupidity. Even her father's history of running around on her mother was common knowledge on the island, much to her mom's keen embarrassment.

'Will it be snowing at the zoo?'

Sammi's mind switched back to the present, and she smiled down at her son, her heart swelling with love. 'I hope not.' Doubly so because Toby's father had always seemed slightly irritated at the limitations placed on their son due to his asthma. A die-hard sports fan, Brad often hinted that Toby's condition wouldn't be as bad if Sammi didn't coddle him so much.

But she didn't. At least, she didn't think she did. What else was she supposed to do when he was gasping and wheezing for breath? Tell him to 'man up' and deal with it?

It was another reason she'd always accompanied Toby on these trips, rather than just ask Brad to come to the island and pick him up. It's not like her ex didn't have the money to fly over for their bi-weekly visits. Neither did she begrudge Toby the time with his father. Brad was a good man, and a decent father—at least he'd never begged off having Toby come and see him—but Sammi also wanted to be somewhere close, in case something went terribly wrong. So she'd sit in a hotel room all day while Brad, along with his new wife and daughter, took Toby on their usual one-day jaunt. She'd stare at her cellphone and will it not to ring. But Toby had always been dropped off at the end of the day healthy, happy, and singularly untraumatized. He never knew his mother went to hell and back until he was delivered safely into her care once again.

At least she and Molly—who'd come back from her

honeymoon a week ago—could go out and enjoy a meal. If her friend was off duty for the day. And if she could drag herself away from Blake long enough for them to get in some girl time.

'There it is, Mom!'

Sure enough, off in the distance was a pinpoint strip of land that could only signal they were getting close to docking. 'Do you have all your stuff?'

Toby glanced down at his wheeled backpack. 'I think so. I'm coming back to the hotel room tonight, right? Or am I staying with Daddy?'

'Nope. It's you and me, popcorn and a movie.' She tucked the tail of his scarf into his coat a little better. 'What do you want to see?'

'How about something scary? With zombies and stuff.'

Her brows went up. 'Try again. This time come down a couple of ratings to something within the PG range.'

'Awww, Mom…'

It was a familiar fight, but Sammi wasn't irritated. She knew it was part of Toby's search for independence, but she also knew that at six, he still needed limits. Lots of them. She could be his friend when he was an adult. Until then, she was fully prepared to be the bad guy.

'Hmm… How about that penguin movie you love so much?'

'We've seen that like six thousand times.'

'That's a lot. I had no idea.' She gave him a mock roll of her eyes. 'We can decide once you get back to the hotel, then.'

The next half-hour was spent making sure they weren't forgetting anything on board before the ferry drew up at the docking. When Toby acted like he was going to bolt toward the exit, she took his arm. 'Wait.' She didn't particularly want to be trampled on the way out. So they hung back, allowing the bulk of the passengers to disembark before making their own getaway.

Brad and his family met them in the parking area. There were so many people around that they didn't have to worry about making small talk or about whether or not Sammi should invite them inside her hotel room. She wanted to keep things as cordial as possible, for Toby's sake.

A small pang of envy went through her as Brad bent down and wrapped his son in a big hug. His wife also knelt to say hello, their four-year-old daughter holding tightly to her hand. Sammi wanted to dislike the woman, especially since they'd started their own family almost before the ink had been dry on the divorce papers, but she couldn't. Maribel had never been anything but nice to her, and she seemed to really like Toby. That was all that mattered. That her son was happy and well taken care of.

Brad stood, keeping hold of Toby's hand. 'Do you want to do this like we usually do? We can bring him to the hotel room around eight or nine?'

Something about the way he said it made Sammi fidget. Yes, that was their normal arrangement, so it wasn't like she could suddenly say Toby couldn't go. She just had a funny feeling. The weather had been iffy for the two-day trip on the ferry, but nothing in the forecast seemed to predict anything unusual for a day in mid-October. 'That sounds fine.'

No one asked which hotel, because she always stayed at the same place. And she was always alone when they arrived.

Alone. What an awful-sounding word.

Maybe she needed to put herself back on the market.

Toby was growing up quickly. And Brad seemed to have gone on with his life. So why hadn't she?

Certainly not because she was still in love with Brad. She'd been fond of him—had convinced herself he was the stable, steady presence she craved in a husband. Not like her father or Mark who had been there one minute and gone the next. But, in the end, stable and steady hadn't been enough to make the marriage work.

She leaned down and kissed Toby, making sure his backpack was zipped up tight. 'I guess you're all set.'

'Ready for the zoo?' Brad asked his wife and daughter. Little squeals went up from both the girls, while Toby stood motionless.

Strange. A little while ago he'd been excited about the prospect of being with his dad. Maybe he'd sensed her mood, which he seemed to have an uncanny knack of doing. She hoped not. The last thing she wanted to do was spoil his outing.

'Oh, wait.' Lord, she couldn't believe she'd almost forgotten. Reaching into her jacket pocket, she pulled out Toby's inhaler and handed it to her ex. The skin between Brad's brows puckered a bit, but he said nothing. Instead, he shoved the small canister into the pocket of his own jacket. Her trepidation grew. Brad wouldn't let anything bad happen to Toby. He was *his* son as well. And they'd been through this same routine for the last four years without a hint of trouble.

They turned to go, and Sammi waved them off with a smile that she hoped hid the kernel of sadness that appeared whenever she watched her son walk away from her. She then trudged over to the car rental place, anxious to get to the hotel and kick back and relax.

Right. Kick back and mope was more like it.

Lucky for her, Molly was home when she called and was currently husbandless, since Blake was off on a flight. Maybe today wouldn't be as bad as she feared. Molly swung by the hotel and picked Sammi up, refusing to let her drive all the way out to the house.

'It was on the way to the restaurant,' her friend insisted, once they sat at the table of a popular seafood place.

The aroma of garlic and fresh fish swirled around the foyer, and Sammi gave an appreciative sniff, beginning to relax a little. 'It's been a while since I've been out to eat.'

It was true. Normally on these jaunts she simply grabbed some Chinese takeout and carried it back to the room, as it felt pathetic to sit at a table all by herself. But with Molly there, things seemed a little more festive, a little less sad.

Once they were seated, she cracked open the menu and tried not to wince at the prices. Maybe this was why she didn't go out to eat that much. But she'd earned this respite. Toby was safe, and she wouldn't get that many chances to see Molly now that she was back in Anchorage. 'How's Blake?'

'He's fine. In fact, he's more than fine.' Molly leaned forward, her glance darting around the room before coming back to rest on Sammi with a smile. 'Okay, so we weren't going to tell anyone yet, but…I'm pregnant.'

'What?' So this was why her friend had been practically glowing when she'd arrived at the hotel. 'Holy cow. Are you serious?'

'I am. You wouldn't believe how hard it was to squeeze into my wedding gown.' She laughed. 'But you have to promise not to tell anyone. Blake and I wanted to announce it together once the pregnancy was further along. But you're so far away…and I wanted you to be the first to know.'

Sammi's eyes pricked unexpectedly, remembering her own excitement when she'd discovered she was pregnant with Toby. 'Oh, Molly, I'm so happy for you. You're going to make a wonderful mother.'

'You think so? I wasn't actually sure I wanted to have children, but...' She laid her menu down. 'Here we are.'

'You're going to love it. Having Toby changed my life. For the better,' she was quick to add. 'You'll be exhausted and frustrated and scared...and you'll love every second of it.'

Molly reached over and squeezed her hand. 'Thank you. I may be calling you for advice at some point.'

The waiter came and took their order, leaving them to chat. About halfway through the meal, Blake strode into the restaurant, his eyes fastening immediately on Molly, who bit her lip and stood as he reached them. 'I thought you said you'd be gone until tomorrow.'

He grinned and dropped a kiss on her mouth, then hugged Sammi. Pulling up a chair next to his wife's, he looped an arm around her shoulders. 'I missed you and decided to come back early. So what have you girls been talking about?'

Molly's cheeks immediately turned pink, causing Blake to lean back in his chair, brows raised. 'I thought so.'

'I know we decided not to tell anyone, but...Sammi is family.'

Blake's mouth quirked. 'Yeah, kind of like an annoying little sister.'

Sammi, although the same age as Blake, had been the runt of the class during their childhood days. He'd never let her forget it, even though she was now five feet seven.

Sammi leaned across the table and swatted his arm. 'Molly doesn't seem to think so.' She paused, letting her eyes convey her true thoughts. 'Seriously, though. Congratulations.'

'Thanks.'

Molly smiled up at him. 'Do you want to order something?'

He plucked a huge battered shrimp from her plate, munching it before he answered. 'No, I ate on the way. I'm stuffed.'

'I can tell,' she said, when he snagged a second piece.

He laughed. 'I'm meeting a friend for drinks later, anyway, so I can't stay. I just wanted to see you first.'

'I see. And just who is this friend?'

Sammi's phone buzzed, indicating she was getting a text. She scrunched her nose. 'Sorry guys, I know it's not polite, but I told Brad to let me know if their plans were going to change. Do you mind?'

'It's fine.' Molly waved her fork.

Retrieving the phone from her handbag, she pressed a button to retrieve the message. The low lighting in the restaurant caused her to squint as she tried to make out the letters, but once she did, she gasped, her heart dropping. 'Oh, God, I have to go.' She threw her napkin on the table and stood.

Alarmed, her friends got to their feet as well. 'What is it?'

She stuffed her phone back in her purse. Her voice shook as she tried to get the words out. 'They're rushing Toby to the hospital.'

# CHAPTER FOUR

SAMMI raced through the doors of the emergency room, while Molly parked the car. They'd left Blake at the restaurant to pay the bill and follow in his own vehicle.

Brad met her in the reception area, his wife and daughter nowhere to be seen. 'Where is he?' she demanded, her breath rushing from her lungs.

'Calm down. He's with one of the doctors.'

'Then why the hell are you out here, instead of back there with him?' Toby had to be frightened out of his wits.

Her ex's eyes narrowed in warning. 'I did go with him. But I didn't want you to hear what happened from some stranger.'

'Sorry.' Her anger deflated. 'Was it his asthma?'

'Yes.' He stuffed his hands into his pockets. 'He's never had an attack while with us. I thought it wasn't really that serious…that he'd be okay.'

She remembered his face when she'd handed over the inhaler. He'd thought she was just babying Toby yet again. 'You left his medicine in the car, didn't you?'

'Not on purpose. I had it in my pocket when we left, then asked Toby to put it in his backpack for safekeeping. When we got to the zoo…well, I didn't want him lugging the pack with him all day.'

'I'm going back there to see him.'

By that time, Molly had joined them. 'I'll see where he is.'

'Why didn't you just go and get his inhaler once you realized he was having trouble?'

'It came on so fast. He couldn't get enough air.' His lips tightened. 'I didn't know how long it would take to work. I—I panicked, Sammi.'

She touched his arm, compassion sweeping over her. She knew how frightening Toby's attacks could be. 'You did the right thing getting him here as fast as possible.'

Molly returned. 'He's okay. I'll take you back to him.'

'Thank you.' She glanced at Brad. 'Are you coming?'

'I'll wait for Maribel. She's dropping Jessie off at the sitter's.'

Molly led her back to an exam room, where her son sat on a table holding a nebulizer mask over his mouth and nose. Hurrying over to him, she leaned down and looked into his face. She raised her brows in the wordless question they'd devised to communicate during these times. He answered with a thumbs-up sign, although his breathing still sounded a little ragged to her ears. His color looked good, so Brad had told the truth about not wasting any time getting him here. She pressed her lips to his forehead, then checked the amount of medication remaining in the nebulizer cup. The treatment was about half-finished.

'Did you talk to the doctor?' She glanced at Molly, who was standing by the door.

Molly nodded. 'It was serious…' she glanced toward Toby as if unsure how much to say in front of him '…but manageable. They want to observe him for a couple of hours before they discharge him. They've got a call in to the pulmonologist, who should be here in a few minutes.'

'I—I don't know if Brad still has his inhaler. Can I get a new prescription just in case?'

'I'm sure we've got some extras here at the hospital. I'll give you one to take home with you. Albuterol, right?'

'Yes.' Sammi hopped up onto the bed beside Toby and put her arms around him, a surge of love and thankfulness going through her. She kissed the top of his head. 'I'm going to leave in a minute or two to give Daddy a chance to see you, okay? He's pretty worried.'

Toby pulled the mask down. 'I want to go home.'

'We will.' She put her hand over his, steering the mask back into place. 'As soon as the doctor says it's safe. We've got a long trip ahead of us tomorrow.'

Molly touched her arm and nodded toward the door. 'The doctor's in the hall.'

'I'm going with Aunt Molly for a minute. I'll be right outside that door, if you need me.' She gave him one last kiss and slid off the table.

Going into the hallway with Molly, she was able to speak with the doctor who'd treated her son. He assured her Toby was going to be fine. His breathing was already better, but they wanted to do a pulmonary function test as soon as he finished with the nebulizer.

Sammi smiled. 'That's Toby's favorite part of any hospital visit.' She sighed. 'Actually, that's the *only* part he likes. It's like a challenge to see if he can beat his last set of results.'

'It's my favorite part too.' Dr. Donnelly's kind blue eyes twinkled, helping to reassure her. 'Believe me, I want our buddy in there to ace that test as much as you do.'

'Thanks for everything you've done. I'm going to run and get his father, okay?'

'Of course,' he answered.

Sammi wasn't sure, but she thought she detected a hint of interest in the man's look at her. The doctor was attractive enough, his dark, conservatively cut hair falling neatly over his forehead. Nothing like Mark's slightly shaggy locks that seemed as loose and free as the rest of him.

Why had she thought of him, of all people?

Besides, despite her earlier thoughts about putting herself back on the market, now was not the time. Not with her son sitting in that room fighting for each breath. 'I'll go and get his father.'

She headed for the waiting room. Brad, his back to her, stood at one of the large windows, staring outside. Maribel had arrived and was leaning against him, whispering in his ear. Sammi hesitated before touching his arm. 'You can see him now. He's better.'

'Thank God.' He turned part way around and met her eyes. 'I think I'll keep an extra inhaler or two on hand from now on. Can you help me get them?'

'I think that's a great idea. Molly's going to see if she can find a couple.' She dropped her hand to her side. 'Go ahead. He's waiting for you.'

Brad and his wife walked away, pushing through the double doors that led to the various exam rooms. She stood there for a few moments, her arms wrapped around her waist, trying to convince herself things were going to be all right. It was a losing battle.

'How is he?' The sudden question raised the hair on her neck. Actually, it wasn't the question itself but the familiar voice behind it. Low and mellow, the tone slid over her like warm honey.

Sammi whirled around to find Mark standing there, both hands shoved into the pockets of his jacket. She could have sworn he wasn't there a second ago. 'How—? What are you doing—?'

'I dropped off some clients this afternoon and was supposed to meet up with Blake later for drinks. He called my cell on his way to the hospital.'

So this was the friend Blake had mentioned meeting earlier. 'He did? Why?'

'He wanted to let me know he might be late.' His jaw tightened. 'Don't worry. He wasn't trying to invade your privacy.'

'I didn't think that.'

So what had she thought? That Mark wouldn't care one way or the other what happened to her or her son? Yep. But trying to explain that in a way that didn't sound bitter—or like she was stuck in some sad version of the past—was impossible. So she decided to answer his original question instead. 'Toby's better. Brad's with him now.'

'I know. I saw him when I came in.'

There'd never been any love lost between the two men, although she wasn't quite sure why. In school they'd all run in different circles. She'd been a geek, while Mark had hung out with the rougher crowd. Brad had been firmly in the jock camp—the all-American-hero type. Her ex had always kind of looked down on Mark when they'd been kids. Maybe Mark had sensed that

She crossed her arms over her chest. 'Did you see Blake? He should be here by now.'

'He's waiting for Molly in the cafeteria. We decided to cancel our plans.'

Uh-oh. She'd assumed he was killing time until Blake arrived. Maybe she should start looking for an exit. 'Are you going back to the island tomorrow?'

'If Toby is released by then.'

She blinked, not sure what that had to do with anything. 'What do you mean?'

'Are they planning to hold him overnight?'

Was she missing something? 'No, just observe him for a couple more hours to make sure the attack is over.'

'Good. We should be able to leave in the morning, then.'

'We?'

Okay, there was something strange going on. Where exactly were *they* going?

'I'm flying you back to the island.'

'We bought round trip tickets for the ferry, we can…'

The words died in her throat when he took a step closer, brushing back a strand of hair that had come loose from her braid. 'There's no way in hell I'm letting you take that ferry back to the island. Not with Toby sick.'

His fingers were warm against her skin, and she wanted more than anything to lean into his palm, to hand over a tiny portion of her burden. But she didn't dare. Mark had proved he could—and would—walk away without a backward glance. That's not what she wanted for her son. He was already enamored with Mark as it was. Watching him pilot a plane would only make it worse. The thought made her stiffen against his touch. 'We'll be okay.'

'You're right. You will.' His hand dropped to her shoulder. 'Because you're flying back with me. Both of you.'

Driving Toby and Sammi back to the hotel, Mark wasn't quite sure why she'd seemed so averse to flying with him. Being out in that frigid air couldn't be good for Toby's lungs. Not right after an attack that had landed him in the hospital. And especially not after the way she'd angled her face toward his hand for a second as he'd brushed his fingers across her cheek in the emergency room. His breath had caught, memories of her doing that very same thing in the past sweeping over him.

But neither of them were the kids they'd once been. And Sammi evidently had an easier time accepting that than he did, because she'd pulled away. He, on the other hand, had been lost the moment he'd touched her. All he'd wanted to do was press his lips to hers and feel the response that used to set his world on fire.

He'd told Molly and Blake he'd make sure Sammi got back to the hotel, as her rental car was still there. She hadn't seemed very happy about that either, although she'd kept silent. Glancing over at her as she stared out the passenger window, he wondered if he'd done the right thing in demanding she accept his offer. But she couldn't take Toby on that ferry, dammit. Even *she* had to see that.

'You doing okay back there, buddy?' He peered into the rear-view mirror to find Toby leaning against the window in the back, eyes shut, mouth open. A thrill of anxiety went through him, along with a flashing image of a different boy—blood everywhere as the medics worked on the horrific wounds covering his small body. The same child who inhabited many of his current nightmares.

But Toby wasn't that boy. And he wasn't injured, just asleep. Mark forced his hands to ease their grip on the wheel, and thankfully the memory faded away.

He glanced at Sammi to make sure she hadn't noticed anything. 'He's out.'

'I'm sure he's exhausted.' Sammi twisted around in her seat to look, her dark braid looped over her left shoulder. He'd teased her about that long length of hair in high school, tugging on it repeatedly. Those had been during the light times, when they'd just been good friends. Later, when they'd been more than friends, he could remember wrapping that braid around his hand to hold her in place as he kissed her. Or removing the band and unwinding those thick lustrous strands so that they could fall loose and free.

This was a mistake, and he knew it. Being around her and Toby was reawakening the very things he'd tried to wipe from his mind. But he had no choice. It was time he thought about someone other than himself.

He was. He had been. It's why he'd left Dutch Harbor all those years ago.

So why had he moved back to his hometown? Why hadn't he just stayed away?

Because his mother needed him. At least that's what he told himself.

Soon they were parked in front of the hotel's check-in area. 'Which room?'

'Four-oh-two.' Sammi's voice remained soft. 'Thank you, Mark. I know I didn't seem very grateful back at the hospital, but you're right. It's better for Toby if we fly back. We're not taking you away from a customer?'

It wouldn't matter if they were. This was more important than a tourist. 'Nope. I don't have another charter trip on the docket until Tuesday, and that's just a quick little island hop.'

Mark found the room number and pulled up in front of it. 'I'll help you get him inside, then I'll check in. I'll call you with my room number.'

'Wait. Weren't you going to stay with Blake and Molly?' In the dark, he could just make out her frown.

'I thought it might be easier to leave first thing if I stayed here. They're forecasting sleet in the morning, and I'd like to be in the air before it hits.' He hesitated. 'And if something happens, you might need someone nearby.'

His chest tightened at the thought.

She unbuckled her seat belt then shoved her arms through the sleeves of her down jacket. She didn't say anything as she clicked open the door and stepped from the car, so Mark had no idea if she was happy or furious that he was staying at the hotel. It didn't matter either way. It was the right thing to do.

Getting out of the car as well, he pulled Toby's door open and carefully released the latch on the seat belt. Then he slid his arms under the boy's shoulders and knees and eased him from the car, thankful the kid's jacket was still buttoned up tight. He was light. Almost as light as the boy he'd once carried to his chopper. That seemed like a lifetime ago now.

*Had it only been a year?*

*It's over. Done. You can't undo the past.*

Mark used his own body to block the wind, backing towards the door that Sammi had already opened.

'He likes the far bed,' she whispered as they went past.

'His backpack is still in the car.' Mark walked toward the bed, glancing down at the child's slack face and dark lashes fanned out against his cheeks. A shard of loss went through his chest, and he suddenly had trouble catching his breath.

After setting the boy down on the blue bedspread, he carefully unzipped his coat, thankful the heat had been left on in the room. The weather conditions had turned frigid outside. So different from the stifling heat of Afghanistan and its twin scents of blood and fear that would often sweep through their camp like a dust storm, coating everything in sight. Even now it stung his nostrils, filled his lungs—

'Mark?'

He jerked upright, turning toward her. 'Yes?'

'I—I wanted to thank you for what you're doing. It means a lot to me.' Before he could prepare himself, she stood on tiptoe and pressed her lips to his cheek. The touch was as light as a feather, but it was as if something in his heart clicked back on. Fear—and something much stronger—began racing through his veins.

He had to take a step back before he wrapped an arm around her waist and dragged her into his arms, hoping her very presence could banish the memories he'd locked deep inside himself. 'Don't worry about it. I'd do the same for anyone.'

Something flared behind her eyes, and he damned himself for not thinking before he opened his big mouth. Yes, he'd do it for anyone, but the suggestion had been so much more than the casual offer from one stranger to another.

As she said goodbye and closed the door on him, he had his first inkling that he might be headed on a dangerous course. He couldn't save the world, he'd already proved that to himself and everyone around him. He'd left Dutch Harbor eight years ago a scared and messed-up kid. He'd returned an even more screwed-up man. One who could barely take care of himself, much less anyone else. He'd do well to keep that in mind before making any other big promises he couldn't keep.

Like promising a little boy he'd be fine? That he wouldn't die like his mother and father had?

Mark set off for the lobby, a wave of exhaustion going through him. If there was one thing he'd learned, it was that promises were the stuff of fairy-tales—not worth more than the hot air used to voice them. He'd broken one too many of them over the course of his life.

But not any more.

He pulled off his clothes and slid beneath the bulky covers of his bed, the chill from the sheets clinging to skin like the ice that sometimes coated the props on his plane.

No more promises from him. Not to Toby. And especially not to Sammi.

Mark frowned as he peered over the steaming surface of the desert. The wind from his chopper's rotors whipped a woman's dark hair around her face as she pushed toward the aircraft. Even from a hundred yards away, something about her looked familiar.

The wife of their translator, who was now dead at the hands of insurgents. His eyes went to the bundle she carried in her arms.

*A bomb!*

The thought scrabbled through his mind, sending fear spiking through his veins.

The medics had just raced to help several downed soldiers who'd gotten caught in the crossfire, leaving Mark alone.

She moved a few yards closer. Mark motioned for her to stay away that it was too dangerous for her to be here, but she shook her head, taking another step. The swirling currents caused the cloth to fall away from the top portion of the object, allowing Mark to catch a glimpse of what was inside. Instead of a hardwired mass of explosives, a small face appeared, a vicious smear of red across his temple...his cheek.

*Ahmed, her child!*

Without thinking, he shoved open his door and hopped down to her level, blocking the wind with his body like he'd done with Toby earlier.

*No. Toby wasn't here. He was far away.*

Before he could reach them, she set the child down, then turned and began running in the opposite direction.

*What the hell? Why was she abandoning him?*

Mark raced toward the boy, just as a blinding explosion came from the direction of the boy's mother. He fell to his knees as something struck his chest. A piece of shrapnel. His eyes went to the woman, but she was gone, smoke still drifting from the spot where she'd been.

It had been a bomb after all.

The boy! Reaching him, he ripped open the blanket and gasped as large sucking chest wounds met his eyes.

He forced his lips to move, but they did so in slow motion, his voice a garbled distortion of human speech. 'Hang…on…I've…got you.' He picked the bundle up, ignoring the sting in his chest, then he climbed back aboard the plane, setting the child down in the seat next to him. Things went from slow motion to rapid fire as bodies suddenly piled inside the aircraft—mouths gaping, eyes staring—crowding every available inch of space.

Sharp pinging sounds against the metal skin of the chopper let him know they were under attack.

Mark's eyes flew open. He blinked rapidly as he tried to figure out what to do next, where to go as darkness swallowed him whole. The pinging continued, growing louder by the second.

No, not gunfire. Something else.

His chest heaved as he tried to suck down breath after breath and push through his terror.

Something weighed him down, and he kicked out at it, finding the object soft and light—fabric—rather than the heavy, solid mass he expected to encounter. Cold air hit him as the cloth fell away, and a shudder rolled through him. He was drenched with sweat. Naked.

Where was his uniform? His chopper?

Gone. Like the woman and the boy.

He blinked again and his surroundings came into sharp focus. He was lying in a bed, not face down in blistering sand. No screams. No blood. Just the sound of something hitting the glass windowpane to his left.

Sleet.

Reality swept over him in a rush as his brain clicked back into gear. He was in a hotel room in Anchorage, far from the horror and carnage he'd lived through in Afghanistan.

But the mother and child, although nothing more than figments of his imagination now, had once been living, breathing souls. And the promise he'd made to them both had been snatched away in the space of a few mismatched heartbeats, leaving him cold. Empty.

Carrying nothing, except regret.

# CHAPTER FIVE

'COOL! I get to ride on Uncle Mark's plane?'

*Uncle? What's with that?*

'Yes, so we need to hurry and get ready.' A light dusting of snow had fallen just after midnight, leaving a shimmery coating on the tree branches—almost as if Mother Nature had uncapped a jar of silvery glitter and let the wind sift it across the landscape. The effect this morning, as she peered out the drapes of the hotel room, was gorgeous.

As beautiful as it was, the icy conditions also made her nervous. Mark had mentioned wanting to leave *before* the snow hit. His plane was an amphibian type, so he could land directly on the water if need be, but that wouldn't help them during take-off, as his plane was parked at the Merrill Field airport.

Even as she thought it, she squinted skywards and found it a menacing shade of grey. She could only pray the runway stayed clear a little while longer. And that the weather en route to Dutch Harbor co-operated. She wasn't needed at the clinic today, but she was on the schedule for Monday. She really didn't want to sit around in Anchorage for the next couple of days if conditions turned ugly. Especially since she'd already called the rental car agency this morning and had them pick up the vehicle.

Dropping the curtain, she swung back to her son, assessing his condition. He was lounging on the bed, his attention focused on his handheld game unit—cheeks bright with excitement, breathing normal. You'd never know by looking at him that he'd endured a serious asthma attack less than twelve hours ago.

She double-checked his backpack for his inhaler, removed it and put it inside her own jacket pocket for safe-keeping. 'I'll bet your dad is glad you're all better.'

Brad had called first thing that morning to check on Toby. He hadn't wasted any time with chit-chat but had asked to speak with his son. Once reassured that everything was okay, he'd rung off.

'Yep, he is.'

Sammi had just retrieved Toby's coat from the small closet when a knock at the door made her jump. Mark. She glanced at her watch. Right on time, too.

Her son didn't wait for her to make the first move. He leaped from the bed and yanked the door wide open before she could stop him.

She put a hand on his shoulder. 'Hey, remember what we discussed a few weeks ago? Never open the door without checking to see who it is, first. It could be someone who's not very nice.'

'Sorry, Mom.'

Her eyes went to Mark, noting the still damp hair slicked back from his face and just starting to curl slightly at the ends. Toby shrugged away from her and attached himself to the other man's hand.

Mark's lips tightened. 'Your mom is right, bud. It could definitely be someone who's not very nice. It could even be someone like me.'

'But you *are* nice,' said Toby.

Mark's eyes went to hers and stuck there for a moment. 'There are not-so-nice sides to everyone.'

There was a brittle edge to his words that she didn't understand.

*Find a safer subject, then.*

'How are the conditions out there?'

*Or you could always go for the obvious choice and ask about the weather.*

Toby let go of him to pull his backpack closer, and she could have sworn Mark's hand gave a subtle swipe against the fabric of his jeans as if wiping away every trace of her son's touch. What could the man possibly have against Toby? He seemed to stiffen up whenever he was around. She shrugged it off. Some people just didn't like kids.

Except he'd offered to fly them to Dutch Harbor to keep him safe.

'We'll make it into the air, if that's what you're asking.' Mark stepped to the side, putting another foot or so of space between him and Toby. 'But we should get going if we want to take off before the worst of it hits.'

'I'm okay with doing whatever it takes to avoid the storm.'

'So am I.'

She blinked. Again, there seemed to be some weird intensity behind the words as if he was talking about something other than the weather. 'Um, did you eat breakfast?'

He shifted his weight. 'Yes. You?'

'I packed some cereal bars before we left home. We'll be fine until we get back.'

'I have some juice and snacks on the plane if you get hungry on the way.'

So she could be beholden to him more than she already was? She didn't think so. 'I've got extras as well.'

They stared at each other for a few more seconds as if performing a delicate dance in which neither one wanted to upset the balance and send the other careening over some unseen edge—or tumble over it themselves.

Toby broke the uneasy silence, peering into his backpack. 'Mom, I can't find my inhaler.' The slight panic in his voice brought her attention fully back to him, her heart cramping. No six-year-old should have to worry about whether or not he'd be able to take his next breath.

Pulling the small canister out of her pocket, she held it up. 'I have it. Sorry.' *Wait, was he okay?* 'Do you need it? *Please, God, no.*

He shook his head. 'I just didn't want to not have it like…'

Like yesterday. Her chest tightened further. His pediatrician said there was a good chance he'd outgrow some of his breathing problems—some children did. She could only hope Toby was one of the lucky ones.

Mark nudged the curtain aside to glance out the window. 'Are we ready, then? The sky's getting darker.'

'I think so.' She made a quick sweep of the room, zeroing in on Toby's hand held game system, which he'd tossed on the bed in order to answer the door. 'Um, missing something, Tobe?'

'Oh, yeah.' He gave her a sheepish grin as he went over to retrieve it. 'But I did check on my medicine.'

'You did. And I appreciate you taking responsibility for it.' She reached for her overnight case, only to have Mark take it from her. He then picked up Toby's backpack as well, holding it out so her son could stuff the game system inside one of the back zippered compartments.

They made it to the airport in record time, and Mark filed their flight plan. When he opened the plane, Toby scrambled up, heading straight for the copilot seat, but Mark stopped him. 'I think it's safer for you to buckle up in that seat right over there.' He pointed to the chair directly behind the pilot's seat. 'It's got a really great view.'

Toby groaned in disappointment, but plopped down into the seat indicated, pulling his game out of his backpack and plugging in his earbuds.

So much for the view. Surely once they took off, Toby would lose interest in his game and enjoy his first flight.

Sammi took a moment to look around. She'd only seen Mark's plane from a distance. It looked a lot smaller inside than it did on the outside, which surprised her. She was also surprised by the sudden sense of anticipation that swept over her. Flying had always been a luxury she couldn't afford.

Three hours in the air versus two days on a ferry. How was that even possible?

Mark stood beside her as she continued to study her surroundings. Besides the pilot and copilot seats, there were four additional seats. A grey curtain walled off whatever lay behind them. 'What's back there?'

'I had a couple of seats taken out, as I'll be taking on most of Blake's medevacing duties. I still need to outfit the rest of it, but I've been…waiting to find out exactly what I'll need.'

She nodded, wandering back and pulling aside the curtain, only to find the space devoid of anything but a lone stretcher on wheels that was clamped down along the far wall. No other medical equipment, at least none that she could see. 'Where're your supplies?'

'Blake's been planning on helping with that but, seeing as he just got married, I figured he had other things on his mind right now.' Red crept up his neck. 'I mean—'

'I know what you mean.' She tried not to let those gears switch in her head, but the heat traveling through her own system said she wasn't entirely successful.

'I, er, figured we could grab whatever was needed from the clinic if we had a medevac before I'm completely set up.'

Things were normally so chaotic during those times that trying to do anything other than care for the patient and get off the ground as fast as possible was neither wise nor an efficient use of time. 'I could help you pull some stuff together, if you want.'

His brows drew together, so she hurried to add, 'If you've ever done a medevac before you know it's better to have everything in place long before you need it.'

What was she thinking? She obviously wasn't. But she also didn't want to have to scramble during an emergency if Mark's plane ended up being called into service.

'I guess you're right.' His eyes traveled over the empty space. 'If you could get me a list…'

She hesitated. 'Will filling this area with medical supplies put a crimp in your regular job?'

'I don't normally haul more than four people at a time, and I'm cutting back to a couple of times a week, so the seats I've left up front should be plenty. I'm also going to try to stick to day trips, so I'll be on hand if something comes up at night.'

'I see. As far as a list, I'll need to order some things from Anchorage.' They moved back towards the front, and Sammi stopped in mid-thought. This was the perfect opportunity to make sure she knew exactly where every piece of equipment was. No digging around for IVs or other items. She could set up the back of Mark's airplane like one of the exam rooms at the clinic with certain crucial instruments paired together for ease of use. 'If you have a free weekend coming up, we could make up an inventory and put everything in place.'

Toby's head popped up from his game. 'Can I help?'

Sammi glanced at Mark to see how he'd react to having her son hanging around.

Just as expected, he stiffened for a second then relaxed. 'I don't see why not. In fact, that's a great idea.'

*A great idea?*

A sudden sense of relief seemed to color his voice. Almost as if he'd rather have Toby there than…

An ache went through her chest. *The man didn't want to be alone with her.*

Why? Did he think she'd try to take a quick trip down memory lane by pinning him to one of the passenger seats and having her way with him?

If so, he could dream on.

She wasn't about to revisit old times, because all they'd brought her had been heartache.

And if Mark could use a child as a shield, so could she.

'Good, it's settled, then,' she said. 'Toby and I will both be at the hangar first thing Saturday morning.'

Something white drifted past the window, just as Sammi made her pronouncement. If they were going to get out of here, now would be a good time. He glanced at her tilted chin, catching a familiar glint of defiance in her eyes.

The sight made him smile, despite the lingering effects of the nightmare he'd had last night. 'In that case, let's get this show on the road.'

He put a hand on the arm of Toby's seat and waited until the boy looked up at him. 'I need you to stay buckled in during the flight, okay? Do you need to use the restroom before we go?'

Toby seemed to consider his question. 'How long is the trip?'

'You've never flown from the mainland before?'

'I don't think so.' He looked to his mother for confirmation. She shook her head.

For some reason, that made Mark's mood plummet even further, as if he'd once again let down a mother and her son.

Ridiculous. He'd never promised to take care of them. 'It takes around three and a half hours.'

The child nodded. 'Then I'd probably better try to go.'

'The bathroom's in the very back, through those curtains.'

Toby removed his earbuds and carefully zipped his game system back into his knapsack. It seemed a very adult thing to do. Most kids he knew would have just tossed the thing onto the seat.

When Toby was out of sight, Mark turned to Sammi. 'Do you not like to fly or something?'

'Flying's fine.' She stared at the curtain between her and her son. 'We just can't afford to hop on a plane every time we want to head to the mainland.'

'But you're a doctor.'

'I'm a community health aide,' she corrected. 'I fly when there's a patient who needs to be transported, not for personal convenience. Besides, with what I make... well, the clinic operates on a shoestring budget. It's why Molly had to go back to Anchorage until she can talk the hospital into funding her for another year.'

If anything, that made him feel worse. 'You could let me know when you need to go and I'll take you. It won't cost you anything.'

*Why the hell had he just done that?*

Her chin lifted, as it had done several times this morning. 'I prefer to pay my own way, thank you.'

'Even if it means risking your son's health?' The words came out harsher than he'd meant them to, and he immediately wanted to swallow them back. Especially when Sammi looked stricken, her teeth digging into the softness of her lower lip. 'Ah, hell, Sam, I didn't mean that the way it sounded.'

She didn't reply, but wrapped her arms around her midsection and turned away. Mark could swear he saw a sheen of moisture in her eyes as she did so. Desperate to undo the damage he'd caused, he moved behind her and laid his hands on her shoulders. Giving them a gentle squeeze, he leaned down to keep his words quiet. 'I know you love that boy…that you'd do anything for him. Let me help. If you feel you have to pay me something, you can take it out in trade.'

'Why bother?' The whispered words made his heart contract.

'Because I can.' He hesitated. 'Because I want to.'

He did. And Mark knew he was treading on dangerous ground here. His dream last night should have warned him, if nothing else. But was this really about his personal comfort? What about doing the right thing?

And offering to fly her was the right thing. He was certain of it.

And maybe by doing so, he could set a few things right between them. Make up for the heartache he'd caused. Even if it couldn't lead anywhere, he might be able to ease Sammi's burden just a bit. If she'd let him. But even as he decided to try, he wondered at the stupidity of such a move. Even now, her warm, feminine scent was drifting over him, bringing back memories that were better off locked away in some deep corner of his mind. But he'd have to find a way to deal with it. This wasn't about him, it was about helping a fellow human being. Someone he'd once cared about deeply.

Deeply enough to leave her behind.

He rested his chin on top of her head, knowing he'd likely never get another chance, and kept his voice low, hoping to coax her into agreeing. 'I'll tell you what, Sam. You help me trick out the plane like a flying ambulance, and…'

*Say it!*

'And I'll take you back and forth to the mainland as many times as you want.'

# CHAPTER SIX

THE murmured words slid past her ear, sending a shiver over her.

Agreeing to his suggestion would be like committing emotional suicide. But the steady pressure of Mark's hands on her shoulders, the warmth of his body filling the gap between them muddled her thoughts. The squeaked 'Okay' was out of her mouth before she could stop it.

All she had to do was take one step back and she'd be in his arms.

She took a shaky breath instead.

As if he'd guessed her thoughts, he lifted his head and gently turned her to face him. His thumb brushed across a track of moisture on her cheek she hadn't realized was there. 'I'm sorry. For what I said a few minutes ago.'

She lifted a shoulder, not trusting her voice.

'It can't be easy,' he murmured, 'raising him alone. Keeping him safe.'

All her insecurities washed over her in an instant. Plenty of women raised children by themselves, and they seemed to have it so together. But there were days when the loneliness of shouldering the burden closed in around her, stealing her breath as surely as her son's asthma stole his.

His eyes searched hers, seeming to read her every

thought. God, he must think she was the most pitiful creature he'd ever come across. 'We manage.'

Her voice cracked, much to her horror. She tried to clear her throat, but that sounded strangled as well.

'Sam.' The thumb that had brushed across her cheek moved sideways as his fingers slid beneath the braid at her nape, his palm so very warm against her skin. His gaze dropped to her mouth.

*He was going to kiss her.*

The realization swept through her, just as the curtain behind her swished open, and Toby came trotting into the space, his 'All done!' cracking through the air like a whip.

Sammi yanked free so fast that she stumbled backwards, Mark grabbing her arms to keep her from falling into the seat behind her.

She pulled away again without looking at him and gripped the back of Toby's seat, her hands shaking. 'Go ahead and get buckled in, then.'

Through the tiny window, the snow seemed to be falling a little harder, and her nerves, already on edge, took a turn for the worse. She glanced toward Mark, but avoided looking directly at him. 'Are we going to be able to take off in this?'

'It shouldn't be a problem. But we're also leaving a little later than I'd hoped.'

Because he'd been about to kiss her? Because she would have welcomed it, like a fool?

She made sure Toby was secured and then sat in the copilot seat without a word, fastening her own seat belt.

Mark went through the pre-flight checks like the pro he was, inspecting gauges and switches and communicating with the flight tower.

Was she smart to have taken him up on his offer? A

single trip was one thing. An open-ended arrangement was something else entirely.

It felt like charity.

Only he did need to get the plane ready for patients. Maybe he didn't want to be beholden to her either. By agreeing to a fair exchange of services, neither party would owe the other a thing.

Yes. That's how she'd look at it. A business deal that had nothing to do with their personal history or whatever feelings she may or may not have once harbored. Those emotions would stay where they belonged.

In the past.

If she was smart, she'd clearly set the tone for how they were going to handle this little exchange. By keeping things businesslike and impersonal, she'd send him a message that said *hands off.* No more freebies or anything else were heading his way.

The adult playboy Mark might be able to get any woman he laid his eyes on, but she wasn't going to be one of them. Not this time. The touching, the whispered words had almost broken through her barriers and taken her to a place where things would not end well.

As he revved up the engines and taxied toward the runway, she kept her mind fixed on that. Letting things get personal—again—would only end in heartache for both of them. If she couldn't do it for herself, she had to do it for the one person who mattered more than anything in this world.

Her son.

Within minutes, they were in the air. Sammi forced her eyes closed, letting the sound of the engines wash over her.

*Go to sleep. It's the best thing you can do. For everyone involved.*

Besides, if she was asleep, she wouldn't have to talk. And if she didn't have to talk, she could get off this plane without doing or saying anything else stupid. She needed time alone to sort through things and come up with a plan of attack.

That was it. She'd go on the offensive, rather than sit back and worry about how she was going to react to seeing him and Toby working together.

She didn't expect to really sleep, so when Mark's voice came through the headset, telling her they'd be landing in about ten minutes, she jerked upright in her seat, blinking.

Oh Lord, if she'd known she was actually going to fall asleep, she'd have taken the stupid thing off. Better that than have him hear what her ex claimed she did at night. He'd had to shake her awake on more than one occasion. She could only imagine how mortified she'd be if that sound was magnified and piped directly into Mark's ear.

A wave of heat washed over her. She glanced over at him to find him staring at her with raised brows.

*Uh-oh.*

'Um…I didn't…'

'Snore?'

She put a hand to her forehead. *Heavens.* 'Sorry about that. Couldn't you turn the sound off or something? I'm sure it's not something you'd choose to listen to for three hours straight.'

He smiled, turning on every part of her that she'd just finished switching off.

'I've always kind of liked it, remember?' he said, reminding her that he had indeed heard it on more than one occasion. 'You sound like a kitten purring.'

That's certainly not how Brad had described it. No wonder women fell at Mark's feet in droves. He had those pretty little lines down pat.

'I've heard I sound more like chainsaw, but thanks, anyway.'

'Someone actually said that to you?'

'Oh, yeah. I've heard it from more than one person.' Toby had also teased her about her snoring. Relentlessly. She'd retaliated by buying him a package of multicolored earplugs for Christmas.

Mark's smile disappeared and a muscle tightened in his jaw. 'I see.'

*Huh?* What was with the stiff answer? He'd been cracking jokes a minute ago.

Only when he avoided her eyes and turned to face forward did she realize how he'd taken her words. That she'd heard about her snoring from more than one *man*.

A spike of anger charged through her gut. What if she had? It was none of his business who she'd slept with. He'd made no secret of hopping from the bed of one beautiful woman to another. Did he think she wasn't attractive enough to land anyone other than him—although look where that had gotten her—and her ex-husband? She could sleep with a million men and it would still have nothing to do with him.

If he'd been a normal person, she might have corrected his misconception. As it was, she didn't feel she owed him any explanation whatsoever.

Fine. Hopefully they'd be on the ground in short order and she could get away from him as fast as humanly possible. Twisting around in her seat, she saw that Toby was still playing his game. He hadn't overheard their conversation, which was a good thing.

Even without his earbuds, the rumble of the twin propellers filled the space, creating a constant drone that was louder than her supposed snoring could ever be.

She hoped Mark liked the sound of those engines, because that's all he'd be hearing from now until they were on the ground.

She needn't have worried, because he didn't try to fill up the time with chatter anyway. He maintained his rigid silence until they whipped down the tiny runway at Dutch Harbor.

As soon as they slowed to a crawl, coasting toward the nearest hangar, Sammi unlatched her seat belt and started to scoot out of her chair. 'Thanks for the lift. I appreciate it.'

'Mind staying in your seat for another minute or two?'

'Why? I don't think it's really—'

The plane came to a sudden halt, and the momentum that should have been absorbed by her seat belt threw her body forward into the instrument panel a few feet away. Her elbow landed with a thud against the nearest metal object. 'Ouch!'

She dropped back into her seat, rubbing her injured limb.

'That's why.' He didn't look the slightest bit sorry that he'd just about killed her.

'You did that on purpose!' she fumed

'I did ask you to stay seated.'

'Mom, are you okay?' Toby was looking at her with his brows puckered. 'You're not supposed to stand up until the seat belt sign goes off.'

Except there was no sign. Just a smart-ass who evidently had a Napoleon complex. Except this particular Napoleon could never be considered short.

Short-tempered, maybe. She remembered the black eyes

he'd sported on more than one occasion from fights he'd been in during their middle- and high-school years. He'd thought he was hiding the truth from her…from everybody, but she'd seen right through the act. Knew his father was responsible for some of those bruises.

'I'm okay. And you're right.' She sent a glare Mark's way. 'You should never stand up while a plane is in motion. *Someone* might get hurt.'

Mark gave a quick sigh as he shut down the engines. 'If I say I'm sorry, can we call a truce?'

'Depends what you're sorry for.'

'Making you fall?'

Would that be making her fall right now? Or making her fall for him years ago?

She'd go with the former option. It was the only smart one. Because the other was unthinkable.

Because no matter what else she did in this lifetime, she wasn't going to fall for Mark Branson ever again.

# CHAPTER SEVEN

SAMMI smiled as yet another clucking sound came from the woman beside her. Apparently Hannah, resident physician's assistant and all-round worrywart, had found another problem.

'Okay, spill it.'

Hannah tapped the sheet of paper on the counter between them. 'I see three bags of saline on this list, but no warmer.'

'A warmer. You're right, I didn't even think about it. I'm used to keeping a unit of saline in the glove compartment while en route to a patient, but I guess planes don't have glove compartments, do they?' Sammi slid the paper closer and jotted down a note to check the prices on fluid warmers.

Hannah wrinkled her nose. 'You're kidding right? You don't actually do that.'

'In Unalaska? Where hypothermia is a constant threat? Um…yeah. Pumping cold saline into an already chilled patient isn't going to do him any good. My glove compartment must be near a heater vent because it gets nice and toasty in there. I've heard of throwing them on the dashboard as well.'

The PA's mouth opened and closed a time or two, before

anything came out. 'Okay, I guess I'm a little too sheltered. I wasn't saying you should administer cold fluids. Been there, had one of those, and it's not a pleasant experience. I'm saying that's what *war-mers* are for.'

'Warmers cost *mon-ey*.' Sammi mimicked her friend's inflection. 'Maybe I could use that baby wipe warmer I got as a gift when Toby was born.'

'A baby wipe warmer. Really?'

Sammi laughed. Okay, so maybe Hannah was right. But when funds were tight, you found ways to make do. Hannah wasn't from the Aleutians or even Alaska, she'd grown up in Idaho and had moved to the island a little over three months ago, taking the place of the PA who'd retired last year. The lanky redhead had arrived just in time, too, as Molly was no longer around. But the young woman still had a thing or two to learn about medicine in the Aleutians.

'I'm going to bring it in and check it for size. You never know, it might just fit. If not, maybe I can kind of squeeze it inside…'

Hannah rolled her eyes and giggled. 'Squeeze it inside? What if it breaks in the process? I don't think you want to be electrocuted. Just bite the bullet and ask someone for the real thing.'

They'd been so intent on their list that Sammi hadn't heard the door open, but she definitely heard the low drawl that came from somewhere behind her. 'I would ask what it is that might break if it's the wrong size but, quite frankly, I'm afraid to.'

A rush of heat washed through her face as she whirled around and found Mark leaning against the wall beside the entrance. His lazy smile said what his words hadn't quite spelled out: that finding two women giggling over something's size couldn't be good.

She licked her lips, trying to get herself under control, but a nervous laugh came out before she could stop it. 'We weren't talking about… I mean we were trying to figure out how to…'

Hannah came to her rescue. 'We're trying to decide whether to buy an IV warmer for your plane.'

'As opposed to a…' He paused and waited for someone to fill in the blank.

'A—a baby wipe warmer.'

The look on Mark's face was priceless. His eyes widened, his mouth moving as if to repeat the words. Then he laughed. Sounding nothing like Sammi's pitiful snicker of humiliation, Mark's chuckle filled the room with light and mirth, bringing back memories of a younger, less cynical Mark. The joyous sound sent a shiver down her spine.

She stared at him for a few seconds, glancing over at Hannah to find her with her hands plastered over her mouth, shaking with silent laughter of her own.

*Okay, it wasn't that funny.*

Then why were her lips curving higher as Mark's laughter made its way past a cold, isolated area in her heart, warming it instantly?

She stood a little taller, needing to get control of this situation *and* her silly emotions. 'We'll see who has the last laugh when I bring that baby wipe warmer in tomorrow.'

'This I've got to see.' Mark was still smiling, as if her idea was the most ridiculous thing he'd ever heard.

'Prepare to hear "I told you so." Both of you.'

Hannah choked out, 'You could always put it in the restroom if that doesn't work out. No one likes a cold roll of t-toilet paper.'

'Very funny.' Sammi shook her finger at the two of them. 'Did you both graduate from the same school of future comedians? If so, I don't think you should quit your day jobs.'

Hannah took a deep breath in and let it back out, then crossed to Mark and held out her hand. 'Hannah Lassiter, Unalaska's resident spendthrift, if you believe what Sammi says. Seriously, I'm the new PA.'

Taking her hand and giving it a quick shake, Mark introduced himself as well. Surprisingly enough, he didn't immediately lay on the charm that seemed to have most women clinging to his arm by the end of the encounter. Instead, he was businesslike and professional.

It made her nervous.

What was he up to? She'd never known him to pass up an opportunity like this. He'd even put the moves on Molly when she'd first arrived on the island.

'Did you want something?' she asked, the waspish edge back in her voice.

'I came to make sure we were still on for Saturday. I have to run a tourist to Akutan and won't be back until tomorrow afternoon. Didn't want you to worry.'

Why on earth did he think she would?

She'd been frantic when he'd left that first time. Had hoped and prayed he'd change his mind and come back. Well, he hadn't, and she'd learned her lesson. If he disappeared tomorrow, never to return, she'd barely raise an eyebrow. 'Don't worry. I won't.'

He ignored her churlish words. 'Do you need anything from the island?'

A more civilized tongue, maybe? Except if she suggested it, he might get the idea she was ready to let bygones be bygones. She hadn't quite made it to that point yet, despite the whole turn-the-other-cheek lessons she'd learned in Sunday school years ago.

Besides, she was fresh out of cheeks.

'I can't think of anything.' She glanced at Hannah. 'How about you?'

'Do they have a coffee chain outlet?'

Sammi thought for a second she might be serious, but the other woman's smile gave her away. 'Nope, just the same kind of sludge we have here.' She had a thought. 'Hey, are you heading to Anchorage afterwards?'

'I was planning to. Why?'

She gave Hannah a mock glare. 'Ask Molly if the hospital has any spare IV warmers lying around.'

'You got it. Anything else?'

As she looked at his warm green eyes and solid, steady presence, she found she did want something else despite her best efforts. She wanted a time machine. One that would take her back to simpler days and a very different Mark.

She bit her lip. But then she wouldn't have her son, and he meant everything to her.

She couldn't go back, and neither could Mark. But maybe they could turn a page on their past and start afresh, bypassing the blips and complications that came with a more intimate relationship.

Maybe they could learn to be colleagues. And if they were very lucky, someday they might even become... friends.

He was losing his touch. And maybe even his nerve.

Pulling into his mother's driveway, he made no move to get out of the car. There was a new woman on the island, and he hadn't given her a second glance. The PA was beautiful enough, with reddish mahogany locks that curled loose and free around high classical cheekbones and a delicate upturned nose. He'd willed himself to smile at her, but the knowledge that Sammi was standing right there, probably waiting for him to do just that, kept him from acting.

Or maybe it was the pang of regret that had come from listening to Sammi's laughter as she'd joked with the other woman.

Until she'd seen him standing there.

Then the light in her eyes had flickered out, her chin going up in a defensive move she probably wasn't even aware of. As if waiting for him to hurt her. Again.

It brought back memories of his father and the way the bastard had disappointed his mother repeatedly. And that wasn't the worst of it. Even the thought made his hands ball into fists at his side, something he'd seen his old man do time and time again—just before he'd let loose and used them on whoever was the closest. Mark forced his own fingers to flex and relax.

The second his father had found that engagement ring, Mark had known he had to leave the island, that he couldn't allow Sammi to be drawn into his nightmare. But in doing so, he'd felt tremendous guilt at leaving his mother alone.

No, that wasn't entirely true. From the time he'd turned eighteen, Mark had pleaded with his mother to leave…to report his father to the authorities, but she'd always refused. Had made up excuses until the day he'd died.

And in running away from one terrible situation, Mark had found himself in the middle of a nightmare of a different sort. One he still struggled with.

He finally went to the door of his childhood home and knocked, before peeking inside. 'Mom? You home?'

'I'm in the kitchen,' she called out.

Walking into the other room, he found her slicing apples over a low table and tipping them into a bowl of water.

Fresh lemon slices floated on the surface. He leaned down to kiss her cheek. 'What are you doing?'

'Making an apple pie.' She smiled up at him. 'Your favorite.'

'It is indeed.' He pulled a chair from the small kitchen table that sat in the corner of the room and parked it next to her wheelchair. 'Do you want some help?'

Her brows went up. 'Do I usually?'

'No.'

They never talked about his father. In fact, Mark had never once been to his grave, although he knew his mother put flowers on it from time to time.

Sammi had sent them a sympathy card that had almost made him laugh. Because sorrow had been the last thing he'd felt. He'd felt relief that his mother was finally safe, that she could now live her life without being afraid.

For a few brief moments he'd toyed with the idea that he could come home and make things right with Sammi now that the threat was over, that she might somehow forgive him for leaving her in the first place. In fact, he'd kept the ring all these years, just for that reason.

But his first night back, he'd had a nightmare. The second night had brought another one. Then he'd seen Toby, and the whole scene at his chopper had played through his mind in agonizing slow motion. How would Sammi feel if she discovered what her son did to his own insides? That when the child's blanket fell away in his dreams, it was sometimes Toby's face he saw and not the dying boy's.

He hated it, despised his mind for playing those kinds of tricks on him, but he was powerless to stop it.

The best he'd been able to accomplish was to hold himself at bay with a string of meaningless relationships—

hoping Sammi would take the hint that they were over and done.

Of course, working with her on the plane shot those plans to hell.

He swallowed, forcing back his thoughts by ducking his hand into the icy lemon-water and plucking a slice of apple. The tartness hit his tongue with an acidic rush, forcing his lips to draw up in protest. 'Sour.'

His mom laughed. 'I haven't added the sugar yet. The lemons keep the slices from turning dark and ruining the pie.'

Kind of like the happy-go-lucky attitude Mark had adopted after leaving the military. It kept his mind from wandering into dark places. Or ruining lives. After all, no one wanted to wake up next to a man who cowered beneath the covers whenever he heard a branch crack under the weight of ice, or one who zoned out and saw the death of a child time and time again.

'I came by to let you know I have to work this weekend. I promised Sammi I'd get the plane ready for service.'

'Sammi?' Her knife stopped in mid-slice.

There was such hope in that single word that Mark had to grit his teeth to keep from immediately setting her straight. He knew his mom wanted him to get married someday and provide her with grandchildren, but it wasn't on the cards right now. Maybe it would never be.

He forced a smile and dipped into the water for another slice, taking a bite of the crisp, sour fruit. He studied the flesh before popping the rest into his mouth. His mom was right. The lemon kept the apples as white as snow.

If he could do the same thing, keep his true feelings submerged, he might just get through his time with Sammi unscathed.

But more importantly, so would she.

# CHAPTER EIGHT

'HEY, Mom, can I try out the bed?' Toby pushed his hand against the thin mattress of the stretcher.

They'd come to the airport loaded with supplies and equipment. Hannah had insisted on showing up at the clinic and helping her pile everything into her tiny car. Sammi had been tempted to ask the other woman to come to the airport with them, but couldn't bring herself to. Hannah's week had been hectic, and she deserved some downtime. So Sammi and Toby went to face Mark together. At least she had her son along with her for the ride.

She started to tell Toby not to climb on the stretcher, but Mark came over with another box of bandages, catching the tail end of his question. 'Sure, bud, go ahead. It's not very comfortable, though.'

How on earth did Mark know that? Yeah, well, some thoughts were better left unexplored.

Her son scrambled onto the mattress and sat there, legs dangling over the side. 'If I get hurt really bad, is this where I'll have to stay? I couldn't ride in the seat like I did last time, right?'

Sammi's heart crawled into her throat and lodged there. She'd had nightmares of him having an attack serious enough to require a medevac. It was one thing to be a half-hour from a hospital like he'd been during his episode at the zoo. It was another thing entirely to get onto a plane knowing it would take three and a half hours to reach a medical facility. So many things could happen in that time.

When she glanced at Mark, she noted his face was devoid of any color and his hands gripped the back of a seat with such force that his knuckles stood out. Before she could ask him what was wrong, he seemed to recover, pulling in a deep breath. 'Yes. This is where you'd be. But you don't have to worry about that. We're going to try to make sure you stay good and healthy.'

*We?* The lump in her throat grew.

'I have asthma, you know.'

'I know.' Mark didn't try to minimize her son's announcement, he simply acknowledged it.

That satisfied Toby, and he quickly switched to another subject. 'My mom is going to help with the patients, isn't she?'

'Sometimes.'

Mark seemed completely at ease again. The relaxed façade he showed to the world was back in place. But she'd just glimpsed something she might have missed had she not been watching.

Her son glanced up at her. 'Will I stay with Grandma when you're helping sick people?'

'Yes.' Sammi's mother already knew this was a possibility, and she was more than thrilled to keep Toby. It made Sammi nervous to leave him alone overnight, but she'd done it before Molly had come to the island. The problem was she'd gotten used to going home every night, safe in the knowledge she wouldn't have to make any sudden runs to Anchorage. Yep, she was definitely spoiled.

Her eyes fastened on a shoebox-sized box Mark was

cutting open with a knife. She caught the words "*Fluid War*—*" before the top opened and revealed what looked like a rectangular insulated bag.

She couldn't remember ordering anything that looked like… 'What's that?'

Glancing down, then back up, his eyes met hers. 'My contribution to the supplies.'

'An IV warmer? Is that from Alaska Regional?'

'No. I know funds are tight, so—'

'You bought one? I told you I'd try my baby wipe warmer. Toby's growing up, so I don't need it any more.'

'You never know.' Something flashed behind Mark's eyes before he extinguished it. 'You might have another child someday.'

Right. It wasn't as if she had men lined up, waiting to take her out. And after her failed marriage, she couldn't see herself jumping into another relationship.

She wasn't like Mark. Or her father who—like Mark—oozed charm and had used it every chance he'd got…to the chagrin of his wife. Sammi couldn't bounce from relationship to relationship. She needed a strong connection before getting involved. Something in common. Because of that, she'd always thought she'd be married for life.

How quickly things could change.

Staring at the zippered warmer, an ache went through her chest. She wanted someone who really heard her. Someone who went the extra mile to make sure she knew she was loved.

That someone wasn't Mark, despite the fact that his purchase made her gushy inside, made her want to wrap her arms around him with a sigh and absorb some of his warmth and strength.

In fact, it might just be one of the nicest things anyone had ever done for her.

That damned moisture was gathering in the back of her eyes again.

Mark must have sensed something was wrong, because he added, 'I know the clinic doesn't have the funds to buy one, but Hannah made it sound pretty important.'

'She's right. It is.' She hesitated, trying to figure out a way to thank him that wouldn't come across as pathetic and needy. Or make the stinging in her eyes even worse. 'Thank you. I'm sure the patients will appreciate it.'

'I'm sure they will.' A beat went by. 'But what about you, Sam? Did I do the right thing?'

Something about the way he said it—the almost pleading note that hovered between them—caused little sparks to go off in her stomach, spreading outward and setting off more explosive charges along the way.

*Act like you don't care one way or the other.*

But she did care. And lying wouldn't do anyone any good. He'd made an effort. The least she could do was acknowledge it.

'You did.' The words came out as a whisper.

Mark straightened, standing far too close for her emotional well-being, the warmer still gripped in his hand.

Her lips parted as he brushed back a strand of hair that had drifted across her cheek.

'What the heck's an IV warmer?' Just like that, Toby shattered the moment by jumping off the stretcher.

As jarring as it was, Sammi could have kissed him for yanking her back to her senses. She sidestepped Mark and did just that. 'It keeps bags of medicine warm so the patients don't get cold when we give it to them.'

'Oh.'

When she glanced at Mark, she saw he was staring at his hand, a far-away look in his eyes. The shadow of a bruise was still visible from where she'd slammed the door on it.

Was he thinking about her?

Of course not.

A thread of anger twisted inside her. This was getting ridiculous. She wasn't an eighteen-year-old girl any more. She couldn't turn starry-eyed every time Mark said or did something nice. He'd do the same for any woman. He'd proved that time and time again.

She was no one special.

He'd driven that home in the cruelest possible way. And she needed to be on her guard from here on out. That mark on his hand pulled at her conscience, though, as did the memory of those old breaks.

'How's your hand, by the way?'

He blinked, his face hardening slightly. 'My hand?'

'Where the door caught it.' She touched the bruise, the yellow color signifying it was healing. 'Any lingering problems?'

He stuffed the IV warmer into an overhead bin, effectively pulling away from her touch. 'None. I'd almost forgotten about it.'

A pang went through her. Maybe she'd better just leave him to do the rest of the set-up on his own. 'Well, I guess we're about done here—'

The buzzer sounded on her phone, stopping her from making a quick getaway. She glanced at the readout. Hannah.

Clicking the talk button, she put the phone to her ear. The receiver crackled with static. 'Hey, Hannah. What's up?'

'I…' The voice faded, the one word sounding shaky and uncertain.

'Hannah? Is everything okay?'

'Not sure…' The PA seemed to be struggling with her thoughts.

'Do you have a patient?'

'Y-yes.'

Sammi waited, but only heard the sound of heavy breathing. 'Hannah? Who's the patient?'

'I…' a groan came across the line. 'I think…I think it's me.'

Mark's glance traveled beyond the flashing lights of the police car and found the wreck itself. The front of the car was crumpled, and two officers were working on the driver's-side door, trying to force it open. Sammi gasped from the seat beside him. 'Oh, God. Hannah.'

She leaped from the vehicle almost before they'd pulled to a complete stop, her medical bag gripped in her right hand.

'Mom!' Toby's frightened voice came from the back seat. 'What's happening?'

Putting the car in park and feeling more impotent than he ever had in his life, Mark twisted in his seat to face Toby, the child's pale, scared features pulling at him in the worst possible way. 'Your mom went to help Hannah. It's okay.'

The back of the plane wasn't even completely set up yet. If they had to medevac her out…

Could Sammi do it?

Yes, she'd proved herself to be competent and inventive. She'd be able to handle just about anything.

Unlike him. Maybe he shouldn't have agreed to take

on this gig. His military flight training should have prepared him for any eventuality. He'd had to ferry injured soldiers back from distant battlegrounds. Had had to watch helpless as a young child died inside his chopper, as that child's mother, swathed with explosive charges, had run away from the plane at the last minute, trying to spare Mark and her son.

He swallowed the sour taste that rose in the back of his throat.

Those memories had the power to make him lose track of where he was…of who he was with.

But he wasn't in his chopper now. He was here in Dutch Harbor with a little boy who needed him to keep it together.

'Toby.' He faced the child again. 'This is important. Do you know your grandmother's phone number?'

'Of course. I'm not three.' Color poured back into the child's face.

'I'm going to ask her to come pick you up.' He handed over his cell phone. 'Can you punch in the number?'

Toby nodded, taking the phone from him and jabbing the buttons in rapid succession. 'There.' He gave the phone back.

Three rings…four…

*Come on, pick up.*

The screech of metal giving way met his ears and he saw the door pull free of the car. Sammi was next to it in an instant.

'Hello?'

'Mrs. Trenton? This is Mark Branson, remember me?'

There was a slight pause then her voice came over the line, the chill in it unmistakable. 'Yes, of course I do.'

He ignored the pointed words, knowing he deserved whatever censure she tossed at him, but it would have to wait until later. 'Can you come and pick up Toby? There's been an accident—'

'Sammi?' The coolness in her tone gave way to fear.

'No, no, she's fine. We're at an accident scene and may have to do a medevac. I think she said you were to watch Toby if that happened.'

'I'll be right there. Tell me where you are.'

Mark quickly relayed their location and clicked off when Sammi's mom said she'd be there in less than ten minutes.

'Get your stuff together, buddy.'

'I don't have any.'

Mark frowned. 'What about your inhaler?'

The child's eyes widened. 'I think I left it on the plane.' Then Toby breathed out a sigh. 'But Grandma always has an extra one at her house.'

'Good.' Mark made a mental note to ask, then focused on keeping Toby's attention away from the ruined vehicle once he noted efforts to extricate Hannah were under way. He sent up a quick prayer, hoping it wasn't as bad as it looked, then said, 'Hey, do you know how to play I Spy?'

The next several minutes were taken up with searching out innocuous items, making sure to choose things in or near the ocean, which faced away from the scene of the accident.

'No, it's not the rock,' Mark said.

A small grey Toyota pulled up behind them, and Mark saw with relief that it was Sammi's mother. 'Wait here for a second, okay?'

He clicked his door open and waved to the older woman, who hurried toward them.

'Oh, my God, who's in there, do you know?'

'Hannah Lassiter. She works at the clinic with Sammi.'

Grace Trenton shook her head. 'I know Hannah. Poor girl, is she going to be okay?'

'I don't know. I've been letting Sammi and the police do their jobs.'

'Toby?'

'In the car.' He touched Grace's arm. 'Listen, Toby said you had another inhaler. He left his on my plane when we were over there, setting up.'

'I do. I keep a couple of extras on hand.' She glanced again toward the accident. 'Looks like I'll be keeping my grandson for the night.'

'Is that okay?'

'Of course. I'll take him now so she doesn't worry.' She gave Mark a hard look. 'I'm going to say this one time then you won't hear me mention it again. I know you have to work together, and Sammi may look and act tough. She's not. Neither is Toby. For my daughter's sake, please… *please* don't start something you don't intend to finish.'

Before he had a chance to understand what she meant, she'd moved away and had opened the car door to collect Toby. The child leaped out and hugged his grandmother around the waist. Grace took his hand and led him to her car, the boy turning to wave wildly at Mark as he went, a smile plastered to his face.

Mark started to wave back, then Grace's warning went through his head, her meaning finally taking hold and burrowing deep: *Don't start something you don't intend to finish.*

*Like he had eight years ago?*

If that's what she meant, Mark couldn't agree more. And he intended to keep reminding himself of that advice over and over.

For as long as it took to make himself believe it.

# CHAPTER NINE

'HELP me!'

Sammi threw the words at Mark, who stood frozen beside the closed door of the plane, his eyes vacant.

Why wasn't he moving?

They'd made it to the airfield, but she didn't dare let him go to the cockpit until they'd stabilized Hannah's breathing, which had grown increasingly labored as they'd rushed to the airport. The steering-wheel that had pinned the still unconscious PA to her seat had almost certainly sent a rib through the woman's left lung, as Sammi wasn't getting many breath sounds when she listened on that side. Hannah's blood pressure was also dropping. And Mark hadn't moved in the last two or three minutes.

'Hey!' she yelled again. 'Come on. I need you over here, dammit. Now!'

He appeared to shake himself back to the present and crossed over to her. 'Sorry. What do you want me to do?'

Ripping open Hannah's white blouse, and praying she was right, she splashed some Betadine high on Hannah's chest, making sure it hit the area where the second intercostal space was located.

'I have to decompress her chest, so she can breathe better. There should be a box of needles in one of the drawers.

I know we haven't separated them yet, but I need you to dig through the container and find one that says fourteen gauge. If you can't find it, just get me the biggest needle you can find. And the longest.'

Mark, seemingly back to his old self, tore through the supplies, while Sammi scrambled to get an IV set up.

'Sorry, honey,' she murmured to Hannah as she inserted a line. 'I don't have time to get the warmer out.' And with the temperature outside dropping rapidly, the interior of the plane was growing ever colder. So much so that a quick shudder rippled through her as she hung the bag of saline on a nearby hook. She forced it back, knowing she couldn't afford to let the tremors move down to her hands.

Eyes burning, she remembered laughing with Hannah about the dangers of pumping cold fluids into a patient. She'd never dreamed it would be one of them lying on that table.

She straightened up and caught herself. Now was not the time to be emotional. Hannah would do exactly the same thing if she were in her shoes.

'Found one.'

'Open the wrapper and hand it to me.' Sammi had already slapped on a pair of gloves, but didn't have time to tell Mark to do the same. It should be okay, as long as he didn't click off the protective cover.

He put it into her waiting palm, and Sammi twisted the cap, exposing the needle. Using her free hand, she found Hannah's clavicle then moved down to the second rib and the space just beneath it. 'Stand back.'

No time for a mask. No time for second thoughts.

*Please let it be air compressing that lung and not blood from an internal bleeder.*

Before she had time to change her mind, she pressed

the needle home. She felt the quick *pop* as it entered the pleura, followed by a gurgle, then air hissed from the site.

*Air!*

No symphony ever written was as beautiful as that sound.

The left side of Hannah's chest deflated as the trapped air continued to escape. Within a minute the woman's breathing eased, and Sammi was able to gently retract the needle.

'Hell, Sam. I can't believe you just did that.'

She glanced up to find Mark staring at her, every bit of color drained from his face.

'If I hadn't, she'd have died.'

'I know, it's just…' He swallowed, his Adam's apple dipping before coming back up. 'You've changed.'

'Yeah, well, so have you.' The paralyzed version of Mark she'd seen a few minutes ago had scared her almost as much as Hannah's injuries. And the look on his face as he'd watched her work… A sliver of fear skittered through her. Was there something wrong with him?

No time to think about that right now.

She turned away and checked Hannah's vitals. Her blood pressure had come back up. 'We can take off now.'

'Right.' Without another word, Mark turned away. Out of the corner of her eye she noted the shaky fingers raking through his thick dark hair, the jerky movements as he did what she asked.

What was going on? He was always so cool. So sure of himself.

Something had shaken him. Hannah's condition? No, she didn't think that was it.

*Forget about it.*

She could try to figure it out later. Right now she needed

to concentrate on her friend and pray all three of them could hold it together for the next three hours. Until they reached Anchorage.

She'd had to perform the needle decompression twice more on the trip, and she damned herself for not making sure a catheter had been loaded onto the plane. But there was nothing to do about it now, except make sure Hannah's chest cavity stayed clear of air.

'Better?' she asked.

Hannah had regained consciousness minutes after they were airborne, and while that was an encouraging sign, Sammi cringed each time she had to stick her to relieve the growing pressure.

'Yes.'

'I'm so sorry, Hannah.'

The other woman reached out and touched Sammi's hand, her voice gravelly and weak. 'Don't. It's better than suffocating.'

Sammi gritted her teeth, unable to answer. She busied herself checking her friend's vitals, which were still holding steady. 'How do your ribs feel?'

'Like I've been hit. With a baseball bat,' Hannah managed to get out.

'You were, kind of. The steering-wheel had pinned you to the seat. It's a wonder you were able to call me.'

Hannah shook her head. 'I knew if I didn't try...'

Neither of them needed her to finish that phrase, knowing what probably would have happened if she hadn't.

Glancing at her watch, she patted Hannah on the shoulder. 'Let me see how much longer.'

A storm had been riding their tail almost the whole way, making it a bumpy flight. She moved to the front, where Mark was working the controls with a much steadier hand than he'd had earlier. 'You okay? You were acting kind of strange a while back.'

His jaw tightened. 'Fine. How's the patient?'

'No signs of internal bleeding or head trauma. Do we have an ETA?'

He glanced up at her. No sign of the haunted look he'd worn as she'd worked on Hannah. 'Around ten minutes.'

'Good. I'm hoping the broken rib and punctured lung are as bad as things get. No way to know the full extent of the damage until they get some chest CTs.'

'CTs?'

'Cat scans. Sorry. I keep forgetting you're not an EMT.'

'That's probably a good thing.'

She smiled. 'At least you didn't faint. Although you had me worried for a few minutes there.'

Her second attempt to get him to open up was met with as much enthusiasm as her first. Something flickered behind his eyes for a second then he turned his attention back to the sky in front of him.

'You're good,' he said. 'If I were injured, I'd want you working on me.'

A quick jab of shock went through her. If she hadn't seen his face, she'd think he was joking, but the tight lines around his eyes said he was dead serious. She had no idea why he'd felt the need to say something like that, but the thought of him lying on that stretcher—hurting—did ugly things to her composure. 'Let's hope it never comes to that.'

He nodded. 'I'll let you get back to it.'

Sammi studied his stiff profile for a second longer before heading back to Hannah's side. Her patient's eyes were closed, and she frowned.

'Hannah?'

The other woman groaned. 'Can't a body get some sleep?'

'No.' The tension drained from her lungs. 'Not on my watch. No sleeping until we get you to the hospital.'

Mark called for them to prepare for landing. Already she could sense the floor beneath her feet tilting as they made their descent.

Checking the wheels on the stretcher yet again to be sure they were locked in place, she sat in the seat next to the bed, and held Hannah's hand. 'The landing's probably not going to feel good on those ribs.'

'Nothing feels good right now.' She glanced over her head at the IV bag, which was swaying on its hook. 'I guess I didn't rate the baby wipe warmer.'

Sammi laughed, glad Hannah was feeling well enough to joke. 'No time to test it, remember?'

The wheels touched down with a couple of hard bumps, and Hannah's smile transformed into a grimace as they jostled and bounced their way to a stop.

'You holding on okay?'

Hannah gasped. 'Remind me…to lodge a complaint… with the pilot.'

'I will. Once we get you back on your feet again.'

Thankfully Molly was on duty today and had promised to meet them. One of the legs of the runway ran almost up to the hospital's entrance so they could basically wheel Hannah down the ramp of the plane and through the sliding glass doors.

Mark powered down, then came back to help ready Hannah for transport. Sure enough, as soon as the door to the plane swung open, a small contingent of doctors and nurses came into view, Molly's familiar face among them.

They wheeled Hannah down to ground level, Molly running over to meet them. 'What have we got?'

Everyone was all business. 'Hannah Lassiter, twenty-nine years old, car accident, possible broken rib with accompanying pneumothorax on the left side. I did three needle decompressions, but the chest keeps filling back up. She'll probably need a chest tube and a CT. Vitals are stable, BP one-twenty over eighty, pulse eighty-five. I couldn't measure her pulse ox.'

Molly nodded, leaning over the gurney with her stethoscope. 'Hannah, how are you doing? Any pain?'

'What do you think?' Hannah took a breath, gasping as she did. 'I think I'm going to need that chest tube pretty quickly.'

'We'll get you one.' Molly motioned to a nearby attendant. 'Let's get her inside.'

Turning to Sammi, she smiled. 'You know the routine. We'll take it from here.'

Sammi nodded, leaning down to kiss Hannah's cheek. 'You'd better come home soon.' She glanced at Molly. 'And you had *better* call me as soon as I can see her.'

'Will do.' Molly followed the stretcher into the hospital, already calling out orders for tests and treatments.

A minute or two went by as she and Mark stood just inside the entrance.

'Well, I guess that's that,' she said. 'Feels kind of weird, huh?'

'Hmm.' Hands propped low on his hips, he didn't seem to be in a hurry to talk about anything.

Okay, so this was going to be awkward if every medevac wound up like this. She wrapped her arms around her waist to ward off the chilly air that had followed them inside. 'Do you need to take the plane to the hangar?'

'I guess I do.' He didn't move, though, and Sammi wasn't sure why he was hesitating all of a sudden. Maybe he was trying to figure out a subtle way to head back to the island. Now.

Although Mark didn't normally do subtle.

As if reading her thoughts, he touched her arm. 'Listen, I'm sorry about earlier.'

'Earlier?'

'Before we took off. I was…distracted.'

That wasn't quite the word Sammi would have chosen, but she was at a loss to find a better one.

Horrified? Scared?

No, neither of those fit either.

A nurse walking down the corridor glanced toward them, and then did a double take. 'Mark?'

His hand fell away from Sammi's arm as the woman crossed over to them. Tall and slender, her blonde hair was twisted into an elegant knot. Not a single strand was out of place.

Sammi fingered her own messy braid, wishing she'd had time to do something different with it. She tossed it over her shoulder in an effort to hide it.

*Ridiculous. Who cares what you look like? You just saved a friend's life.*

The woman stopped in front of them. 'Molly said we'd be seeing a lot more of you around here.' Her voice was low and husky, the smile she sent him matching it to perfection.

Throwing a quick glance Sammi's way before he answered, Mark shifted his weight from the balls of his feet to his heels. 'I don't know about that. It depends on how many patients we have to transport.'

Maybe she should try to make a quick exit. This woman certainly seemed like she knew Mark. Quite well, in fact.

What if he wanted to pick up where he'd left off, but didn't want to do it in front of her? Far be it from her to cramp his style.

She looked at the glass doors behind them, where the plane still sat. 'Do you need to get back to Dutch Harbor? If so, don't let me keep you. I'm going to head to the cafeteria and wait for word on Hannah's condition.'

When she started to move away, Mark's fingers circled her wrist, stopping her in her tracks. 'I was planning on spending the night. I try not to do round trips in a single day, if I can help it. Once the plane's put away, I'll join you.'

A shivery sensation went through her that had nothing to do with the cold. He hadn't tried to get rid of her. In fact, he seemed to be using her as a way to give Gorgeous Nurse What's-Her-Name the royal brush-off.

The other woman evidently took the hint, since her delicately carved brows lifted. 'I'll catch you next time you come in, then.' Her sharp gaze zeroed in on Sammi. 'Good luck.'

The acid tone behind the words said it all: *good luck pinning this one down.*

With that the nurse swung away, her hips twitching as if to let Mark know exactly what he'd turned down. Sammi could imagine far too well. And there was no way she'd be able to compete with a woman like that. Ever.

Even if she wanted to. *Which* she didn't.

She tugged her wrist free. 'Okay, then. I'll see you when you're done.'

'Give me about thirty minutes to hand the plane off.'

Sammi nodded. 'As soon as Molly returns and we have a quick cup of coffee, I'll help you get the plane cleaned up. Probably not a good idea to leave the back the way it is.'

'Right. I hadn't thought about that.' He dragged a hand through his hair, looking like he wanted to say something more, but if he did, the words didn't make it out. 'I'll be back as soon as I can.'

'No hurry.'

Mark gave her one last enigmatic look, then turned and walked through the sliding doors.

She shook off her unease. Ever since Hannah had been injured he'd been acting strangely. Scratch that. He'd been this way ever since he'd returned home from the military.

Well, she wasn't going to figure it out by standing here. Besides, she needed to call her mom and let her know she'd made it, and check on Toby.

She wandered to the emergency-room waiting area and dropped into the nearest chair. Not too busy for this time of day. Dialing the number and reaching her mom on the second ring, she was glad to hear laughter in the background.

'Sounds like everything's going okay there.'

Her mom's voice was slightly breathless. 'We're playing duck, duck, goose.'

'Huh? There are only two of you.'

'No, there's also Woody, a penguin and some kind of shark.'

Sammi laughed. 'I'm sure those guys are getting a lot of the action. Don't let him wear you out.'

'He's not. I'm doing the stuff I should have done when you were little.'

'You did, Mom.' Her chest ached every time her mother went down this road. 'You were working, and there was a lot of…stuff to deal with.'

'You're a good daughter, Sammi.'

'And you're a good mother.' The two of them had played this same game many times before. Their relationship was good, and Sammi was more grateful for her than ever. 'Does he want to talk to me?'

A second later, Toby came on the line. 'Hi, Mom. Is Hannah okay?'

'She will be. The doctors are taking good care of her.'

'Oh.' There was a pause. 'Are you coming home soon?'

Was that a tinge of disappointment she heard in his voice? 'I think I'll need to stay here tonight. Is that okay?'

'Sure! Oh, I mean…sure.' His voice went from happy to dejected in an instant. Trying not to sound too relieved to have his doting grandmother as a playmate for the evening.

*Poor Mom.*

She smiled. 'Okay. Put Grandma back on, then. Love you.'

Her mom reassured her that they were fine, that she wouldn't let Toby eat too many sweets or stay up too late. And, yes, she had his inhaler nearby.

Ringing off, Sammi sighed and stared at the wall-mounted television, letting the drone of strangers' voices wash over her for a while, glad to have a little time to recuperate before facing Mark again. She glanced down at her watch. Hannah had been in the back for close to an hour.

Just as she started to get up to hunt someone down to see if there was any news, Molly hurried down the corridor, her normally cheerful smile absent as she spotted her and headed over.

Sammi lurched to her feet, a sliver of worry lodging in her gut. Hannah had seemed stable when they'd brought her in, despite the pneumothorax. Had she taken a turn for the worse?

Once Molly reached her, her friend put a hand on her arm. 'Sorry to take so long, the emergency room had another serious case to deal with. I just finished with it.'

'Is Hannah okay?'

'Yes. She's in surgery to repair the damage to her ribs. It shouldn't be much longer.'

'Thank God.'

'It's a good thing you guys got her here when you did, though. The hole in her lung was bigger than expected. Another hour and she might not have made it.'

The words brought back the memory of Mark pressed flat against the metal skin of the plane, something terrible behind his eyes. If he hadn't snapped out of it, what would have happened? Dozens of different scenarios played through her mind, none of them reassuring, because they all ended with Mark paralyzed while Hannah slipped away into darkness.

'Yes,' she said slowly. 'It's a very good thing.'

# CHAPTER TEN

MARK made his way across the tarmac, hunched against the snow. The word in the hangar was that the storm that had trailed them from the Aleutians was definitely headed ashore. That storm, however, could be no worse than the one currently raging within his gut.

Why had he ever thought he could run medevacs without being affected by them? Without remembering what had happened in Afghanistan? He could kill Blake for talking him into it.

Therapeutic, his ass.

As was Blake's assertion that battlefield evacs were very different from the sterile medical evacuations practiced in civilian circles. What a crock. The war that Sammi had fought in the belly of his plane had been anything but sterile.

And he hadn't been able to move a muscle as memories of chest compressions and severed limbs paraded through his skull in rapid succession. And that child he'd flown back to the M.A.S.H. unit—little Ahmed. He could still hear the shouts of the medics as they'd worked on him, willing the boy to fight, to breathe. But the damage had been too great.

His breath hitched, even now. Heaven help him, it was

still hard for him to look at Toby without remembering that horrific night.

And what if Toby's asthma took a turn for the worse? He'd already been to the emergency room once.

Mark firmed his chin. He might not have been able save one child, but he could make sure Toby didn't ride on the open deck of a boat to reach the mainland.

He was doubly glad Toby wouldn't be on that boat during the incoming storm.

According to the guys at the hangar, the weather would only get worse as the evening wore on, which meant his comment about spending the night was probably carved in stone at this point. The problem was, the icy conditions were supposed to last through tomorrow as well.

The episode at the plane had left him shaken and tired. Having that run-in with the nurse hadn't helped. It had made him take a hard look at his lifestyle and wonder if his strategy for shaking the horror of the past eight years was even feasible. Maybe he'd never be rid of it, no matter what kind of mind games he played with himself.

It was one thing when Sammi hadn't been around to witness him in action, it was another thing entirely to do it right under her nose. He couldn't even remember the nurse's name. That fact ate at him like a school of piranhas tearing flesh from the bone.

How had he gotten to this point?

Becoming a hermit suddenly looked pretty damn good. One thing was certain. He couldn't go on the way he had. Something had to give.

He made it through the hospital entrance and noted that Sammi was no longer standing where he'd left her. Neither was she in the waiting room. He could only hope she'd gone to the cafeteria like she'd mentioned doing. Turning down the corridor to the right, he made his way there, seeing Sammi's dark braid even before he entered the room. Facing away from him, her shoulders were rolled forward, a white coffee cup sitting in front of her.

He moved in front of the table and waited for her to glance up at him. 'You okay?'

'Yes.'

Her one-word reply put him on edge. She'd seen him flip out on the plane, was probably wondering just what she'd been saddled with. Hell, sometimes he wondered that about himself. Blake had left the military without any lasting effects, while he...

*Block it out.*

'How's Hannah?'

'She's in surgery, but Molly thinks she'll make it through just fine.'

He pulled out the chair across from hers. 'That's great.'

She sighed and fingered her coffee cup. 'I haven't been on one of these runs in a long time. And to have to work on someone I'm close to, this first time...'

'I know.' He reached out and took her hand, trying not to let the relief swamp him. There was no hint that she was hung up on what had happened earlier.

'Just a few days ago we were laughing about stuffing a saline bag into a baby wipe warmer. And then to see her lying on that stretcher, not sure if she was going to live or die...'

He knew exactly what she meant. He'd seen close buddies wheeled off his plane and wondered if he'd ever see them again.

'She's going to be fine, Sammi.'

She tightened her fingers around his. 'I know.'

He glanced down at their joined hands, trying not to

think about how natural the act felt. As if he was coming home. As if this was where he belonged.

*Wrong.* He belonged on the periphery. Arm's length from everyone who mattered. Tonight had proved that beyond a shadow of a doubt. What if Sammi had been lying on that stretcher and he'd zoned out, unable to move... to help.

He should pull away, but somehow he couldn't force himself to budge. This was a one-time thing. He was simply letting her know he understood how she felt. More so than she might realize.

'Do you need to call Hannah's family and let them know?'

Her eyes met his. 'I never thought to ask for her contact numbers. Maybe in her file...' Her teeth came down on her lip. 'How could I not know if she has family?'

'She has you, Sam. And I can't think of anyone I'd rather have on my side.'

It was the truth. And if he'd been born in a different time and place, he could have ended up with everything he'd ever dreamed of.

She squeezed his hand and let it go. 'Thank you for saying that.'

'So do you want to wait here?'

'I do. Molly's supposed to let me know when I can see her.' She wrapped her hands around her mug and shivered. 'My coffee's cold.'

He eased her fingers away and picked up the cup. 'I'll get you a fresh one. Still cream and sugar?'

'Yes, the same as I...'

She stopped, but Mark knew what she'd been about to say. *The same as I always take it.*

Out of all the women he'd dated since Sammi, how was

it that he remembered exactly how she took her coffee, even after all these years? He couldn't recall the name of the nurse in the hallway but he seemed to remember everything about Sammi.

*Because she happened during your formative years. Because her memory—and that ring—were what kept you going for the last eight years.*

He stood in a rush to shake off that last thought and went to the coffee pot, refilling Sammi's mug and getting one for himself. By the time he made it back to the table, he'd pulled himself together. Partially, anyway.

Sitting down and sliding the cup over to her, he said, 'Let me know if it's not sweet enough.'

She took a sip, not quite meeting his eyes. 'It's fine, thank you.'

Taking a swig of his own coffee and letting it sear its way down his throat, he hoped the caffeine would kick-start his brain and set it down on safer ground. 'Did they say how long surgery would take? You can't sit here all night.'

'No. But I can't leave without seeing her.' Her eyes finally made contact with his. 'Go ahead to the hotel, Mark. No sense in both of us waiting. I know you need to get some rest for the flight tomorrow.'

Should he tell her about the storm coming in?

No. It was just one more thing for her to worry about. 'Did you get a hold of your mom?'

She nodded. 'She and Toby were in the middle of playing a game.'

'He's stayed with her before.'

'Lots of times.' A tiny smile appeared. 'They're best of friends. Since Toby's father isn't…around, it's been nice that Mom has been willing to watch him.'

'Your mom is a great person,' he said.

'She is.' Sammi's brows went up. 'So is yours. I could never figure out why she didn't leave, though.'

'Leave?'

Her eyes held his, relaying her meaning without the words having to be said.

He sighed. 'I don't know. I wanted her to.'

'You did, though.' She glanced down at her cup. 'Leave, I mean.'

Is that what she thought? That he'd left to save his own skin? That he'd put his comfort above what they'd had together?

And if she did? Maybe it was better to leave it that way. To let her to draw whatever conclusions she wanted.

'It was complicated, Sammi.' He downed the last of his coffee, forcing the bitter liquid past the lump in his throat. 'Do you want another one?'

'No, I'm good.' She stood. 'I think I'll go back to the waiting room and see if there's any news.'

'Hannah's going to be fine.' He hesitated. 'But are you?'

'What do you mean?'

'If she's here for the next week or so recovering, how are you going to handle the workload?'

'I'll manage.'

He frowned. 'You're already working yourself into the ground. What about Toby?'

Her teeth came down on her lip. 'What else can I do? I can't just walk away from my patients when the going gets tough. The people relying on me are not just tourists looking for thrills. They have real problems.'

As soon as the words came out of her mouth she put her hand to her face, eyes wide. 'Oh, Mark, I didn't mean that the way it came out.'

Yes, she did, and although the inference stung, she was right. He'd purposely chosen a career that didn't involve life-or-death races against the clock. Or downing one too many whiskeys when the clock won.

Hell, he'd drunk himself into a stupor after Ahmed's death. Had had to be carried back to his tent.

It was then the nightmares had begun.

He'd done his best to work through them. Had thought he'd finally succeeded in pushing past the worst of it. Until he'd seen Toby, and the downward spiral had begun all over again.

'It's okay.' He picked up both their cups. 'Are you ready?'

'Yes, but, really, you don't have to sta—'

'No buts. For once, I'm not walking away.' Yes, part of that statement was referring to her earlier words, but he was also talking about his decision eight years ago. When he'd walked away from the best thing that had ever happened to him.

She laid her hand on his arm, her fingers finally warm again after their flight. 'I'm sorry for saying that. I don't deal well with uncertainty.'

He smiled and covered her hand with his own. 'Are you kidding? You've always been a rock. Whereas I, on the other hand, was always a royal screw-up.'

Retrieving his coat from the back of the chair, they made their way to the waiting room and sat in chairs next to each other. An uneasy truce seemed to have sprung up between them, one he was loath to mess up. So he stuck to small talk, which he murmured in a low voice to avoid disturbing others who also waited for word on their loved ones. He figured that by droning on and on, Sammi didn't have to think, she could just sit back and not expend any more energy than she already had. So it was a shock when in the middle of a sentence, he felt something land on his shoulder.

He turned his head slightly, and his chin brushed Sammi's forehead.

She was asleep. Exhausted.

No longer needing to talk, he sat there and absorbed each tiny nuance of her. The pressure of her cheek against his shoulder, the slightly medicinal scent of lemon and antiseptic that now clung to her. The heavy breathing that he knew from experience could quickly turn into that cute kittenish snore. Leaning a little closer, he let the wall he'd erected between them lower a couple of inches. Just enough so that he could allow his jaw to rest on the silky hair on top of her head.

'Your wife's tired.'

A whispered voice came from a woman two chairs over.

Shock went through him, and he started to correct her assumption, explaining they were just coworkers. But how many colleagues would drape themselves over each other like this?

Okay, so Sammi falling asleep on him had been an innocent gesture. Not so innocent was his rubbing against her like a cat. So he settled for nodding slightly and scooting down in his chair, hoping that by closing his eyes, he could pretend he too had fallen asleep and prevent any more misunderstandings.

But an even bigger reason was to flee the nagging thought of what it might be like if the woman's words were true, and there were no nightmares to deal with. No war. And if Sammi was indeed his wife.

# CHAPTER ELEVEN

SOMETHING touched her face.

Mark.

Pulling herself from the bottom of a drugged pool, she blinked open her eyes to find her head trapped between two hard surfaces.

She took in her surroundings. White walls, astringent bite that hung on the air, reception desk.

Her glance moved back. Reception desk. She was at the hospital. But why?

Everything came back in a rush. Seeing Hannah trapped in her car, the needle decompressions she'd had to perform.

But that didn't explain why she couldn't move her head.

Then she saw the masculine thigh lying next to her own. Touching it. Her attention moved to her fingers which were wrapped around a muscular biceps.

It really was Mark. His head was lying on top of her cheek, hence the feeling of being pinned in place.

She must have fallen asleep, and then he'd done the same.

Heat rushed to her face, until she realized he probably wasn't aware of what either of them had done. The last thing she remembered was him talking in hushed tones that had soothed her jangled nerves. All the worry about

Hannah and her own exhaustion had just seemed to slide away. She'd relaxed and found herself drifting, following wherever his voice led her. Her head had dipped a couple of times before settling on a solid perch. Which, evidently, had been his shoulder.

But he was asleep as well, so that was a relief. She could just ease her head from beneath his…

She attempted to do just that, but she really was trapped. If she jerked too hard, he'd wake up with a bump.

Gearing up for another try, he suddenly shifted upright, dragging his hand through his hair.

*Pretend you're still asleep? Or let him know you're awake and get it over with?*

She voted for the latter, since the continued contact was making her heart lurch around like a drunk on a binge. Sitting up, she rubbed her eyes as if she'd just awoken, feeling like a fraud. But what other choice was there? Just keep on sitting there with her head propped on his shoulder and have him wonder if she was making a move on him?

The thought made her stomach give an ominous twist.

'Looks like we both fell asleep,' she said, thanking her lucky stars her voice was indeed low and scratchy.

Glancing across the room, she saw another woman smiling at them. 'Your husband said you were exhausted. But he evidently was as well.'

*Husband?* Had she done more than drool on his shoulder?

Before she could open her mouth to ask what she meant, Mark said in a low voice, 'It was a little complicated to explain at the time.'

*I'll bet.*

She forced herself to smile at the older woman. 'It's been quite a night.'

'I think it has been for everyone.' A man showed up behind the older woman and handed her a coat, waiting as she rose to her feet. 'Best of luck with your loved one.'

Okay, this conversation was a little odd. 'Thank you. To you as well.'

The man helped her slip on the coat, then the pair made their way to the door, the woman using a cane to help her progress.

Once they were out of sight, Mark said, 'She assumed… you were asleep. It seemed harmless.'

Harmless. Maybe for him. But having the woman refer to Mark as her husband made something zing through her chest.

A flash of hope?

Surely not. Most probably regret. Regret for her failed marriage. Regret that her son didn't have a live-in father.

Regret that her youthful dreams had been crushed before they'd ever been fully realized.

'It's fine. It's not like we'll ever see them again.' She sat a little straighter. 'Any more news on Hannah?'

'No. It's only been a couple of hours.'

'How long can it take to repair her ribs?'

'Maybe the situation was a little more complicated than they anticipated.'

Panic shot through her stomach.

'Molly said the tear was worse than they expected. There was air leaking into her chest during the flight, but it wasn't filling up with every breath she took.'

Mark put his arm around her and squeezed. 'Let's not jump to conclusions before we know what's going on.' He stood. 'I'm going to run for more coffee, would you like some?'

She shook her head. 'My nerves are on edge enough as

it is. It'll just make me jittery, especially this late at night.' Glancing at her watch, she saw that it was only ten-thirty. It felt so much later. 'On second thoughts, if they have some decaf or a cappuccino in the vending machine, I'd accept that. Let me dig out some money.'

'I've got it.' He turned on his heel and headed down the corridor that led to the cafeteria.

Sammi sat back and checked out the waiting room. Still quiet. Sending up a quick prayer that Hannah would come through surgery without any major problems, she toyed with whether or not to call her mom again. She decided against it, worried she might wake Toby. While he was probably out like a light, her mom was a night owl who stayed up until all hours. An old habit ingrained by a husband who'd consistently come home late.

Even though deep down her mother had known their marriage vows had been purely one-sided, she'd stuck with him. She'd asked Mark why his mother had stayed with his father. But Sammi could very well ask herself that same question: why had her mother stayed with someone who'd cheated on her? Sammi's schoolmates had all known who her dad was sleeping with on any given week and had teased her about it. It was one of the reasons Mark's current behavior appalled her so much. He hadn't been like this while they'd been together, never even hinted that he'd wanted to see other people. In fact, at one point she'd been sure he was gearing up to ask her to marry him.

*But he hadn't.*

And now he couldn't seem to stick with any one woman for very long. What had changed?

He wasn't in a committed relationship, so it technically wasn't cheating, but it seemed wrong to skid from one woman to another, never waiting around to see if things felt right.

She sensed there was more to Mark's actions than met the eye—at least she hoped there was—because he had so many other great qualities. But she felt for the woman who eventually *did* get involved with him. Who fell head over heels for him.

Did she really believe he'd cheat on someone he'd given his word to?

No.

Maybe that's why he'd never given it in the first place. Why he'd left her all those years ago. He'd known he was incapable of being monogamous, so he'd simply never committed.

To anyone.

At least he hadn't put on a front, like her father had…as if he were an upstanding husband and a pillar of the community. Her dad had finally moved on to another wife, and Mark's dad had died of a heart attack just months before Mark had come home. Both women were now free to live their lives as they saw fit.

She spied Mark at the far end of the hallway carrying two paper mugs. His concentration was fastened on the cups, giving her the chance to study him.

Loose-limbed, he moved with ease, his tall build and broad shoulders giving off a kind of steady confidence that turned heads. Dark hair fell over his forehead, long enough to need strong fingers to sweep it back again and again. She could still remember how those silky locks had felt sliding through her own fingertips. A trace of dark stubble now lined his jaw, although he'd been clean-shaven that morning at the plane. And the man made her mouth water as much now as he had when they'd tiptoed from their teenage years and fallen headlong into young adulthood.

Yes, the man was gorgeous, but Sammi was smarter and hopefully wiser now than she'd been all those years ago.

He reached her and handed over a cup. A mountain of foam covered the dark liquid and a dusting of—cinnamon?—lay on top. She eyed it. 'I didn't know the vending machines did cinnamon.'

'They don't. I broke into the kitchen supply cupboard.'

Her eyes widened. 'You didn't!'

'Well, not exactly. I picked the lock.' At her still shocked look, he added, 'Don't worry, I put the container back and relocked the cabinet.'

Sammi laughed, despite herself, and sipped the coffee. It was rich and luscious and she could just about bet he'd nabbed some flavored creamer from somewhere as well. Her tongue darted out to lick the clinging sweetness from her lips, noting that Mark followed the movement. Her laughter died in her throat.

So he wasn't as immune to her as she'd thought. She didn't know whether the idea pleased her or terrified her. Scrabbling for something safe to say, she blurted out, 'What did you get?'

He held his cup down so she could see inside. 'Espresso. Black.'

Not a hint of foam, which meant he'd broken into the cupboard just for her. It was a typical Mark thing to do. At least the Mark she'd once known. She willed herself to stay indifferent, but it warmed her from the inside in a way the doctored-up cup of java never could. 'Wow. Espresso. You're going to be up all night. I promise.'

As soon as the words tumbled out, she cringed. She took a deep gulp of her coffee, scalding her tonsils and a good part of her throat in the process. Sucking in a deep breath to ease the burn, she turned toward one of the windows, watching the snow as it blanketed the parking lot and walkways. 'It's coming down faster.'

The heat of his body reached her as he took his seat again. 'I meant to tell you earlier, but with everything else going on I didn't get a chance. A storm front is moving through, with some heavy winds and snow predicted over the next couple of days.'

'Are you kidding me?'

'It's a good thing we got Hannah here when we did, because I doubt the airport will be clear for much longer.'

'It'll be gone by tomorrow, when we need to leave, right?'

He didn't say anything, and she looked into his face, which was lined with something she didn't understand.

'Mark, will we be able to fly home tomorrow?'

'I don't know.'

A spear of panic shot through her. 'I have to get home to my son!'

He hesitated, then used his thumb to brush back a strand of hair that had fallen into her eyes. Something he'd done repeatedly. 'I checked with Toby when we were at the scene of the accident. He said your mom keeps a couple extra inhalers on hand, so he should be fine. We'll call and let her know what's going on. She'll understand.'

She started to relax in her seat then tensed again as another thought hit her.

Toby and her mother might be okay, but what about her? The last thing she needed right now was to be stranded in Anchorage with Mark.

But it looked like that was exactly what was going to happen.

# CHAPTER TWELVE

*'Heavy snows continue in our area for the next twenty-four to forty-eight hours, delaying flights and making roads impassable.'*

Sammi rolled over in bed at the hotel and groaned at the forecaster on TV. Yes, she knew winter was closing in on them—and brutal storms often blew into Alaska with little notice—but couldn't it have waited until she got back home? Maybe if they'd flown out right away, they could have reached Dutch Harbor before it hit.

But Mark had said he didn't like to fly back and forth in one day.

Besides, she'd needed to know how Hannah was doing.

Molly had come out three hours after surgery had started and said the PA was in Recovery. Her rib and lung had been patched up, and she was not in pain at the moment.

Sammi had gone back and held Hannah's hand as she'd slowly emerged from the effects of anesthesia.

'How are you doing, kiddo?' She'd sensed Mark standing slightly behind her, but had forced herself to keep her attention focused on her friend.

'I feel like someone stabbed me with every needle in their arsenal.'

Sammi had smiled. 'That would be me. We had to de-flate all that hot air you were storing.'

'Gee. Thanks.' She'd shifted in bed, wincing as she did. 'They put a U-plate on my rib to hold it in place, so it doesn't wander back into my lung. Looks like I'll be stuck here for a week or so.'

'You deserve some vacation time, anyway.'

'Some vacation. Are you going to be okay?'

'Sure.' She leaned down and kissed her cheek. 'Lynn and I can hold the fort until you're better.'

'But—'

'*Don't worry about tomorrow, because today has enough worries of its own*. Wasn't that the quote you taped to the clinic wall, right behind the reception desk?'

Hannah nodded. 'My daddy was a preacher. Some of it stuck.'

'He was right. You've got plenty to keep you busy for today and the next several days. Just concentrate on healing.'

Her thoughts returned to Mark, even as the meteorologist continued relaying storm warnings in the background. She scowled, throwing back the covers and climbing from the cocooning warmth of her bed. Why was he always right at the periphery of her mind?

*Because he's flying you back to Dutch Harbor, you ninny.*

She dragged herself to the bathroom, her frown deepening as she looked at herself. She'd had to sleep in the buff, since she hadn't brought any extra clothes, but at least the panties she'd washed out by hand seemed dry enough. Her hair was an absolute rat's nest…and that was currently her best feature. Not a good sign. Just because she was stranded it didn't mean she could hide out naked for the next day or so.

She dragged on her clothes, which were wrinkled both from sitting on the plane and from the wait at the hospital. Maybe she could run the hotel's blow-dryer over them and relax the worst of the creases. Besides, the warm air would be a welcome change from the constant chill the storm had dragged with it. Once she washed her face and scrubbed her teeth as best she could with a washcloth, she undid her braid. It was still damp from her shower last night. Better to leave it down until it dried out some more. As she was brushing the tangles out, her stomach gave an angry rumble.

Food.

*Do you still have that candy bar from last week stuffed in your purse?*

She went to the other room and rummaged around for a minute or two, but the chocolate had mysteriously vanished. Stolen. Um, yeah. Probably by her own hand. The hotel had a couple of vending machines if she remembered right, so she wouldn't starve. She just had to get up the nerve to venture out in the snow.

Someone knocked on the door, and she froze.

The sound came again, this time accompanied by a voice. 'Sam? If you're in there, could you open up? It's freezing out here.'

Mark. Who else would it be?

She hurried to the door and found him standing hunched in his coat, snowflakes sticking to his hair. His arms were full of bags. She realized she was just staring at him when his brows went up in question.

'Oh, for heaven's sake. Sorry. Come in.' She stood to the side and let him through the door. 'What is all that?'

'Food. Toothbrushes. Stuff.'

Had the man read her mind?

She took several of the packages from him, noticing he also had two coffee cups tucked into the crook of his elbow. Fragrant steam wafted from beneath the lids. Tossing everything else onto the bed, she rescued what she considered to be the most precious commodity right now.

'Um, you might want to be careful with some of those.' But as she sniffed first one cup and then the other to see which held a whiff of vanilla creamer, he smiled. 'I thought that might hit the spot.'

She gave what she hoped was a nonchalant grunt as she peeled back the tab on top of the cup and took a cautious sip, groaning in ecstasy. 'Mmm…still so hot.'

'I assume you're referring to the coffee and not to me.' He shook the moisture from his hair and raked his fingers through it a couple of times. 'Although I think I deserve a bone for braving this weather to make sure your pearly whites stay clean and cavity-free.'

Heat washed over her face. Okay, so the man was still hot as well, even with a nose that was red from the cold, but no way was she going to admit that out loud. Especially since he did in one sweep of his hand what had taken her at least twenty minutes to do: restore order to his hair. 'The coffee has earned you something. And if you have a Boston cream donut in one of those bags, you're getting extra points for sure.'

A slow smile appeared on his face, and he shrugged out of his coat, tossing it onto one of the chairs next to a minuscule table. He seemed awfully chipper this morning. Maybe he'd gotten a better night's sleep than she had.

Sorting through the bags, he pulled out a napkin and then opened a box. He soon had cradled within his palms a perfect round disk of pleasure, its chocolate icing in pristine condition. 'It's fresh. I made sure.'

Sammi gulped, the caffeine hitting her system and sparking a rush of emotions…giddiness being one of the first she recognized.

*No grabbing.*

Instead she reached out and gingerly took the offering from him with a sniff. 'I'll be the judge of that.' She bit into the donut and the powder-soft dough was indeed extremely fresh. Probably made just minutes earlier. As hard as she tried, she couldn't suppress yet another moan as the vanilla cream center mixed with the warm chocolate frosting.

'I take it the verdict is in?'

She nodded, her mouth full of donut and her heart squeezing with happiness. She gave a thumbs-up sign the best she could with her hand still wrapped around the coffee cup.

Mark took a donut of his own, simple glazed, and bit into it, taking a seat at the table. Okay, so was it too much to expect for him to leave the box of donuts and venture back into the storm to go to his own room?

Of course it was. She set her coffee on the table across from him and took the other seat. The one with Mark's coat draped across the back. The chill of icy raindrops penetrated her thin cotton top. Despite the moisture, the scent of Mark's body clung to the leather, and she just wanted to pull it around her shoulders.

'Sorry,' he said, retrieving the coat and hanging it on the hook behind the door.

'It's okay.' She gave a deep sigh. 'Thanks for bringing this. I didn't realize how hungry I was.'

*Well, it was only a tiny lie.*

Mark reached over and grabbed the box of donuts and put the whole thing in front of her. Donuts of every shape and size met her glance. 'Oh my gosh. I'm going to gain ten pounds.'

'Doubtful. Besides, you work hard enough to burn off those calories and more.'

'A nice thought, but not true.' She glanced at the rest of the packages. 'Surely you didn't bring more food.'

'Nope. Just the stuff that's bad for you.' He glanced over as well. 'I thought you might like a toothbrush. I know I would.'

Her brows shot up. 'You needed three bags to carry two toothbrushes?'

'No, I also brought you a book. I wasn't sure what you'd like so I guessed.' He paused and glanced away. 'I also got a little something for Toby.'

'Toby?' She blinked at him, her mind running through the dates, horrified that she might have forgotten something crucial. 'His birthday isn't until next month.'

'It's nothing big. I just saw it and thought he might like it.'

Sammi's gaze went to the window out front. The snow was piled deep, although the parking lot had already seen the blade of a snowplow. 'You drove in this?'

'It's not as bad as it looks, actually.'

Hope flared in her chest. 'So we might make it out of here today?'

His lips twisted. 'Sorry. Driving in it and taking off in it are two different things. The worst of the storm is still out over the ocean. We'd have to fly right through it, not something I particularly want to do.'

'Oh.' She sagged back in her seat, nibbling her donut.

'I did bring some playing cards, if you're interested.'

Sammi's heart stopped for a minute before taking off at a gallop. Their game had been poker. And they hadn't played for money. 'Um…'

How exactly did you ask what seemed to be an obvious question? Was this regular poker or the naughty kind?

'I seem to remember always losing.' His innocent blink did nothing to quell her suspicions.

He had indeed. Repeatedly. At first, Sammi had thought it was because she was an awesome player. Later, she'd realized he stayed one step ahead of her so she wouldn't be the one who shed the last piece of clothing at the end. He hadn't wanted her to be embarrassed. Although he'd seen every inch of her body by then. And she'd traced every contour of his with her fingertips. In fact, they'd rarely made it to the end of a game.

Not a good memory to dwell on when she was currently in a hotel room all alone with the man.

Time to be evasive. 'I haven't played cards in a long time. I've probably forgotten how.'

A brow quirked up. 'Really? Is it possible to forget?'

What was with him? She couldn't imagine him wanting to take a trip down memory lane. Especially since he was the one who'd run away from it in the first place.

'Yes. It is possible. And sometimes it's better not to pick up old habits.'

Zing! That should have earned her a point or two. And sent him a message that she wasn't looking to heat things up between them.

Liar. She might not be looking to, but she was definitely warmer than she'd been before he'd shown up at her door.

He closed the top on the box of the donuts, and Sammi imagined he was also closing the lid on this particular conversation.

'So what do we do until the storm passes?' she asked.

'I offered a simple game of cards, but you shot that down. I'm all out of options.'

The cellphone on the end table went off, the vibration sending the thing careening toward the edge. She hurried over and grabbed it before it fell. Glancing at the screen, she swore softly. Just what she needed.

'Hello?'

'Samantha? Where the hell are you? I've been calling the house since yesterday afternoon.'

Brad. And he was not happy.

'Why didn't you call my cell?'

'That's what I'm doing now.' Her ex's voice was tight and angry, which was unusual for him.

'Sorry. I had a medevac yesterday, and I'm having to stay in Anchorage because of the storm. Don't worry, I haven't forgotten that you have Toby next weekend.'

'You're in Anchorage? You told me you weren't doing medevacs any more.'

'Molly got married, remember? We talked about this.'

'I still don't like it. And what is our son going to do, while you're gallivanting around?'

*Gallivanting around?*

A knot of anger twisted in her gut. She glanced at Mark and then away, embarrassment crawling over her. Brad's phone voice tended to be twenty times louder than his normal speaking voice, so Sammi had to hold the cell slightly away from her ear. No doubt Mark could hear every word the man said. 'Toby's staying with my mother.'

'You couldn't have brought him with you? He could have stayed with Maribel and me. At least he'd be with *one* of his parents.'

The knot tightened. 'I was with a patient, Brad. Car

accident. It wouldn't have been the best thing for Toby to witness.'

There was a moment of silence. 'If you're going to be away from home a lot, maybe we should rethink this custody thing. Make it a more even split. I talked to Maribel, and she wouldn't mind having Toby around more often. Wouldn't it be better for him to be a part of a *whole* family? It's not good for him to be shuffled from person to person. Especially with his condition. What if he has an attack, and you're not there?'

Her growing fury morphed into terror in a split second. He'd hit on the very thing she feared the most. That Toby would need her and she wouldn't be there.

But to change their custody agreement? She'd never in a million years thought Brad would want to go there. Toby was all she had. Brad had his own family now. Would he really try to take their son away from her?

She knew she was overreacting, but couldn't seem to stop herself.

Brad's voice came back over the line. 'Toby needs stability. He needs to know at least one of his parents will be there at all times.'

'You travel, sometimes, too.' Her words tumbled over themselves. *Breathe. Do not let him rattle you.*

'Yes, but Maribel would be here. And Jessica. He'd be able to stay at home. Attend a good school.'

'His school is fine. And my mother is a wonderful caregiver.'

Brad's volume went up another decibel. 'Your *mother* hasn't always made the best choices, though, has she? What if she gets involved with another sleazebag like your father? Is that really who you want Toby to be around? The example you want him to see?'

Oh, God. Mark's eyes had narrowed, zeroing in on hers. Something dark and angry lurked below the surface.

'Can we please discuss this later? I—I'm not alone.'

A poisonous silence lit up the line between them, and she realized how her words might have sounded.

'What do you mean you're not alone?' The words were shouted so loudly, her ear rang, even with the phone held a couple inches away. 'I thought you flew in with a *patient*? If I find out you left Toby in Unalaska so you could—'

Before Brad could finish his sentence, Mark strode across the room and took the phone from her hand, her ex's voice still raging in the background. Pressing the phone to his ear, he said, 'Brad, this is Mark.'

Unlike Sammi, he evidently had no problem absorbing Brad's full volume directly into his ear canal. All she heard was the mumble of her ex-husband's voice, but his outrage came through loud and clear.

Mark's answering smile held a tinge of cruelty as he answered. 'I'm the medevac pilot who flew Sammi and her patient into Anchorage. I'd advise you to dial back the accusations. This isn't doing anyone any good. You can call the hospital and check with them, if you don't believe her. You, more than anyone, should know that Sammi doesn't lie.'

Although Mark's voice was low and even, there was an undercurrent of steel running through it, and a muscle spasmed in his jaw. He was furious. For her.

Sudden warmth bloomed in her stomach and flowed to parts that had frozen over when Brad had suggested he might fight her over custody. She sagged onto the bed, relief washing over her. There was something primitive about the way Mark handled Brad, like a sleek, lethal cat who had no qualms about dealing a death blow if crossed.

She could no longer hear Brad at all, but he'd apparently taken Mark's advice and toned down the threats, because after a moment or two the conversation ended.

Mark set the phone back on the end table and stared at it for a second or two. 'Bastard.'

Biting her lip, she wasn't sure what to say, but he evidently wasn't done talking, because he went on, 'You don't have to put up with that, you know.'

'He's not normally like that. Besides, he's Toby's father. I should have called to let him know where I'd be, but I forgot.' She had. With all the stuff that had gone on with Hannah, notifying Brad had completely slipped her mind.

Mark sat on the bed next to her, his fingers going to her chin and forcing her to look at him. 'I don't know what happened between the two of you during your marriage, but I don't like him yelling at you—accusing you of things that aren't true.' His eyes bored into hers, anger and something else pulsing in their depths. 'I have to ask, Sam. Did it ever go further than that? Further than yelling? Further than empty threats?'

'I—I'm not sure what you mean.'

His fingers tightened fractionally, not allowing her to pull from his grip. 'Sammi, did that man ever raise a hand to you? To Toby?'

# CHAPTER THIRTEEN

PROTECT and Defend.

Those words had been drilled into him as a new recruit. And they echoed what he'd tried to do his entire life. First with his mom, and then with his buddies in the service. Finally with Ahmed, who had lain dying in the back of his chopper.

And now with Sammi.

But as soon as he saw the dismay on her face, he realized he'd overstepped his bounds.

'If you're asking if he hit us, no. Never. How could you think I'd ever allow *anyone* to put Toby in danger? Or myself?' Her shoulders relaxed, and she gave a small smile. 'I can take care of myself, so no need to go all caveman on me.'

Caveman.

His fingers gentled on her chin, and he smiled back. Okay, so maybe he had overreacted. As he stared at her, something inside him shifted, and his fingers left her chin to trace across her cheek, gently tucking her hair behind her ear.

'I like your hair down.' He rubbed the strands between his fingers, the satiny texture whispering against his skin. 'It's softer than anything I've ever felt.'

'Thank you.' Her tongue swiped at her lower lip, leaving it moist and inviting. 'I...'

The words died away as if she'd seen his eyes follow the movement.

She was so beautiful. So incredibly strong.

'Sam...' Unable to resist any longer, his head lowered, mouth touching hers, seeing if she'd allow it—if she'd feel the need to defend herself against him.

She held completely still.

And he...hell, he couldn't stop the surge of emotions that erupted within him—neither could he seal the bevy of cracks that appeared in the concrete wall encircling his heart. The wall he'd cemented shut the second his father had uttered that obscure threat against Sammi. He'd reinforced that barrier when he'd learned she'd gotten married...had had a child with someone else. But her kiss had just blown the cover off, exposing every hope and fear he'd shoved inside.

Sammi's hands went to his shoulders, and he could have sworn it was with the intent of pushing him away, but instead they curled into his shirt and hung on, tugging him closer.

The fingers that had touched her hair now tunneled beneath the shiny locks, his palm cupping the back of her head and holding her close as his mouth increased its pressure.

*Ahhh...hell.*

He relaxed into the swirling sensations, telling himself he could stop any time he wanted.

No, that was a lie. He couldn't stop. Not yet.

His tongue moved along the seam of her mouth, licking across her lower lip, tasting the last traces of sugar from the donut she'd eaten earlier. A shudder rippled through her, and her mouth opened, inviting him in.

There was no hesitation, only action, and he slid home with a low growl of need. The blood rushed to his head and immediately pumped back down into other areas, filling...swelling.

How could a simple kiss do that?

Because nothing was simple where Sammi Trenton was concerned. She provoked emotions that were complex—that ran deeper than anything he'd ever experienced. And he'd stayed away for eight long years.

Almost long enough to forget how it had been with her. The release he'd found in her arms.

Almost. But not quite. And this woman could touch him in ways no other ever had. And he'd been damned glad of it. At least that's what he'd told himself.

So why now?

*Forget it. You can figure it out later.*

Mark's other hand came up and cupped her jaw, his thumb strumming along its length before moving to where their mouths were fused together, needing tangible evidence of what was happening between them.

The sensation was erotic, crazy, and when the tip of her tongue darted out to slide over the pad of his finger a blast of need ricocheted through his skull. The subtle friction put all his nerve endings on high alert. She coaxed his thumb inside her mouth, abandoning his lips in order to fully wrap around his digit, her tongue swirling over it before sucking it deeper.

'*Sam.*' The word whispered against her mouth was low and tortured. A half-hearted plea for her to stop.

Except she didn't. And the soft moan that met his ears said she was as lost in the moment as he was.

Enough of this. He eased his thumb from her mouth, sliding its wetness across her lips before he claimed them again, his kiss no longer gentle.

Something tugged at the bottom of his shirt, freeing it from the waistband of his jeans, then her hands were on his skin, sliding up and over before splaying across his chest. The slight coolness of her palms did nothing to cool his ardor. In fact, all it did was make him pull her closer, trapping her hands between their bodies. He didn't want them wandering to other areas. Not when he was still drinking in the luscious sensation of her mouth on his, her tongue cradled against the curve of his. She could do all the exploring she wanted to. Later.

Angling his head to the left, he somehow managed to get closer, although he wasn't sure how. He could have sworn a second ago that was impossible.

He itched to touch her, and found his hands wandering from the back of her head to her shoulders, and then down her arms, the soft shirt she wore keeping him from skin to skin contact. He glided lower, encountering the lower band of the garment, which, unlike his own, wasn't tucked into her slacks.

*Don't do it.*

His body ignored that command completely, pulling back just enough so his fingers could tunnel beneath the shirt, his breath imprisoned in his lungs as he waited for her reaction.

It only took a second. The tiny whimper…the press of her body into his hands. He wrapped his fingers around her rib cage, his thumbs exploring the long, lean bones before moving higher to the place where her bra met the warmth of her skin.

He swallowed, forcing himself to stay there, rather than

move any higher, his mouth going to the line of her neck. Nibbling, tasting.

Biting.

'Oh.' Her breathy sigh only heightened his senses, bringing them to a frenzy of want, need...and something he shied away from. Instead, he concentrated on the here and now. The sound of her breathing, the sweet scent of her bare skin beneath his lips.

As if she suddenly realized her hands were free to roam, they crept to his shoulders, sliding over them, her fingers pressing into his flesh—he wasn't sure of the reason, but he liked it.

Things seemed to move fast forward, and what he'd been satisfied with a minute earlier became a gnawing discontent that ate at him. Tempted him to leap ahead. The second her fingertips slid across his nipples, an arc of electricity went through him before settling in his groin, which was already pulsing with impatience.

He came back up and covered her mouth with his. 'Slow.'

His plea went unanswered and her fingers left their perch, moving in a beeline toward his...

Catching her hands just before she reached the danger zone, he imprisoned them, easing her back onto the bed and leaning over her. He stared into her eyes, huge dark pupils meeting his own.

'Say no,' he whispered, some sane part of him still looking for an escape.

Her throat moved, then she slowly shook her head. 'I can't.'

'You can't do this? Or you can't say no?'

As much as his mind wanted her to answer the former, his heart wanted something far different. But he had to hear the words—to know for sure. If she didn't want him, he'd find the strength to let her up. Even as the thought went through his head, his hands tightened on her wrists.

'I…'

Her lips parted as if she was battling something inside herself. Then, instead of answering, she raised her head and drew her tongue from the base of his throat all the way up to his chin, a slow deliberate move that told him everything he needed to know.

The world swirled around him in slow motion, then he sat up and dragged his shirt over his head, his mind already on his wallet, hoping he had something inside.

Sammi's fingers immediately trailed over his nipples again before they moon-walked down his abs. His stomach muscles rippled in that half ticklish, half tormented sensation that skated the line between eroticism and…

*Oh, sweet Jesus.*

She'd reached his waistband and flipped open the button in a quick move that left him breathless.

'Sam.' He injected a hint of warning into his voice and lifted her hands above her head, pressing them into the mattress and holding them there for a second or two to emphasize his point. 'Don't move.'

When he let her go, she stayed right where he'd placed her, and a feeling of power flowed through him. Until she arched her back slightly, her lips curving in a smile that turned the tables in an instant.

His fingers again went to the bottom of her blouse, but this time, instead of sliding beneath it, he pulled the garment up and over her head, until she was free of it. He wrapped one of his hands around her wrists, making sure she stayed put as his eyes roamed over the bared flesh before him.

Her lacy black bra played peek-a-boo with her breasts, giving hints of where the rosy center met pale white flesh. Her flat stomach rose and fell in time with her quickening breaths, and she squirmed a bit beneath his gaze. He splayed his hand across her lower tummy, amazed at the difference between them, his rough, tanned skin, her soft white curves.

Unable to wait, he palmed her breast, loving the way it filled his hand to perfection, the way she rose to meet his touch. He released her, undoing the front hook on her bra and slowly easing it away until she lay exposed…her gorgeous body a work of art.

Kissing her mouth, then pressing his lips against her throat, he made his way down until he reached his goal, her quick gasp heightening his pleasure as he suckled first one breast and then the other.

Her hands left the pillow and slid down his sides, and he didn't stop her this time when she reached his zipper. The tab inched its way down as she wrestled with it, stopping a time or two when he employed his teeth, holding her in place while his tongue lapped over her. Dark mutterings mixed with sighs until she finally had the zipper undone. She soon had him in her palm and his body tightened to the point of pain.

*Too soon.*

He wouldn't last much longer at this rate. Lifting his head, he went to work on her own jeans, surprised by how unsteady his hands were. He'd never had a problem before. He released the snap and tugged the slacks over her hips until she helped him kick them off the rest of the way.

Panties next. They matched her bra, and he fingered the elastic for a few seconds knowing once this final barrier was removed it was all over. There'd be no going back.

'Are you sure?'

Her response was to bat his hands away and push the garment down her legs, making short work of them. Once she was naked, her delicate brows arched. 'I think it's your move, fly boy.'

He gave a low laugh. The woman he'd known as a girl had always waited for him to take the lead. He'd stayed one step ahead of her in their card games for just this reason. There was no longer any need. She'd grown into a witch who knew exactly what to do to drive him crazy. He suppressed the slight flare of jealousy that someone else had led her to this point.

*Your fault.*

He'd chosen to leave, no matter what the reasons, therefore he had no say as to how she lived her life. 'I have to check something first.'

He didn't bother to cover himself, and as he wrestled his wallet from his back pocket she ran her index finger down his exposed flesh, making it—and him—jump.

*Be in here, dammit.* He flipped open his billfold and checked the tiny compartment. *Success.*

There was only one, though, so he'd better make this count.

He tossed the condom onto the bed, standing on the floor to rid himself of the rest of his clothes. When he came back down, covering her with his body, the shock of her flesh against his made his pulse run wild. He kissed her, his hand sliding between their bodies to the heart of her, finding moist heat. Ready. All he had to do was slide home…

*Not quite yet.*

Continuing to kiss her, he gritted his teeth and stroked

her, swallowing her moans, murmuring nonsensical phrases that meant nothing…and everything.

'Mark.' The whispered word carried a plea he gladly heeded.

Ripping open the square packet and sheathing himself, he nudged her knees apart, settling between them with a muttered threat to his own body which was screaming for release.

He surged forward, the tightness he found almost pushing him over the edge. When she tried to lift her hips he used his weight to hold her in place. 'Shh. Just give me a minute.'

'Mark…no…I…' Her body bucked against his.

At first he thought she was fighting him, that she'd changed her mind, then realized she was right on the brink. He gave up trying to hold on and let go, meeting her thrust for thrust as she arched and retreated, her head twisting from side to side.

She stiffened, with him buried deep inside her, eyes flying open to fasten on his just as her body gave way to a series of glorious spasms that catapulted him into the stratosphere. He groaned as he pumped into her, riding out his own release, until he was empty.

No, not empty.

Full. Like he'd never been in his life. Like he'd never dreamed he *could* be.

Gathering her to him, he rolled onto his side, carrying her with him, relishing the slight sheen of moisture that covered her body, the breathlessness as she buried her head in the crook of his neck.

He swallowed hard, a sudden wetness appearing behind his eyes that he didn't understand. Was afraid to explore.

It had to be the stress of the flight. The emotional tension that came with Hannah's injury followed by that phone call. He'd soon feel like he did with every other woman. A physical release that began and ended there.

Except he'd never carried more than one condom in his wallet, because he'd never felt the need to stage an instant replay.

Until now.

He and Sammi had just expended violent amounts of energy in a short period of time. Instead of feeling replete and sleepy, he wanted her again. Was already hardening within her—the temptation to just say to hell with it all and take her despite the risks.

And that terrified him.

He'd lived the past several years in a way that kept any explosive emotions under a tight leash. Contained within an iron fist.

He was never out of control. *Never*.

Until now.

# CHAPTER FOURTEEN

'THERE you go, Sarah. A little bandage and you're all set.'

Sammi smoothed the adhesive edges of the large square gauze pad on the child's forearm, which covered six brand new stitches. They looked kind of like the set Sammi now sported across the center of her heart. Six days and counting since she'd returned to Dutch Harbor after her disastrous encounter with Mark. The storm had let up unexpectedly, and they'd been able to fly out that day after all. Thank God!

She'd sworn she'd never fall at his feet like the legions of other women he'd been with. And yet she'd toppled like a sapling in a hurricane after he'd picked up that phone and tried to defend her honor. At his concern for her well-being.

'Will it leave a scar?' the girl's mother asked, bringing Sammi back to the present with a bump.

'Probably a little one. Make sure you keep the sun off the new skin as it heals. Either cover it with a bandage whenever you're outside or load it down with a good-quality sunscreen, once the stitches come out.'

Sarah, who'd surprised both women by not uttering a peep during the administration of the anesthetic or during the stitching itself, said, 'Now Johnny Riker can't say he's the only one with a battle car.'

Her mom smiled. 'I think you mean *scar*.'

'Huh? You mean I don't get a car?' The six-year-old crossed her arms over her chest and scowled.

Becky sighed. 'Nothing prissy about my daughter.'

'That's quite all right. I wasn't either when I was her age. I'm still not.' Sammi forced a smile.

The same age as her son, Sarah had her whole life in front of her. She could be anything she dreamed, do anything she wanted. Well, maybe not drive a 'battle car'.

Actually, an armored vehicle didn't sound like a bad idea right now. She needed something with dark bullet-proof glass, so Mark wouldn't see how their time together had affected her. He was used to the whole love 'em and leave 'em philosophy, but she wasn't. She'd been with exactly two men in her life. Mark and her ex-husband. She had no experience to draw from.

Maybe he'd just keep on avoiding her, and they could all get back to their normal lives.

Except he was still the medevac go-to for the foreseeable future. And Sammi wanted nothing more than to have him go back to hauling tourists.

Liar. She wanted something else entirely, but that was never going to happen. Not with a man like Mark.

*Okay, enough! You are* not *going to spend all day mooning over him.*

Sammi went to the cupboard and pulled down a big glass jar filled with colorful lollypops. Setting it on the counter, she spun it around until the hand-written list of ouchies came into view. Each ailment had a color-coded pop to go with it. It wasn't a perfect system, by any means, but it made the kids feel special.

If only there was a color for her particular boo-boo. Maybe she should add a new one to the bottom of the list.

Except there were no more colors available. She should check to see if there were licorice-flavored suckers. Then she could hand one to Mark to go along with his black heart.

*Not his fault, Sammi. It takes two.*

She went over and helped Sarah hop off the exam table. 'You've earned a treat. You've got a big choice in front of you. See the list here?'

Sarah nodded. 'Red—valor, green—broken bones, yellow—sunny disposition, purple—vac…vac…'

'Vaccinations.'

'Purple—vaccinations, Orange—courage, Blue—stitches.'

What to call the yellow pops had stumped her, until Lynn had suggested putting a positive spin on it. 'See? You have quite a decision to make.'

The child glanced down at her arm. 'I think my stitches will last longer than my courage.'

Sammi knelt in front of her, thanking her lucky stars she'd refilled the popular blue suckers. 'You know, I don't think that's true. I think bravery is something you either have or you don't. You definitely have it.'

Unlike she herself, who was displaying all the hallmarks of a coward.

After that, the choice was easy. Sarah picked orange.

She leaned the jar toward the child and let her retrieve the candy herself. 'As you can see, there are a lot of orange suckers left. Not too many kids are as brave as you.'

After hugging the child, she sent the pair on their way. She started to put the lid back on the lollypop jar but stopped, reaching in to grab an orange lollypop of her own. Maybe the candy itself could infuse her with a dose of courage.

The waiting room was empty, a strange sight. She glanced at Lynn, who shrugged. 'It's a rare sunny day. People evidently have better things to do than get sick or injured.'

'I think I'll go see how Mrs. Litchfield is doing, then. Can you call, if anyone comes in?' The pianist she'd seen a couple of weeks back had been to Anchorage for a consult with the rheumatologist, and Sammi wanted to see if the new medication was helping control her symptoms.

'Are we talking *patients*?' Lynn asked, answering her original question. 'Or are we talking *anyone*?'

Sammi knew exactly who the receptionist was referring to, but chose to ignore it. 'Patients. Anyone else can wait.'

She hurried to her car, wondering if she should call first. But Mrs. Litchfield had told her to drop by whenever she had some spare time, which had been almost nil. Hannah had been in the hospital for almost a week now, which meant Sammi had been pulling double duty. She needed a breath of fresh air.

Pulling up to a stop sign at the end of the road, she watched another car pull up in the opposite direction. Her eyes widened.

Mark's car. Of all the dumb luck.

She scooched down in her seat, realizing how ridiculous it was. He knew what kind of vehicle she drove. Plus, it was kind of hard to steer when you couldn't see a thing.

She started across the road, noting he hadn't moved. Tempted just to bolt past, she tensed when his window started down. It was either be rude or do the same.

Rude sounded good. Really good, but her foot came off the gas and her finger hit the power window button.

*But you are not going to be the first one to talk!*

'Hey,' she said. Okay, so that orange sucker was kicking in at just the wrong moment. Great.

'Hey, yourself.' Mark paused, his eyes trailing over her face in a way that made the interior of the car turn warm, despite the puff of mist her breath gave off. 'I've been meaning to call, but I've had tourists this week. Are you okay?'

*Okay?*

Ah, he meant after their fateful encounter. If he was asking if she was so destroyed by their one-night stand that she'd jump off a bridge, she could reassure him she was quite safe.

'I'm fine. Why wouldn't I be?'

*There! That should put any fears to rest.*

Thank God she had *not* been waiting around by her phone. And since Toby's dad had visitation tomorrow, she'd have to catch the ferry this afternoon. Despite Mark's earlier offer, he probably wanted to be with her even less than she wanted to be with him.

He nodded, his eyes narrowing on her face. 'When's Toby's next trip to the mainland?'

She blinked. Had he read her mind? What now? Lie? Or tell the truth.

Mark had once told her she was a terrible liar, so better just to get it over with. 'His dad is meeting us at the dock tomorrow.'

She glanced in the rear-view mirror to make sure no one was behind her, the chilly air beginning to permeate the car.

'I thought we had a deal.' His voice was so low she had to strain to make out the words, but even so, she knew better than to think he was taking her announcement in his stride. His tone was identical to the one he'd used on the phone with Brad.

Before she could respond, he took a deep breath, seeming to fight for composure, his hands white on the wheel. 'You've bought tickets for the ferry?'

'Not yet, but—'

'Then don't. I'll take you.'

'But your tourists…'

'I flew them back yesterday. I have the weekend off.'

Her brain worked to find another excuse, but came up empty. 'Oh. But I thought…'

'You thought what?' His eyes bored into hers.

She shook her head, unwilling to say it aloud, terrified she'd burst into tears if she even tried.

Suddenly Mark's car door clicked open, and he unlatched his seat belt.

Panic welled up in her throat as he stepped from the vehicle. *What on earth?*

He hadn't bothered putting on a coat, but crossed the space between them, placing his hand on the top of her car and bending down to look inside. 'Did you think I wouldn't want to take you to Anchorage any more after what happened on Sunday?'

'I…I…assumed it would be easier this way.'

'You assumed wrong.' Mark bent closer, his scent carried to her on a stray current of air. It was warm and familiar, and she thought she'd never be rid of it after their time together. 'It's not easier.'

The intensity of the words sent a shiver over her, even though she had no idea what they meant.

His hand came off the door frame and cupped the back of her head. He stared at her for a long moment before leaning through the window and meeting her lips in a hard kiss.

The surge of need was immediate, flooding her system and overflowing the flimsy barriers she'd tried to erect. A soft sound came from her throat. When his fingers tangled in her messy French braid, his tongue seeking entrance, her breath caught in her lungs.

The kiss was abrupt, harsh, like something he'd tried to keep himself from doing and failed. That alone caused her mouth to open, allowing him in. Because she'd done the same thing. Tried to act indifferent…nonchalant, but her insides were a seething cauldron, emotions bubbling to the surface and sinking back down. And as hard as she fought it, at his touch the tension hissed from her in a tight stream, like a balloon that was stretched to its limit.

Had she put the car in neutral? She wasn't sure and at the moment she didn't care. He invaded her mouth the same way he invaded whatever space he inhabited. And she welcomed the assault, tried to force her way past the barrier of the door, only to have her seat belt restrain her.

Then it was over. He backed off, her lips humiliatingly following his for a half-second longer.

He gave a low laugh that rumbled through her chest as he took a step backward. 'No, it's not easier. Not by a long shot.'

The nightmares had gotten worse, and it was all Sammi's fault. Because they'd gone from nightly reruns of seeing that boy die on his plane to watching a Jeep Sammi was driving hit an IED, shattering into a thousand pieces as he watched it happen in slow motion.

And that IED represented him and his current stupidity. He'd already hurt her once, did he really want to do it again? Mark was no longer the kid he'd once been. The war had marked him. Changed him. And he wasn't sure he could find his way back to 'normal'.

He spent the rest of the day getting his plane ready for their flight, his thoughts a mass of jumbled emotions and regrets. Resting his hand against the metal skin, he shook his head for the hundredth time. He wasn't fit to have a relationship with Sammi or anyone, so kissing her again was tantamount to emotional suicide. But her assurance she was fine and that it was 'easier this way' caused something to snap within him because he'd been through hell and back since their night together, while she'd seemed to have gotten through it with ease.

So that kiss had been as much about seeing her reaction as it had been about needing to touch her again.

Instead of slugging him like the old Sammi might have done, though, she'd made that sexy little sound in the back of her throat and moved into his kiss. The exact same way she'd kissed him when they'd fallen into bed together.

He was screwed. He'd spent the last six months keeping his emotional involvements to a minimum. And he hadn't spent the entire night with a woman in all that time…because he knew what might happen once he fell asleep. There was no way he wanted Sammi—or anyone else—to see him in that condition.

He had to keep his distance.

*Kind of hard when you're committed to flying her back and forth so Toby can visit his father.*

Oh, hell. That also meant Sammi would be alone in that hotel room once again. And exactly where did Mark expect to sleep?

He knew one thing for damned sure.

It wouldn't be in Sammi's bed.

# CHAPTER FIFTEEN

'You have your inhaler?'

A lump caught in Mark's throat as Sammi leant down to kiss Toby's cheek, tension thick in the air. Sammi had been adamant about meeting Brad at their usual place rather than having her ex meet them at the airport, and Mark had insisted on going with her. If the jerk wanted to accuse them of something, it would be in his presence.

Not that the man would be wrong. They *had* been together. For one night. That didn't mean they were routinely getting it on every time Toby was out of his mother's sight…or that it would ever happen again. Besides, Sammi had mentioned Hannah might catch a ride home with them, if the doctors were ready to discharge her, *and* that she'd be staying in Sammi's hotel room tonight. The inference was that he shouldn't hope for a repeat of their last encounter.

And damn if it hadn't sent a wave of disappointment crashing over him.

Sammi was smart, he had to hand it to her. She wasn't taking any chances that he'd have a relapse and end up back in her bed.

It was for the best. He rolled his eyes. Now, if he could only convince that ticking thing in his chest of that.

Brad gathered Toby's stuff and hustled him off to the car with a curt goodbye that made Mark's shoulders tense.

That tension grew when Sammi turned to him with a bright smile. 'Well, I guess that's that. I'm off to the hospital to visit Hannah. Shall we meet at the plane tomorrow afternoon for the return flight?'

'How is she?' He ignored the hint that she wanted to get away from him as fast as she could.

'The doctor's going to check her over this afternoon and hopefully release her.'

'Does that seem likely?'

'Unless something changes.' She hesitated. 'She'll still have to rest at home for a few weeks.'

That meant Sammi would still be all alone at the clinic, something he'd hoped wouldn't happen. There were already tell-tale smudges of exhaustion beneath her eyes that would only get worse.

'Can I help?' The words were out before he could stop them.

'What do you mean?'

'How are you going to handle the clinic by yourself?'

'The same way Dr. Stevers used to handle it. It's only for a couple of weeks.'

Was she kidding? Paul Stevers, the general practitioner who'd single-handedly manned the clinic when they'd been kids, had died of a heart attack at age fifty-five.

'You're a mother, Sammi. Is that really fair to Toby?'

She popped her chin into the air, eyes flashing. 'I know exactly what I am. I don't need you—or anyone else—reminding me.'

A clear reference to her argument with Brad last week.

'Hey, I'm sorry.' He took a step closer, his fingers curving around her upper arms to encourage her to look at him.

'I'm worried about you, that's all. I wasn't trying to imply anything about your parenting skills. You've done an awesome job with Toby. Everyone can see that.'

She squinched her nose. 'Ugh. Sorry for snapping. I don't know what's wrong with me.'

'Don't worry about it.' He stroked a finger down the length of her nose, teasing out the crinkles. 'Listen, why don't you let me take you to the hospital? Afterwards, if Hannah feels up to it, I can take you both out to eat and drop you off at the hotel room. That is, if you don't already have plans.'

'Hannah will still be pretty sore from her surgery, I imagine.' She eased back, forcing him to release her.

The emptiness collecting in his chest was just from the cold air hitting where her warmth had rested. He was almost sure of it. And if Hannah wasn't well enough to leave the hospital or go out to eat, that let him off the hook.

Instead of relief, however, he was filled with a sense of longing he hadn't felt in a very long time.

Not since the day he'd left Dutch Harbor eight years ago.

On Wednesday morning, the red heart on her calendar glared at her from across the kitchen.

'It's only one day,' she muttered, taking her cereal bowl and moving to the two-person dinette.

'What is?' Toby was already there, slurping down the contents of his dish.

'Can we be a little quieter when we eat?' Maybe she could distract him, because no way was she talking to a six-year-old about late periods.

*One day.*

She'd been late before.

'Sorry.' He proceeded to finish with a little more delicacy until the end, when he held up the bowl with a questioning look.

Sammi laughed. 'Go ahead, since it's the only way I can get you to drink milk.'

Up went the bowl to Toby's lips, where he emptied it. Setting it back on the table, he grinned. 'It tastes like cereal this way.'

Kids were inventive, she'd give them that. If you wouldn't give them chocolate milk to drink in the morning, they'd find a work-around. Human nature never changed.

There was no way she could be pregnant. They'd used a condom. And Mark had pulled away with a rueful grin when she'd reached for him again. A no-more-supplies explanation followed by a quick kiss to the mouth had softened the rejection.

She'd been tempted to chuck caution to the wind, but his actions had been surprisingly responsible, something she might not have given the 'new' Mark credit for. Maybe he wasn't as reckless as he'd seemed in recent months.

The thought wasn't something she wanted to dwell on. It was a whole lot easier to cast him in the role of villain and stay well away from him than to wonder if there were deeper motives for his actions.

For leaving the island all those years ago.

Uh, yeah. He'd wanted to join the military. And he hadn't wanted *her*. That was all she needed to know.

She ate quickly, needing to get Toby off to school and head to the clinic. They were both going to be late if she didn't get a move on.

*And what if you are...late?* the little voice whispered in the back of her head, renewing the panic she'd awoken to this morning.

*Stress.*

It wasn't as if she wasn't under a ton of it nowadays. First there had been Toby's asthma attack, then Hannah's accident.

And then there'd been that lovemaking with Mark. World-altering.

Possibly in a more literal sense.

*No, it was impossible.* She'd taken every precaution.

Actually, Mark had. But she was smart enough to know that one in every fifty condom-alone users would get pregnant. She should have taken some precautions of her own. But she wasn't sexually active.

She still wasn't. So what were the odds?

*This is you we're talking about, Sammi. Since when have your odds ever been good? Your mom married a womanizer and then you followed in her footsteps and let yourself get charmed into bed by one.*

Except she could swear Mark hadn't done that. He hadn't set out to make her one of his conquests. In fact, after that day in her hotel room, he'd not given any indication that he'd be interested in a repeat. Except for that amazing kiss beside her car last week.

That had flipped her tummy inside out.

It was why she'd asked Hannah to fly back to Dutch Harbor with them. It was a whole lot easier not to send off some kind of weird needy vibes if she had another adult along for the ride.

She sent Toby to brush his teeth while she gathered up the dishes and loaded them in her old rattletrap of a dishwasher that she somehow kept nursing along. It needed to be replaced, as did her refrigerator, but she just didn't have the money. Not with Toby's chronic condition and the co-pay on his inhalers.

And if she was pregnant…

*Oh, Lord.*

Her hand went to her stomach for a second, shoving back the quick flash of hope. No way did she want Mark's baby. It was crazy thinking.

Was there some kind of stupid gene that could be passed down from mother to daughter?

No, and it wasn't nice to think of her mother in those terms. She'd grown so much since divorcing her father and becoming a grandmother. It seemed she was trying to right all the mistakes of her past. And doing a damned good job of it. Sammi could honestly say she was proud of her mom in a way she'd never been as a teenager or young adult.

*You'll start your period tomorrow.*

With that positive affirmation ringing in her head, she ran Toby to school then turned her tiny car toward the clinic.

Lynn was already there, as was Hannah.

'What the hell do you think you're doing?' she asked the PA.

'Working?'

'Um…no. You had surgery less than two weeks ago. Car accident…punctured lung…broken rib? Does any of this ring a bell?'

Hannah straightened some charts behind the reception desk, moving slowly and carefully. 'I'm bored out of my skull at home. I need to do something besides dwell on my aches and pains.'

Words Sammi could definitely relate to. She'd been relieved to come to work herself, so she could keep her mind off her own emotional aches and pains.

*And if you are pregnant?*

What was she going to do about Mark? Tell him?

Uh…yeah. It was the right thing to do. Besides, it wasn't

like she was playing leapfrog over the line of guys waiting to take her out. He'd know the baby was his the second she started showing.

She could move away and take Toby with her.

Again, that wouldn't be fair to Mark. She would never keep a child's father from knowing the truth, no matter how awkward things might become. She had no doubt that Mark wanted nothing to do with kids. Why else would he still be single? He was over thirty, and even though that was well within the time range for children nowadays, he didn't seem interested. He'd always seemed kind of uncomfortable around Toby, in fact.

Her hand went unconsciously to her stomach again.

'Are you feeling okay?'

She realized she'd zoned out and that Hannah and Lynn were both staring at her with concerned eyes. 'I'm fine. It's just been a crazy morning.'

Hannah came around the desk and touched her arm. 'I know you've been having to do a lot of extra work, so why don't you take the day off.'

'Didn't we just talk about that broken rib a few minutes ago?'

'I'm fine, just a little tender. Besides, it feels better when I'm on my feet than when I'm sitting down or lying in bed.'

'And if some excited little kid wants to give you a bear hug?'

Hannah's face paled, and Lynn stepped up. 'I'll help with the kids. She can just tell me what to do. I know how to take temperatures and blood pressure. All she has to do is sign her name on the prescription pad. Besides, it's been slow the last couple of days—you said so yourself yesterday.'

Before Sammi could refuse again, the PA insisted, saying, 'Please, Sammi. Let me at least sit behind the desk so I have someone to talk to.' Hannah and Lynn exchanged a meaningful glance.

'I don't know...'

Lynn made a shooing motion with her hands. 'If we get into trouble we'll call someone from the clinic across town. Go have fun while Toby is in school. Or take a nap, whatever sounds good.'

'I think I will, then. Thanks.' She glanced at Hannah. 'I'll have my cellphone, if you need anything.'

'We won't, but thanks.'

The first patient of the day, sporting a cut on her finger, pushed through the double doors and Lynn scooted behind the desk, greeting her and taking down pertinent information. Hannah took Sammi's arm and edged her toward the exit. 'Go before you change your mind. I'll call you if we need you.'

She zipped up her jacket and headed across the parking lot just as Mark pulled up. Her heart lurched, and her steps faltered. Then she sucked down a deep breath and walked over to his car. 'Everything okay?'

'Yep, just wanted to let you know I was flying a pair of tourists over to Umnak. Do you want to come?' He opened the door and got out.

That was strange. Why would he think she was off today?

'Um, I'm not sure I should.'

'Do you have to work?'

'No.'

'So, come with me.' Shoving his hands into the pockets of his jeans, he rocked back on his heels. 'I only have two passengers, so I have some extra room. You could do a little sightseeing. Get away from the clinic for a while.'

'I don't know. I have to be home when Toby gets out of school at four.'

'I told the Parnells I'd have them back by dinner. So that's just about the right time. You could call your mom, if it looks like it's going to be late.'

She hesitated. She hadn't been to Umnak in ages, and she had been putting in a lot of extra hours the last couple of weeks. Sightseeing did sound like fun…and there would be chaperons along for the ride. 'Let me check and make sure she's okay with watching Toby, just in case.'

Mark reached through the window and turned off his engine as she dialed the number. Her mom answered on the second ring.

'Hello?'

'Mom?' Why did this seem so awkward all of a sudden? *Just blurt it out.* 'I'm thinking of flying over to Umnak with Mark and a couple other people. I should be home by the time Toby gets out, but just in case—'

'You're going with Mark?' There was a pause, then her mom's voice came back on the line. 'Oh, that's right. I'd almost forgotten. You should go. I'll be at your house when the Tobe-man gets off. If you're already home, maybe we can order a pizza and watch a movie. If you're not, we'll be fine.'

'Are you sure?' Something about her mom's voice made her uneasy. First Mark was acting strangely, and now her mom.

'Of course I am. It's about time you went out with young men your own age.'

'Oh, uh…' She snuck a panicked glance at Mark. 'It's just as friends.'

A slight frown appeared between his brows. Heaven only knew what he thought her mother had said. It was

kind of hard to call them friends after the night they'd
spent together two weeks ago. With what might be growing inside her.

She quickly signed off, promising to call her mother if
she was late or if their plans changed. To her relief, Mark
said nothing once she ended the call.

'Do you want to leave your car here, or should I follow you home?'

Safer to leave the vehicle at the clinic, since her house
was empty. She didn't want to go over there, knowing that.
Mark might be above temptation, but she, obviously, was
not. She was still hopeful her period might start soon, so
she already had some supplies tucked into her purse, just
in case.

'We can go straight to the airport, if you don't mind
dropping me off here when we get back.'

'No problem.'

The pair of tourists was already there when they arrived. Young and obviously in love, the couple held hands
and did a whole lot of whispering. That meant Sammi
was stuck in the co-pilot's seat, since there was no way
the young lovers were going to want to be separated. She
sighed as she strapped herself in. As if he knew exactly
what she was thinking, Mark gave her a quick smile, one
brow lifted in question. 'We're going to do a water landing. One of the boats will meet us in the bay.'

'Why? There's an airstrip on Umnak.'

Mark pushed buttons and pulled levers and glanced
back toward his other passengers. She got what he was saying. The customers wanted to see what a real amphibian
plane landing was like. Sammi couldn't blame them. If
she were in their shoes, she'd probably opt for the same.

'Sounds like fun.' Ha! Then why did her voice sound so glum?

He radioed the tower that they were ready for take-off and got the okay. Taxiing into position, they waited behind another plane, which was next on the line-up. Soon they were in the air, leaving the island behind them.

Flying had always been something Sammi loved, she just didn't get to do it very often. The fact that they could be somewhere in an hour that would have taken three or more by boat still amazed her. So much so that small planes like Mark's didn't faze her.

She stared at the clouds as they passed through them and then leaned over to look at the ocean once they were in the clear. The deep silver water glinted up at her, the whitecaps barely visible from their height. 'It's so beautiful up here. It looks like something out of a movie.'

'I like it too.' His smile was warmer than it had been in recent days. Her system responded with an answering heat.

The man in the back spoke up. 'How long is the flight again?'

'About an hour. Not enough time for our flight attendant to serve drinks, I'm afraid.'

Sammi sent him a glare, thinking at first he meant her, but the passengers' laughter made her realize he was just joking.

*Calm down.*

'You said the village is small?' The woman, who'd introduced herself as Nancy, asked.

'There are about thirty-nine folks, I think. It's struggling to stay alive, like several of the more remote islands. A lot of the young people have already moved to Anchorage or Unalaska—the island where Sammi and I live. But it's beautiful. The volcano will make some nice background photos.'

*The island where Sammi and I live.* Those words made an ache settle in her chest. If things had been different, she and Mark could have been like this young couple. Toby could have been...

No. If she and Mark had stayed together, there would be no Toby.

He glanced at her, something dark coming and going in his eyes. It was almost as if he could read her thoughts. Heat rushed to her face, and she turned to look out the window in case her cheeks were as pink as they felt.

His voice came again. 'There are no cars, so we'll be walking once we're back on land.'

'Understood. Thanks for agreeing to take us.'

'My pleasure.'

Those low words washed over her, and Sammi closed her eyes, pressing her forehead against the icy glass next to her. The chill soon cooled her off enough to face forward again without fearing she'd give herself away.

Despite the awkward silences that fell between the two of them from time to time, the flight passed quickly, and before she knew it they were swooping towards the bay.

Once they landed, the choppy waters rocked the small plane in a quick *one-two...pause* rhythm that she feared might make her seasick, but thankfully she could already see a boat being launched from shore. Someone was waiting for their arrival, just like Mark had said.

He turned to her. 'Once we're on land, do you think you could go somewhere with me? I have an errand to run.'

'An errand?' What could he possibly have to do on the tiny island?

'Yep. I talked to a friend here. She has something I

thought Toby might like.' He smiled. 'Don't worry, I've already cleared it with your mother. I promised her I'd make it a surprise.'

# CHAPTER SIXTEEN

WOULD she kill him?

Mark sincerely hoped not. He wasn't just doing this for Sammi and Toby, he was also doing it to help a fallen comrade-in-arms. Or at least that comrade's wife.

Sammi's mother—who'd been surprisingly cordial on the phone—had assured him that Toby had always wanted one, and that Sammi had actually looked into the possibility. She just hadn't been able to scrape together the funds yet. So Mark had decided to take matters into his own hands. He just hoped he was doing the right thing in making this trip with her.

The dreams about Sammi had eased over the past week, and he attributed that to the distance he'd kept between them. But he hadn't been able to pass up this opportunity.

If he believed in fate, he might think his father's death meant he and Sammi could finally be together, but it seemed like fate had thrown yet another spanner in the works. It wasn't safe for him to be with Sammi or anyone right now.

No matter how much he might want it.

He'd accepted the fact that this was one woman he'd regret letting slip through his fingers, which was why he'd been very careful to keep recent relationships superficial. Nothing got under his skin nowadays.

Okay, maybe *one* thing. But it was the very thing he couldn't have.

The trip to shore was a little rougher than he'd expected, and he glanced back at his plane, which was still bobbing in place. One of the village men had promised to keep an eye on it and Mark had handed him a walkie-talkie so they could keep in touch, just in case. The villager knew his plans and had already called ahead to let Vonnie know they were on their way.

Sammi sat across the boat, huddled into her coat, looking a bit on the greenish side. He remembered she wasn't a big fan of the water, but she was being pretty stoic about it. She'd leapt onto the dinghy without complaint and had hunkered down in a seat.

He leaned across. 'You okay?'

'Peachy.' Her eyes told a different story. She was wondering what the heck she was doing here. Hopefully she'd soon realize why he'd asked. Even the girls at the clinic had been in on it, making sure Sammi was told in no uncertain terms that she was not welcome at work today. He couldn't believe she'd given in without a fight, though.

The bottom of the boat scraped against shore and the owner got out to drag it a few yards further. Mark glanced at Sammi's feet, relieved to see she had on some sturdy boots. It was one thing he hadn't thought about when he'd planned this crazy outing.

'You two have everything you need?' he asked the pair in the back of the boat.

'Yep. Camera, coffee and a packed lunch.' The man patted his backpack.

'Pick a sheltered spot, since it gets pretty nippy this time of year.' Nippy was an understatement. He and Sammi would be eating at Vonnie's, but he'd given a third walkie-talkie to the pair, telling them to make sure they kept in contact and to call immediately if they got into trouble.

Once off the boat, the lovebirds took off gloved hand in gloved hand, leaving Mark and Sammi alone on the shore.

Sammi shoved her hands into the pockets of her jacket, glancing with suspicion at his backpack. 'What's this errand you were talking about?'

'I told Vonnie I'd stop in and hang a light for her.'

'Vonnie?' Her brows puckered.

'Donald's sister. You remember him from school?'

'No, I don't... Wait, little Donny Mosely?'

'Yep. His sister moved to Umnak when she got married.'

Her face cleared. 'She's married.'

'Widowed. Her husband died in Afghanistan six months ago, why?' He'd attended his friend's memorial service in Anchorage—one more child left without a father. So many deaths.

'He died? I'm so sorry.' She hesitated. 'I thought you said this trip had something to do with Toby.'

'It does, but you have to promise you're not going to get mad.'

Her feet stopped moving. 'What's going on, Mark?'

'Like I said, it's a surprise.'

Not only did she not start walking again, her hands went to her hips. 'What kind of surprise?'

He took hold of her wrist and started walking, leaving her no choice but to tag along. 'If I told you, it wouldn't be a surprise.'

'I don't even know Vonnie, so I don't understand.'

'If you keep dragging your feet, you're never going to find out, are you?'

'Have I ever told you I hate surprises?'

Did she? That wasn't a good sign. Grace could have told him she might not agree to it before he'd put down a deposit. But if she didn't want it, he'd take it for himself. That way the boy would still get some enjoyment from it, even if it was at Mark's house rather than Sammi's. Although why he thought Sammi would allow Toby to come over was still a little fuzzy in his head.

But at least she was walking next to him willingly, now. Somehow he couldn't bring himself to drop her hand, and she made no move to yank free of his grip. Instead, he threaded his fingers through hers, a strange feeling of rightness again coming over him. He could still remember when he and Sammi had taken walks by the stream in Unalaska, high on the mountain. Just the two of them. And the intimate kisses in the shadow of the salmonberry bushes.

*Better not to remember things like that.*

They were soon at Vonnie's tiny house and already he could hear sounds of barking coming from the back. The door was flung open, and Vonnie stood in the doorway, her burgeoning abdomen sending a shock wave through him.

She hadn't mentioned being pregnant at the memorial service. It must have happened just before Greg had shipped out. He'd been killed within two months of leaving the States. How terrible that the father would never know the joy of seeing his child's birth.

'Oh.' Sammi's quiet murmur came from beside him, her hand reflexively going to her own stomach.

He swallowed, trying not to put her in Vonnie's place and imagine what it might be like to come home to find her waiting in the doorway, her abdomen just as swollen with child. Except that image soon morphed into that of a young child, who bled out while he watched helplessly.

No kids for him. Not now. Not ever. They were not on his bucket list.

'Mark. You're right on time.' Vonnie's low voice was filled with welcome and a small boy appeared next to her legs. The child couldn't have been older than two or three. 'This is Aaron.'

Mark swallowed hard, trying not to think of Greg or the milestones his friend would be missing in his children's lives. He nodded toward Sammi and introduced her as well. Then he got to the point. 'You have a light for me to hang?'

'Yes.' She held the door open for them to pass through. 'But that's really enough payment for the puppy.'

His eyes went to Sammi's face. She was staring at him, her mouth opening and then closing, her teeth catching her lower lip.

He squeezed her hand before releasing it. '*That* was the surprise. Vonnie's dog had a litter of pups not too long ago, and she needed to find homes for them. I asked her to hold one in the hope that you'd accept it. For Toby.' He kept the money situation to himself.

'A puppy?' A smile started to form before it slid away. 'But, I can't...I couldn't.'

His fingers swept across her cheek, the skin smooth and silky to the touch. 'It'll be good for the boy to have a dog of his own. Please don't say no.'

She leaned into his hand. 'I won't. Thank you.'

Vonnie beamed. 'You can have your pick. They're chocolate Labs. I have two males and a female left in the litter.'

'Can I see them?' Sammi's voice held a hint of wonder, and Mark knew it was going to be all right. She was going to accept. If not for herself then for her child.

'Of course you can.' Aaron latched onto his mother's hand, popping his thumb into his mouth as he glanced from one to the other.

Vonnie led the way to the back of the house, through a closed door that passed through the kitchen. Behind a white child gate stood a beautiful Lab, her fur a glossy mahogany color that matched soft, liquid eyes. The animal gave a muted woof, her thick tail wagging back and forth. 'I have to keep them back here so Aaron doesn't bother them. He'd sleep with the little ones if he could.'

Reaching over the barrier, Vonnie stroked the dog's silky head. 'Her name is Brenda. She's wonderful with all people and with children especially. I imagine her pups will be the same.'

Sammi moved beside the woman and petted the animal. 'Hi, girl. Aren't you a beauty?'

The dog's tail made loud thumping sounds as it struck a nearby wall with each and every wag, making the little boy squeal in delight. Vonnie laughed. 'That's her only downside. Her tail is a lethal weapon. She knocks over everything in reach. And if you get hit by it, it stings.'

Mark could well imagine. The animal's tail was thick and muscular, a classic sign of the breed, from what he'd read.

Vonnie unlatched the gate and, instead of barreling in and knocking the child over, Brenda came into the room and sat right in front of Aaron, her head lifting with a whine as if asking him to give her a pat. The child obliged and then wrapped his thin arms around her neck. The dog sighed and almost seemed to smile. Mark's chest tightened.

'The puppies are just inside. The males are normal sized, but the female is a runt. She's healthy but pretty small. She also has one ear that cocks up higher than the other.'

As soon as Sammi knelt in the midst of three brown squirming bodies, Mark knew which puppy she was going to choose. The female was in her arms in an instant, lapping at Sammi's face with little yips of excitement, her whole back end moving in time with her tail.

Vonnie peered round the corner and smiled. 'She's not worth as much as the other two as she's never going to be up to show standards, but she's as cute as a button.'

'She's perfect for Toby.' Sammi snuggled the pup closer.

Mark had to blink back the rush of emotion that came with the words. Sammi's awed voice said it all. Her son, who railed at his asthma, could learn so much from a dog that was considered less than perfect in some eyes.

But what about a man who was less than perfect? A man who had scars and nightmares and who still cringed at sudden sounds? Who had trouble looking at children like Aaron and Toby without remembering another child who would never grow up?

But while the puppy might be every bit as valuable as her two more robust siblings in Sammi's eyes and would become a wonderful companion, Mark wouldn't. He was missing some important pieces. He doubted he'd be a suitable companion for anyone.

Watching the two of them together, though, it was hard to make himself accept that fact.

'Is she old enough to leave her mother?'

Vonnie nodded. 'She's eight weeks old and weaned. I've already found homes for three of her littermates.'

He needed to get working on that light, before Sammi noticed his face. 'Where's that fixture you wanted hung?'

'Oh, it's in the living room. I've set a toolbox in there

as well.' She glanced from one to the other. 'Would you like some coffee first?'

'Maybe in a little while.' He nodded toward Sammi. 'I think you're going to have to prise her out of there.'

Vonnie rubbed her tummy. 'I'm hoping to find them all homes before the baby comes.'

That's right. She was going to be all alone with a young child and a new baby. 'Your parents?'

'They're in Anchorage.' She bowed her head. 'I'll be moving back there once… I should have left earlier, but I just couldn't bring myself to say goodbye to this place. Greg and I worked hard on this home.'

'I'm sorry, Vonnie.'

She gave him a watery smile. 'I knew what I was getting into when I married him. We had three good years together before he was called to active duty.'

Unlike he and Sammi, who'd never gotten a real shot at happiness.

With one last glance at Sammi and the puppies, he pulled in deep breath. 'Why don't you show me the light fixture.'


Seated at the dinette table with a cup of coffee in front of her, Sammi smiled at the puppy curled up in her lap. The second she'd tried to put the young dog back in its bed with the others, the tiny animal had lifted her head and howled, glancing at Sammi out of the corner of her eye. She'd laughed and picked her up again, carrying the puppy with her into the kitchen. 'Don't think you're going to get this kind of treatment once you get home.'

The dog's ears perked as if to say, We'll see about that.

Mark was in the other room, balanced on top of a ladder, installing a new pendant light Vonnie's parents had sent for the house. 'Your light is going to be really pretty.'

'Much better than the bare bulb I've had hanging there for the last year.' Instead of coffee, the other woman nursed a glass of milk.

Sammi tried not to stare at her midsection, but it was impossible. Was that what she was going to look like eight months down the road?

No, because she was not pregnant. She'd even been snippy this morning with Mark. That had to prove she was heading for that time of the month. She'd never been really crabby or PMS-y, but right now she was willing to grab at any straw she could find.

Her hand headed for her tummy, something she'd found herself doing several times today, but she stopped it.

*This is ridiculous. You're not pregnant!*

Every time she repeated that mantra, something inside her shifted. Mourned for something that could never be.

Damn. What was wrong with her? If it had been with anyone else, she would have been horrified at the possibility.

And she was. But this was Mark. Someone she'd known since her childhood days. Someone she'd grown up with, laughed with…loved. Someone she…

Her throat grew tight as a sudden suffocating realization swept through her.

*No. It can't be.*

But it was.

She was in love with Mark. A man who'd left without a backward glance eight years ago and had gone the speed-dating route in the six months he'd been back.

Only she hadn't heard rumors of him going out with

*anyone* in the last month or two. And he'd blown off the nurse at the hospital. Why was that?

She listened to him work in the other room and tried to produce an ounce or two of self-righteous anger, but she couldn't. Because this was a man who cared enough about a pregnant widow to hang a light fixture for her. Who'd bought an IV warmer just because she had mentioned doing without. Who'd not only thought of Toby when he'd heard about this litter of puppies but had schemed with her mother and her colleagues to bring her on this outing. He'd brought warm donuts to her hotel room without being asked—had expressed outrage when he thought someone might have harmed her. And when he found out that no one had, had held her and…

*Loved her.*

She took a big gulp of her coffee, the liquid now cool, but she needed something to wash down the expanding lump that seemed stuck in her gullet.

And what was she going to do if she was indeed pregnant? Mark couldn't commit to a snowdrop if he were a snowman, so how in the world did she expect him to stick around to raise a child? And would she even want him to hang around for a reason like that?

No. If it came down to it, she'd raise this child on her own. She'd done it with Toby, she could do it again. And Vonnie was living proof that women were strong enough to handle just about anything.

Just then a rattling noise came from the living room, followed by a shout and then the sound of glass shattering. The adult dog rushed to the other room, while the pup in Sammi's lap lifted her head and whined softly.

After a split second of shock Sammi leaped up, holding the puppy in her arms, while Vonnie prised herself from her chair.

'Mark!'

A groan came from the other room.

Cradling the puppy, she hurried to the doorway, Vonnie right beside her.

Her free hand went to her throat just as Vonnie grabbed her dog's collar to prevent her from venturing further into the room. Sammi saw why in an instant.

The pendant light was up and lit, the glow from the light bulb making the linoleum floor glitter as if covered with thousands of tiny diamonds. Mark lay among them, gripping one of his arms.

Glass! Everywhere.

She spied the broken coffee table and overturned ladder. 'Oh, God, Mark, are you okay? What happened?'

'The boy! Where is he?' His glazed eyes latched onto hers. 'Have to stop the bleeding...too much blood.'

Sammi blinked, the panicked words making no sense. She then realized he was probably asking about Vonnie's son. 'Aaron's playing in his room, it's okay.'

It was as if she hadn't spoken. Mark gazed right through her, the expression on his face sending a chill through her. 'Ahmed! He's bleeding.'

It was then that something dripped off Mark's elbow and pinged silently against the floor, joining countless other drops that had already fallen. More were diving into the growing pool, the unmistakable scent of iron finally reaching her nose.

Blood. Lots of it.

# CHAPTER SEVENTEEN

'I DON'T need stitches.' Mark's stubborn voice repeated the phrase.

Back at the plane, Sammi tamped down her rising exasperation. But it was better than the raw terror she'd felt when Mark had spouted off stuff that made no sense. He'd recovered within a couple of minutes, insisting he'd just been stunned from the fall.

She wasn't so sure. Yes, the names Ahmed and Aaron both started with the same letter, but there was no way in hell she'd confuse the two. She'd even checked Mark for a head injury, thinking he might have a concussion, but there was no sign of anything but the cut on his arm. Nothing that could explain what had happened in that living room.

'I think I know better than you do when a wound needs to be closed,' she snapped.

'You are not sewing me up. Just slap a butterfly on it, and I'll be good to go.'

'You're being ridiculous. It's in the crook of your elbow, Mark. If I don't suture it, you'll just keep opening it back up every time you bend your arm. The last thing you need is to have it get infected or not heal properly.' She reached for him. 'Besides, I want to look at it a little more closely.'

The puppy, safely tucked into an extra dog crate Vonnie

had on hand, whined. Sammi sighed. 'See? Even she knows you need stitches. Now, hop on the stretcher.'

Mark rolled his eyes, but did as she asked. He still seemed tense and distracted. 'It's only a little cut.'

Unwinding the bandages, which turned more and more crimson with every layer she removed, she glared at him. 'A little cut? I've seen some pretty nasty injuries caused by falls through glass tables.'

'I forgot the coffee table was behind the ladder. When I stepped off it, I caught the edge, and...' He shrugged. 'It broke.'

She bent over his arm. 'So did you. You're lucky you didn't slice through something important. Do you know how many nerves and vessels are located in this area?'

'No, but I'm sure you're about to enlighten me.'

His glare was acid, but in reality Sammi was relieved. The old Mark had returned with a vengeance.

She studied the wound. He'd cut all the way through his skin, revealing the rich red muscle tissue below but, despite the continued bleeding, nothing was spurting. 'Bend your fingers.'

Mark made a fist. 'Don't you think you're overreacting just a little?'

*About this, or about that flight of fancy you went on a little while ago?*

'No. And if I even suspect ligament or nerve damage, we're heading straight to Anchorage.'

'I have tourists to take back to Dutch Harbor, in case you've forgotten. In fact, they're due back in a couple of hours.'

'Then let me do my job, so you can do yours.' She didn't argue with him, but if this was serious, she wasn't going to wait around. They could radio the tourists and tell them to hightail it back in. Although asking Mark to fly a plane with a bad injury was suicidal. If she thought he was critical, she'd call for help. Blake could be here in four hours, if need be.

Laying a clean piece of gauze over the wound, she kept pressure on it as she assessed his tactile senses, making sure the nerves were still intact. She pressed one of his fingers with her free hand. 'Can you feel that?'

His white face and pinched lips turned in her direction. 'If you mean can I feel the cloth you're grinding into my cut, then damn straight. I feel it.'

'Sorry. I'll give you something for the pain in a minute.' She knew it hurt. But she hadn't wanted to inject him with lidocaine until she was sure she could do the stitching herself. She didn't want to cause any more damage than the glass had already done.

Keeping her voice calm, and her eyes on her work, she couldn't help but ask. 'Who's Ahmed?'

'Excuse me?'

'Ahmed. You called out his name when you were on the floor.'

He tried to pull his arm away, but she grabbed his wrist and held tight.

'I don't know what you're talking about.'

When she glanced into his face, she noted the bunched muscles in his jaw, the way his lips had thinned.

He was lying. He knew exactly who she was talking about, and it wasn't Vonnie's little boy.

'Mark?'

'Leave it alone.'

She sighed. He wasn't going to tell her anything. It was there in the stubborn set to his chin, the tight words.

'Fine, then take off your shirt.'

He finally met her gaze. 'I'm sorry?'

'Your sleeves are long and it's hard to maneuver around them.' She wasn't going to pry. From here on out, she'd show him nothing but professional interest.

'Right.' He helped her peel off the black sweater, the blood soaking his right sleeve not noticeable. Good thing. The tourist couple might be freaked out if they could see what Mark had done to himself.

She clenched her teeth, trying to remember her resolve as taut skin and toned muscle came into view, but the heat level in her tummy rose about ten degrees. Easing the piece of gauze away, she studied the injury itself. It was still oozing, but it was no longer dripping like it had been at Vonnie's when he'd talked about stopping the bleeding. About two inches long, the gash ran part way along the crease of his elbow and wrapped around to the outside. A piece of glass must have followed the curve of his arm as he'd gone down, because it hadn't sliced straight through to deeper tissues. He didn't know how lucky he was.

'I think it'll take seven or eight stitches. You okay with me doing them?'

'Come on, Sam. Are you sure this is necessary?'

'Yes. Are *you* going to make this as difficult as possible?'

One side of his mouth curved up, some of the tautness easing from his jaw, 'It's what I seem to be good at.'

'No kidding.' She grumbled the words while digging around for the supplies she needed, but underneath the growl a bit of her panic finally subsided. He could keep his secrets as long as he really was okay.

Sammi found everything then laid them beside Mark. 'I need to sterilize the area before I give the injection so I don't push any bacteria into your system. It's going to sting a bit.' Tipping the bottle, she sluiced alcohol over the wound, hearing his muffled curse as the liquid washed across his skin.

'You just want me to suffer as much as possible.'

For being so mean to her a little while ago? Yeah... maybe. 'What, a big bad navy pilot can't take a little sting?'

'Oh, I can take the little ones. It's the big ones that get to me.' Something dark peeked around the corners of his eyes, then sank back into the depths.

Her laughter died in her throat, and she drew some lidocaine into a syringe. 'You might want to look away. It makes it easier.'

'It really doesn't.' Again, there was something in the words that made her uneasiness come back in full force.

Was he talking about his father, and what the man had done to him? His time in the service?

*Ahmed.* The name whispered through her mind like puff of air then faded away.

Blake had never mentioned anything happening to Mark but, then she wasn't really sure they discussed those kinds of things, even within their own ranks. Shaking off the feeling, she slid the needle into the cut and pushed the plunger, working it slowly back out as she did. She repeated the stick a couple more times, never once feeling him wince as she did, even though he'd complained about the alcohol not three minutes earlier.

Maybe she should put in a call to Blake and see if the name Ahmed rang a bell, or if he knew anything.

She immediately dismissed it. Would Mark really appreciate her digging into something he was so reluctant to talk about?

Hardly.

Once she was satisfied he wouldn't feel anything, she

threaded the suture material through the tiny needle and started closing the injury, taking her time and making sure she lined each flap of skin up as best she could. 'You're going to have a little scar, sorry.'

'Plenty more where that came from.' This time it wasn't her imagination. She'd definitely heard a hint of bitterness in his voice as he'd said it. You'd think he had tons of the things. But she'd studied every inch of that gleaming bronzed skin as they'd made love and aside from a single sickle-shaped scar marring the hard flesh of his left pec, he was about as good as they came. So if it wasn't a physical scar, what was it? Emotional?

Mark didn't seem like the type of man to dwell on what had happened to him as a child. Yes, his father had been a piece of work, but Mark had been able to function in school. And he'd never had an episode like the one in Vonnie's living room.

Her eyes widened. Neither had he ever gotten that haunted look he'd had when Hannah had been injured. He'd frozen up then as well.

Damn. So many questions. But she didn't dare ask.

She finished stitching him up as quickly as she could and tied the last knot, checking her work. Not bad. It should heal cleanly. 'You'll want to come into the clinic in a week to have those taken back out.'

'I'll just take them out myself.'

She moved around in front of him until he met her eyes. 'Don't. You. Dare.'

He laughed, and the sound made her nerves again settle into place. 'Okay, Doc. Point taken.'

'Good.'

Setting her instruments into a metal tray then dropping the whole thing into a plastic bag to be sterilized later, she wet a clean piece of gauze and gently scrubbed the caked blood from his elbow, sliding the cloth down his forearm as she followed the trail. She did the same with his hand, dipping in and around each finger, leaning close to check for more places the stuff had dripped. 'Almost done.'

'Sam.'

The low murmured sound of her name caused her to glance up at him. 'What?'

There was no hint of the man who'd sent her into a panic an hour earlier. Instead, the Mark from the hotel room was back, eyes burning. 'I think you've done enough.'

It was then she realized his pupils had widened, almost obliterating the green of his irises. Before she fully absorbed his meaning, his uninjured hand came up and cupped the back of her head, fingers easing through her hair.

Her voice came out as a squeak when his meaning hit her. 'My patients don't normally react this way to getting stitches.'

'No?' The one syllable held a wealth of meaning. 'How do they react?'

'Mostly by groaning. Moaning. Sometimes cursing.'

He chuckled again. 'You're not helping me here, Sam. I can imagine myself doing each and every one of those things. For very different reasons.'

With that, he tugged her head down until her lips were a breath away from his. 'But for now I have a better idea. Let's see exactly which of those I can make *you* do.'

Mark heard the ooing and ahhing from the back of the plane as the tourists played with Sammi's new puppy. But his attention wasn't on what was happening in the back but what was going on in the seat beside his.

Sammi couldn't seem to get comfortable, shifting from side to side, looking anywhere but at him.

It made him feel like a first-class bastard. He wouldn't tell her about Ahmed when she'd asked, but he'd had no qualms about kissing her…and more. What was worse was that he'd pulled her towards him partially to stop her from probing further, but things had spiraled out of control. Just like they had in Vonnie's living room.

The second he'd seen the blood on the floor, the horrific scene from the back of his chopper had come to mind. He couldn't even remember what he'd said, but he must have said the boy's name…scared Sam enough to make the name stick.

Why couldn't he tell her?

Because it would be tantamount to voicing aloud what he'd never admitted even to himself: that he was having trouble dealing with what had happened on his plane that day. Yes, his dreams had eased, and he hadn't had one about Sam in almost a week. But it was as if his mind was playing a cruel joke, pulling back on a stretched rubber band and then letting it snap when he least expected it.

If he even suspected his flying would be affected or that he was putting people in danger, he'd stop going up. But the air was the one place where his concentration was so fixed on the tasks needing completion that it left no room for anything else.

What was he doing?

He'd made love to her. On his plane. And while it didn't quite qualify for the mile-high club, he was pretty sure he'd floated higher than that afterwards.

And it made him edgy. Because he had no idea what Sammi was thinking. Almost as soon as she'd caught her breath, she'd been clearing away the remainder of the medical materials she'd used while stitching his elbow, leaving him seated on the stretcher unable to move a muscle.

'Hey,' he said through the headset, knowing that while she could hear him, his passengers couldn't. 'Are you okay?'

*Shift. Shift. Shift.*

It took a full minute for her to actually turn and look at him. 'Fine.' Her face colored, glancing at the seats a few yards behind theirs. 'You don't think they know, do you?'

His gaze fell to the collar of her shirt and the mark hidden just beneath the fabric, remembering the way she'd squirmed, a moan coming from the far reaches of her stomach as he'd bitten down on the sensitive flesh.

*Tell her!*

He wanted to…wanted her to understand why he couldn't…

Hell, he loved the woman, knew the emotions had never truly disappeared even after all the time apart. And he could do nothing about it.

He settled for answering her question. 'No, they don't know.'

Her eyes clouded, her hands going to her braid and tugging it to the side. 'Let's get something straight. We've been down this road once before, and it didn't have a good ending. I'm not looking to repeat the mistakes I made in the past.'

Mistakes she'd made. Did she really consider their time together a mistake?

Who was he to ask something like that? Hadn't he treated it like one by taking off eight years ago? By never once writing her or telling her the truth after his father had died and he'd come back to Dutch Harbor?

Wasn't he treating today as a mistake by keeping his past a secret?

He could tell her the truth about why he'd left all those years ago. The truth about what happened on his chopper.

Where did he start?

Maybe it was better to start in the near past and work his way back to the distant past—if he even got that far.

He put his hands on the yoke of the plane and squeezed, trying to drum up the courage to do now what he should have done eight years ago.

Before he could back out, he opened his mouth, letting the words come out in a rush.

'Ahmed was a boy I knew in Afghanistan. His father was one of our medical translators, until insurgents found out he was helping us and gunned him down in front of his house. In front of his family. We felt responsible—if he hadn't been seen with us…' He swallowed before continuing. 'His wife was left with nothing but their son. We got together and took up a collection, buying food and helping to pay Ahmed's tuition in a private elementary school. We moved them to another part of the city. A place we thought they'd be safe.'

But they hadn't been. The insurgents had tracked them down hell bent on making her pay for accepting the 'infidels'' help, as they called all the UN troops. They'd wounded Ahmed and strapped his mother with a bomb, knowing she'd run right to his squadron to get help for her boy. She'd been smarter than they had, though, setting her son on the ground about a hundred yards away from Mark's chopper. She'd run the other way just as the bomb had gone off…

Why tell Sammi any more than he already had, though? He'd admitted to knowing the boy and helping him. She could make believe the story had a happy ending. Just the way he sometimes imagined it.

Only he evidently wasn't all that convincing, even to himself, as evidenced by his nightmares. Or by the way he'd called out Ahmed's name the second he'd fallen through that coffee table. He'd heard the explosion of glass and had thought it was the damned bomb all over again.

Sammi was staring at him, her brow puckered as she waited for him to continue, trying to put the pieces together all by herself. Suddenly a look of horror slid through her eyes, her hand coming up to cover her mouth for a long moment.

Then she reached out, her fingers going to his on the yoke and prising them loose, holding them tight in her own.

'Ahmed died, didn't he?'

# CHAPTER EIGHTEEN

SAMMI waited in the hangar as Mark took care of the plane and his passengers, her mind a jumble of shock and dismay. The puppy was fast asleep in the animal crate by her feet, his soft breathing rising to meet her ears.

That poor child.

The second she'd asked the question, she'd known it was the truth. The boy had died. Mark hadn't denied it, neither had he responded, but his hand had given hers a quick squeeze before releasing her to scrub the back of it over his eyes.

The man had been on the verge of tears.

It was unthinkable. The happy-go-lucky, fun-loving guy who'd come home from the navy, duffle bag slung over one shoulder and a big smile plastered to his face as he'd disembarked, wasn't as carefree as he seemed. Had it all been an act— his way of dealing with the horrors he'd lived through overseas?

Had he talked to anyone about all this?

Before she could process her thoughts and organize them, Mark joined her, reaching behind her to tweak her braid. 'Ready to go?'

No, she didn't want to go anywhere until they could sit down and have a heart-to-heart discussion, but Toby was due home from school in about a half hour. Besides, there was something in her that needed to hug her son tightly and give him a silent promise that no one would ever hurt him. Even the thought brought an ache to her chest that squeezed harder and harder until she couldn't breathe. So she said the only thing she could right now: 'Yes, I'm ready.'

His eyes searched hers for a second, and she willed herself not to break down and sob in front of him. Somehow she knew that was the worst thing she could do. He'd take it as a sign that she pitied him for what he'd had to endure.

She didn't pity him. She hurt for him in a way she'd never hurt for another human being in her life. Not her ex-husband, not her patients...not even her son. She ached for the man who'd done his damnedest to help a family and had ended up feeling like he'd hurt them instead.

Mark was silent as he drove Sammi back to the clinic. She struggled to find something to say, but everything she came up with just seemed shallow and trite. She wanted to ask him to pull over and let her hold him, but she didn't.

How did you heal a wound that had become part of the man himself?

Maybe you didn't. Maybe you simply acknowledged the scar without trying to pick it back open again.

They pulled into the parking lot, and Sammi put her hand through the crook of his uninjured arm and leaned her head against his shoulder. He stiffened for the tiniest fraction of a second before relaxing. 'What's this for?'

She sat back up. 'I just felt like it.'

'Thanks.'

'You're welcome.' She paused, trying to figure out where they went from here, or if they even did. There was a fork in the road, and Sammi wasn't sure which path to choose.

Could she risk her heart and Toby's on a man who might never be quite whole?

She wasn't sure. She'd slept with the man twice, might even be carrying his child. A decision had to be made.

And if he decided he didn't want a relationship?

One way or the other, she had to tell him the truth. Which meant, if she hadn't started her period within a week or so, she'd have to choose a venue. Since she didn't know when she would see him again, it was better to go ahead and plan something.

Could she do it?

'Listen,' she said, trying to find her way in unfamiliar territory, 'you wouldn't be interested in having a picnic with me and Toby, would you?'

She held her breath as she waited on his response.

'You want to go on a picnic this time of year?'

That didn't sound very promising. 'I never said it had to be outside. We could have it at my place. Just throw a couple of blankets on the floor and have some traditional grub. Fried chicken. Potato salad. I'll do all the cooking.'

He shifted to look at her. 'How could I refuse an offer like that?'

Her breath left her lungs in a relieved whoosh. 'I do make a pretty mean fried chicken.'

'When were you thinking?'

'Shall we plan it for Friday afternoon? Toby won't have school the next day.'

Hmm…that could be taken the wrong way. Maybe she should clarify things. 'I wouldn't feel comfortable having you spend the night with my son in the next room, though.

Not at his age.' She smiled to soften the words, but tensed when he didn't smile back.

'Of course not.'

She gave a nervous laugh and tried to backtrack a little bit further, in case she'd insulted him. 'Okay, so you might have to remind me about the no-spending-the-night clause. Because I have a feeling you may be stronger in that area than I am.'

The first hint of a smile pulled at the corners of his lips. 'I doubt that, Sam. I sincerely doubt that.'

Sammi stared at the pregnancy test in her hands.

The week at the clinic had flown by, despite the fact that Mark hadn't put in an appearance. It was just as well. She needed time and a little bit of space to think things through. Was she wrong to put herself in a situation like this? The man had hurt her once. And she was more than a little vulnerable at the moment as she was now over a week late with her period.

Why now? Why not next year, when she was better able to tell what Mark was thinking—see how he acted?

Still staring at the test, she tried to get up the courage to actually take it. If she was pregnant, it was early on, but this particular test was pretty sensitive to any shift in hormones. Did she really want to do this now? Wouldn't it be better to wait a while longer so she could have plausible deniability in case things went horribly wrong on their picnic?

Yes. But she wasn't sure it was the right thing to do.

*Just take it and get it over with. It's killing you not to know.*

Firming her resolve, she went into the small restroom at the clinic and locked the door. Putting her hands on the edge of the sink, she leaned forward and stared at herself in the mirror.

*You might be having Mark's baby. How do you feel about that?*

Elated. Terrified.

She smiled at her reflection. But most of all full of hope.

The test strip came out of the package and she eyed the blank space where she would soon see a pink plus or a blue minus.

No time like the present. She went into the stall and sat on the toilet for a few seconds before getting up the nerve to actually do the deed. Once she did, the second temptation was to toss it into the medical waste receptacle without giving it a glance. But she didn't.

She left the stall and laid the strip on top of the box, washing her hands and then splashing cool water over her face. Her reflection no longer smiled back at her, but was pale and sober. Somehow she already knew without having to look.

Still, she took a deep breath and blew it back out, then forced her eyes to the little plastic case.

The first thing that stood out was the color. Pink. She didn't need to see the plus to know what it meant.

She was pregnant. *They* were pregnant.

And Sammi had no idea how to break the news to Mark.

Something was wrong.

Mark wasn't sure how he knew, but there was a hitch in Sammi's smile as she sat on the blanket across from him—and that smile seemed overly bright, even to his untrained eyes. And beneath her quick laugh lay a serious undertone that made him wonder if she'd changed her mind.

Maybe she was regretting asking him here.

Who could blame her? He'd hurt her once before, maybe she wasn't going to give him the chance to do it again. But he'd done a lot of thinking. He hadn't had a nightmare all week. Maybe Sammi was good for him. Maybe this was what he needed.

The problem was, how could he prove to her that he wasn't out to repeat the mistakes of the past?

And leaving her had been a mistake. No matter what his father had said or done, he should have been honest with her. But he hadn't wanted what they'd had to be tainted by threats or be afraid for Sammi's safety every time he was out of the house.

Maybe they could have even run away together. But he'd been too terrified to think straight at the time. He'd just wanted to get as far away as possible, giving his dad no reason to set his sights on Sammi. He'd wanted to keep her safe.

The way he and his buddies had tried to keep Ahmed and his mother safe?

He realized now that something terrible could have happened to Sammi while he'd been away. But it hadn't. His father hadn't dared touch anyone outside his immediate family, because then someone might finally discover his secret.

Shaking off his thoughts, he scraped the last of the potato salad from his plate and popped it into his mouth. 'Delicious. Is there more of this stuff?'

Toby eyed him, his small nose wrinkling. 'It has mayonnaise in it, you know.'

'Yes, it does.' Mark kept his voice serious, trying not to let the smile that tumbled around in his gut come to the surface. His feelings for the boy had grown over the past month, the real child overshadowing any likeness to Ahmed. 'I happen to like mayonnaise.'

'Yuck. It tastes like white slime.'

'Toby.' Sammi's voice held a light warning as she scooped more potato salad onto Mark's plate. 'Remember what we talked about? Not everyone has the same likes and dislikes as you.'

'I know.' He picked up his chicken leg and took a big bite out of it, glancing at his puppy, who'd been corralled in a playpen.

Belly—Sammi said the name Bella had morphed into Belly, due to the puppy's round stomach and the fact that she was always hungry—seemed to sense her master's attention and took the opportunity to whine.

Funny that Sammi had kept the playpen around long after Toby had outgrown it. She'd also kept that baby wipe warmer she'd mentioned a while back. Something about the smiling moons on a dark blue background made him nervous. Would Sammi want more children someday? He had been so sure he'd never want any of his own after his time in the Middle East. And yet here he was with Toby, smiling and almost completely at ease.

Almost.

He turned his attention to Sammi, reaching out to touch her hand. 'Everything okay?'

'Fine.' Bright smile. The same one she'd flashed the last two times he'd asked that question.

'Are you regretting having me over?' Despite the baby contraption across the room, sitting on the ancient quilt in the middle of Sammi's living room felt right. Too right.

'No. Oh, no.' She wrapped her fingers around his, squeezing tight. 'I know I seem distracted. It's just a lot to absorb, you know? Two months ago we were standing at Molly and Blake's wedding doing everything we could not to even look at each other, and now we might be having…' Her eyes widened, her voice falling away.

'We might be having what?'

Toby's head came up, his jaws grinding yet another bite of chicken. 'Yeah, we might be having what?'

Sammi sighed and pulled her hand away to ruffle her son's hair. 'You, my dear, have very big ears.'

'I do not!' He reached up to finger one of his ears, a line of worry puckering the skin between his brows. 'Do I?'

She leaned down to kiss his head. 'No, silly. That's another way to say that you hear everything that goes on around you.'

'My teacher says I'm a great listener.'

'She does indeed.' Sammi glanced at Mark and gave him the knowing smile that one parent might give to another. He allowed himself to relax.

Belly yipped, then gave a mournful howl.

'Mom, can we let her out yet?'

'When everyone's done eating. Plates on the floor are too much of a temptation for that little lady.'

Mark scraped the last of his potato salad onto his fork and slid it into his mouth, then swallowed. 'Better than any restaurant could have made.'

'There's nothing quite like home-made.'

He reached out and touched her face, loving the smoothness of her skin. 'You're right. There's also nothing quite like home.'

'No. There really isn't.' She studied him. 'Does this feel like home? Being back on the island, I mean.'

'It didn't when I first came back.' He couldn't resist leaning forward to drop a quick kiss on her cheek. 'But it does now.'

'I'm glad.' She reached over to gently close Toby's gaping mouth, bringing a smile to Mark's face. 'Now, I think we should get this cleaned up so Belly Bella can come out to play.'

Helping Sammi pick up the plates and serving bowls, the feeling of rightness still hung in the air. That had to be a good thing, didn't it? He hadn't felt the urge to slam through the front door and flee into the night yet. Neither had he pictured flaming helicopters filled with wounded soldiers at every turn. He'd even been a little less jumpy over the past week.

Every day seemed to have wrought more and more of a change in his heart and mind. Puttering around his house seemed unbearably lonely, even though he still made it a point to check in on his mother every day. He was encouraged by the fact that she seemed to be getting out of the house more and mingling with her old friends.

What would she think about all this?

She'd definitely approve. She'd wanted Mark to settle down for a long, long time. There was no way she could understand why he hadn't, or why his legs had turned rubbery when he'd pulled that ring box out of the back of his sock drawer.

Was he actually thinking of…?

Yes. He'd clicked open the top of that box more than once over the last week. But it was too soon. He needed to take things slower than they had the first time. But despite wrenching open his closet door and letting her see the big bad skeleton he'd hidden inside, she hadn't looked at him any differently. Hadn't kept Toby close to her side as if afraid he might snap under the pressure at any second.

His heart swelled with love that what he'd once thought impossible might be not only possible but easier than he'd ever imagined. Sammi had invited him to her house to eat with her and Toby. That had to mean she cared at least a little, right?

They got everything up off the floor just in time for Toby to reach into the playpen and lift out the tiny dog. Racing around the room a time or two, she skidded on the tile floor, paddling with her legs until she finally got them back under herself.

Mark bent down and scrubbed behind the pup's ears, then lifted one of her paws, staring at the oversized pads. 'Have you seen the size of these? She might have been the runt, but I have a feeling she's going to catch up, and fast. She's already grown since the last time I saw her.'

'They don't stay small for ever,' Sammi murmured, putting her hand on Toby's head.

The doorbell rang, startling him. Belly took off for the entrance, four legs going in all directions, looking like a cross between a drunken ice-skater and cross-country skier.

Standing, he glanced at Sammi, who gave him a quick smile. 'Toby, get your backpack, honey, Grandma's here.'

'Why would he need to—?'

'My mom's agreed to watch Toby and Belly for the night.'

His brain tried to compute as Sammi started for the front door. Just before she opened it, she looked back at him. 'Like I said at the clinic, I never claimed to be the strong one.'

# CHAPTER NINETEEN

SAMMI sat up quickly, the sheets tangled around her. The room was dark, and she tried to figure out what had awoken her. A rustling to her left met her ears, followed by a groan.

Mark.

She started to turn toward him, but his legs— hidden somewhere beneath the covers—jerked, freezing her in place. A pained growl issued from his chest, sending a chill skittering down her spine. Not quite a wail, the sound was low and feral—like an animal that had been cornered and was fighting for its life.

He must be dreaming. She blinked the rest of the way awake, letting her eyes adjust to the darkness.

Naked. Why was she…?

It all came rushing back. The night before, her mom had taken Toby and Belly home with her, giving Sammi a knowing wink when she saw Mark standing behind her. Then, finally alone with him, she'd led him back to her bedroom, where they'd spent hours rediscovering all those secret places they had once known. No stolen moments, no rushing. Just her…and Mark.

He'd tried to leave afterwards, murmuring that he didn't want Toby to find them in the morning.

No need, she'd said. Toby wouldn't be back until tomorrow afternoon. He'd tensed, but in the end had allowed himself to be coaxed back to bed. Besides, she couldn't let him leave without telling him about the baby. She'd meant to do it beforehand, but he'd looked at her with such need that she'd decided to follow his lead.

His thrashing grew more intense, and she placed her hand on his chest to wake him up. 'Mark?'

His reaction wasn't what she expected. He lunged up from the mattress, grabbed her arms and rolled over on top her, his naked body pressing hers deep into the soft surface. She gave a little screech at the suddenness of the move but arched toward him to show him she was more than willing. Instead of feeling that ready heat pressing against her center, she was shocked to find him soft. No sign of the urgency that vibrated off the rest of his body.

Well, she could fix that. She tried to move her hand down his stomach, but found she couldn't.

What was happening?

'Mark?' She looked into his face, realizing his fingers weren't just snug around her upper arms, they were actually tightening more as the seconds passed, hurting her. His mouth moved, but no sound came out.

She tried to gain some wiggle room and failed. 'Are you okay?'

No response. It was as if he hadn't heard her.

Panic welled up inside of her, along with a sense of claustrophobia she hadn't felt since she'd allowed friends to bury her in the sand as a young child. They'd run off, leaving her trapped and helpless. This was the exact same sensation.

'Mark, let me up, you're scaring me.'

'You won't get her.' The words were a low snarl.

Terror clogged her pores, collected in her lungs, and she began struggling in earnest, bucking beneath him and finally letting out a scream that could have woken the dead.

And it did. Mark stiffened above her, then rolled away, the pressure on her chest gone, leaving her gasping down huge lungfuls of air. Her heart gave a series of palpitations as the surge of adrenaline eased.

She sat up, her hand at her throat as she turned to look at him.

He hadn't bothered to cover himself, and lay on the bed completely exposed, his arm thrown over his eyes. Deep shudders wracked his body, which was slick with sweat.

Fear morphed into concern. 'Mark?'

'Don't say anything.' His voice shook, but at least it was his own again. Not that mindless creature who'd hulked over her looking like he wanted nothing more than to strangle the life out of her.

She touched him, and he flinched, then he moved his arm and let her see into his eyes, which were deep pools of anguish.

'Wh-what happened?' she asked.

'I had a dream.'

*Holy hell.*

'That was a dream?'

'I have them sometimes. It's why I didn't want to stay over.' He turned his head to look at her. 'I'm sorry for scaring you.'

He'd done more than frighten her. And his words told her those so-called 'dreams' happened often enough that he was wary about spending the night anywhere. Was that why he'd dated so many women? Because he knew what could happen if he got too involved? If they wanted him for longer than just an hour or two? 'Why didn't you say something last night?'

'Because I hadn't had one in a while. I thought it was safe.'

What if Toby had been in the house? What if he'd heard her scream and had come running into the room to find Mark leaning over her like a maniac?

She swallowed. Or what if Toby had come into the room and saw Mark moving in his sleep and tried to wake him up? Would Mark have lashed out at her son without realizing what he was doing? What if she'd been further along in her pregnancy and he'd somehow hurt the baby?

She'd told him she'd never let anyone hurt her or her child. Did she mean what she said? Even if that 'anyone' was Mark Branson himself? Someone she loved? Someone she was pretty sure might feel something toward her as well?

Her thoughts rolled over and over, tangled and chaotic.

'Have you talked to anyone about these dreams?'

He sat up and scrubbed a hand through his hair. 'I don't need to. They're just dreams.'

Were they? She thought about his other odd behavior. Like calling out Ahmed's name at Vonnie's house and the way he'd zoned out during Hannah's injury. They had to be connected.

Flashbacks, maybe?

'You can't be serious, Mark.' She laid her hand back on his chest, his heartbeat pounding against her palm. 'Are these dreams about your time in the military? About Ahmed?'

'You wouldn't understand.'

She pushed forward, not allowing him to brush off her

concerns. 'You're right. There's probably no way I could. But someone will. There are people who are trained to—'

'No.' Swinging his feet off the bed, he found his briefs and tugged them up over his lean hips. His other clothing followed in short order, leaving her with the sheet pulled up to her waist.

'Mark, let's talk about this.' Sammi had so much she wanted to know, desperately wanted to understand what was going on in his head.

'Nothing to talk about. This was a mistake.' He picked his wallet up off the nightstand and stuffed it into the back pocket of his jeans.

*A mistake.* She recoiled against the headboard, her hand automatically going to her stomach as if to protect the child inside. Then she pulled the sheet up to cover her breasts, although the act did nothing to make her feel any less naked and exposed.

Would he consider their baby a mistake as well? Want nothing to do with it?

He moved toward the door in the dark and put his hand on the knob.

Turned it.

'I'm pregnant.'

She'd planned to do this gently, break the news to him after serving him breakfast in bed. But he was leaving, and unless she could do something to change his mind, he might never come back. Never know the truth.

Mark went very still then looked at her, his eyes glittering from across the room. 'What did you say?'

'I—I'm pregnant.' She gripped the sheets harder, wondering if the Egyptian cotton she'd splurged on a few years ago would withstand the strain. But nothing ripped.

Except her heart.

Because after the briefest of pauses, when she could have sworn he was going to respond to her words, he swore softly instead. Then he pushed through the door, leaving her more alone than she'd ever been in her life.

Sammi took her time showering, allowing the water to cascade over her. If only it could wash away her tears as easily as it did her shampoo. But nothing could erase them, because they weren't pouring from her tear ducts but were locked deep inside her, in a remote corner of her heart.

Her eyes remained dry as she dressed, taking the time to do her hair and make-up. They stayed dry on the trip to Mark's house, where she parked in front of his white garage door.

She sat there for several minutes, trying to drum up the courage to go and knock on the door. His car was there, so she knew he was home.

Sucking down a deep breath, she finally climbed out of her car. Before she made it halfway up the walk, the front door opened and Mark stood there, one hand on top of his doorframe, watching her approach.

Neither of them said a word as she reached him.

'I'm not here to ask you for anything. You had a right to know.'

'I appreciate you telling me.'

Those words told her nothing.

Sammi swallowed, not sure exactly how to do what she'd come to do. 'I care about you, Mark. More than I should, probably. But I want you to think back to that day in the hotel room when you asked about Brad. I told you I wouldn't let anyone hurt Toby or me. Do you remember?'

'Yes.'

'You scared me this morning.'

'I've already apologized for that.' His face was an empty mask, the words slow and mechanical.

'Yes. You did.' Her mind blanked out for a second or two as she faced her future, the front stoop doing a slow twirl as if circling an imaginary drain.

*Stop it.*

She forced herself to stand up straight and continue. She had to do this now or she'd back out. 'I can't risk Toby seeing what I saw—or worse. Not with his asthma.'

Mark didn't say anything, but the color drained from his face.

Sammi's heart squeezed inside her, agony turning her blood to dust in her veins. 'I don't know how you feel about us…about me. But I can't get involved with someone whose refusal to admit he might have a problem makes him a danger not only to himself but to those he's around.'

A muscle worked in his jaw. 'I'm sure you're getting around to saying something profound.'

Damn him! How could he stand there and act like none of this mattered? Like she didn't matter?

Because she didn't. It was why he'd been able to walk away from her eight years ago with barely a wave of his hand.

She backed up a step, anger flaring through her system. 'You always were a smart guy, Mark. You're right. I'm getting around to saying this: unless you talk to someone about what's going on with you, I don't want to see you again. I don't want to fly with you on medevacs. And I especially don't want you stopping by to see Toby. Understood?'

A few seconds of silence blanketed the area then his hand came off the doorframe, and he took a step forward, winding up on the front stoop, mere inches from where she stood. Something dark pooled behind his pupils, turning them inky black as he stared down at her.

Panic skittered up her spine, but she didn't move from her spot. She was not going to stumble back to her car like a frightened little mouse. He wasn't going to hurt her. He might be a soldier, but he was still a man, and she knew her words had struck deep.

He'd confided in her on their trip home from Umnak, and again this morning, and now she was using those confessions against him. Maybe he thought she was holding the pregnancy over his head as emotional blackmail. But the baby had nothing to do with this. Not really.

This was about Mark.

How much was she willing to bet on her position…on the belief that she was right?

As he went back inside without a word and shut the door behind him with a soft click, she had her answer about what she was giving up.

Everything.

# CHAPTER TWENTY

BLAKE met him at the airport. 'Are you sure about this?'

'No, but I don't have a choice.' The blow Sammi had dealt had sent him into a spiral over the past couple of weeks.

What did she know? He was fine. Fine! She didn't want to see him again? Didn't want him near her kid? Well, that was fine, too. He'd chucked the ring to the farthest reaches of his closet and then cancelled all his flights for the foreseeable future.

He'd spent the majority of his time at the local watering hole, drinking away his cares. Or at least trying to. Then a drunk had slammed a glass down on the bar with a little too much enthusiasm, sending a loud crack of sound ricocheting to the corners of the bar. Mark had landed in a defensive crouch, fists raised, eyes darting from person to person. Only when he'd realized everyone was staring at him, that the place had gone deadly silent, did he realize what he'd done, and how far out of the norm it seemed to be for the world around him. His body may have come home from the war unscathed, but his mind seemed to have dragged something extra back with it. Something that had scared Sammi enough to order him to stay away from her.

Blake gripped his shoulder and looked into his face. 'Let's go, then. They're waiting for you.'

'Hannah! What's up, girl?'

Sammi held the cellphone against her ear as she stirred the hamburger helper, the one 'fun' food she permitted Toby to have every Friday night—doctored up, of course, with broccoli florets. Belly sat beside the stove, her doggy gaze fixed on the food preparations that were under way. Toby was in the living room, assembling the new construction set his father had given him on their last visit.

'I'm thinking of renting a movie,' her friend said. 'Are you game?'

'What movie?'

Four weeks and counting. Mark had evidently taken her at her word and was steering clear not only of her but the entire island. Rumor had it that he'd gone to Anchorage. Sammi had no idea if it was a permanent thing or if he was coming back. But she wasn't going to put her life on hold, waiting for something that might never materialize.

'What is Toby allowed to watch?'

'We try to stick to the three Gs around here.'

Hannah laughed. 'Do I even want to know what that means?'

'Yes, since it'll narrow your choices down to a manageable few.' She ticked off her fingers. 'Gore-less, Grunt-less, and Ghost-less.'

'Grunt-less?'

'You know...*grunting*.' She emphasized the word enough to let Hannah in on the codeword.

'Oh...grunting.' Hannah laughed. 'Well, that knocks out all the fun movies.'

'Sorry about that.' She crooked her shoulder to hold

the phone as she dished some food onto Toby's plate and walked over to the tiny dinette table. She motioned to him, pointing at the food. He leaped up and came running…and so did Belly. 'Hold on a second, would you?'

She grabbed the dog just before she tried to scramble onto the chair ahead of Toby. 'Where do you think you're going, young lady?'

Carrying the pup to the playpen, she set her inside, realizing just how fast the dog was growing. Soon she'd be big enough to leap out of the confined area. But it was just as well. She'd have to sterilize the playpen to use for the baby. She'd shared her secret with Hannah and Molly, but no one else. She couldn't. Not quite yet. She'd eventually have to tell her mother, which wasn't going to be a lot of fun.

Making sure Toby was eating, she put the phone back to her ear. 'Sorry about that. I had to—' The sound of the doorbell pealing stopped her in mid-sentence.

*Good heavens.* Why did things always come in waves?

'Hannah, I have to get the door. Can I call you back?'

'It's okay, I'll call you from the movie store.'

'You sure?'

'Yep. Talk to you soon.'

'Okay. Don't forget the rules—' she swung the door open ' I told you about…' She stared in disbelief, the phone falling from her hand and clattering to the floor.

'Sammi? Sammi?' She heard Hannah's voice calling out to her but couldn't tear her eyes from the person in front of her.

Mark, a little bit thinner than he'd been four weeks ago, stared at her. 'I'm back.'

'So I see,' she whispered. Why was he there?

He nodded at the floor, where Hannah's voice was growing more distressed. 'You'd better get that.'

Sammi swallowed, then bent down to retrieve the phone. 'Sorry, Hannah. I—I dropped the phone.'

'You scared me to death. Is everything all right?'

She searched Mark's eyes, seeing the corners crinkle as he gave her a slight smile. 'You know what? I think it just might be, but we'll have to cancel our movie plans for tonight, okay? I'll talk to you later.'

Clicking the phone shut and stepping through the entryway so that Toby wouldn't see Mark before she had a chance to find out what was going on, she pulled the door closed behind her. She'd told him not to contact her again, unless…

*Could it be?*

She waited, but he didn't seem in any hurry to say anything, his eyes trailing over her as if he couldn't get enough.

'How's Toby? The baby?' he asked.

Hearing him acknowledge their child sent a flash of joy shooting through her system, which she immediately tried to tamp down. 'They're both fine.'

He nodded. 'I did as you asked. I went to see a therapist. In Anchorage. Someone who specializes in post-traumatic stress disorder. Blake went to the same guy after he got out of the navy.'

A feeling of shock went through her. Blake had gone to a therapist too?

'How did it go?'

'I learned that some things shouldn't be handled on your own. That lots of other guys have the same issues. It's not just about me being too weak to handle things on my own.'

'Weak?' She closed the gap between them and leaned

her head on his chest. 'You're not weak. *God,* Mark. You're the strongest man I've ever known.'

His cheek came down to rest on top of her head. 'I love you, Sammi. I always have. Always will.'

'Always?' She leaned back to look at him, not sure she'd heard him right. 'But…but you left. Why?'

He let go of her and reached into his pocket and pulled out a little box. Cracking it open, she saw the ring inside, its small stone glittering up at her. 'Because my father found this in my room. Said some things that led me to believe that my being involved with you could put you in danger.'

'My God.' She stared at the ring, not believing he'd bought it all those years ago. Her heart went to her throat and stuck there. 'Why didn't you tell me?'

'Because I knew you'd try to talk me out of leaving. I realize now it wasn't the smartest move, but we were both young. I didn't know what else to do at the time.'

There was a tiny part of her that wondered if this was really happening. If Mark Branson was really standing on her doorstep, declaring his undying love for her. She blinked the world in and out of focus. Still there. 'You had this ring eight years ago? You kept it all this time?'

'Yes.'

She leaned back, pulling in a deep breath to let his scent fill her, surround her. All the hurt and bitterness of the past faded away. He was real. He loved her. 'Why are you showing it to me now?'

'Because I hoped that you might…' He ground to a halt. 'I don't want you to think I went to see someone just because you told me to. I did it for me. For us.'

'Is there an "us"?'

He nodded. 'I hope so.'

'So do I. I love you too, Mark. I don't think I ever stopped.'

He pulled her tight against him for a long moment. This time the sensation wasn't scary. It filled her with hope. Joy. So many other things.

'I know this is too soon but…' he let her go and prised the ring from its velvety bed '…would you consider becoming my wife? I still have a lot of work to do, and I'll want you there with me for some of my sessions, so you'll know what to expect—how to help me as I recover.'

Tears blurred her vision. 'I'll be right there beside you, every step of the way.'

'No more running. No more lies.' He folded her in his arms and kissed the top of her head.

She reached up on tiptoe and kissed him back, her lips searching his, clinging to them when he immediately deepened the kiss. By the time she pulled back, gasping for breath, she was laughing. 'I'd better remember those three Gs myself.'

When he looked at her, puzzled, she shook her head. 'I'll explain later. Come inside. I know Toby's going to want to see you.' Everything else could wait: explanations, discussions about the future.

'Wait a second.' He took her left hand and lowered himself to one knee. 'Samantha Grey Trenton, I don't deserve you, but would you do me the honor of becoming my wife?'

The ring slipped onto her finger like magic, the fit perfect.

'Are you sure this is what you want?'

'It's all I've ever wanted.'

She smiled and drew him to his feet, her heart kicking up its heels and sprinting towards the finish line. 'Then welcome home, Mark. We're glad you're back.'

# EPILOGUE

'I FOUND some!'

Toby's voice came from the other side of the salmon-berry patch, interrupting the kiss Mark had tried to sneak from Sammi. She looked up at him with a smile, her growing belly pressed tightly against his, causing all kinds of strange and wonderful sensations inside his skull and elsewhere.

He couldn't get enough of her, even now when she was mere weeks away from delivering their child.

A little girl. They'd chosen Melody for her name, after his maternal grandmother, something Sammi had insisted on.

He'd finished his treatments for post-traumatic stress syndrome a few months ago, and Sammi, true to her word, had been right there for many of the sessions, which they'd scheduled for days when Toby was visiting his father. The nightmares were gone. And both he and Sammi had learned coping mechanisms in case any problems arose in the future.

Toby's shout came again, 'Mom! I found some!'

Mark nuzzled her cheek, nipping her earlobe. 'I think he found something.'

'Mmm,' she murmured. 'So did you.'

'Did I?' He kept his voice low. 'You know the doctor says we have to be good from here on out, until after the baby's born.'

'What does he know?' That little kitten purr she had drove him crazy with need, just like it always did.

Mark took a deep breath then stepped back, gritting his teeth as he tried to pull himself together.

'Party pooper,' she said.

'Hey, don't blame me.'

Sammi cupped her stomach. 'You see there, Melody? You daddy is blaming you for having to keep his—'

'Don't say it.'

'What? I was going to say "for having to keep his plane in the hangar".'

'Very funny.' They both knew she wasn't talking about his actual plane, which was also grounded until after the baby was born. He wasn't going to take any chances on her going into labor while he was off on a charter flight.

Belly and Toby came running toward them, Toby's mouth smeared with a suspicious red substance. 'Toby, I promised those berries to a doctor in Anchorage.'

'Sorry, Mom. I'll go and find some more.' He turned and raced away again, Belly hard on his heels.

Mark eyed her. 'Exactly how many pints of jam do you owe people?'

'Um…' She twisted her hands. 'Maybe thirty.'

'Thirty? And how do you expect to can thirty jars of jelly before you give birth?'

'Well…' She drew out the word as she looked him up and down.

'Oh, no. I don't know anything about making stuff like that.'

'I could talk you through it.'

Mark laughed, a rush of love spiraling through his chest as he looked at the beautiful woman he'd married a month ago. 'I'm sure you could. And just what would I get for my trouble?'

She sidled up to him and ran a finger down his chest, before hooking it into his waistband and giving a suggestive little tug. 'You'd get something *very* special. Something reserved for only a select few.'

His mouth went dry. 'Which is?

She gave him a slow smile. 'Why…a pint of salmon-berry jam.'

\* \* \* \* \*

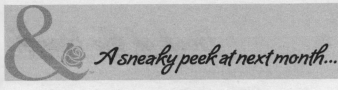

*A sneaky peek at next month...*

## Medical Romance™

**CAPTIVATING MEDICAL DRAMA—WITH HEART**

### My wish list for next month's titles...

In stores from 2nd November 2012:

☐ Maybe This Christmas...? – Alison Roberts

& A Doctor, A Fling & A Wedding Ring – Fiona McArthur

☐ Dr Chandler's Sleeping Beauty – Melanie Milburne

& Her Christmas Eve Diamond – Scarlet Wilson

☐ Newborn Baby for Christmas – Fiona Lowe

& The War Hero's Locked-Away Heart – Louisa George

**Available at WHSmith, Tesco, Asda, Eason, Amazon and Apple**

### Just can't wait?

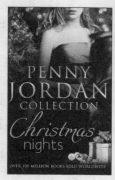